**Praise for Award-Winning Author
Mary Balogh**

"An incomparable talent."   —Jill Barnett

"Once you start a Mary Balogh book, you won't be able
to stop reading."
                    —*New York Times* bestselling author
                    Susan Elizabeth Phillips

"Mary Balogh has the gift of making a relationship
seem utterly real and utterly compelling."
                    —Mary Jo Putney

"Mary Balogh just keeps getting better and better . . . interesting characters and great stories to tell . . . well
worth your time."   —*The Atlanta Journal-Constitution*

"Mary Balogh is a superb author whose narrative voice
comments on the characters and events of her novel in
an ironic tone reminiscent of Jane Austen."
                    —*Milwaukee Journal Sentinel*

"Winning, witty, and engaging . . . fulfilled all of my romantic fantasies."   —Teresa Medeiros

"Mary Balogh reaches deep and touches the heart."
      —*New York Times* bestselling author Joan Johnston

continued . . .

Under The Mistletoe

Mary Balogh

A SIGNET ECLIPSE BOOK

SIGNET ECLIPSE
Published by New American Library, a division of
Penguin Group (USA) Inc., 375 Hudson Street,
New York, New York 10014, USA
Penguin Group (Canada), 90 Eglinton Avenue East, Suite 700, Toronto,
Ontario M4P 2Y3, Canada (a division of Pearson Penguin Canada Inc.)
Penguin Books Ltd., 80 Strand, London WC2R 0RL, England
Penguin Ireland, 25 St. Stephen's Green, Dublin 2,
Ireland (a division of Penguin Books Ltd.)
Penguin Group (Australia), 250 Camberwell Road, Camberwell, Victoria 3124,
Australia (a division of Pearson Australia Group Pty. Ltd.)
Penguin Books India Pvt. Ltd., 11 Community Centre, Panchsheel Park,
New Delhi - 110 017, India
Penguin Group (NZ), 67 Apollo Drive, Rosedale, North Shore 0632,
New Zealand (a division of Pearson New Zealand Ltd.)
Penguin Books (South Africa) (Pty.) Ltd., 24 Sturdee Avenue,
Rosebank, Johannesburg 2196, South Africa

Penguin Books Ltd., Registered Offices:
80 Strand, London WC2R 0RL, England

Published by Signet Eclipse, an imprint of New American Library, a division of
Penguin Group (USA) Inc. Previously published in a New American Library
edition.

First Signet Eclipse Printing, October 2006
First Signet Eclipse Printing ($4.99 Edition), November 2007
10 9 8 7 6 5 4 3 2 1

Contents

A
Family
Christmas

"*W*ell?" Lady Templar watched impatiently as her daughter folded her letter and set it down beside her plate on the breakfast table.

"Mr. Chambers will be coming for Christmas," Elizabeth replied, rearranging the napkin across her lap.

"*Here?* To Wyldwood Hall?" Her mother looked aghast. "How dreadfully inconvenient."

"It *is* his home, Mama," Elizabeth reminded her.

"His father purchased it as a trophy," Lady Templar said disdainfully, as if that fact made it less a possession. "He thought it would elevate him into the ranks of the beau monde and erase the vulgar smell of commerce from his person. He thought to make doubly sure by purchasing a well-bred bride for his son. Well, the son may have both the home and the bride, but he is as much a cit as his father, Lizzie. He is an embarrassment. I wish in my heart now that we had not invited the whole family to spend Christmas here. But it is too late to change our plans. Tomorrow everyone will be arriving. How very provoking, to be sure, that Mr. Chambers will be here too."

We? Elizabeth thought. *Our plans?* It was her mother who had invited everyone to Wyldwood. She had written the invitations and sent them on their way before

Elizabeth had even known about her plan for a family Christmas.

Elizabeth folded her napkin again, set it neatly beside her plate, and rose to her feet. She had not eaten, but she had lost her appetite. Mr. Chambers was coming home.

"Will you excuse me?" she asked. "There are a thousand and one tasks I must attend to."

"All of which you will leave to me, Lizzie," her mother said firmly. "You know I am far more experienced than you in managing servants and organizing large house parties."

Elizabeth smiled at her but did not sit down again. She left the room and made her way straight up to the nursery. It was not time to feed Jeremy yet. There would have been time first to complete several of the tasks she had spoken of. But she needed to compose herself. The letter had upset her. So had her mother's open contempt for Mr. Chambers. Lord and Lady Templar had come to Wyldwood in August to be close to their daughter during her confinement in September, and they still had not returned home. Lady Templar had taken over the running of the household, and it had run smoothly ever since.

Elizabeth could not dispute the truth of what her mother had just said about her superior competence. But oh, how she longed to have her home back to herself again, even if she *was* less experienced at running a large house. But how could she say anything to hurt her mother? She had never been an assertive person.

Now all of her aunts and uncles and cousins, as well as her brother and his wife and son, were coming for Christmas—and so was Mr. Chambers. She really had not expected that he would come. She had not even written to inform him of the family Christmas that her mother had planned and to which she had acquiesced after the fact because it was always easier to let Lady Templar have her way than try to fight her.

The baby's nurse was sitting close to the window, sewing. Elizabeth indicated with one raised hand that she was not to get up. Jeremy was awake in the crib, making little baby noises, though he was not crying. She bent over him, smiling and cooing to him, and lifted him out. She could never resist holding him; he was so soft and cuddly, even though her mother had warned her during the month after his birth that she would spoil him if she gave him too much attention. If love could spoil a person, then so be it.

It was her one little rebellion against her mother.

Mr. Chambers was coming home. *Edwin.* She formed his name with her lips, though she did not speak it aloud. She never had said it aloud—except during their nuptial service.

Her mother had just spoken with the utmost disdain of Mr. Chambers's father, who had attempted to buy his way into the upper classes by purchasing a viscount's daughter for his son. But Mama had been quite as eager for the marriage, Elizabeth thought with some bitterness, and Papa had voiced no complaint. The marriage settlement had enabled them to pay off all the considerable family debts, the result of years of gaming and extravagant living. It had not seemed to matter then that Mr. Chambers's father was a city merchant without birth or connections and spoke with a hearty Cockney accent. The only important consideration had been that he was as wealthy as a nabob. Privately, of course, they had considered it lowering to have to marry their only daughter to his son, but sacrifices had to be made if they were to maintain the style of living to which their consequence entitled them.

Elizabeth had been the sacrifice. She had been married off to Mr. Edwin Chambers a little over a year ago, early in December, two weeks before the elder Mr. Chambers died of a heart seizure. During those two weeks Jeremy had been conceived. After the funeral of his father, the younger Mr. Chambers had settled his wife on the grand estate his father had purchased less than a year before, and returned to London to manage the family business. She had seen him on only one occasion since. He had come to Wyldwood after the birth of their son in September. He had visited her in her bedchamber for ten minutes each day, but even during those brief sessions her mother had always been present and had dominated the conversation, choosing topics— deliberately, it had seemed to Elizabeth—designed to exclude her son-in-law or demand only one-word answers from him. He had returned to London after less than a week, with only a few brief words of good-bye to Elizabeth—in her mother's company.

He was a stiff, proud, humorless, morose man. As handsome as sin, it was true, with his blond hair and regular features and trim, elegant figure, but with no character or personality or human warmth with which to attract even the mildest affection. He had been a dreadful disappointment to Elizabeth. Nevertheless, he was her husband, and it hurt to hear her mother belittle him.

When the nurse went downstairs to fetch more mending, Elizabeth sat down. She set the baby on her lap, his head nestled between her knees. She held him by the ankles and lifted his legs one at a time to kiss the soft soles of his feet.

"And he is your papa, my precious," she said aloud. "He is coming home for Christmas."

Jeremy blew a bubble.

Perhaps, she thought, if he stayed for a week or two he could leave her with child again. It was not an entirely unwelcome prospect. Jeremy gave meaning to her lonely life. Another child could only enliven her existence even more. It was only the process she dreaded. He had not treated her roughly during the two weeks following their wedding—not by any means. He had done only what her mother had warned her he would do. It had not even been painful, except a little the first time. But she had been chilled and humiliated by the impersonality of it all.

"But I will say this," Elizabeth told her son, taking his little hands in hers and clapping them while he cooed at her. "You were worth every minute of it. And your brother or sister would be worth as many minutes more."

It was strange how sometimes she ached for what she had found so terribly disappointing.

Sometimes Edwin thought that perhaps he had been too fond of his father, who had loved him with every beat of his great, generous heart. His father had worked for years longer than necessary in order to make sure that his son would live the life of a gentleman. Edwin had had an expensive tutor and had later gone to one of the best schools in England and then to Cambridge. He had been given, in fact, every social and educational advantage that money could buy, as well as oceans of love. Wyldwood Hall had been bought for him. So had his bride, with the idea that she would provide him with an entrée to the highest ranks of the society into which he had not been born but for which he had been raised and educated. If it was possible to die happy, the elder Mr. Chambers had done it.

His son had made him happy by allowing himself to be formed into the sort of person he would rather not have been and placed in the sort of world he would rather not live in with a wife not of his own choosing. He had loved his father—perhaps too much.

It was a gray, blustery, raw day, two days before Christmas, when Edwin Chambers rode up the long

driveway toward Wyldwood Hall. He looked ahead to
the imposing stone mansion with a sinking heart. It was
his, but it did not feel like home. It never had. He would
rather be going almost anywhere else on earth to spend
Christmas, he thought—except that his wife was here.
And his child. And when all was said and done, he was
sufficiently his father's son that he could not simply turn
from what was his or shirk his responsibilities altogether.

His father had never understood that all Edwin had
ever wanted was to be proudly his son, to allow him into
the family business, to speak with a Cockney accent if
he so wished, to marry a woman of his own choosing
from his own world and bring up sons and daughters to
be proud of their heritage. But it was not his father's
fault that he had never understood. Edwin had never
told him, had never been willing to dash the dearest
dream of his father's life. In addition, he had known for
a number of years that his father was dying of a heart
disease.

Perhaps it was wrong to allow one's life to be manip-
ulated, even when the motive was nothing more
heinous than love. But he had done it, and he must live
with the consequences.

Lord and Lady Templar would still be here, he did not
doubt. They had come for a month or so and stayed for
almost five. They would continue to live here, he supposed, for the rest of their lives. Their own home was
shabby and in dire need of all sorts of repairs, none of
which they could afford. And so Christmas must be
spent, not only with his wife and son, but with his
mother- and father-in-law, who had never made any secret of the disdain they felt for their daughter's husband. They had driven him away in September. He had
been unwilling to assert his will against them—most
particularly his mother-in-law—while his wife was still

so weak after giving birth to Jeremy. They would not drive him away this time until he was ready to leave. But the thought of the inevitable conflict was a dreary one.

He swung down from the saddle outside the great double front doors and handed the reins to a groom, who had materialized from the stables without having to be summoned. He wondered if his approach had been noted from the house too, if it had been watched for with as much reluctance as he felt. Even as he wondered, the front doors swung open from within, and the butler was bowing regally to him and welcoming him home.

Edwin nodded affably and bade the butler a good afternoon.

"Is Mrs. Chambers at home?" he asked.

But she was coming through the stairway arch even as he spoke, and he was struck again, as he had been thirteen months or so ago, when he had set eyes on her for the first time, by her breathtaking beauty. She was on the tall side, slender and yet shapely. She bore herself with an aristocratic grace that was bred into her very bones. She had dark golden hair, large blue eyes, and perfect features.

She was like an icicle, he had thought from the start—and nothing had happened since to cause him to change that initial impression—ethereally lovely, but icy cold, frigid to the heart. Everything about her bearing and manner proclaimed her contempt for the man who had allowed his father to purchase her as a trophy for his son.

She curtsied. "Mr. Chambers," she said. "I trust you had a pleasant journey?"

He inclined his head to her as he handed a footman his hat and greatcoat and gloves. She had never called him by his given name, though he had invited her to do so when he had called upon her to go through the farce

of proposing marriage to her. He had deliberately called
her by hers after their nuptials, though she had never invited him to do so. Her greeting chilled and irritated
him. The married couples from his world did not address each another with such impersonal formality.

"Yes, thank you, Elizabeth," he said. "You are well?
You have recovered your health?"

"Yes, thank you," she said.

"And my son?"

The tightening of her lips was almost imperceptible,
but it suggested unexpressed annoyance. He wished he
could recall his words and speak them again to refer to
Jeremy as *their* son. But he was accustomed to boasting
to his friends about his golden-haired boy—*my* son—
whom he had last seen when the child was ten days old.

"He is well, thank you," she said.

If, he thought ruefully, he had married a woman from
his own world, she would perhaps have greeted him
each evening of the past year on his return home from
work with a smile and a kiss and warm, open arms and
an eagerness to share her day with him and to hear
about his. He would naturally have thought of their
child as *ours*. He would have seen their son every day of
the child's life.

But he had only himself to blame that things were not
so. His father had not forced him into this marriage. Indeed, he would have been horrified if he had realized
that Edwin did not really want it.

"Would you like to go to your room to freshen up?"
she asked, her eyes moving over him and making him
intensely aware of the less than pristine state of the
clothes in which he had been riding for the better part
of the day. "I have guests in the drawing room."

"Lord and Lady Templar?" he said. "I trust they are
well?"

"Yes, thank you," she said. Her chin rose a notch, and

she suddenly looked arrogant as well as cold. "We decided to have a family Christmas here. All the members of my family arrived yesterday."

What? Good Lord! Without any consultation with him? Was he even to have been informed? How disastrous his own decision to come home at such short notice must have seemed to his wife and her family. How disastrous it seemed to him! If he could, he would have turned and left the house without further ado and ridden away back to London. *All* her family? He had never even met most of them. Their wedding had been a fair-sized affair, but apart from Lord and Lady Templar and their son and daughter-in-law, all the guests had been his family and his friends and his father's. He could not leave now, though.

He *would* not leave. This was, after all *his* home.

"I will meet and welcome them to Wyldwood later," he said. "But first I would like to go to the nursery. Will you come there with me?"

"Of course." She turned to accompany him through the arch to the staircase. She clasped her hands gracefully in front of her, discouraging him from offering his arm.

"How many guests?" he asked as they ascended the stairs. He could hear the chill in his own voice. He had never been able to inject warmth into it when speaking with his wife. How could one hold a warm conversation with an icicle?

"Thirty-two adults altogether," she said. "Thirty-three now."

He winced inwardly. Under different circumstances he might have felt some amusement over the realization that he had made the numbers odd. Doubtless his wife and his mother-in-law had planned meticulously in order to ensure even numbers. He would even be willing to wager that of the other thirty-two adults sixteen

were gentlemen and sixteen ladies, even though normally one would not expect a family to fall into such a
neat pattern.

He was surprised when he opened the nursery door
and stood to one side to allow his wife to precede him
inside. He had expected a hush appropriate for a sleeping baby. Instead there was a noisy, cheerful hubbub.
But of course—there must be children as well as adults
in her family. There was a vast number of the former, it
seemed, all rushing about at play, all talking—or, rather,
yelling—at once. A few nurses were supervising, but by
no means subduing them.

Several of the children stopped what they were doing
to see who was coming in. A few of them came closer,
and a copper-haired, freckled little boy demanded to
know who Edwin was.

"You must remember to mind your manners,
Charles," Elizabeth said, nevertheless showing a human
touch by ruffling the hair of the offender. "This is
your . . . uncle. Charles is Bertie's eldest," she explained, naming her brother. She identified the other
children in the group, all of them cousins or the children
of cousins.

"What is *your* name?" Charles asked.

"Charles!" Elizabeth exclaimed, sounding embarrassed.

But Edwin held up a hand. "Have you noticed," he
asked, winking at the boy, "that when a lad does not
know something he ought to know, adults invariably tell
him he should have asked? Yet when he does ask, he is
treated as if he had been impertinent?"

"Ye-e-es!" The children were all in loud agreement,
and Edwin grinned at them all.

"He is Uncle . . . Edwin," Elizabeth explained.

There was a chorus of requests that Uncle Edwin
come and play with them. He held up a staying hand

again, chuckling as he did so. Almost all his closest friends had young families, who for some inexplicable reason always saw him as a potential playmate. His friends claimed that it happened because he was still a child at heart. He liked children.

"Tomorrow," he promised. "We will play so hard that you will not have to be told to go to bed in the evening. In fact, you will beg your nurses to let you go there."

There was a swell of derisive denials. Charles, who was obviously something of a leader, snorted.

"It is a promise," Edwin told them. "But today I have come to see a certain baby by the name of Jeremy, who is mine. Has anyone seen him running around here, by any chance?" He looked around him with a frown of concentration.

"Nah," a plump little boy told him, the utmost contempt in his voice. "He's just a *baby*."

"I wanted to play with him," a little girl added, "but he had to go to sleep. Is he yours? He is Aunt Lizzie's too."

Elizabeth led the way to a room beyond the nursery.

"You ought not to have said that about tomorrow," she said with quiet reproach. "They will be disappointed when you do not keep your promise. Children do not forget, you know."

He did not answer. The room was quiet and in semidarkness with the curtains drawn across the window. But the baby was not asleep. Edwin could hear him cooing and could see him waving his fists in the air as he lay on his back in his crib. His eyes focused on his father when Edwin stepped closer. Edwin swallowed hard and was glad that his wife was standing well behind him. He had ached for this moment for almost three months.

Being separated from his child was the most bitter experience of his life. He had considered a number of schemes for bringing him closer, including buying a second house in London for Elizabeth to live in. But there would be too many awkward questions if he and his wife both lived in London but not together. Yet it seemed somehow impossible to set his family up in his own London home, formerly his father's, even though it was large and tastefully decorated and furnished and well staffed and situated in a fashionable part of town. It was, nevertheless, well-known as the home of a prosperous merchant.

"He has grown," Edwin said.

"Of course. You have not seen him for almost three months."

Was it an accusation?

"He has lost much of his hair," he said.

"That is natural," she told him. "It will grow back."

"Do you still . . . nurse him?" He could remember his surprise when her mother and the doctor had been united in their protest against her decision not to hire a wet nurse. It was one issue on which she had held out against her mother's will.

"Yes."

She made no move to pick up the child, who admittedly seemed happy enough where he was. Edwin longed to do so himself, but he was afraid even to touch him.

"He looks healthy enough," he said.

Why was it that with Elizabeth words never came naturally to him, and that the ones he chose to speak were stiff and banal? They had never had a conversation. They had been bedfellows for two weeks he would prefer to forget—she had been a cold, unresponsive, sacrificial lamb beneath him on the bed each night—but they had remained awkward, near-silent strangers.

"You will wish to go to your room," she informed him. "Will you join us for tea later?"

"I believe I will forgo the pleasure of meeting our guests until dinnertime," he told her.

She nodded. Even through the cold impassivity of her

face he thought he could detect her relief. He gestured to the door so that she would precede him. He did not offer his arm.

It had been a mistake to come—and that was a colossal understatement. He should have stayed in London, where he had had numerous invitations to spend the holiday with friends whose company he found congenial and in whose presence he could relax and be himself. But he had remembered his father and imagined how sad he would be if he could see his son apart from his wife and child at Christmas, just one year after the wedding that had brought all the elderly man's dreams to happy fulfillment.

Elizabeth, dressed with greater care than usual in an evening gown of pale blue, a color she knew became her well, went down early to the drawing room before dinner. Even so, Mr. Chambers was there before her, standing before the marble fireplace, his hands clasped behind his back, looking like the master of the house. She was relieved to see that he was clothed severely but immaculately in black and white. Had she expected otherwise? She had never seen him look slovenly or heard him speak in anything other than refined accents. He bowed formally to her and she curtsied. It seemed strange to realize that he had been her husband for longer than a year—and that this was his home.

They had no chance for conversation. The door opened again to admit Lord and Lady Templar and Elizabeth's Aunt Martha and Uncle Randolph.

"Ma'am. Sir," Mr. Chambers said in greeting to his parents-in-law, bowing courteously. "How do you do?"

"Mr. Chambers," Lady Templar said with distant hauteur, her hair plumes nodding as she inclined her head. "I trust you are well?"

Elizabeth introduced her aunt and uncle, and Mr. Chambers greeted them with a bow.

"Welcome to Wyldwood," he said to them. "I am delighted you were able to join Elizabeth and me here for Christmas."

It was a sentiment he repeated over and over again during the next half hour as the rest of the family came down for dinner. Elizabeth stood beside him, making the introductions and feeling enormous relief. She had feared that he would allow himself to be dominated by her mother, that he would allow her to treat him as a guest—an inferior, uninvited guest. How humiliating that would have been.

He was to be put to a further test, though.

When the butler came to announce that dinner was served, Lord and Lady Templar were close to the door and proceeded to the dining room without delay. Everyone else held back until Mr. Chambers had offered his arm to Aunt Martha and followed them. Elizabeth, on Uncle Randolph's arm, cringed at the discourtesy of her parents preceding a man in his own home, and hoped there was to be no unpleasant scene.

"Perhaps, sir," Mr. Chambers said with quiet deference when they entered the dining room, addressing his father-in-law, "you would care to take the place at Elizabeth's right hand at the foot of the table. Ma'am," he added, addressing Elizabeth's mother, "will you honor me by sitting to my right at the head of the table?"

With the rest of the family crowding into the room behind them, Elizabeth looked fearfully at her mother, whose bosom was swelling with outrage.

"Lizzie," she said, ignoring Mr. Chambers, "your papa is the gentleman of highest rank here, and he is head of our family."

But not of Mr. Chambers's family, Elizabeth might have pointed out, and perhaps would have if her father had not saved her by exerting his authority—a rare occurrence.

"Take a damper, Gertrude," he said, and moved off toward the foot of the table.

Lady Templar had no choice then but to proceed in the opposite direction, from which vantage point she displayed her displeasure by ignoring her son-in-law all through dinner and conversing with gracious warmth with Uncle Oswald on her other side. Mr. Chambers conversed with Aunt Martha and Bertie beyond her and looked perfectly composed and agreeable, as if entertaining a tableful of members of the *ton* were something he did every evening of his life.

Had she expected him to be gauche? Certainly she had feared that he might.

He also looked gloriously handsome. Elizabeth, playing the unaccustomed role of hostess in her own home, was nevertheless distracted by the sight of her husband and by the disturbing memories of their two weeks together last year, and wished he had not come to spoil her Christmas and everyone else's—including his own, she did not doubt. At the same time, she regretted the sudden death of his father, whom she had liked. Had he lived, she and Mr. Chambers would very likely not have lived separately for the past year. Perhaps they would have made something workable out of their marriage. Indeed, she had been quite prepared to make it work. Indeed, she had been eager to move away from her mother's often burdensome influence in order to become mistress of her own home.

And she had fallen in love with Mr. Chambers on sight.

Lady Templar was still bristling with indignation when the ladies withdrew to the drawing room after dinner, leaving the gentlemen to their port.

"Well!" she exclaimed. "Of all the impertinence! I must say I am surprised, Lizzie, that you would stand by and watch your father humiliated by a man very far beneath our touch without uttering one word of protest."

"Shhh, Mama," Elizabeth said, mortified, since the words had been overheard by her sister-in-law and by all her cousins and aunts. "This *is* Mr. Chambers's own home." And the man very far beneath their touch was her husband.

"Lizzie!" Her mother's voice quavered with indignation. "Never did I think to live to see the day when you would tell your own mother to hush. And *did* you see what happened, Martha? Did you, Beatrice? When I would have stood, as was perfectly proper given my rank and position in this family, to lead the ladies from the dining room, that man had the effrontery to set four fingers on my arm and nod at *Lizzie* to give the signal."

Elizabeth was both mortified and distressed. She had never been able to stand up to her mother—not even when informed that she was to be sacrificed in matrimony to a wealthy cit in order to recoup the family fortunes. But Mr. Chambers was her *husband,* and she owed him loyalty more than she did anyone else—including her mother.

"Mr. Chambers has a right to expect me to be hostess in his own home, Mama," she said. "I am his wife. It is what all men expect."

"Well!" There were two spots of color high on her mother's cheekbones. "You are the most ungrateful of daughters, Lizzie! I am very vexed with you. Besides, how can you expect to be hostess of such a large house party when you have no experience? And when you have Jeremy to attend to? I have given you almost half a year of my time and this is the thanks I receive?"

"I do appreciate all your help, Mama," Elizabeth said. "You know I do."

But her sister-in-law set a hand on her arm and smiled at her. "Come and join the group about the pianoforte with me, Lizzie," she said. She had had her own conflicts with her mother-in-law during the eight years of her marriage.

Elizabeth, grateful for the excuse to avoid further conversation with her mother, nevertheless felt guilty as Annabelle linked an arm through hers and led her away. She had lied to her mother. She was not grateful. It was with dismay that she had watched September turn into October and October into November without any sign that her parents intended to return home and leave her mistress of Wyldwood again. Despite loneliness and depression over her apparently failed marriage, she had liked being mistress of her own home for a few months.

It was later in the evening, after they were all assembled in the drawing room, that trouble struck again. There were two tables set up for cards. Another group was gathered about the fireplace, conversing. A crowd of younger people was clustered about the pianoforte, listening to young Harriet perform. Elizabeth was on her feet watching the card games and reflecting on the fact that Christmas was already shaping up to be its usual predictable, tedious self. With what high hopes she had embarked upon a totally different life last year. She really had been happy about her arranged marriage, especially after meeting the jolly Mr. Chambers and then receiving his son. But nothing had come of her bright hopes after all, except that she had Jeremy.

Mr. Chambers was moving away from the fireside group and stopped beside her.

"We will be decorating the house tomorrow?" he asked.

"Decorating?" She looked blankly at him.

"For Christmas." He raised his eyebrows. "With holly and ivy and pine branches and mistletoe and all that."

"Oh," she said.

"And a kissing bough."

Harriet had just finished playing. At the same moment a lull had fallen on the conversation by the fire. His words were generally audible.

"A *what*?" Lady Templar asked, looking up from her cards.

"A kissing bough, ma'am," Mr. Chambers repeated. "And other decorations to make the house festive for the season. Have you made no plans, Elizabeth?"

"We have never used Christmas decorations," she said. She had sometimes wished they had. The assembly rooms in the village at home had been decorated one year for a Christmas ball. They had looked gloriously festive, and they had smelled richly of pine.

"Then we will this year," he announced.

There was an audible stirring of interest from the direction of the pianoforte.

"A *kissing* bough," young Sukie said, and there was a titter of self-conscious male laughter and the higher trill of girlish giggles.

"I always did like a few tasteful Christmas decorations in a house," Aunt Martha said with an apologetic glance at Lady Templar. "We had some one year when we remained at home for the holiday. Do you remember, Randolph? But never a kissing bough, I must admit. I believe that might be vulgar."

"There will certainly never be one in *this* house," Lady Templar said in the voice her family recognized as useless to argue with. "Such bourgeois vulgarity would not be tolerated in *this* family. I will direct the servants tomorrow, Lizzie, to bring in some greenery, if it is Mr. Chambers's wish, but I will give strict instructions about what is suitable."

"Oh, it *is* my wish, ma'am," Mr. Chambers assured her. "But the servants need not be burdened with the extra task when I daresay they are already far busier than usual. Half the fun of Christmas decorating is doing it all oneself. I will go out and gather the greenery tomorrow morning. There should be more than enough in the west woods. Would anyone care to join me?"

A number of the young people spoke up with cautious enthusiasm, and a few others stole self-conscious glances at their parents and Lady Templar and would have spoken up if they had dared, Elizabeth thought. She stared silently at her husband, marveling that he would defy her mother yet again. He had seemed so quietly obedient to his father's will last year that she had concluded he was a man easily dominated.

"I must ask the gardeners," he said, "if there is mistletoe anywhere in the park. It would not be Christmas without mistletoe."

The young people tittered and giggled again.

"The children must come too," he said. "I promised to play with them tomorrow. I also promised to exhaust them. Gathering greenery and then decorating the house will serve both functions."

"The offspring of *this* family," Lady Templar said with awful civility, "will remain in the nursery with their nurses, where they belong, Mr. Chambers. Children may be allowed to romp about the houses you are accustomed to frequent, but such is not the case in genteel society."

Elizabeth bit her lip. She dared not look at her husband.

"Well," he replied amiably, "we must allow their parents to decide, ma'am. Now, we will need to be up and out early." He held up a staying hand when there was a collective groan from the direction of the pianoforte. "Tomorrow is Christmas Eve. There will be all the decorating to do afterward, and it must be done well. It is going to be a busy day."

Uncle Oswald cleared his throat and set down his hand of cards. "I do some whittling now and then," he

said, looking embarrassed. "I daresay I could put together some sort of Nativity scene if you wish, Chambers. It seems to me that I did it a few times at
Christmas when the children were young."

"Yes, you did, Papa," Sukie said. "Please, please may
I go out gathering greenery with Cousin Edwin? May I,
Mama?"

"I used to help you, Papa," young Peregrine added. "I
would help again this year, except that I don't want to
miss the outing."

"You can do both," Mr. Chambers assured him. "You
can help your father in the afternoon while the rest of
us hang up the greenery."

"Martha and I were planning to take a drive into the
village tomorrow morning," Aunt Beatrice said. "I daresay we will find some satin ribbon in the shop there if
we look. Will we, Lizzie? It will be needed to make the
decorations pretty," she added without looking at Lady
Templar.

"I doubt you will be able to take the carriage anywhere tomorrow, Beatrice," that lady said, a note of tri-
umph in her voice. "Neither will anyone be able to set
foot beyond the door to gather greenery. It is almost
certain to snow before morning, and we will all be
housebound."

"But I am counting upon its snowing, ma'am," Mr.
Chambers assured her. "All work and no play would
make for a thoroughly dull Christmas Eve. A snowball
fight would be just the thing to lift our spirits, get the
blood moving in our veins, and yet not slow us down fa-
tally. We will definitely need to make an early start,
though."

There was a swell of unabashed excitement from the
younger people at the mention of snow.

Lady Templar got to her feet and surveyed the gathering with haughty disdain. "I, for one, will not stand for

such vulgar nonsense," she declared. "And if Lizzie will not assert herself as mistress of this house, then I—"

"Mama!" Elizabeth cut her off sharply. "If Mr. Chambers says that our home is to be decorated for Christmas, then it will be decorated. Even with a kissing bough."

"Lizzie!" Her mother's bosom swelled with outrage.

"Stow it, Gertrude," Elizabeth's papa advised from the other card table, exerting his authority briefly for the second time in one evening, without raising his eyes from his cards.

Elizabeth met her husband's gaze but then looked sharply away. Her heart was beating a wild tattoo in her bosom. She had just openly defied her mother! But how could she not have done so?

"Excuse me," she said abruptly. "I must go up to Jeremy." He would be ready for his night feeding. She just hoped her milk had not been soured.

She had never seen Mr. Chambers smile before today, she thought as she hurried up the stairs. But he had smiled at the children this afternoon, and he had done more than that to all her young cousins in the drawing room—he had actually grinned at their enthusiasm over his plans for tomorrow. And he had suggested something that sounded so much like fun that her heart ached with longing.

Fighting in the snow.

Gathering greenery in the woods.

Decorating the house.

Making a kissing bough.

She had never been kissed—a ridiculous truth in light of the fact that she was a wife and mother. But he had never kissed her. And she had never had a beau before him.

They were going to decorate the house for Christmas—*they,* not the servants. They were going to have a kissing bough. She hurried lightly along the corridor to the nursery.

They were going to have *fun*.

At least, she thought, amending the idea as her footsteps slowed, the children and young people were going to have fun. But she was not in her dotage, she reminded herself. She was not even twenty yet. It just seemed that somehow, somewhere, she had misplaced her youth.

She was a matron with a child. She would be expected to remain at the house.

Lady Templar's prediction had proved quite correct. Yesterday's gray, raw day had been transformed into today's magical white world. A few inches of snow blanketed the outdoors, and more was falling. They were to enjoy that rare phenomenon, Edwin realized early—a white Christmas.

All the parents of young children not only had given permission for them to join the expedition to gather greenery but also had decided to go outside themselves. Only two babies, Edwin's own included, stayed in the nursery. The remaining children, their parents, and most of the younger cousins gathered in the hall soon after breakfast, bundled up warmly, chattering and laughing and in exuberant high spirits.

Most of the parents and young people were there, Edwin saw. One was conspicuously absent. Had he expected her to come? She had surprised him the evening before by defending him against her mother, but she had done so with a cool dignity that had proclaimed only wifely obedience. There had been no indication that she was enthusiastic about his plans or that she intended to participate in them in any way. It would be as well to take no notice of her absence. She was still the ice maiden he had married, even though she was a maiden no longer. Her cool demeanor had kept him from going to her bed last night, though he had wondered before he arrived at Wyldwood if he would. They were not officially estranged, after all.

But despite himself he hesitated, even as the crowd in the hall looked to him for direction.

"I have forgotten something," he said. "Give me five minutes."

He hurried through the arch and ascended the stairs two at a time, imagining with a certain feeling of amusement what Lady Templar's reaction would be if she should happen to see him. She had ignored him with haughty dignity at breakfast.

Elizabeth was not in her room. She might be anywhere, but he took a chance on finding her in the nursery. He was not mistaken. She was standing at the window of Jeremy's room looking downward, as if she expected the outdoor party to emerge from the door below at any moment. The baby was asleep in his crib.

"We are about to leave," he said.

"Are you?" She turned toward him, straight-backed and regal and unsmiling.

He had wasted his time coming up here to talk to her, he thought. He had probably ruined her Christmas, in fact.

"Does the baby need you?"

"He has just been fed," she told him. "Your eagerness to see him has certainly diminished since yesterday." She spoke softly, but the rebuke was unmistakable.

"I came up here early," he said, feeling a stirring of anger against her. Why had she married him if she despised him so? But the answer to that question was obvious, at least. It had certainly not been from personal choice. "His nurse was changing his nappy, and he was as cross as blazes, though she assured me that he could not possibly be hungry. I held him for half an hour." He had held his tiny son against his shoulder with an intense ache of tenderness. "He almost deafened my right ear for a few minutes, but he finally found amusement in chewing on the brocade collar of his papa's dressing robe."

Not for the first time he wondered how his son would grow up. Would he, too, despise his father and be embarrassed by his origins?

"I did not know that," his wife said. "Nurse did not tell me."

"I suppose," he said, "you do not want to come outside with us?"

"Gathering greenery?" she said. "And engaging in a snowball fight?" She sounded shocked.

"No." He nodded briskly and turned back to the door. "I did not think so. We will probably be back late for luncheon. You may wish to have the meal set back an hour." If her mother would permit such a disruption of the household routine, that was.

He was at the door of the outer nursery—deserted this morning—when her voice stopped him. She had stepped out of Jeremy's bedchamber and was closing the door behind her.

"Mr. Chambers," she called, her formal words of address increasing his irritation, though he turned politely toward her, "do you *want* me to come?"

She looked different somehow, less serene, less sure of herself. There was an expression almost of longing in her eyes. She looked suddenly youthful, and he remembered that indeed she was little more than a girl. She had been eighteen when they married, five years younger than he.

He swallowed his first impulse, which was to tell her that she might please herself.

"Yes," he said abruptly. And it was true. He was as irrationally head-over-ears in love with her as he had been when he first set eyes on her. If she still despised him for his origins and his willingness to have his father purchase her for her birth and rank, well, so be it. But he had come here to see if something could be made of his marriage before their separation had continued for so long that it would be virtually irreversible.

"Very well," she said, her cool, reserved self again. "I will go and change. You need not wait for me."

Had he imagined that look of longing? Was she coming merely because he had asked? Merely because she owed him obedience? Would she be miserable outside in the snow and the cold? Would she spoil the outing for everyone else?

"We will wait outside for you," he said.

It was still snowing. Thick white flakes fluttered down from a heavy gray sky. The steps outside the front doors had been swept recently, but there was a thin film of snow on them again. Elizabeth stepped out onto the top step and felt as if she were walking into an alien, enchanted world.

Snow had always meant being housebound. Snow was something one could slip and break a leg on. Worse, snow was something that had to be waded through with an accompanying loss of dignity, especially if one skidded inelegantly. Walking out into the snow, making slides of it, sledding over it, building snowmen with it, clearing it from a frozen pond or lake in order to make a skating surface, were all activities designed for the lower classes, who had no dignity to lose. Fighting with snowballs was simply beyond imagination, even for children.

There were times when she was a child that Elizabeth had guiltily wished she had been born into the lower classes.

They were out there on the great white expanse that

was the south lawn—all the children, most of the cousins who were in Elizabeth's own age group, her brother Bertie, Annabelle, and Mr. Chambers. The children were dashing about and screeching as they chased one another. The ladies were laughing; the men were whooping as they tried sliding on snow that was too deep, and kept coming to grief. They were all very obviously enjoying themselves.

Even Aunt Amelia and Uncle Horace were outside, standing in the snow on the terrace, watching the activities and laughing.

It was a scene so alien to Elizabeth's experience, so full of wild, uninhibited joy that she felt overwhelmed by it. Could she ever give herself up to such sheer fun? She had been brought up to think that having fun and lacking ladylike dignity were synonymous terms. She almost turned and hurried back inside before anyone saw her. But Mr. Chambers must have been watching for her. He came wading toward her, his eyes bright with animation, his face already flushed from the cold and exertion. He looked incredibly virile and handsome.

"Take my hand," he said when he reached the bottom step.

She set her hand in his outstretched one and remembered with almost painful intensity her first enchanted sight of him when he had come to offer her marriage. He would be her escape, she had thought naively then, from her dull, restricted life into a world where warmth and love and laughter would transform her. She had already met his father and had liked him immensely, despite—or perhaps because of—those qualities her mother had despised as vulgar. Absurdly, she had wanted him as *her* father. The son was so very handsome, and younger than she had expected. It had not taken her long, though, to realize that his very correct, unsmiling demeanor hid scorn for her for allowing herself to be bought. But this morning she would not think of that. He had chosen to come to Wyldwood for Christmas, and he had come to the nursery this morning with the express purpose of inviting her out here.

He released her hand as soon as she was safely down the steps, set two fingers to his lips, and let out a piercing whistle. Elizabeth looked at him in astonishment, as did everyone else.

It was easy to believe over the next couple of minutes that he was a successful businessman, accustomed to organizing and commanding. He announced that the snowball fight was about to begin and soon had everyone divided into two teams of roughly equal numbers and firepower. Elizabeth would gladly have stood watching with her aunt and uncle, but she was given no choice. She was named to a team and waded gingerly out onto the lawn to join her teammates. Annabelle caught her by the hand and squeezed it.

"Lizzie," she said, "I am so glad you have come to enjoy the snow. But however did you escape from Mama-in-law?" She laughed and slapped one mittened hand over her mouth. "Forget I said that. Oh, goodness, I have to face both Bertie and Charles on the other team."

The snow was soft beneath Elizabeth's feet and not as slippery as she had expected it to be. It reached almost to the top of her boots.

"It sparkles," she said, "even though the sun is not shining, as if someone has sprinkled the surface with thousands of miniature sequins. How beautiful it is."

But she was not given long to admire her first real experience of snow. The two teams were facing each other across a neutral expanse of it, and Mr. Chambers whistled again, the signal for the snowball fight to begin. Most of the players, it soon became obvious to Elizabeth, had armed themselves in advance. Snowballs zoomed through the air, and squeals and shouts and laughter revealed that many of them had found their mark.

Elizabeth shied away from all the vigorous action, uncertain what to do herself. She felt the beginnings of misery in the midst of such bubbling animation. She had never been allowed to play and enjoy herself—she did not know how. She was a lady.

And then a snowball collided with her chin and dripped down inside the collar of her cloak before she could brush it away. Another struck her on the shoulder. She could think only of her discomfort, of getting back indoors, where it was warm and quiet and dry and sane and all was familiar to her.

"The best defense is invariably offense," her husband advised from close beside her, and he struck Peregrine, her chief tormentor, on the nose with a large, wet snowball.

Elizabeth laughed and felt suddenly, unexpectedly exhilarated. She stooped to gather a handful of snow, formed it into a ball, and hurled it, also at Peregrine, who was still sputtering and trying to clean off his face. It struck him in the chest, and Elizabeth laughed with delight, even as another snowball from an unidentified assailant shattered against her shoulder.

After that she forgot about discomfort and cold and dignity and hurled snowballs as fast as she could mold them at any foe within her range. Soon, without even realizing it, she was helpless with laughter. She was also liberally caked with snow from head to foot. But several minutes passed before she spared a moment to slap ineffectually at her cloak with snow-clogged mittens.

By that time that fight was losing momentum, the children having discovered an even more amusing activity. They had captured Mr. Chambers, two of them hanging off each arm, one off each leg, while a few others pushed and shoved. With a ferocious roar he went down on his back.

"Bury Uncle Edwin!" Charles shrieked over and over again, and the other children took up the cry until it became a chant.

They proceeded to heap snow over him until only his shoulders and head were visible—and his hat, which had tipped to a rakish angle.

"Poor Mr. Chambers," Aunt Amelia remarked.

"He is a jolly good sport, I must say," Uncle Horace commented. "You would not catch me letting them do that to me."

Elizabeth stood and watched while the other adults and young people slapped themselves and one another relatively free of snow and recovered their breath. Mr. Chambers was laughing good-naturedly and putting up only enough of a struggle to amuse the children. She felt as if she were gazing at a stranger. Where was the cold, humorless, dour man she had married? By some instinct, the children had picked out the very adult who would indulge them and play with them and allow himself to be played with. How had they known?

For the first time Elizabeth could see her husband as the son of that hearty, jolly man who had arranged the marriage with her own parents and insisted upon having a private word with her in order to assure himself that she was not being coerced into anything against her will. Her husband, it seemed, possessed the same generous, fun-loving nature, though he had never displayed it for her benefit.

She felt plunged into sudden depression again. He had not wanted to marry her, of course. He disliked her. He very probably despised her.

Five minutes later the play portion of the morning was over and they were all trudging off in relatively good order toward the west woods. Mr. Chambers had

accomplished the transition without any apparent effort, Elizabeth noticed. And indeed, there was no feeling among them that they were now off to dull work. It
was as if they were merely heading off toward some
new game.

Mr. Chambers had divided them into four groups, two
to cut down pine boughs, one to gather holly, and a
group of four to search for the mistletoe the gardeners
had assured Mr. Chambers was to be found growing on
the older oaks. He was himself a part of the last group,
as was Elizabeth. The other two were Cousin Miranda
and Sir Anthony Wilkins, her betrothed.

Elizabeth could not quite believe she was doing this.
The snow was deep and heavy underfoot, her fingers inside her gloves were tingling from the cold, her cheeks
and nose were almost numb and must be unbecomingly
red, and yet at this point in the morning she would not
go back to the house for all the inducement in the
world. She knew suddenly that she had never enjoyed
herself even half as much as she was enjoying herself
today. And there would be *only* today, and perhaps tomorrow, though Christmas Day had always been one of
her least favorite days of the year. After that Mr. Chambers would surely return to London, and it might be a
long time before she saw him again. She might never see
him quite like this ever again.

"Perhaps you can lead us to where the oaks are," he
said to Elizabeth.

But although she was familiar with the park, she had
never ventured deep into the woods. They searched for
many minutes before finding what they had come for.
Fortunately the snow was not as deep here, as the
canopy of branches overhead acted as a sort of roof.

"As I suspected," Mr. Chambers said when they were
all standing beneath a particularly stout, ancient oak. "It
is rather far from the ground."

It was the mistletoe he was talking about. Elizabeth tipped back her head and saw it an impossible distance overhead. Surely he was not intending . . .

"Are you willing to risk your neck?" he asked, looking at Sir Anthony.

Anthony was in love with Miranda, as everyone knew, and was eager to impress her. And so the two men swung up into the branches of the tree while Miranda gasped nervously and Elizabeth pressed one gloved hand to her mouth. They would kill themselves!

"Don't slip," Miranda admonished her betrothed. She lowered her voice. "Oh, Lizzie, I *do* so admire Mr. Chambers. He is not at all stuffy, is he? Yet he is not vulgar either. I am very happy for you. Mama said last year that it was a great shame you were forced to marry a cit only because Aunt and Uncle were improvident, but this year I do not doubt she will declare that you were fortunate. He is such fun."

Yes, he was. With other people. Not with her, though. He did not like her.

"Oh, Edwin, do be careful!" She clapped a hand to her mouth again. His foot had slipped, but he recovered his balance almost immediately and grinned down at her.

Her knees turned weak. Because he had almost fallen? Or because he had smiled at her? And she had, she realized in some embarrassment, called him by his given name.

Anthony was the first down. He held a clump of mistletoe triumphantly in one hand.

"Now, then," he said while Miranda laughed again, "the victor claims his prize." And he raised his hand aloft, dangled it over her head while he caught her by the waist with his free hand, and kissed her with smacking relish on the lips.

"Tony!" she scolded. "Mama would have a fit of the vapors."

"But we have Mrs. Chambers to act as chaperon," he said.

"Lizzie is *younger* than I," she told him.

He turned to look at Elizabeth in some surprise. She was feeling so embarrassed that she would have been blushing rosily if her cheeks had not already been bright red from the cold. She had never before seen two adults kiss. Mr. Chambers had just reached the ground and was looking down ruefully at a deep scuff mark along the inside of one boot. Elizabeth hoped he had not seen the kiss.

"In that case," Anthony said, grinning, "*you* must chaperon Mrs. Chambers, Miranda."

"Absurd!" she said, laughing too. "Lizzie is *married* to Mr. Chambers. He may kiss her whenever he pleases."

Elizabeth scarcely knew where to look. She had not stepped away from the tree as the gentlemen descended, with the result that she was suddenly almost toe-to-toe with Mr. Chambers, and he was looking into her face, a question in his own. He was holding mistletoe. Did he think she had held her ground deliberately? Did he think . . . ? She stared back at him. She was having trouble with her breathing.

"A man really ought to be rewarded," he murmured, "for risking both his life and his boots."

He intended to *kiss* her?

She had shared the intimacy of the marriage bed with him on fourteen successive nights. She had taken his seed into her womb and borne his child. Yet she felt suddenly as if they had never touched at all. Certainly he had never kissed her.

"Oh, how foolish!" she said in what she hoped was a light tone, turning sharply away. "All the magic will be gone from the mistletoe even before we take it back to the house."

"Well, there is something in that," her husband said

from behind her, his tone matching her own. "But I reserve the right to be the first to test it there after the kissing bough has been made and hung—with the lady of my choice."

Miranda and Anthony laughed. Elizabeth forced herself to turn her head back toward her husband and join in their laughter. Had he really *wanted* to kiss her? He was looking at her with narrowed eyes, an unreadable expression in them.

Had she ruined the morning?

But he strode up beside her, and they led the way out of the deeper woods. Soon they could hear other voices and see the other groups busy about their tasks. Indeed, when they reached their starting point, they found an impressive mound of greenery waiting to be hauled to the house.

"How are we going to get it there?" Cousin Alex asked, lifting his beaver hat in order to scratch his head through unruly chestnut curls.

"Carry it?" Peregrine suggested.

But Mr. Chambers, as they might have expected, had organized everything in advance. Gardeners were to bring carts drawn by teams of horses, he explained. Indeed, they came into sight, raising clouds of snow, almost before he had finished explaining.

And so they all trudged empty-handed back to the house, having to wade through snow that was considerably deeper than it had been when they set out. Elizabeth did not know who it was who began singing "The Holly and the Ivy," but soon they were all singing lustily and not particularly musically and following it with other Christmas carols. Mr. Chambers, who was walking beside her, four-year-old Louisa perched on one of his shoulders, had a good tenor voice, she discovered.

Elizabeth felt awkward and shy with him. Why had she avoided his kiss? She had wanted it. But had he laid claim to kissing her later beneath the kissing bough?

With the lady of my choice. Surely that must be what he had meant. He was not angry with her, then?

She would not think of his being angry. She would not think of her own lost opportunity. There was much to look forward to for the rest of the day. At this particular moment she was chilly, untidy, weary, heavy with milk— and suddenly so filled to the brim with happiness that somehow it seemed more painful than pleasurable.

The children were shooed off to the nursery as soon as they returned to the house. They ate luncheon up there, and some of the younger ones, despite loud protests, were put to bed for a sleep afterward. But all were promised by Edwin, who stayed with them while Elizabeth was feeding Jeremy, that they could come down and help afterward.

"Children have never been allowed out of the nursery during our family gatherings," his wife told him as they made their way downstairs later.

He did not know if she was rebuking him for the promise he had made the children or for suggesting that they bring Jeremy downstairs with them now since he had not gone back to sleep after his feeding. He was tucked into the crook of one of Edwin's arms.

"I was brought up with the idea that children are to be enjoyed as an integral part of a family," he said. "Am I spoiling your Christmas, Elizabeth?"

"No." She spoke quickly, though he was not convinced that she meant it.

And yet he could have sworn that she had enjoyed the morning outdoors after the first few minutes, when he had expected her to return to the house at any moment. She had looked startlingly, vividly lovely while engaging in the snowball fight and laughing helplessly. He had found himself aching with longing to have all that animation and joy focused on him.

"What are your family Christmases usually like?" he asked.

She walked down half a flight of stairs before answering. "There is a great deal of eating," she said. "And drinking. And card playing and billiards. And sleeping."

"Do you enjoy them?"

"I have always *hated* Christmas," she said with quiet vehemence.

There was no chance for further conversation. They were entering the dining room, where everyone else was already gathered. There was a minor sensation, as Edwin had expected, over the appearance of Jeremy. Predictably, Lady Templar, completely ignoring her son-in-law, ordered Elizabeth to summon his nurse to take him back to the nursery.

"It is Mr. Chambers's wish that Jeremy stay with us until he becomes cross or tired, Mama," his wife explained with her usual quiet dignity.

"That child will be ruined," her mother said tartly.

"By spending time with his papa?" Elizabeth said. "Surely not."

"Well, do not say I did not warn you," her mother told her.

Edwin realized suddenly in just how awkward a situation he had placed his wife, who had always obeyed her mother without question, he guessed, and yet who must also have been brought up to believe that she must give the same unquestioned obedience to her husband after she married. Now he was forcing her into making a difficult choice. So far it seemed that she was putting duty to her husband ahead of compliance with her mother's will.

What *her* will was, he did not know. Had she ever exercised it? Had she ever been given a chance? If he had a daughter, he thought, he would want to raise her to think and act for herself, to have opinions, to balance personal identity against duty.

If he had a daughter . . .

He wished suddenly that he could go back and deal differently with his marriage after his father's death last year. He wished he had persevered more to make something workable of what had begun so inauspiciously.

He sat at the table, Jeremy nestled in the crook of one arm, and proceeded to eat his luncheon one-handed. Only for a short while, though. The baby went from hand to hand about the table during the meal, to the delight of most of the lady guests and the silent, haughty disapproval of Lady Templar.

When it came time to decorate the house later, Lady Templar and a few of the other older relatives retreated to the morning room. Elizabeth's uncle Oswald removed to the library with his son, Peregrine, and a couple of the children to work on the carving of the Nativity scene. It would be as well, Edwin thought with an inward chuckle when he peeped in there once, if his mother-in-law did not stray in that direction. There were wood shavings, tools, and unrecognizable wooden objects strewn everywhere.

The drawing room was a hive of industry. A few ladies were tying lavish bows out of the satin ribbon from the village shop and attaching the little brass bells that had been found there too. A few of the more intrepid young people were risking making pincushions out of their fingers as they fashioned wreaths and sprays out of the holly and then attached a bow to each. A large group was earnestly engaged in designing a kissing bough, using all available materials and weaving in the all-important mistletoe. Three young girls, too old for the schoolroom set but not quite old enough to be accepted as adults, took turns holding Jeremy and the other baby, who had also been brought down. A few children darted happily about doing nothing in particular and getting under everyone's feet. A couple of men were balanced on chairs, pinning decorations to wall sconces and pictures and door frames while their womenfolk tilted their heads from one side to another and advised raising the decoration half an inch to the right and then one and a half inches to the left. In the dining room much the same thing was going on. On the grand staircase two footmen and a parlor maid, who had jumped eagerly into the spirit of things, were twining ivy about the banister.

Elizabeth was moving from group to group, helping, advising, encouraging. In the absence of her mother, she had come naturally into her own as hostess, and glowed with what appeared to be pure pleasure.

Edwin did his share of climbing and precarious leaning. But he also recognized the yearning of some of the children to feel useful. He took several of them astride his shoulders while they reached high to balance a pine bough along the top of a picture frame or to spread holly along the top of the mantel. He could do the job at least twice as fast without their "help," of course, but there was no hurry. This was what Christmas was all about.

They were almost finished when Lord and Lady Templar and the others who had retired from the chaos entered the drawing room with the announcement that the tea tray had been sent for. But the kissing bough group had just declared that it was ready for hanging.

"Do let us put it up before the tray arrives," Elizabeth said, looking flushed and animated and quite incredibly beautiful. "In the center of the ceiling between the two chandeliers, I believe. Does everyone agree?"

There was a buzz of acquiescence, a smattering of applause, and a few stray giggles. The family had livened up considerably since the day before, Edwin thought.

"If you believe, Lizzie, that I am going—" Lady Templar began.

"Cut line, Gertrude," Lord Templar said.

Edwin smiled at his wife. "The lady of the house must be humored," he said. "The center of the ceiling it will be, and now, before tea. We will need the ladder. Is it still in the dining room? Jonathan, would you fetch it, please? With Charles to help you?"

Five minutes later, he was perched in his shirtsleeves at the top of the high ladder beneath the coved ceiling, securing the gaily decorated kissing bough in its place while a chorus of conflicting advice came from below. Elizabeth stood at the foot of the ladder, her face upturned, Jeremy asleep openmouthed against her shoulder.

"Oh, that is perfect," she said before he descended carefully.

"Now," he remarked when he was safely down, "kissing boughs are not merely pretty decorations, you know. They have a practical function. And there is an obscure law, I believe, that the master of the house must be first to put it to use."

Elizabeth turned that look of beauty on him. She also blushed and looked the nineteen-year-old she was, even though she was holding the baby. Her lips parted. She did not, as she had done in the woods during the morning, turn abruptly away or try to avoid what was coming.

She closed her eyes just before his lips touched hers. Her lips were trembling. They were also soft and still slightly parted, warm and moist. It was strange that after his wedding to an aristocratic iceberg he had performed his duty in the marriage bed but had never found the courage to kiss her. He had wanted to quite desperately.

But she was not an iceberg after all, he realized— perhaps he had been realizing it all day. Perhaps she did not like him, perhaps she resented his coming here with such little notice, but she was not frigid.

The kiss, very public and therefore very chaste, lasted for perhaps ten seconds.

Then it was over.

Their first kiss.

He slid one arm about Elizabeth's waist, the baby nestled between them, and smiled into her eyes while several members of her family laughed or whistled or clapped their hands. Was it just Christmas that was putting this flush in her cheeks, this glow in her eyes, this warmth in his heart? he wondered.

But this was not the time to muse on the answer.

"I would have to say," he said, looking about him and grinning, "that the kissing bough works very well indeed. I invite any skeptics to try it for themselves."

Bertie drew a laughing Annabelle beneath the bough, and Lady Templar haughtily demanded her husband's arm to lead her to a chair by the fire.

Edwin organized the removal of the ladder and other clearing-up tasks, and the tea trays were carried in while cousins and fiancés and a few older spouses merrily jostled for position beneath the kissing bough. Elizabeth disappeared upstairs, the baby having woken up at the increased noise to the discovery that he was very hungry indeed.

This family, Edwin thought, was really not very unlike any other of his acquaintances once the repressive influence of Lady Templar was challenged and busy activities were offered. There was beginning to be both the look and the feel of Christmas about Wyldwood.

By dinnertime, Elizabeth was feeling quite weary from the unaccustomed activity and excitement, but she also knew that she did not want this day to come to an end. It was by far the happiest of her life. It was also the day during which she had really fallen in love with her husband. Oh, it was true that she had been dazzled by him the first time she saw him, only to be disappointed and disillusioned soon after. But she had been wrong about him for a whole year. He was not humorless or without character or personality. Quite the contrary. He was far more like his father than she had realized.

She wondered if he understood just how totally he had transformed their usual Christmas.

She wondered if he realized how very affected she had been by her first kiss, public and brief as it had been. She had relived it over and over again while feeding Jeremy afterward, her cheeks hot with pleasure. But it was not only the kiss she had recalled, startlingly intimate and wonderful as it had been. She had also remembered his smile, warm, almost tender, and directed fully at her, while his arm had circled her waist and their child had been safely nestled between them.

It was the sort of memory on which she would feed during the lonely times ahead.

But the happy novelty of this Christmas was still not over, as she discovered after dinner, even before she rose to lead the ladies to the drawing room so that the gentlemen might be left to their port. Uncle Oswald cleared his throat and spoke up for everyone at the table to hear.

"The Nativity scene is completed," he announced, "and will be set up in the drawing room after dinner with the help of the children. I have been up to the nursery to arrange it. They will all come down, with your permission, Lizzie."

"Definitely not again today, Oswald," Lady Templar said. "It is far too close to their bedtime. I daresay that even in the homes of the middle classes children are not allowed into the drawing room during the evening."

But Elizabeth had spoken up at the same moment. "Oh, yes, certainly," she said, clasping her hands to her bosom. "What a lovely surprise!"

"It is Christmas Eve," Uncle Oswald continued, "and the story of the Nativity must be told. Edwin has agreed to do it."

So Mr. Chambers had been a part of these secret plans too, had he? He smiled at Elizabeth along the length of the table, and she felt her heart turn over. Was it possible that he liked her a little better today than he had before? But he was speaking to her.

"For such an important family celebration," he asked, "shall we have Jeremy brought down too, Elizabeth?"

"Yes," she said quickly before her mother could finish drawing breath to answer for her. "Having our children about us must be a part of all future family gatherings at Wyldwood. Especially Christmas. Christmas is about children—about a child."

"Oh, I *do* agree with you, Lizzie," Annabelle said fervently. "Don't you, Bertie?"

"You know I do, Bella," he said, though he cast a swift, self-conscious glance at his mother as he spoke.

Half an hour later all the adults and children, except those involved in the unveiling of the Nativity scene, were seated expectantly in the drawing room, one large family group, sharing together the warm anticipation of the approaching holy day.

Finally the door opened and Mr. Chambers came inside. He stepped to one side and opened the great leather-bound Bible he carried, while a hush fell on the gathering.

"'And it came to pass in those days that there went out a decree from Caesar Augustus, that all the world should be taxed,'" he read in a rich, clear voice.

As he read Saint Luke's account of the arrival of Mary and Joseph in Bethlehem, two of the children came through the door, one carrying a folded piece of sacking, which he proceeded to spread out on the floor beneath the center window, and the other a roughly carved manger filled with straw, which she set down on the sacking.

"'And she brought forth her firstborn son, and

wrapped him in swaddling clothes, and laid him in a manager; because there was no room for them in the inn.'"

Three more children entered, one carrying Joseph, another Mary, and the third the baby Jesus, wrapped tightly in a piece of white cloth. He was laid carefully on the straw, and his parents were set down on either side of the manger.

A group of shepherds, all carved together out of one piece of wood, came next.

"'And lo, the angel of the Lord came upon them, and the glory of the Lord shone 'round about them; and they were sore afraid.'"

Two children entered, bearing a paper angel and a paper star, which they pinned to the curtain above the stable.

"'Mary kept all these things, and pondered them in her heart.'" Mr. Chambers closed the book as Uncle Oswald stepped quietly into the room.

There was no applause. It was perhaps the best compliment to the skill of Uncle Oswald, whose figures were large and rudely carved and yet evocative of the ageless wonder of the Christmas story.

There was a moment of silence, during which Elizabeth, holding Jeremy, fought tears and failed to stop one from trickling down each cheek.

"Thank you," she said. She swallowed and spoke more firmly. "Oh, thank you so very much, Uncle Oswald, children, and M . . . and Edwin. This is the crowning moment of a truly wonderful day."

There was a chorus of voices then—the adults complimenting the performers and the carver, the children explaining loudly to anyone who would listen how they had been told to walk *slowly* and had almost forgotten but had remembered at the last moment and then could not remember whether Mary went at the right side of the manger or the left or whether the angel went above

or below the star. Someone wanted to know why there
were no Wise Men, and Uncle Oswald explained that
they appeared only in Saint Matthew's gospel, and he
had had no time to carve them anyway.

Aunt Maria got to her feet and seated herself on the
pianoforte bench. She did not have to call for silence.
Somehow it fell of its own accord as she played the
opening bars of "Lully, Lulla, Thou Little Tiny Child."

They all sang. And they all surely felt the wonder and
warmth and healing power of love in the form of the
baby, invisible inside his swaddling clothes, and of
Christmas itself. Oh, surely they all felt it, Elizabeth
thought. She could not be the only one.

She was aware as Aunt Maria proceeded to a second
Christmas carol that Mr. Chambers was standing beside
her chair. His hand came to rest on her shoulder as he
sang with everyone else, and then, when Jeremy began
to fuss, he leaned over her and picked up the baby, as if
it were the most natural thing in the world to do.

Elizabeth swallowed against the lump in her throat.
How would she ever be able to face her life when
Christmas was over and everyone had left except her
mother and father? But she would not think of that yet.
Not tonight.

They sang for half an hour before the tea tray was
brought in.

"There is a service in the village church at nine
o'clock in the morning, I have been told," Edwin said
after the children had all been sent off to bed, yawning
and protesting.

Everyone looked at him rather as if he had sprouted
a second head. They were not much of a churchgoing
family. But several people had an opinion.

"Much too early," Michael said.

"The carriages could not be taken out in all this
snow."

"We could walk, silly. It is less than two miles."

"Go to *church*? On *Christmas Day*?"

"Peregrine, you will not call your sister silly."

"That is the whole point, my dear."

"I'll come," Elizabeth said, smiling at Mr. Chambers, and remembering how unexpectedly pleasant it had been to speak his given name a few minutes ago.

The chorus of comments continued.

"It *would* be fitting, after all we have done today."

"We could have another snowball fight on the way home."

"The service could not come even close to being as affecting as this little ceremony here this evening, though, could it?"

"And build an appetite for the goose and the plum pudding."

"Does the vicar give long sermons, Lizzie?"

"*You* never lack for appetite, exercise or no."

"Oh, yes, let's go to church," Annabelle said. "Let's walk there through the snow. Together, as a family. What a perfectly delightful Christmas this is turning out to be. The best ever. Thanks to Lizzie and Edwin, that is. You can invite us here every year, you two."

There was a burst of hearty laughter and even a smattering of applause.

"Consider the invitation extended," Mr. Chambers said with a twinkle in his eye. "And after we have feasted and stuffed ourselves tomorrow, we will go down to the lake and make a slide. Unfortunately we have no skates, though I promise there will be some next year. But a slide we will have—and a contest to see who can skid the farthest without coming to grief."

They drank their tea and finally dispersed for the night with warm, cheerful good-nights. Mr. Chambers was talking with a group of uncles and aunts when Elizabeth slipped away to the nursery to give Jeremy his night feeding. Her mother caught up with her on the stairs.

"It is to be hoped, Lizzie," she said, "that tomorrow you will exert more control over your own home than you did today. I cannot tell you how shocked I have been—and all this family has been—over the indiscretion of allowing the children out of the nursery to mingle with the adults when their nurses are being paid to keep them under control in the nursery. And the vulgarity of all those decorations, including the embarrassingly amateurish efforts of Oswald to produce a Nativity scene. And the *kissing bough*. I never thought to live to see such a day in any home occupied by the members of my own family. It comes, of course, of the unfortunate circumstance of your having to marry a cit. Tomorrow you must look to me for guidance. *I* will not be overpowered by such a domineering man."

Elizabeth stopped outside the door of the nursery. She had been hoping to avoid her mother tonight. Mama had been looking sour and outraged all day. Elizabeth still did not know when she drew breath to speak if she would have the courage to say what she wanted to say, what she had been longing to say for the past month or two, in fact.

She had *never* been able to stand up to her mother.

"Mama," she said, "will you and Papa be returning home after Christmas? You have been kind enough to stay with me here far longer than you originally intended, but you must be longing to be at home again."

"Leave you?" Lady Templar said. "When you do not have any idea how to be mistress of your own home, Lizzie, or how to be a good mother to your son? I would not dream of being so selfish. You must not fear that I will desert you when you have such need of me."

"But Mama," Elizabeth said, her heart thumping loudly in her chest and her throat and ears, "I do not. I have much to learn before I can run a household as efficiently as you, but Wyldwood ran smoothly enough before you came here and will do so after you leave. You trained me well when I was a girl. And truth to tell, I look forward to the challenge of managing on my own again. I have been very grateful indeed for your help when I needed it, but I do not need it any longer. And I believe I am a good mother."

"Lizzie!" Lady Templar's bosom swelled, and her face was blotched with red patches. "Never did I think to hear such words of ingratitude from you of all people. It is the influence of that dreadful man, I expect. You were always an impressionable girl."

"I *am* grateful to you," Elizabeth said again. "But I would not keep on expecting you and Papa to sacrifice your own comfort for me, Mama. It would be selfish of me. And against my inclinations," she added lest she weaken.

"You will allow him to make you as vulgar as he is," her mother said disdainfully.

"I do hope so, Mama," Elizabeth said quietly. "A wife ought to allow herself to be influenced by her husband, especially when he was chosen for her by her own parents. Just as I hope Mr. Chambers will allow himself to be influenced by me."

She did not know if her marriage stood any chance of becoming a real one. But she would prefer the aloneness of being a neglected, half-abandoned wife, she had realized today, than the oppression of living under her mother's thumb, as she had all her life except for the few brief months between Christmas last year and her confinement.

Her mother turned and walked away without another word, her back stiff and bristling with righteous indignation. Elizabeth fought the wave of guilt that swept over her. She had been polite. She had been grateful. But she had said what she had wanted and needed to say for a long time. She wanted her home to herself again, to herself and Jeremy and Mr. Chambers whenever he chose to visit them.

Separation from him after Christmas this year was going to be very much more painful than it had been last year, she thought as she let herself quietly into the nursery. Last year she had been upset, but she had also been disillusioned too. Part of her had been relieved to find herself alone. This year, though, she had seen another, warmer, more charming, more fun-loving side to her husband's personality. This year he had kissed her beneath the kissing bough and smiled at her. The house was going to seem empty indeed when he left.

Her life was going to seem empty indeed.

But she had been firm with her mother. She had asserted herself as mistress of Wyldwood. She had made progress. She was proud of herself.

Jeremy was waiting for her with noisy impatience, she heard even before she entered his room. She smiled. For longer than three months he had been her world, her life. He would continue to be after Christmas. How could she even think of emptiness when there was a baby to nurture and love?

Edward Chambers's baby and hers.

Elizabeth was sitting by the window of Jeremy's room in the dim light of one flickering candle, the baby at her breast. She looked up when Edwin opened the door from the nursery quietly and stepped inside, and pulled hastily at Jeremy's blanket in order to cover herself.

"I beg your pardon." He moved a few steps closer to her. "I did not intend to embarrass you."

But he was not going to go away either—not unless she directly asked him to. They had circled about each other for too long, he and his wife. He wanted to be a part of their son's life. Oh, yes, and of hers too.

She gazed at him tensely for a few moments before lowering her eyes and relaxing back into the chair. She smoothed her free hand over the soft golden down of the baby's hair, just visible above the blanket.

Edwin clasped his hands behind his back and watched.

They did not talk. The only sound that broke the silence was the hungry sucking of their child.

If only this moment could be immortalized, carried with him forever, Edwin thought. He felt absurdly close to tears. But he wondered which Elizabeth would leave the nursery with him when she had finished feeding the baby. The cold, dignified aristocrat he had known her as until today? Or the warm, smiling, quietly assertive woman she had been for much of today?

Was it just Christmas that had effected the change in her? Would she be herself again once Christmas was over? Even tomorrow, perhaps? But who *was* her real self? He really did not know her, did he? He had met her twice before their wedding, there had been the two weeks after it, and he had spent a few days here after Jeremy's birth, always with her mother in attendance. They were essentially strangers.

He had never been particularly shy with women. He had not known many sexually, but he was acquainted with many as friends and had looked forward to making a marriage for companionship and affection as well as for physical gratification. He still had female friends. But Elizabeth was different. It was not so much that he was shy with her as that he was a little in awe of her— though he was not in awe of her mother. Elizabeth seemed the perfect lady to him, someone far above him in some indefinable way. The feeling annoyed him. He had never been awed by social rank.

The sucking noises gradually slowed and then stopped altogether. Edwin stepped forward and lifted the sleeping baby from his wife's arms as she set the bodice of her dress to rights. He turned and set the child down gently in his crib after kissing his soft, warm cheek and breathing in the baby smell of him.

It was Christmas Eve, he thought. He did not want to end it.

He held the door open for Elizabeth to precede him into the nursery and then the door into the corridor beyond. He closed it behind them.

She turned to say good night to him. He could read her intent as she drew breath.

"Elizabeth," he said quickly, before he could be caught again in the grip of his eternal awkwardness with her, "may I come to you tonight?"

He knew even as he asked that she would not refuse. She had always been the perfectly obedient wife—he must grant her that. But he desperately wanted to see the light of something more than duty in her eyes.

"Yes, of course," she said with her customary quiet dignity.

He offered his arm and she took it, her hand exerting very little pressure on his sleeve. They did not speak a word as he led her to her room, opened the door for her, and bowed. She stepped inside, and he closed the door from the outside.

What had happened to the warmly happy woman he had seen a few times in the course of the day? he wondered. She seemed to have disappeared. Was this to be an ordeal to her? And why would he want it when the two weeks following their wedding had brought him no pleasure at all?

But he was mortally tired of wondering and guessing. He wanted her. It was up to him, he supposed, to bed her in such a way that at least it would not be a repulsive experience for her. But damn it, that was exactly the attitude with which he had approached her bed during those two ghastly weeks. It was up to him to see to it that their coupling was a pleasurable experience for her.

He turned in the direction of his own room, next to his wife's.

Elizabeth stood looking out through the window. The snow had stopped falling, but the sky must still be cloudy. There was not a star in sight. The snow made the landscape unnaturally bright, though. It was Christmas Eve, soon to be Christmas Day

She shivered. Not that she was really cold. There was a fire burning in the hearth, and she was wearing a long-sleeved, high-necked nightgown—the lace-trimmed one she had worn on her wedding night last year. Indeed, she felt almost too warm.

With what high expectations she had awaited him on that night just a little over a year ago. She had fully expected a happily-ever-after. How disappointed she had been.

And this year? Did she have expectations now? She knew what it would feel like, not unpleasant but . . . disappointing. She longed for it anyway, for that touch of intimacy, that illusion of closeness.

And what were her expectations of the future? *Was* there a future? It was best not to think of it. After all, there never was a future, only an eternal present moment, all too often lost because human nature had a tendency to yearn toward the nonexistent future. What did it matter that he might leave the day after tomorrow and not return for months or even a year? Tonight he was here, and he was coming to her bed.

There was a light tap on the door of her bedchamber even as she thought it, and it opened before she could either cross the room or call out.

He was wearing a long dressing robe of green brocade with slippers. His blond hair had been brushed until it shone. He was freshly shaved.

It was like their wedding night all over again. Elizabeth could hear her heartbeat thudding in her ears. She clasped her hands loosely before her and concentrated upon relaxing, or at least upon not showing any of the turmoil of her feelings.

"You told me you have always hated Christmas," he said, coming closer to her. "Are you hating this one too, Elizabeth?"

"No, of course not," she said.

He stopped a foot or so away from her.

"Because I am the one asking you, and it would not be at all the thing to say yes?" he asked her, tipping his head a little to one side and looking closely at her.

She frowned slightly before smoothing out her expression again. What did he mean? She did not know how to reply.

"I am enjoying it more than I expected when I arrived," he said.

"I am glad," she told him.

"Are you?" He reached out one hand and took one lock of her hair between his fingers—she had had her maid leave it loose.

It was one of their usual conversations, saying nothing and leading nowhere. She had always felt more awkward with him than with any other man of her acquaintance.

He bent his head then and kissed her.

She was taken totally by surprise. *This* was different from their wedding night.

He did not immediately draw back. Instead he parted his lips and settled them more comfortably over her own. She tasted heat and moisture and wine. At the same time he settled his hands on either side of her waist and drew her against him. She lifted her hands and set them on his shoulders—broad, solidly muscled shoulders. He was solid everywhere, she noticed as if for the first time. He seemed terribly male.

She had never really touched him before, she realized. Not with her hands—she had kept them flat on the bed during all their encounters last year. And not really with her body—she had felt his weight and his penetration, that was all.

She felt his tongue prodding against the seam of her lips and jerked back her head—and then wished she had not done so. He stared into her eyes, his hold still firm on her waist, his expression unreadable.

"Is this just duty to you, then, Elizabeth?" he asked her. "Is this what the whole of today has been about for you?"

What did he expect her to say? What did he want her to say? Last year had been easy in a way. He had spoken scarcely a word to her in her bedchamber—or out of it, for that matter.

"I have tried to do my duty," she said. "Have I not pleased you? I am sorry about . . . about just now. I was not . . . expecting it. I am sorry."

He took a half step back from her, though he still kept his hands where they were.

"If this is duty and nothing else, Elizabeth," he said, "say so now and send me on my way."

It was not just duty. She would not have dreamed of saying no to him anyway, of course, but it was not just duty. She had wanted him to come. She wanted him in her bed again even though she knew now from experience that the encounter would not measure up to her dreams. It did not matter. She wanted him inside her again. She wanted to feel like his wife.

She had taken too long in answering. He dropped his hands abruptly, turned, and strode toward the door.

"Mr. Chambers," she said sharply.

"For God's sake, Elizabeth." He stopped and turned back to her, anger in his face. "Call me Edwin or nothing at all."

"I am sorry." She tried not to show her distress. He was angry with her. He had spoken sharply to her. He had said *for God's sake* in her hearing.

"Don't be." He lifted one hand and ran the fingers through his hair. "There is no need to be eternally sorry. You owe me nothing. You married me in obedience to your parents' will, you lay with me in the weeks following our marriage, and you presented me with a son in due course. Your life is essentially your own now. You are not my slave. I have never believed in slavery, especially the marital kind."

"I owe you obedience," she said.

"You owe me *nothing*." For a moment his eyes blazed. Then he shook his head slightly, and his anger faded. "I would far rather hear you consign me to the devil than tell me you owe me obedience. But no matter. It is late and we are both tired. Good night, Elizabeth."

All the joy of the day had been drained away, leaving only an intense pain behind it. His hand was on the doorknob. In another moment he would be gone—and they would be forever estranged. She would not be able to bear it.

"Mr. Chambers," she said. She lifted one hand to her mouth even as he paused without turning. "Edwin. Please don't leave."

He turned his head to look at her.

"Please don't," she whispered.

He did not move and so she did. She crossed the room to the bed, removed her slippers, and lay down on her back, all without looking at him. He stood there at the door for a few moments longer before walking to the mantel and blowing out the candles. There was still plenty of light from the fire and the window to illumine his way to the bed.

And enough light for Elizabeth to see when he removed his dressing robe that he wore nothing beneath it. At first she was shocked, but she did not look away. She had never thought of any man as beautiful. Handsome, yes, but not beautiful. Edwin was beautiful—all well-muscled, perfectly proportioned male beauty.

He lay down beside her and turned to her. He raised himself on one elbow, leaned over her, and kissed her again, his hand cupping her cheek, his fingers pushing into her hair. This time when he parted his lips and touched hers with his tongue, she did not flinch—though she did feel a raw and unfamiliar sensation in her mouth, in her breasts, in her womb, down between her thighs. She parted her lips and opened her mouth, and he pressed his tongue deep inside.

For a few moments she hardly noticed that his hand had moved down to fondle her breasts. She did notice, though, when the hand moved to the ribbons that held her nightgown closed to the waist and pulled them loose one by one. His hand slid along bare flesh to cup her breast. He ran his thumb lightly over her nipple.

She thought she would surely die of pleasure. She heard herself make a sound deep in her throat.

"Touch me," he whispered against her lips.

She set one hand tentatively against his chest—it was hard and dusted with hair. The other arm she set about his waist. She had always wanted to touch him, she realized, but she had never laid claim to him as her own. Hers had always been the passive role of obedient wife. Was it possible for a woman to claim a man? Was it right? Was it seemly?

He was not simply going to lift her nightgown tonight, bring himself down on top of her, and penetrate her. That was already clear. She was enormously thankful. It had always been over so very quickly, long before she could even begin to draw any secret pleasure from it.

She was not prepared, though, for all the things he did

before the inevitable moment came. He touched her everywhere, with his hands, with his mouth, even with his teeth, first through her nightgown, then beneath it. Finally he slid both hands beneath the gown and lifted it up her body and over her head and along her lifted arms.

And they were both naked.

She should have been horribly shocked, especially as there was so much light in the room and the bedcovers had been pushed back. But her body was humming with pleasure, and his hands and his mouth and his eyes made her feel beautiful. She was having a hard time containing the sensations that were pulsing with her blood into every nerve ending in her body. She throbbed between her thighs and up inside, longing for his penetration, not wanting it too soon, knowing that all would be over within moments once it did happen.

She touched him lightly with her hands—above the waist—and said nothing.

When his hand slid between her legs and explored and caressed the soft secret folds, she knew that she was wet and hot—his fingers felt contrastingly cool. He slid a finger up inside her. She kept her eyes closed and tried to concentrate upon her breathing.

And then he moved over her and lowered his weight on her and spread her legs wide with his own. Familiarity returned as he slid his hands beneath her buttocks and she spread her arms across the bed and pressed her palms into the mattress and drew a slow, deep breath.

He came inside slowly, sliding into wetness, stretching her, filling her. He felt gloriously hard. She fought the urge to tighten inner muscles about him, and lay still.

It lasted far longer than she remembered. He worked her with a slow, deep, firm rhythm for a long time, filling her with himself, filling her, too, with a longing so intense that she wondered if indeed there was any difference between pain and pleasure. By the time he quickened and deepened the rhythm, she was digging into the mattress with her fingers and biting hard on her upper lip in an effort to control herself—though what it was she controlled or stopped from happening she did not know.

He made a guttural sound of satisfaction against the side of her face, and she felt the remembered heat at her core. She was taking his seed into herself again. Despite the slight, unidentified dissatisfaction she felt as all his weight relaxed down onto her and he fell still, Elizabeth smiled and felt happiness well inside to replace the raw discomfort of physical desire not quite allowed to complete itself.

They were not estranged.

Perhaps there would be another child.

When he came for an occasional visit to Wyldwood—and surely he would come for Jeremy's sake—they would perhaps share a bed for a few minutes each night and she would be able to feel this pleasure again.

She tried not to feel dejection when he drew free of her and moved off her. He would return to his room now, and she would feel the remembered emptiness of being alone once more. But differently from all those other times, she would have pleasant memories with which to warm herself until she slept. And perhaps he would come back tomorrow night.

He lay beside her for a while, turned toward her. Then he rested a hand on her stomach and made light circles with it. He sighed audibly.

"For a while," he said, "I thought it was perhaps more than duty."

She turned her head sharply to look at him. He was half smiling.

"It was not duty," she said.

"You just do not like me very much, do you?" he said. "Or is it sex you do not like? Or both?"

Joy went crashing out of her again, and she felt her eyes fill with tears.

"I am sorry," she said. "I did not satisfy you. I did my best. I am sorry."

"Damn," he said so softly that she was not even sure he had uttered such a shocking word.

He turned sharply away and sat up on the side of the bed, his elbows on his knees, the fingers of both hands pushing through his hair. Elizabeth felt two tears spill over, one to pool against her nose, the other to plop off onto her pillow.

"I am sorry," she said again. "What did I do wrong? Tell me, and I will do better next time."

"What has she done to you?" he said. "This is all her doing, is it not?"

"Whose?" she asked, bewildered.

"Your mother's," he said. "You are not naturally frigid, are you? I thought so until today, but I have seen you laughing and flushed and happy. You are warmly maternal with Jeremy. Do you hate me so much? Or are you merely a product of your mother's rigid ideas of what a lady should be?"

But she had heard only one thing. She stared at his back in horror.

"I am not frigid," she protested. "I am *not*. I feel things as deeply as anyone else. How could you say such a cruel thing? I am sorry if I do not satisfy you, but I am *not frigid*."

She turned over onto her side, spread her hands over her face, and tried—unsuccessfully—to muffle the sobs she could not control.

"Elizabeth—"

"Go away," she wailed. "Go away. You are horrid, and I hate you. I am not *fr-frigid* I wish you would . . . I wish you would go to the devil." She had never, ever said such a thing aloud, or even thought it, until now.

For a few moments she did not know what he was doing. She waited for the sound of the door opening and closing. But then the bed beside her depressed. He had come around it and sat down. He was wearing his dressing robe. He set the backs of his knuckles against her hot, wet cheek and rubbed them back and forth lightly.

"Forgive me," he said. "Please forgive me."

She turned her face into the mattress, shrugging his hand away.

"No," she said. "How could you say such a thing after . . . after what happened. I thought it was wonderful. Obviously I know nothing. It was not wonderful at all, was it? Go away, then. Go away and never come back. Jeremy and I have lived without you for three months. We can live without you for the rest of our lives."

"Elizabeth," he said, and she had the satisfaction of hearing distress in his voice. "My dearest, I had no intention of hurting you. Curse me for a fool that I ever said such a thing. I do not believe it. We did everything wrong from the start, did we not? We allowed this marriage to be arranged for us. There was nothing too wrong in that—it happens all the time. But we made no attempt to make it our own marriage. We allowed awkwardness and perhaps some resentment to keep us almost silent with each other. And then my father died and everything fell to pieces. It was all my fault. I should have persevered. I should have been more patient, gentler with you. I should have tried to talk with you."

Again, she had heard only one thing, her face still buried in her pillow. *My dearest.* He had called her *my dearest.* No one, in her whole life, had ever called her by any endearment, except the shortened form of her name—Lizzie.

"Is it too late for us?" he asked her. "Is there any chance of making a workable marriage of this one we are in together?"

She shrugged her shoulders but said nothing. She did not trust her voice yet.

"How have you thought of me all year?" he asked her. "I have thought of you as a beautiful, unattainable, aristocratic icicle. You cannot have thought of me in any more flattering terms."

"Morose," she said into her pillow. "Dour, humorless. Wondrously handsome."

"Am I still all those things?" he asked after a short pause.

"You are still wondrously handsome," she said.

"I have assumed," he said, "that you despise me for marrying social position."

She turned her face out of the pillow, though she did not look at him.

"I have assumed," she said, "that you despise me for marrying money."

"Lord God," he said after another pause, "you would think that two reasonably intelligent adults who happen to be married to each other would have found a moment in which to talk to each other in a whole year, would you not?"

"Yes," she said.

He sat there looking down at her for a while. She lay still and did not look directly at him. She felt that a great deal had already been said. But what, really, had changed?

He got to his feet suddenly and turned to slap her lightly on one buttock.

"Get up," he said, his voice brisk and cheerful. "Get dressed."

"Pass me my nightgown, then," she said. He had dropped it over the other side of the bed.

"*Dressed,*" he said with more emphasis. "Put on your warmest clothes."

"Why?"

"We are going out," he said.

"Out?" She stared at him with wide eyes. "Why?"

"Who knows why?" He looked down at her and grinned—her stomach turned a complete somersault inside her, she would swear. "We are going to talk. Perhaps we will build a snowman. Or make snow angels. That would be appropriate for the occasion, would it not?"

"The doors are all bolted," she said foolishly. "It is almost midnight."

He said nothing. He merely continued to look down at her and grin at her.

He was mad. Wondrously, gloriously mad.

Elizabeth laughed.

"You are mad," she said.

"You see?" He pointed a finger at her. "That is something you have not known about me all year. There is a great deal more. And I have not known that you could possibly laugh at the prospect of being dragged outside on a cold, snowy night in order to make snow angels. I daresay there is a great deal I do not know of you. I am going out. Are you coming with me or are you not?"

"I am coming," she said, and laughed again.

"I'll be back here in five minutes," he told her, and he strode to the door and left the room without a backward glance.

Elizabeth gazed after him and laughed again.

And jumped out of bed.

Five minutes! Never let it be said that she had kept him waiting.

"You lie down on your back," he explained, "and spread out your arms and legs and swish them carefully back and forth. Like this." He demonstrated while she watched and then got to his feet again and looked down at the snow angel he had made. "Rather a large one."

"The angel Gabriel," she said softly.

She was wearing a pale, fur-lined cloak with the hood drawn over her head. She looked ethereally lovely in the reflected light from the snow. She also looked very much on her dignity. But she lay down carefully on the snow beside his own angel and made one of her own with slow precision and downcast eyes.

He was so much in love with her that he wanted to howl at the moon. He was also afraid, uncertain. Was this his dutiful wife he had with him? Or was she the repressed daughter of a humorless tyrant, ready to break free, like a butterfly from the cocoon? But would she simply fly past him when she discovered her wings?

"Ah," he said after she had got back to her feet again, "a dainty angel. A guardian angel, I believe. Jeremy's, perhaps. Mine, perhaps."

She looked at him and smiled—and then her eyes went beyond him to the sky.

"Oh, look," she said, "the clouds are moving off. Look at the miracle."

The moon was almost at the full, and suddenly, it seemed, the sky was studded with stars. They looked unusually bright tonight, perhaps because he was in the country rather than in London, as he usually was. One in particular drew his eyes. He stepped a little closer to her and pointed, so that she could look along the length of his arm to that particular star.

"I believe the Wise Men are on their way after all," he said.

"Edwin," she said softly, "have you ever known a more perfect Christmas?"

The sound of his name on her lips warmed him. No, he never had—he had never known a more perfect Christmas or a more perfect moment. If he held his breath, could he hold on to it forever?

"I have not," he told her.

He was about to set one arm about her waist, to draw her to him, to begin, perhaps—one year late but surely not *too* late—to speak the words of the heart, so difficult for a man who spent his days speaking the practical words of business and commerce. But she spun around to face him before he could lift his arm, and in the semidarkness he could see that her body was tense and her expression agitated.

"Take us back with you," she said. "When you go home to London, take us with you."

The words were so stunningly unexpected, so exactly what he wanted to hear that he stared stupidly at her for several moments without speaking.

"Why?"

She stared back at him, still tense, before closing her eyes and turning away from him.

"Jeremy needs you," she said.

Again there was a long pause, during which he dared not ask the question whose answer might shatter his newfound, fragile dream. How foolishly hesitant he was with his wife—so different from the way he was in all other aspects of his life. But she answered the question before he could ask it.

"*I* need you."

"Do you?" His heart felt as if it might burst.

"Edwin," she said in a rush, her voice breathless, her face still turned away, "I should have said no. Even though Mama and Papa were in desperate financial straits, I should not have agreed to buy their reprieve at the cost of your freedom and happiness. But I had met your father and liked him enormously, and I knew that he really wanted me for you. And so I persuaded myself that perhaps you wanted me too. But it was purely selfish of me. I thought I could leave behind the cold, loveless world in which I had grown up and become part of your father's warm, joy-filled world. Instead I killed any joy you might have had. I am so sorry. But let us go home with you, and I will try . . ."

His hand closed tightly about one of her arms, and she stopped talking as he turned her to him and gazed down into her face, bathed in the light of the moon and the Christmas star.

"Elizabeth," he said, "I am the one who destroyed *your* happiness, taking you away from your own world only because I knew my father was dying and I could not say no to him. I despised myself for agreeing to that bargain when you must have dreamed of making a dazzling match with a titled gentleman of the *ton*, someone who was your social equal. All I could think to do after my father died was to bring you here, to a home that at least would be familiar to you in size and grandeur, and to give you a measure of freedom from me and my world. Yet now you want to come back to me?"

She bit her lip. "You did not despise me?"

"*Despise* you?" He took both her arms in his hands and drew her closer. "Elizabeth, I fell head over ears in love with you the moment I set eyes on you. I tried to . . . treat you with restraint and respect. I thought that perhaps after you had grown accustomed . . . But you seemed to turn to stone. And then my father died."

When she lifted one gloved hand to cup his cheek, he could see that it was trembling. He could also see stars reflected in her eyes.

"Edwin," she whispered, "I thought you despised me. I wanted that marriage so very, very much—with you, with your father's son. You were to be my escape from a life I had never enjoyed, and I was so very enchanted when I first saw you. But when you said nothing after our marriage about love or even affection, but were so . . . *respectful*, I thought you despised me."

"We have been such idiots," he said, raising her hand to his cheek and holding it there. He grinned at her. "I thought it was just me, but it was you too. I know so little about pleasing a woman, Elizabeth, especially the woman I love."

Her eyes looked even brighter suddenly, and he knew they were filled with tears.

"You do know," she said. "Today has been the happiest of my life—to see you smile and laugh, to see you hold Jeremy, to have you kiss me beneath the kissing bough, to—" She stopped abruptly and bit her lip again.

He turned his head and kissed her gloved palm.

"I will teach you to enjoy what happens in our marriage bed, Elizabeth," he said. "I promise. Just give me time. I have to learn how to please you."

"You pleased me." She snatched her hand away from his cheek to set it, with her other hand, on his shoulders. She gazed earnestly into his face. "You pleased me, Edwin. I thought I would die of pleasure. But I did not show it, did I? Perhaps I ought to have done so. Mama told me—before our nuptials—that I must always lie still and pray for it to be soon over. But tonight I did not want it to be over. I prayed for it never to end. You pleased me, Edwin. Oh, you did!"

He chuckled and then wrapped his arms about her and held her tight. He laughed aloud, and she joined him.

"I must tell you," she said, "that I have told Mama that she and Papa must leave Wyldwood after Christmas. Even if I must stay here alone with Jeremy, I will be happier without Mama's influence. I want to be your *wife*, even if I am to see you only once or twice a year."

He caught her to him even more tightly.

"My dearest," he said. "Oh, my love. I will not let you out of my sight again for longer than a day at a time—and even that will be too long."

She drew back her head and smiled at him. He smiled back before lowering his head and kissing her. This time there was no audience, as there had been in the drawing room before tea, and this time there was no anxiety or uncertainty, as there had been in their bedchamber earlier. This time there was all of love to be shared openly and joyfully. And the knowledge that a future together stretched ahead of them even after Christmas had passed into a new year and a new spring and a new hope.

When he lifted his head, they smiled at each other again. The house—their house, the house his father had purchased for him, really a rather lovely house—was behind her at the top of the snow-clad lawn. In fancy he could almost see the rudely carved Nativity scene behind the dark drawing room windows. He knew exactly which window Jeremy slept behind, warm and safe in his crib. Their son.

Above them, the sky was moonlit and starlit, the Christmas star beaming softly down on their heads—or so it seemed.

"It must be after midnight," he said, his arms still about her waist, hers about his neck. "Happy Christmas, my dearest."

"Happy Christmas, Edwin," she said.

"I do not know about you," he said, grinning down at her, "but I am frozen out here. Whose idea was this, anyway?"

She smiled back at him, a radiant smile that lit her with beauty.

"It was the most wonderful idea in the world," she said. "I have seen Christmas angels and the Christmas star, and I have taken all the love and joy of Christmas into my heart and my life. But I *am* chilly," she admitted.

"We had better go back to bed, then," he said, "and see if we can warm each other up."

Even in the moonlight he knew that she blushed. But she did not stop smiling or gazing into his eyes.

"Yes," she said. "Oh, yes, Edwin. Let's do that."

The Christmas star shed its radiant light onto Wyldwood long after they had gone inside and warmed each
other and loved each other and fallen asleep, twined together beneath the rumpled bedcovers.

The
Star of
Bethlehem

"I've lost the Star of Bethlehem," she told him bluntly when he came to her room at her maid's bidding. There was some sullenness in her tone, some stubbornness, and something else in addition to both, perhaps.

He stood just inside the door of her bedchamber, his feet apart, his hands clasped behind him, staring at her, showing little emotion.

"You have lost the Star of Bethlehem," he repeated. "Where, Estelle? You were wearing it last night."

"I still have the ring," she said with a nonchalance that was at variance with her fidgeting hands. She noticed the latter, and deliberately and casually brushed at the folds of her morning wrap in order to give her hands something to do. "But the diamond is gone."

"Was it missing last night when we came home?" he asked; his eyes narrowing on her. Having assured herself that her wrap fell in becoming folds, she was now re-tying the satin bow at her throat. She looked as if she cared not one whit about her loss.

"I would have mentioned it if I had noticed, would I not?" she said disdainfully. "I really don't know, Allan. All I do know is that it is missing now." She shrugged.

"It probably came loose when you hurled the ring at

my head last night," he said coolly. "Did you look at it when you picked it up again?"

She regarded him with raised chin and eyes that matched his tone. Only the heightened color of her cheeks suggested the existence of some emotion. "Yes, I did," she said. "This morning. The star was gone. And there is no point in looking about you as if you expect it to pop up at you. Annie and I have been on our knees for half an hour looking for it. It simply is not here. It must have fallen out before we came home."

"I was standing at the foot of the bed when you threw it," he said. "You missed me, of course. The ring passed to the left of me, I believe."

"To the right," she said. "I found it at the far side of the bed."

"To the right, then," he said irritably. "If I were to say that you threw it up into the air, you would probably say that you threw it under the floorboards."

"Don't be ridiculous!" she said coldly.

"The diamond probably landed on the bed," he said.

"What a brilliant suggestion!" She looked at him with something bordering on contempt. "Both Annie and I had similar inspiration. We have had all the bedclothes off the bed. It is not there. It is not in this room, Allan."

She reached into the pocket of her wrap and withdrew a ring, which she handed to him rather unnecessarily. There was certainly no doubt of the fact that the diamond was missing.

The Earl of Lisle took it in the palm of his hand and looked down at it—a wide gold band with a circlet of dark sapphires and an empty hole in the middle where the diamond had nestled. The Star of Bethlehem, she had called it—her eyes glowing like sister stars, her cheeks flushed, her lips parted—when he had given her the ring two years before, on the occasion of their betrothal.

"Look, my lord," she had said—she had not called him by his given name until he had asked her to on their wedding night a few minutes after he had finished consummating their marriage. "Look, my lord, it is a bright star in a dark sky. And this is Christmas. The birthday of Christ. The beginning of all that is wonderful. The beginning for us. How auspicious that you have given me the Star of Bethlehem for our betrothal."

He had smiled at her—beautiful, dark-haired, dark-eyed, vivacious Estelle, the bride his parents had picked out for him, though his father had died a year before and unwittingly caused a delay in the betrothal. And holding her hand, the ring on her finger, he had allowed himself to fall all the way in love with her, though he had thought that at the age of thirty there was no room in his life for such deep sentiment. He had agreed to marry her because marriage was the thing to do at his age and in his position, and because marrying Estelle made him the envy of numerous gentlemen—married and single alike—in London. She would be a dazzling ornament for his home and his life.

It would have been better if he had kept it so, if he had not done anything as foolish as falling in love with her. Perhaps they would have had a workable relationship if he had not done that. Perhaps after almost two years of marriage they would have grown comfortable together.

"Well," he said, looking down at the ring in his hand and carefully keeping both his face and voice expressionless, "it is no great loss, is it, Estelle? It was merely a diamond. Merely money, of which I have an abundance." He tossed the ring up, caught it, and closed his hand around it. "A mere bauble. Put it away." He held it out to her again.

Her chin lifted an inch as she took it from him. "I am sorry to have taken your time," she said, "but I thought you should know. I would not have had you find out at some future time and think that I had been afraid to tell you."

His lips formed into something of a sneer. "We both know that you could not possibly fear my ill opinion, don't we?" he said. "I am merely the man who pays the bills and makes all respectable in your life. Perhaps the diamond fell into the pocket or the neckcloth of Martindale last evening. You spent enough time in his company. You must ask him next time you see him. Later today, perhaps?"

She ignored his last words. "Or about the person of Lord Peterson or Mr. Hayward or Sir Caspar Rhodes," she said. "I danced with them all last evening, and enticed them all into anterooms for secret dalliances." Her chin was high, her voice heavy with sarcasm.

"I believe we said—or rather yelled—all that needs to be expressed about your behavior at the Eastman ball—or your lack of behavior—last night," he said. "I choose not to reopen the quarrel, Estelle. But I have thought further about what I said heatedly then. And I repeat it now when my temper is down. When Christmas is over and your parents return to the country, I believe it will be as well for you to return with them for a visit."

"Banishment?" she said. "Is that not a little gothic, Allan?"

"We need some time apart," he said. "Although for the past few months we have seen each other only when necessary, we have still contrived to quarrel with tedious frequency. We need a month or two in which to rethink our relationship."

"How about a lifetime or two?" she said.

"If necessary." He looked at her steadily from cold blue eyes. Beautiful, headstrong Estelle. Incurably flirtatious. Not caring the snap of a finger for him beyond the fact that he had had it in his power to make her the

Countess of Lisle and to finance her whims for the rest of a pampered life, despite the occasional flaring of hot passion that always had him wondering when it was all over and she lay sleeping in his arms if she had ever gifted other men with such favors. And always hating himself for such unfounded suspicions.

She shivered suddenly. "It is so cold in here," she said petulantly. "How can we be without fires in December? It is quite unreasonable."

"You are the one being unreasonable," he said. "You might be in the morning room now or in the library, where there are fires. You might have slept in a bed-chamber where there was a fire. Chimneys have to be swept occasionally if they are not to catch fire. Half the house yesterday; the other half today. It is not such a great inconvenience, is it?"

"It should be done in the summertime," she said.

"During the summer you said it could wait until the winter, when we would be going into the country," he reminded her. "And then you had this whim about having Christmas here this year with both our families. Well, I have given you your way about that, Estelle—as usual. But the chimneys have been smoking. They must be cleaned before our guests arrive next week. By to-morrow all will be set to rights again."

"I hate it when you talk to me in that voice," she said, "as if I were a little child of defective understanding."

"You hate it when I talk to you in any voice," he said. "And sometimes you behave like a child of defective understanding."

"Thank you," she said, opening her hand and looking down at the ring. "I wish to get dressed, Allan, and go in search of a room with a warm fire. I am grateful that you have seen fit not to beat me over the loss of the diamond."

"Estelle!" All his carefully suppressed anger boiled to the surface and exploded in the one word.

She tossed her head up and glared across at him with dark and hostile eyes. He strode from the room without another word.

Estelle returned her gaze to the ring in the palm of her hand. The back of her nose and throat all the way down to her chest were a raw ache. The diamond was gone. It was all ruined. All of it. Two years was not such a very long time, but it seemed like another Estelle who had watched as he slid the ring onto her finger and rested her hand on his so that she could see it.

It had been Christmas, and she had been caught up in the usual euphoric feelings of love and goodwill, and the unrealistic conviction that every day could be Christmas if everyone would just try hard enough. She had looked at the diamond and the sapphires, and they had seemed like a bright symbol of hope. Hope that the arranged marriage she had agreed to because Mama and Papa had thought it such a splendid opportunity for her would be a happy marriage. Hope that the tall, golden-haired, unsmiling, rather austere figure of her betrothed would turn out to be a man she could like and be comfortable with—perhaps even love.

The ring had been the Star of Bethlehem to her from the start and without any effort of thought. And he had smiled one of his rare smiles when she had looked up at him and named the ring that. Looking into his blue eyes at that moment, she had thought that perhaps he would grow fond of her. She had thought that perhaps he would kiss her. He had not, though he had raised her hand to his lips and kissed both it and the ring.

He had not kissed her mouth at all before their marriage. But he had kissed her afterward on their wedding night in their marriage bed. And he had made a tender and beautiful and almost painless experience out of what she had anticipated with some fright.

She had thought . . . She had hoped . . .

But it did not matter. The only really tender and passionate moments of their marriage had happened in her bed. Always actions of the body. Never words.

They had not really grown close. He never revealed much of himself to her. And she shared only trivialities with him. They never really talked.

They were lovers only in fits and starts. Sometimes wild passion for three or four nights in a row. And then perhaps weeks of nothing in between.

She had never conceived. Not, at least ... But she was not at all sure.

The only thing consistent in their relationship was the quarrels. Almost always over her behavior toward other gentlemen. His accusations had been unjust at first. It was in her nature to be smiling and friendly, flirtatious even. She had meant nothing by it. All her loyalty had been given to her new husband. She had been hurt and bewildered by his disapproval. But in the last year, she had begun to flirt quite deliberately. Never enough to deceive the gentlemen concerned. No one except Allan had ever been offered her lips or any other part of her body except her hand. And never even one small corner of her heart. But she had taken an almost fiendish glee in noting her husband's expression across a crowded drawing room or ballroom, and anticipating the wild rages they would both let loose when they came home.

Sometimes after the quarrels he would retire to his room, slamming the door that connected their dressing rooms behind him. Sometimes they would end up together in her bed, the heat of anger turned to the heat of sexual passion.

The night before had not been one of those latter occasions. She had dragged the Star of Bethlehem from her finger and hurled it at his head and screeched something to the effect that since the ring had become meaningless, he might have it back and welcome to it. And he had yelled something about its being less likely to scratch the cheeks of her lovers if she were not wearing it. And he had stalked out, leaving the door vibrating on its hinges.

And now she really was without the ring. No, worse. She had the shell of it left, just as the shell of her marriage still remained. The star was gone—from the ring and from her marriage.

She was taken by surprise when a loud and painful hiccup of a sob broke the silence of the room, and even more surprised when she realized that the sound had come from her. But it was a wonderful balm to her self-pity, she found. She allowed herself the rare indulgence of an extended and noisy cry.

It was all his fault. Nasty, unfeeling, sneering, cold, jealous monster! She hated him. She did not care that the ring was ruined. What did she care for his ring? Or for him? Or for their marriage? She would be delighted to go home with Mama and Papa when Christmas was over. She would stay with them, surrounded by all the peace and familiarity of her childhood home. She would forget about the turmoil and nightmare of the past two years. She would forget about Allan.

"Allan."

The name was spoken on a wail. She looked down at the ring and sniffed wetly and noisily.

"Allan."

She drew back her arm suddenly and hurled the ring with all her strength across the room. She heard it tinkle as it hit something, but she did not go in pursuit of it. She rushed into her dressing room and slammed the door firmly behind her.

Two minutes passed after the slamming of the door before there came a rustling from the direction of the cold chimney followed by a quiet plop and the appearance of a tiny, ragged, soot-smeared figure among the ashes. After looking cautiously around and stooping for a moment to grub about among the ashes, it stepped gingerly out into the room and revealed itself as a child.

The chimney sweep's boy looked briefly down at the diamond in his hand, a jewel he had mistaken for a shard of glass until he had overheard the conversation of the man and woman. His eyes darted about the room, taking in the door through which the woman had disappeared, and close to which she must have been standing while she was crying and when he had heard the tinkling sound.

She must have thrown the ring they had been talking about. It was just the sort of thing women did when they were in a temper.

His mind tried to narrow the search by guessing in which direction she would have thrown the ring from that particular door. But his wits really did not need sharpening, he saw as soon as he turned his eyes in the direction that seemed most likely. It was lying on the carpet in the open, the light from the window sparkling off the gold band.

What queer coves these rich people were, giving up the search for the diamond after only half an hour, if the woman was to be believed—and the man had not even searched at all. And throwing a gold band set full of precious stones across a room and leaving it lying there on the floor for anyone to take.

The child darted across the room, scooped up the ring, and pulled a dirty rag from somewhere about his person. He stopped when he had one foot back among the ashes, and tied his two treasures securely inside the rag. He must get back to old Thomas. The sweep would be hopping mad by now, and the old excuse of getting lost among the maze of chimneys had been used only three days before.

However, the child thought with a philosophy born of necessity, today's haul would probably be worth every stinging stroke of old Thomas's hand. As long as he did not use his belt. Even the costliest jewel did not seem quite consolation enough for the strappings he sometimes got from the sweep's belt.

The boy had both feet in the grate and was about to pull himself up into the darkness and soot of the chimney when the door through which the lady had disappeared opened abruptly again. He started to cry pitifully.

Estelle, now clad in a morning dress of fine white wool, even though her hair was still about her shoulders in a dark cloud, stopped in amazement.

The child wailed and scrubbed his clenched fists at his eyes.

"What is it?" she said, hurrying across the room to the fireplace and stooping down to have a better look at the apparition standing there. "You must be the chimney sweep's boy. Oh, you poor child."

The last words were spoken after she had had a good look at the grimy, skeletal frame of the child and the indescribable filth of his person and of his rags. Hair of indeterminate color stood up from his head in stiff and matted spikes. Two muddy tracks flowed from his eyes to his chin. He looked as if he were no older than five or six.

"It's dark up there," he wailed. "I can't breathe."

"You shouldn't be climbing chimneys," she said. "You are just a baby."

The child sniffed wetly and breathed out on a shuddering sob. "I got lost," he said. "It's dark up there."

"Oh, you poor child." Estelle reached out a hand to touch him, hesitated, and took hold of one thin arm. "Step out here. The ashes will cut your poor feet."

The boy started to cry in noisy earnest again.

"He'll . . . thrash . . . me," he got out on three separate sobs. "I got lost."

"He will not thrash you," Estelle said indignantly, taking hold of the child's other arm with her free hand and helping him step out onto the carpet. He was skin and bones, she thought in some horror. He was just a frightened, half-starved little baby. "He will certainly not thrash you. I shall see to that. What is your name?"

"N-Nicky, missus," the boy said, and he hung his head and wrapped one skinny leg about the other and sniffed loudly.

"Nicky," she said, and she reached out and tried to smooth down the hair on top of his head. But it was stiff with dirt. "Nicky, when did you last eat?"

The child began to wail.

"Have you eaten today?" she asked.

He shuffled his shoulders back and forth and swayed on one leg. He muttered something.

"What?" she said gently. She was down on her knees looking into his face. "Have you eaten?"

"I don't know, missus," he said, his chin buried on his thin chest. And he rubbed the back of his hand over his wet nose.

"Did your master not give you anything to eat this morning?" she asked.

"I ain't to get fat," he said, and the wails grew to a new crescendo. "I'm so hungry."

"Oh, you poor, poor child." There were tears in Estelle's eyes. "Does your mama know that you are kept half-starved? Have you told her?"

"I ain't got no maw." His sobs occupied the child for several seconds. "I got took from the orphinige, missus."

"Oh, Nicky." Estelle laid one gentle hand against his cheek, only half noticing how dirty her hand was already.

"He'll belt me for sure." The child scratched the back

of one leg with the heel of the other foot and scrubbed at his eyes again with his fists. "I got lost. It's dark and I can't get me breath up there."

"He will not hurt you. You have my word on it." Estelle straightened up and crossed the room to the bellpull to summon her maid. "Sit down on the floor, Nicky. I shall see that you have some food inside you, if nothing else. Does he beat you often?"

The child heaved one leftover sob as he sat down cross-legged on the carpet. "No more nor three or four times a day when I'm good," he said. "But I keep getting lost."

"Three or four times a day!" she said, and turned to instruct her maid to sit with the child for a few minutes. "I will be back, Nicky, and you shall have some food. I promise."

Annie looked at the apparition in some disbelief as her mistress disappeared from the room. She sat on the edge of the bed a good twenty feet away from him, and gathered her skirts close about her as if she were afraid that they would brush against a mote of soot floating about in his vicinity.

Estelle swept down the marble stairway to the hall below, her chin high, her jaw set in a firm line. At one glance from her eyes, a footman scurried across the tiles and threw open the doors of his lordship's study without even knocking first. His mistress swept past him and glared at her husband's man of business, who had the misfortune to be closeted with the earl at that particular moment.

"Can I be of service to you, my dear?" his lordship asked, as both men jumped to their feet.

"I wish to speak with you," she said, continuing her progress across the room until she stood at the window, gazing out at the gray, wintry street beyond. She did not even listen to the hurried leave-taking that the visitor took.

"Was that necessary, Estelle?" her husband's quiet voice asked as the doors of the study closed. "Porter is a busy man and has taken the time to come half across town at my request this morning. Such men have to work for a living. They ought not to be subject to the whims of the aristocracy."

She turned from the window. She ignored his cold reproof. "Allan," she said, "there is a child in my bedchamber. A thin, dirty, frightened, and hungry child."

He frowned. "The sweep's climbing boy?" he said. "But what is he doing there? He has no business being in any room where his master or one of our servants is not. I am sorry. I shall see to it. It will not happen again."

"He is frightened," she said. "The chimneys are dark and he cannot breathe. He gets lost up there. And then he is whipped when he gets back to the sweep."

He took a few steps toward her, his hands clasped behind his back. "They do not have an enviable lot," he said. "Poor little urchins."

"He is like a scarecrow," she said. "He cannot remember if he has eaten today. But he is not allowed to eat too much for fear he will get fat."

"They get stuck in the chimneys if they are too fat," he said, "or too big."

"He gets beaten three or four times a day, Allan," she said. "He does not have a mother or father to protect him. He comes from an orphanage."

He looked at her, his brows drawn together in a frown. "You ought not to be subjected to such painful realities," he said. "I shall have a word with Stebbins, Estelle. It will not happen again. And I shall see to it that the child is not chastised this time. I'm sorry. You are upset." He crossed the room to stand a couple of feet in front of her.

She looked up at him. "He is a baby, Allan," she said. "A frightened, starving little baby."

He lifted a hand to rest his fingertips against her cheek. "I will have a word with the sweep myself," he said. "Something will be done, I promise."

She caught at his hand and nestled her cheek against his palm. "You will do something?" she asked, her dark eyes pleading with him. "You will? You promise? Allan"—her voice became thin and high-pitched—"he is just a little baby."

"Is he still in your room?" he asked.

"Yes," she said. "I have promised him food."

"Have some taken to him, then," he said. "And keep him there for a while. I will come to you there."

"You will?" Her eyes were bright with tears, and she turned her head in order to kiss his wrist. "Thank you, Allan. Oh, thank you."

He held the door of the study open for her, his face as stern and impassive as usual, and summoned a footman with the lift of an eyebrow. He sent the man running in search of the butler and the chimney sweep.

A little more than half an hour later the Earl of Lisle was standing in his wife's bedchamber, his hands clasped behind his back, looking down at a tiny bundle of rags and bones huddled over a plate that held nothing except two perfectly clean chicken bones and a few crumbs of bread. The bundle looked up at him with wide and wary eyes. The countess's eyes were also wide, and questioning.

"You are Nicholas?" his lordship asked.

"Nicky, guv'nor," the child said in a high, piping voice.

"Well, Nicky," the earl said, looking steadily down at him. "And how would you like to stay here and not have to climb chimneys ever again?"

The boy stared, openmouthed. The countess clasped her hands to her bosom and continued to stare silently at her husband.

"I have talked with Mr. Thomas," the earl said, "and

made arrangements with him. And I have instructed Mrs. Ainsford, the housekeeper, to find employment for you belowstairs. You will live here and be adequately fed and clothed. And you will continue to have employment with me for as long as you wish, provided you do the work assigned to you. You will never be whipped."

He paused and looked down at the boy, who continued to stare up at him openmouthed.

"Do you have anything to say?" he asked.

"No more chimbleys?" the child asked.

"No more chimneys."

Nicky's jaw dropped again.

"Does this please you?" the earl asked. "Would you like to be a part of this household?"

"Cor blimey, guv'nor," the boy said.

Which words the earl interpreted as cautious assent. He assigned his new servant to the tender care of the housekeeper, who was waiting outside the door and who considered that her position in the household was an exalted enough one that she could permit herself a cluck of the tongue and a look tossed at the ceiling before she took the little ragamuffin by the hand and marched him down the back stairs to the kitchen and the large tin bathtub that two maids had been instructed to fill with steaming water.

Estelle smiled dazzlingly at her husband and hurried after them. Her white dress, he noticed, standing and watching her go, his hands still clasped behind his back, was smudged with dirt in several places.

She looked more beautiful even than usual.

Estelle was lying in her husband's arms, feeling relaxed and drowsy, but not wanting to give in to sleep. It had been a happy and exciting day and she was reluctant to let it go.

The best part of it was that Allan had come to her

after she had gone to bed, for the first time in two weeks. He had said nothing—he almost never did on such occasions—but he had made slow love to her, his hands and his mouth gentle and arousing, his body coaxing her response and waiting for it. They were good in bed together. They always had been, right back to that first time, when she had been nervous and quite ignorant of what she was to do. Even when there was anger between them, there was always passion too. But too often there was anger, and it always left a bitterness when the body's cravings had been satiated.

It was best of all when there was no anger. And when he held her afterward and did not immediately return to his own room. She liked to fall asleep in his arms, the warmth and the smell of him lulling her.

Except that she did not want to fall asleep tonight. Not yet.

"Allan," she whispered hesitantly. They almost never talked when they were in bed. And very rarely when they were out of it, except when they were yelling at each other.

"Yes?" His voice sounded almost tense.

"Thank you," she said. "Thank you for what you did for Nicky. I think he will be happy here, don't you? You have taken him out of hell and brought him into heaven."

"Our home, heaven?" he said quietly, jarring her mood slightly. "But he will be safe here, Estelle, and warm and well fed. It is all we can do."

"He has a new home in time for Christmas," she said. "Poor little orphan child. He must be so very happy, Allan, and grateful to you."

"He has merely exchanged one servitude for another," he said. "But at least he will not be mistreated here."

"What did you say to the sweep?" she asked. "Did you threaten him with jail?"

"He was doing nothing that every other sweep in the country is not doing," he said. "The problem does not end with the rescue of the boy, Estelle. I merely bought him for twice his apprenticeship fee. The man made a handsome profit."

"Oh, Allan!" Her hand spread across his chest over the fabric of his nightshirt. "The poor little boys."

She felt him swallow. "Some members of the House are concerned over the matter," he said, "and over the whole question of child labor. I shall speak with them, find out more, perhaps even speak in the House myself."

"Will you?" She burrowed her head more deeply into the warmth of his shoulder. She wanted to find his mouth in the darkness. But she only ever had the courage to do that when he had aroused passion in her.

"In the meantime," he said, "you can console yourself with the thought that at least your little Nicky has a warm and soft bed for the night and a full stomach."

And then a wonderful thing happened. Something that had never happened before in almost two years of marriage. He turned his head and kissed her, long minutes after their lovemaking was over, and turned onto his side and stroked the hair back from her face with gentle fingers. And before another minute had passed, she knew that he was going to come to her again.

She fell asleep almost immediately after it was over. It was not until later in the night, when she had awoken and nestled closer to the sleeping form of her husband, who was still beside her, that reality took away some of the magic of the previous day. He had done a wonderful thing for Nicky, she thought. They would be able to watch him grow into a healthy and carefree childhood, long after this particular Christmas was past.

They would be able to watch him? *He* would, perhaps. Allan would. But would she? She was to be ban-

ished to Papa's home after Christmas for a stay that
would surely extend itself beyond weeks into months.
Perhaps even years. Perhaps forever. Perhaps she would
only ever see Allan again on brief visits, for form's sake.

He was sending her away. So that they might rethink
their relationship, he had said. So that he might end
their marriage to all intents and purposes. He didn't
want her anymore. He did not want their marriage to
continue. And even if he were forced to continue their
marriage to some degree, even if her suspicion and
hardly admitted hope proved right, it would be an
empty thing, only a third person holding them together.

And there was that other thing. That thing that she
had not allowed to come between her and her joy the
previous day. The missing ring. Not just the diamond,
but the whole ring. She had hunted for it until she had
felt almost sick enough to vomit. But she had not found
it. Or told Allan about its disappearance. She had repressed her panic and the terrible sense of loss that had
threatened to overwhelm her.

Where could it have gone? Had it been swept up by
the maids? She had even thought briefly of Nicky, but
had shaken the thought off immediately. It had just disappeared, as the diamond had.

Christmas was coming, and there would be no Star of
Bethlehem for her. No joy or love or hope.

But she would not think such depressing and self-pity-
ing thoughts. She settled her cheek more comfortably
against her husband's broad shoulder and rested a hand
on his warm arm. And she deliberately thought back on
the brighter part of the previous day. She smiled.

Nicky not wanting to be parted from his filthy rags
and bursting into pitiful wailings when Mrs. Ainsford
snatched away the rag of a handkerchief he clutched
even after he had relinquished all else. He had a curl of
his mother's hair in the little bundle, he had claimed,

and a seashell that someone had given him at the orphanage. All his worldly possessions. Mrs. Ainsford had given the rag back to him and another clean one to use instead. But the child had not unpacked his treasures to their interested gaze.

Estelle smiled again, listened for a few moments to the deep and even breathing of the man beside her, and turned her head to kiss his shoulder before allowing herself to slip back into sleep.

The earl had not slept for a while after making love to his wife for the second time. He ought not to have come. Relations between them had been strained enough for several months, and the bitter quarrel of the night before had brought matters to a crisis. He had made the decision that they should live apart, at least for a time. They must keep up the charade over Christmas, of course, for the sake of her family and his own. But the pretense did not at least have to extend to the bedchamber.

There was no harmony between them—none—except in what passed between them in silence between the sheets of her bed. He had often wanted to try to extend that harmony into other aspects of their life by talking to her in the aftermath of passion, when they would perhaps feel more kindly disposed to each other than at any other time.

But he had never done so. He was no good at talking. He had always been afraid to talk to Estelle, afraid that he would not be able to convey his inner self to her. He had chosen to keep himself closed to her rather than try to communicate and know himself a failure. He had always been mortally afraid of having his love thrown back in his face. Better that she did not know. And so he had contented himself with giving his love only the one outlet. Only the physical.

But he should not have come tonight. The events of the day had created the illusion of closeness between them. And so he had come to her, and she had received him with something more than the usual passion, which he knew himself capable of arousing. There had been an eagerness in her, a tenderness almost. A gratitude for what he had done for her little climbing boy.

He should not have come. How would he do without her after she had left with her parents after Christmas?

How would he live without her?

What would he give her as a Christmas gift? It must be something very special, something that would perhaps tell her, as he could never do, that despite everything he cared.

Some jewels perhaps? Something to dazzle her?

He smiled bitterly into the darkness as Estelle made low noises in her sleep and burrowed more closely into his warmth. Something to remind her that she had a wealthy husband. More baubles for her to lose or to cast aside with that look of disdain that she was so expert at when he was angry with her for some reason.

Like that ring. He stared upward at the dark canopy over his head. The Star of Bethlehem. The ring that had told him as soon as he slid it onto her finger two years before that she was the jewel of his life, the star of his life. It was not a bauble. Not merely a symbol of wealth.

It was a symbol of his love, of his great hope for what their marriage might have been.

If he could replace the diamond . . .

Where had she put the ring? It had probably been tossed into a drawer somewhere. It should not be hard to find. He could probably find it with ease if he waited for her to go out and then searched her rooms.

He would have the diamond replaced for her. She had been careless about its loss. It had not really mattered to her. She had told him about it merely to avoid a scolding if he had discovered it for himself at a later date.

But surely if he could put it on her finger again this Christmas, whole again, the Star of Bethlehem new again, as Christmas was always new even more than eighteen hundred years after the first one, then it would mean something to her.

Perhaps she would be pleased. And perhaps in the months to come, when she had not seen him for a while, when the bitterness of their quarrels had faded, she would look at it and realize that he had put more than his money into the gift.

He turned his head and kissed his sleeping wife with warm tenderness just above her ear. There was an excitement in him that would surely make it difficult to get to sleep.

Estelle had been happy about Nicky. He remembered the look she had given him as she left this very room after Mrs. Ainsford and the child—a bright and sparkling look all focused on him. The sort of look he had dreamed of inspiring before he married her. Before he knew himself quite incapable of drawing to himself those looks that she bestowed so willingly on other men. Before he realized that he would find himself quite incapable of communicating with her.

He would bask in the memory. And the child had been saved from a brutal life. That poor little skeletal baby, who was probably sleeping peacefully at that very moment in another part of the house, as babies ought.

At that precise moment the former climbing boy, whom his new master thought to be peacefully asleep, was sitting cross-legged on the floor of a room in quite another part of London—a dingy, dirty attic room that was sparsely furnished and strewn with rags and stale remnants of food and empty jugs.

"I tell you, Mags," he was saying in his piping voice, which nevertheless did not sound as pathetic as it had sounded in the countess's bedchamber the previous day, "I took me life in me 'ands comin' 'ere in these togs." He indicated the white shirt and breeches, obviously of an expensive cut and equally obviously part of a suit of livery belonging to some grand house. "But there weren't nothin' else. They burned all me other things."

The Mags referred to shook with silent laughter. "I scarce knew you, young Nick," he said. "I always thought you 'ad black hair."

The child touched his soft fair hair. "Such a scrubbin' you never did 'ear tell of," he said in some disgust. "I thought she'd rub me skin away for sure."

"So yer can't be up to the old lark no more," Mags said, the laughter passing as silently as it had come.

"Naw." Nicky scratched his head from old habit. "Thought she was bein' a blessed angel, she did, that woman. And 'im standin' there arskin' me if I wanted to stay at their 'ouse. Exceptin' I couldn't say no. I would've given an 'ole farthin' to 'ave seen old Thomas's face." He giggled, sounding for a moment very much like the baby the Earl and Countess of Lisle had taken him for. He was in reality almost eleven years old.

"This might be better," Mags said, rubbing his hands together thoughtfully. "You can go 'round the 'ouse at leisure, young Nick, and lift a fork 'ere and a jeweled pin there. P'raps they'll take you to other 'ouses, and yer can 'ave a snoop around them too."

"It'll be almost too easy," Nicky said, rubbing the side of his nose with one finger. His voice was contemptuous. "They're a soft touch if ever I seen one, Mags."

"Got anythin' for me tonight?" Mags asked.

The child shifted position and scratched his rump. "Naw," he said after a few moments' consideration. "Nothin' tonight, Mags. Next time."

"It weren't hardly worth comin', then, were it?" the older man said, his narrowed eyes on the child.

"Just wanted yer to know that me fairy godmother come," the child said, leaping lightly to his feet. "Did yer give the money to me maw for that thimble I brought you last week?"

"'Tweren't worth much," Mags said quickly. "But yes. Yer maw got her food money." He laughed silently again. "And yer sister got 'er vittles to grow on. Another two or three years, young Nick, and yer maw'll be rich with the two of yer."

"I got to go," the child said. And he climbed down the stairs from the attic and went out into the street, where for the first time in his life he had something to fear. His appearance made him fair game for attack. Only the filthy stream of curses he had been quite capable of producing had discouraged one pair of tough-looking urchins when he had been on his way to Mags's attic.

And unexpectedly he still had something to protect on his way back home. He still had the ring and the diamond pressed between the band of his breeches and his skin, although the main reason for his night's outing had been to deliver them to Mags for payment. One of his better hauls. But he had not given them up. That woman, whom he had been told he must call "your ladyship," had bawled like a baby after the man had left her, and flung the ring across the room.

And she had had food brought to him, and had sat and watched him eat it, and smiled at him. And she was the one who had told the big, sour-faced, big-bosomed woman to give him back his bundle—the bundle that held her ring and diamond, and who had stooped down and kissed him on the cheek before he got dumped in that hot water up to the neck and scrubbed raw.

She was pretty. Silly of course, and not a brain in her brainbox—calling him a baby, indeed, and believing his story about the orphanage and about his mother's lock of hair! But very pretty. Well, he would keep her ring for a day or two and sell it to Mags the next time he came. He would have more things by then, though not much. The reason he had never been caught was probably that he had never been greedy. He had learned his lesson well from Mags. He had never taken more than one thing from each house, and never anything that he had thought would be sorely missed.

Nicky darted in his bare feet along a dark street in the shadows of the buildings and cursed his clean hair and skin, which would make him more noticeable, and his clothes, which would be like a red flag to a bull if the wrong people were to spot him on these particular streets.

The bed was empty beside Estelle when she woke up the following morning. She felt only a fleeting disappointment. After all, he never had stayed until morning. And if he had been there, there would have been an awkwardness between them. What would they say to each other, how would they look at each other if they awoke in bed together in the daylight? And remembered the hot passion they had shared before they had fallen asleep.

When she met him downstairs—in the breakfast room perhaps, or later in some other part of the house—he would be, as always, his immaculate, taciturn, rather severe self again. It would be easy to look at him then. He would seem like a different man from the one whose hands and mouth and body had created their magic on her during the darkness of the night.

It was a good thing that he was not there this morning. The night had had its double dose of lovemaking and silent tenderness. At least she could imagine it was tenderness until she saw him again and knew him incapable of such a very human emotion.

Estelle threw back the bedclothes even though Annie had not yet arrived and even though the fire was all but extinguished in the fireplace. She shivered and stood very still, wondering if she really felt nausea or if she were merely willing the feeling on herself. She shrugged, and resumed the futile search for her ring. She had combed through every inch of the room the day before, more than once. It was not to be found.

What she should do was repeat what she had done the day before. She should send for Allan before she had time to think and tell him the truth. If he ripped up at her, if he yelled at her, or—worse—if he turned cold and looked at her with frozen blue eyes and thinned lips, then she would think of some suitably cutting retort. And she need not fear him. He had never beaten her, and she did not think she could ever do anything bad enough that he would.

And what could he do that he had not already done? He had already decided to banish her. There was nothing he could do worse than that. Nothing.

"Oh, my lady," Annie said a few minutes later, coming into the room with her morning chocolate and finding her standing in the corner of the room where she had thrown the ring, "you will catch your death."

Estelle glanced down at herself and realized that she had not even put on a wrap over her nightgown. She shivered. And looked at her maid and opened her mouth to tell the girl to go summon his lordship.

"It is rather cold in here," she said instead. "Will you have some coals sent up, Annie?"

The girl curtsied and disappeared from the room.

And Estelle knew immediately that the moment had been lost. In the second that had elapsed between the opening of her mouth and the speaking of the words about coal being brought for the fire, she had turned coward.

It had been easy the morning before to have Allan called and to tell him about the missing diamond. She had still been smarting from the accusations he had hurled at her the night before, and the sentence he had passed on her. She had derived a perverse sort of pleasure from telling him of the ruin of his first gift to her.

This morning it was different. This morning she could remember his kindness to a little child. And his gentle tenderness to her the night before. And she could hope that perhaps it would be repeated that night if nothing happened during the day to arouse the hostility that always lurked just below the surface of their relationship—except when it boiled up above the surface, that was.

This morning she was a coward. This morning she could not tell him.

She had arranged to go shopping with her friend Isabella Lawrence. There were all sorts of Christmas gifts to be purchased before their houseguests began to arrive to take up all her time. There was Allan's gift to be chosen, and she did not know what she would get him. She did have one gift for him already, of course. She had persuaded Lord Humber, that elderly miser, to part with a silver snuffbox Allan had admired months before, and she had kept it as a Christmas gift. But that had been a long time ago. And Lord Humber had refused to take anything but a token payment. Besides, she had given him a snuffbox the year before too. She wanted something else, something very special. But what did one buy for a man who had everything? Still, she would enjoy the morning despite the problem. Isabella could always cheer her up with her bright chatter and incessant gossiping.

She ate her breakfast in lone state, her husband having already removed to his study, Stebbins told her. She did not know whether to be glad or sorry.

But there was one thing she had to do before going out. She had Annie bring Nicky to her dressing room.

She smiled at him when he stood inside the door, his chin tucked against his chest, one leg wrapping itself around the other. He was clean and dressed smartly in the livery of the house. But he was still, of course, pathetically thin and endearingly small.

"Good morning, Nicky," she said.

He muttered something into the front of his coat.

She crossed the room in a rush, stooped down in front of him, and set her hands on his thin shoulders. "Did you have a good breakfast?" she asked. "And did you sleep well?"

"Yes, missus," he said. "I mean . . ."

"That is all right," she said, lifting a hand to smooth back his hair. "You do look splendid. Such shiny blond hair. Are you happy, Nicky, now that you have a real home of your own?"

"Yes, missus," he said, sniffing and drawing his cuff across his nose.

"Nicky," she said, "I lost a ring yesterday. In my bedchamber. You did not see it there when you came down the chimney, I suppose?"

The child returned his foot to the floor and scratched the back of his leg with his other heel.

"No, of course you did not," she said, putting her arms about his thin little body and hugging him warmly. "Oh, Nicky, his lordship gave me the ring when we were betrothed. And now I have lost it. It was without question my most precious possession. Like the lock of your mama's hair is to you. And the seashell." She sighed. "But no matter. Something else very precious came into my life yesterday. Even more precious perhaps because it is living." She smiled at his bowed head and kissed his cheek. "You came into my life, dear. I want you to be happy here. I want you to grow up happy and healthy.

There will never be any more chimneys, I promise you. His lordship would not allow it."

Nicky rubbed his chin back and forth on his chest and rocked dangerously on one leg.

"Annie is waiting outside for you," Estelle said. "She will take you back to the kitchen, and Mrs. Ainsford will find you jobs to do. But nothing too hard, I assure you. Run along now. I shall buy you a present for Christmas while I am out. And I will not add 'if you are good.' I shall give you a gift even if you are not good. Everyone should have a Christmas gift whether he deserves it or not."

Nicky looked up at her for the first time, with eyes that seemed far too large for his pale, thin face. Then his hand found the doorknob and opened the door. He darted out to join the waiting maid.

Estelle tied the strings of her bonnet beneath her chin and knew what she was going to buy for her husband for Christmas. It was not really a gift for him, she supposed. But it would do. It would be the best she could do, and perhaps after she had gone away into her banishment he would understand why she had chosen to give him such a strange gift. Perhaps—oh, just perhaps—her exile would not last a lifetime.

The Earl of Lisle felt very guilty. He had often accused his wife of flirting, on the basis of very hard evidence he had seen with his own eyes. He had a few times accused her of doing more than flirting. She had always hotly denied the charges, though she had usually ended the arguments with a toss of the head and that look of disdain and the comment that he might believe what he pleased. And who, apart from him, would blame her anyway for taking a lover, when she was tied for the rest of a lifetime to such a husband?

He had never looked for evidence. And it was not be-

cause he was afraid of what he might discover. Rather it
was out of a deep conviction that even though he was
her husband, he did not own her. Although in the eyes
of the law she was his possession, he would never look
on her as such. She was Estelle. His wife. The woman he
had secretly loved since before his marriage to her. And
if she chose to flirt with other men, if she chose to be unfaithful to him with one or more of those men, then he
would rant and rave and perhaps put her away from
him forever. But he would never spy on her, never publicly accuse her, never publicly disown her.

He would endure if he must, as dozens of wives were
expected to endure when their husbands chose to take
mistresses.

It was with the greatest of unease, then, that he
searched his wife's rooms after she had left on her shopping trip with Isabella Lawrence. He was looking for the
ring. He was terrified of finding something else. Something that he did not want to find. Something that would
incriminate her and destroy him.

He found nothing. Nothing to confirm some of his
worst suspicions. And not the ring either. Wherever she
had put it, it certainly was not in either her bedchamber
or her dressing room.

It seemed to him, as he wandered through into his
own dressing room, that he must now abandon the plan
that had so delighted him the night before. But not necessarily so, he thought after a while. The diamond would
have been new anyway. Why not the whole ring? Why
not have the whole thing copied for her? A wholly new
gift.

A wholly new love offering.

The trouble was, of course, that he would have to de-
scribe the ring very exactly to a jeweler in order that it
could be duplicated. He had bought the ring for her two
years before. He had put it on her hand. He had looked

at it there, with mingled pride and love and despair, a thousand times and more. And yet he found that he could not be clear in his mind whether there had been eight sapphires or nine. And exactly how wide had the gold band been?

He tried sketching the ring, but he had never been much of an artist.

He would have to do the best he could. After all, it was not as if he were going to try to pretend to her that it was the original ring.

The idea of the gift excited him again. Perhaps he would even be able to explain to her when he gave it. Explain why he had done it, what the ring meant to him. What she meant to him.

Perhaps. Perhaps if he did so she would look at him in incomprehension. Or with that look of disdain.

Or perhaps—just perhaps—with a look similar to the one she had given him the day before, after he had told the little climbing boy that he would be staying with them.

He would go immediately, he decided. The ring would have to be made specially. And there were less than two weeks left before Christmas. He must go without delay.

He decided on eight sapphires when the moment came to give directions to the jeweler he had chosen. And he picked out a diamond that looked to him almost identical to the Star of Bethlehem. And left the shop on Oxford Street feeling pleased with the morning's work and filled with a cautious hope for the future. Christmas was coming. Who would not feel hopeful at such a season of the year?

But his mood was short-lived. As he walked past the bow windows of a confectioner's shop, he turned his head absently to look inside and saw his wife sitting at a table there with Lady Lawrence. And with Lord Martindale and Sir Cyril Porchester. Estelle's face was flushed and animated. She was laughing, as were they all.

She did not see him. He walked on past.

Estelle, inside the confectioner's shop, stopped laughing and shook her head at the plate of cakes that Sir Cyril offered to her. "What a perfectly horrid thing to say," she said to Lord Martindale, her eyes still dancing with merriment. "As if I would buy Allan an expensive gift and have the bill sent to him."

"There are plenty of wives who do just that, my dear Lady Lisle," he said.

"I save my money for Christmas," she said, "so that I can buy whatever I want without having to run to Allan."

"But you still refuse to tell us what you are going to buy him, the lucky man?" Sir Cyril asked.

"Absolutely," she said, bright-eyed and smiling. "I have not even told Isabella. It is to be a surprise. For Allan alone."

Lord Martindale helped himself to another cake. "One would like to know what Lisle had done to deserve such devotion, would one not, Porchester?"

Estelle patted him lightly on the arm. "He married me," she said, and looked at Lady Lawrence and laughed gaily.

"Oh, unfair, ma'am," Lord Martindale said. "Since he has already done so, you see, the rest of us poor mortals are unable to compete."

"We could find some excuse to slap a glove in his face and shoot him," Sir Cyril said.

They all laughed.

"But I should not like that at all," Estelle said. "I would be an inconsolable widow for the rest of my life, I warn you."

"In that case," Sir Cyril said with a mock sigh, getting

to his feet and circling the table in order to pull out
Lady Lawrence's chair, "I suppose we might as well
allow Lisle to live. Lucky devil!"

When they were all outside the shop, the gentlemen
bowed and took their leave, and Estelle promised to
meet Lady Lawrence at the library as soon as she had
completed her errand. She did not want her friend to
come into the jeweler's shop with her—a different jeweler from the one her husband had visited half an hour
before.

She was very excited. Surely he would understand
when he saw it, even though strictly speaking it would
not seem like a gift for him.

She had the advantage over the earl. She remembered quite clearly that there had been nine sapphires.
And she was able to tell the jeweler exactly how wide
the gold band was to be made. She took a long time
picking out a diamond, and did so eventually only because she must do so unless the whole idea was to be
abandoned, for none of them looked quite like the Star
of Bethlehem.

But it did not matter. She was not going to try to deceive Allan. There was no question of trying to pass off
this new ring as the lost one. She would give it to him
only because she wanted him to know that the betrothal
ring had been important enough to her that she would
spend almost all she had on replacing it. She wanted
him to know that there was still the hope in her that she
had worn on her finger for two years.

The hope that one day he would come to love her as
she loved him.

She was going to ask him to keep the ring until she
came home to stay. Perhaps he would understand that
she wanted that day to come.

Perhaps.

But she would want him to have it anyway.

She hurried along the street in the direction of the library a short while later, her cheeks still flushed, her eyes still bright. Everyone around her seemed to be loaded down with parcels. Everyone looked happy and smiled back at her.

What a wonderful time of year Christmas was. If only every day could be Christmas!

The Earl of Lisle was sitting in one corner of his darkened town carriage, his wife in the other. Heavy velvet curtains were drawn across the windows, it being late at night. Estelle's gaze was necessarily confined within the carriage, then. But she did not need to see out. Her gaze was fixed on an imaginary scene of some magnificence.

"'For unto us a child is born,'" she sang quietly to herself. "'Unto us a son is given; unto us a son is given.'" She looked across to her husband's darkened face. "Or is it 'a child is born' twice and 'a son is given' once?" she asked. "But no matter. Mr. Handel's *Messiah* must be the most glorious music ever composed, don't you agree, Allan?"

"Very splendid," he agreed. "But I am surprised you heard any of it, Estelle. You did so much talking." He had meant the words to be teasing, but he never found it easy to lighten the tone of his voice.

"But only before the music began and during the interval," she said. "Oh, come now, Allan, you must admit it is true. I did not chatter through the music. How could I have done so when I was so enthralled? And how could I have sat silent between times when we were in company with friends? They would have thought I was sickening for something."

Her eyes fixed on the upholstery of the seat opposite her, and soon she was singing softly again. "'There were shepherds abiding in the field, keeping watch over their flocks by night.'" She hummed the orchestra's part.

The earl watched her broodingly. He could not see her clearly in the darkness, but he would wager that her cheeks still glowed and that her eyes still shone. As they had done through dinner at the Mayfields', through the performance of Handel's *Messiah* they had attended in company with six friends, and through late-evening tea and cards at the Bellamys'.

She was so looking forward to Christmas, she had told everyone who had been willing to listen—and everyone was always willing to listen to Estelle, it seemed. The first that she and her husband had spent at their own home. And her mama and papa were coming, and her married brother with his wife and two children, and her unmarried brother. And her husband's mother and his two sisters with their families. And two aunts and a few cousins. One more week and they would begin to arrive.

She had been pleased when he had agreed a couple of months before to stay in London and host the family Christmas that year. But she had not bubbled over so with high spirits to him. He could not seem to inspire such brightness in her.

"I spent a fortune this morning, Allan," she said to him now, turning her head in his direction. And he could tell from her voice that she was still bubbling, though she had only him for audience. "I bought so many presents that Jasper looked dubious when I staggered along to the coach. I think he wondered how we were to get all the parcels inside." She laughed.

"Did you enjoy yourself?" he asked.

"I love Christmas," she said. "I live like the world's worst miser from summer on just so that I can be extravagant at Christmas. I think I enjoy choosing gifts more than I like receiving them. I bought Nicky a little silver watch for his pocket. Such a dear little child's thing. You should just see it." She giggled. "I suppose he cannot tell time. I will have to teach him."

"Did you buy such lavish gifts for the other servants?" he asked.

"Oh, of course not." She laughed again. "I would have to live like a beggar for five years. But I did buy them all something, Allan. And they will not mind my giving Nicky something special, will they? He is just a child, and has doubtless never had a gift in his life. Except for his seashell, of course."

"Did you meet anyone you knew?" he asked.

"I was with Isabella," she said. "We nodded to a few acquaintances." There was the smallest of hesitations. "No one special."

"Martindale is not special?" he asked quietly. "Or Porchester?"

There was a small pause again. "Someone told you," she said. "We met them on Oxford Street and they invited us for tea and cakes. I was glad to sit down for half an hour. My feet were sore."

"Were they?" he said. "You did not look as if you were in pain."

She looked sharply at him. "You saw us," she said. "You were there, Allan. Why did you not come inside?"

"And break up the party?" he said. "And make odd numbers? I am more of a sport than that, Estelle."

"Oh," she cried, "you are cross. You think that I was doing something I ought not to have been doing. It is quite unexceptionable for two married ladies to take tea with two gentlemen friends at a public confectioner's. It is too bad of you to imply that it was some clandestine meeting."

His voice was cold. "One wonders why you decided not to tell me about it if it was so unexceptionable," he said.

"Oh!" she said, exasperated. "For just this reason, Allan. For just this reason. I knew you would read into it something that just was not there. It was easier not to tell you at all. And now I have put myself in the wrong. But if you will spy on me, then I suppose you must expect sometimes to be disappointed. Though when I think about that last statement, I don't suppose you were disappointed. Unless it was over the fact that it was not just me and one of the gentlemen. That would have suited you better, would it not?"

"One is hardly spying on one's wife by walking along Oxford Street in the middle of the day," he said.

"Then why did you ask me those questions?" she said. "In the hope that I would lie or suppress the truth? Why did you not simply remark that you had seen me with Isabella and Lord Martindale and Sir Cyril?"

"I should not have had to either ask or make the comment," he said. "If it was all so innocent, Estelle, you would have come home and told me about the afternoon and your encounters. You find it very easy to talk to all our friends and acquaintances, it seems. You never stop talking when we are out. Yet you have very little to say to me. How can I escape the conclusion sometimes that you have something to hide?"

"What nonsense you speak!" she said. "I have been talking to you tonight, have I not? I talked to you about the concert and you remarked that I had chattered too much. I told you about my Christmas gifts and you suggested that I had spent too much on Nicky. Do you think I enjoy such conversation? Do you think I enjoy always being at fault? I don't think I am capable of any goodness in your eyes."

"There is no need to yell," he said. "We are in a small space and I am not deaf."

"I am not yelling!" she said. "Oh, yes, I am, and I yell because I choose to do so. And if you were not so odious and so determined to put me in the wrong, you would yell too. I know you have lost your temper. You speak quietly only so that I will lose mine more."

"You are a child!" he said coldly. "You have never grown up, Estelle. That is your trouble."

"Oh!" she said. And then with a loudly indrawn breath, "I would rather be a child than a marble statue. At least a child has feelings. You have none, do you? Except a fanatical attachment to propriety. You would like a little mouse of a wife to mince along at your side, quiet and obedient and adding to your consequence. You have no human feelings whatsoever. You are incapable of having any."

"We had best be quiet," he said. "We neither of us have anything to say except what will most surely wound the other. Be quiet, Estelle."

"Oh, yes, lord and master," she said, her voice suddenly matching his in both volume and temperature. "Certainly, sir. Beg pardon for being alive to disturb you, my lord. Console yourself that you will have to put up with me for only another few weeks. Then I will be gone with Mama and Papa."

"Something to be looked forward to with eager anticipation," he said.

"Yes," she said.

They sat side by side for the remainder of the journey home in frigid silence.

Estelle had to keep swallowing against the lump in her throat. It had been another lovely day, though she had seen very little of her husband until the evening, when they had been in company. She had so hoped that they could get to the end of the day without trouble. She had hoped that he would come back to her that night so they might recapture the tenderness of the night before. And they had come so close.

She took his hand as he helped her from the carriage, and tilted her chin up at such an angle that he would know her unappeased. His jaw was set hard and his eyes were cold, she saw in one disdainful glance up at him.

He unlocked the door and stood aside to allow her to precede him into the hallway. Although the coachman had been necessarily kept up very late indeed, all the other servants were in bed. The Earl of Lisle refused to keep them up after midnight when he was perfectly capable of turning a key in a lock. He had explained his strange theories to his butler three years before, on his acquisition of the title and the town house.

Estelle waited in cold silence while he took her cloak and laid it on a hall stand, and picked up a branch of lit candles. But before she could reach out a hand to place on his sleeve so that he might escort her to her room, he set a warning hand on her arm and stood very still, in a listening attitude.

Estelle looked at him questioningly. He handed her the candlestick slowly and without a word, his eyes on a marble statue that stood to one side of the staircase, between the library and his study. A hand gesture told her that she was to stay exactly where she was. He moved silently toward the statue.

A child's treble wailing broke the silence before the earl reached his destination. The sounds of a child whose heart was breaking.

"What are you doing here?" the earl asked, stopping beside the statue and looking down. His voice was not ungentle.

Estelle hurried across the tiles to his side. Nicky was standing between the statue and the wall, his fists pressed to his eyes, one bare foot scratching the other leg through his breeches.

"I was thirsty," he said through his sobs. "I got lost."

The earl stooped down on his haunches. "You wanted a drink of water?" he asked. "Did you not go down the back stairs to the kitchen? How do you come to be here?"

The sobs sounded as if they were tearing the child's chest in two. "I got lost," he said eventually.

"Nicky." The earl reached out a hand and pushed back the boy's hair from his forehead. "Why did you hide?"

"I got scared," the boy said. "Are you goin' ter beat me?" His fists were still pressed to his eyes.

"I told you yesterday that you would not be beaten here, did I not?" the earl said.

Estelle went down on her knees and set the candlestick on the tiled floor. "You are in a strange house and you are frightened," she said. "Poor little Nicky. But you are quite safe, you know, and we are not cross with you." She took the thin, huddled shoulders in her hands and drew the child against her. She patted his back gently while his sobs gradually subsided. She glanced across at her husband. He was still stooped down beside her.

The sobs were succeeded by a noisy and prolonged yawn. The earl and his countess found themselves smiling with some amusement into each other's eyes.

"Come on," Estelle said, "we will take you back to your bed, and you shall have your drink."

"I'll take him, Estelle," the earl said, and he stood up, scooping the small child into his arms as he did so. Nicky yawned again.

She picked up the candlestick and preceded them down the stone stairs to the kitchen for a cup of water and up the back stairs to the servants' quarters and the little room that she had been to once the day before. She helped a yawning Nicky off with his shirt and on with his nightshirt while her husband removed the child's breeches.

She smoothed back his hair when he was lying in his bed, looking sleepily up at her. "Sleep now, Nicky," she said softly. "You are quite safe here and must not be afraid of his lordship and me or of anyone else in the house. Good night." She stooped down and kissed him on the cheek.

"Bring a cup to bed with you at nights," the earl said, glancing to the washstand and its full jug of water. "And no more wanderings, Nicky. Go to sleep now. And there must be no more fear of beatings either." He touched the backs of two fingers to the child's cheek, and his lips twitched when a loud yawn was his only answer.

The yawning stopped abruptly when his door closed softly behind his new master and mistress. Nicky clasped his hands behind his head and stared rather glumly at the ceiling. Mags would kill him if he didn't show up with something within the next few days. More to the point, there would be no money for his mother.

But he was, after all, only ten years old. And the hour was something after two in the morning. Sleep overtook him. She smelled like a garden, he thought as he drifted off. Or as he imagined a garden would smell. A really soft touch, of course, as was the governor, for all his stern looks. But she smelled like a garden for all that.

The Earl of Lisle had taken the candlestick from his wife's hand. He held it high to light their way back to the main part of the house and their own rooms.

Estelle turned to face him when they entered her dressing room. Her eyes were soft and luminous, he saw. They had lost their cold disdain.

"Oh, Allan," she said, "how my heart goes out to that child. Poor little orphan, with no one to love him and hug him and tuck him into his bed at night."

"You were doing quite well a few minutes ago," he said.

There were tears in her eyes. "He is so thin," she said. "And he was so frightened. Thank you for being gentle with him, Allan. He did not expect you to be."

"I would not imagine he knows a great deal about gentleness or kindness," he said.

"He should not be working," she said. "He should be playing. He should be carefree."

He smiled. "Children cannot play all the time," he said. "Even children of our class have their lessons to do. Mrs. Ainsford will not overwork him. If you fear it, you must have a word with her tomorrow."

"Yes," she said. "I will. How old do you think he is, Allan? He did not know when I asked him."

"I think a little older than he looks," he said. "I will see what I can do, Estelle. I need to make a few inquiries."

Her face brightened. She smiled up at him. "For Nicky?" she said. "You will do something for him? Will you, Allan?"

He nodded and touched her cheek lightly with his knuckles as he had touched the child's a few minutes before. "Good night," he said softly, before taking one of the candles and going into his own dressing room. He shut the door quietly behind him.

Estelle looked at the closed door before beginning to undress herself rather than summon her maid from sleep. She wished fleetingly that she had apologized for calling him a marble statue. He was not. He did have feelings. They had shown in his dealings with Nicky. But what was the point of apologizing? If she could not call him that in all truth, there were a hundred other nasty things she would call him when next he angered her. And his own words and suspicions were unpardonable.

She climbed into bed ten minutes later and tried not to think of the night before. Soon enough she would have to accustom herself to doing without altogether. She needed to sleep anyway. It was very late.

But even before she had found a totally comfortable position in which to lie and quieted her mind for sleep, the door of her dressing room opened and closed and she knew that after all she was not to be alone. Not for a while anyway.

And as soon as he climbed into the bed beside her and touched her face with one hand so that his mouth could find hers in the darkness, she knew that he had not come to her in anger. She put one arm about his strongly muscled chest and opened her mouth to his seeking tongue.

During the week before their guests began to arrive and the Christmas celebrations could begin in earnest, Estelle kept herself happily busy with preparations. Not that there was a great deal for her to do beyond a little extra shopping. She was not the one who cleaned the house from top to bottom or warmed the extra bedrooms and changed their bed linen and generally readied them for the reception of their temporary occupants. She was not the one who would cook and bake all the mounds of extra food.

But she did confer with Mrs. Ainsford about the allocation of rooms and with the cook on the organization of meals. And she insisted, the day before her parents were to arrive, and her husband's mother, and a few of the other relatives, on decorating the drawing room herself with mounds of holly and crepe streamers and bows and a bunch of mistletoe.

The earl was called in to help, and it was generally he who was having to risk having all his fingers pricked to the bone, he complained, handling the holly and placing it and re-placing it while Estelle stood in the middle of the room, one finger to her chin, directing its exact placement.

But there was not a great deal of rancor in his complaints. There had been no more quarrels since the night of the concert. And Estelle seemed to be happy to be at home, aglow with the anticipation of Christmas. She smiled at him frequently. And he basked in her smiles, pretending to himself that it was he and not the festive season that had aroused them.

"Oh, poor Allan," she said with a laugh after one particularly loud exclamation of protest as he pricked his finger on a holly leaf. "Do you think you will survive? I will kiss it better if you come over here."

"I am being a martyr in a good cause," he said, not looking over his shoulder to note her blush as she realized what she had said.

The mistletoe had to be moved three times before it was in a place that satisfied her. Not over the doorway, she decided on second thought, or everyone would get mortally tired of kissing everyone else, and Allan's cousin Alma, who was seventeen, with all the giddiness of her age, would be forever in and out of the room. And not over the pianoforte, or only the musical people would ever be kissed.

"This is just right," she said, standing beneath its final resting place to one side of the fireplace. "Perfect." She smiled at her husband, and he half smiled back, his hands clasped behind his back. But he did not kiss her.

She made some excuse to see Nicky every day. Mrs. Ainsford would despair of ever training him to be a proper servant, the earl warned her at breakfast one morning when the child had come into the room to bring him his paper, if she persisted in putting her arm about his shoulders whenever he appeared, whispering into his ear, and kissing him on the cheek. And the poor housekeeper would doubtless have an apoplexy if she knew that her mistress was taking a cup of chocolate to the child's room each night after he was in bed.

But he did not forbid her to do either of those things. For entirely selfish reasons, he admitted to himself. Estelle was happy with the child in the house, and somehow her happiness extended to him, as if he were solely responsible for saving the little climbing boy from a life of drudgery. She smiled at him; her eyes shone at him; she gave him tenderness as well as passion at night.

The Earl of Lisle was not entirely idle as far as his new servant was concerned, though. He had learned during his interview with the chimney sweep, of course, that Nicky was no orphan, but that there was a mother at least and perhaps a father, and probably also some brothers and sisters somewhere in the slums of London. The mother had paid to have the boy apprenticed. The sweep had shrugged when questioned on that point. Someone had probably given her the money. He did not know who, and why should he care?

The mother had not come to protest the ending of the apprenticeship. Neither had anyone else. His lordship had not tried to penetrate the mystery further. He had decided not to question the child, not to confront him with his lie. Not that first lie, anyway. But the second? Had Estelle really believed that the boy had been in search of a drink and had got lost? Yes, doubtless she had. She had seen only a thin and weeping orphan, alone in the dark.

The earl had still not done anything about the matter five days after the incident. But on the fifth day he entered his study in the middle of the morning to find Nicky close to his desk, his eyes wide and startled.

"Good morning, Nicky," he said, closing the door behind him.

"I brought the post," the boy said in his piping voice, indicating the small pile on the desk and making his way to the door.

Lord Lisle did not stand aside. His eyes scanned the desktop. His hands were behind his back. "Where is it, Nicky?" he asked eventually.

"What?" The eyes looked innocently back into his.

"The top of the inkwell," the earl said. "The *silver* top." He held out one hand palm-up.

The child looked at the hand and up into the steady eyes of his master. He lifted one closed fist slowly and set the missing top in the earl's outstretched hand. "I was just lookin' at it," he said.

"And clutched it in your hand when I came in?"

"I was scared," the child said, and dropped his head on his chest. He began to cry.

Lord Lisle strolled over to his desk, and sat in the chair behind it. "Come here, Nicky," he said.

The boy came and stood before the desk. His sobs were painful to hear.

"Here," the earl directed. "Come and stand in front of me."

The child came.

The earl held out a handkerchief. "Dry your eyes and blow your nose," he said. "And no more crying. Do you understand me? Men do not cry—except under very exceptional circumstances."

The boy obeyed.

"Now," the earl said, taking the crumpled handkerchief and laying it on one corner of the desk, "look at me, Nicky." The boy lifted his eyes to his master's chin. "I want you to tell me the truth. It must be the truth, if you please. You meant to take the inkwell top?"

"I didn't think you'd miss it," the boy said after a pause.

"Have you taken anything else since you have been here?"

"No." Nicky lifted his eyes imploringly to the earl's and shook his head. "I ain't took nothin' else."

"But you meant to a few nights ago when we found you outside this door?"

His lordship's eyes advised the truth. Nicky hung his head. "Nothin' big," he said. "Nothin' you'd miss."

"What do you do with what you steal, Nicky?" the earl asked.

"I ain't never stole nothin' before," the child whispered.

A firm hand came beneath his chin and lifted it.

"What do you do with what you steal, Nicky?"

The boy swallowed against the strong hand. "Sell it," he said.

"You must have a lot of money hidden away somewhere then," the earl said. "In that little bundle of yours, perhaps?"

Nicky shook his head. "I ain't got no money," he said.

The earl looked into the frightened eyes and frowned. "The man you sell to," he said, "is he the same man who apprenticed you to the sweep?"

The eyes grew rounder. The child nodded.

"Who gets the money?" the earl asked.

There was no answer for a while. "Someone," the boy whispered eventually.

"Your mother, Nicky?"

"Maw's dead," the boy said quickly. "I was in the orphinige."

The earl's tone was persistent, though not ungentle. "Your mother, Nicky?" he asked again.

The eyes, which were too old for the face, looked back into his. "Paw left," the child said. "Maw 'ad me an' Elsie to feed. 'E said we would all 'ave plenty if I done it."

The earl removed his hand from the child's chin at last. He leaned back in his chair and steepled his fingers against his mouth. The boy stood before him, his head hanging low, one foot scuffing rhythmically against the carpet.

"Nicky," Lord Lisle said at last, "I will need to know this man's name and where he may be found."

The boy shook his head slowly.

The earl sighed. "Your mother's direction, then," he

said. "She will perhaps be worried about you. I will need to communicate with her. You will tell me where she may be found. Not now. A little later, perhaps. I want to ask you something. Will you look at me?"

Nicky did so at last.

"Do you like her ladyship?" the earl asked.

The child nodded. And since some words seemed to be required of him in response, he said, "She's pretty." And when his master still did not say anything, "She smells pretty."

"Would you want her to know that I found you with the silver top in your hand?" the earl asked.

The child shook his head.

"Neither would I," the earl said. "We are in entire agreement on that. What do you think she would do if she knew?"

Nicky swallowed. "She would cry," he said.

"Yes, she would," the earl agreed gently. "Very hard and very bitterly. She will not be told about this, Nicky. But if it happens again, perhaps she would have to know. Perhaps she would be the one to discover you. I don't want that to happen. Her ladyship is more important to me that anyone or anything else in this life. Do you know what a promise is?"

The child nodded.

"Do you keep your promises?"

Another nod.

"Are you able to look me in the eye and promise me that you will never steal again, no matter how small the object and no matter how little it will be missed?" Lord Lisle looked gravely and steadily back into the child's eyes when he looked up.

Another nod.

"In words, Nicky, if you please."

"Yes, guv'nor," he whispered.

"Good man. You may leave now." But before the

child could turn to go, the earl set a hand on his head and shook it slightly. "I am not angry with you," he said. "And you must remember that we are now in a conspiracy together to make her ladyship happy."

He removed his hand, and the child whisked himself from the room without further ado. Lord Lisle stared at the door for a long while.

Estelle was not entirely pleased with the ring when she returned to the jeweler's to fetch it. It was very beautiful, of course, but she did not think she would have called it the Star of Bethlehem if this had been the one Allan had put on her finger. The diamond no longer looked like a star in a night sky. She did not know why. It was surely no larger or no smaller than the other had been, and yet it looked more prominent. It did not nestle among the sapphires.

But no matter. She had not expected it to look the same, anyway. There could be no real substitute for the original ring. This one would serve its purpose—perhaps. She took it home and packed it away with the rest of her gifts.

The following day the guests would begin to arrive. She would see her parents for the first time in six months. She had missed them. And everyone else would be coming, too, either on the same day or within the few days following. And Christmas would begin.

She was going to enjoy it more than any other Christmas in her life. It might be her last with Allan. The last during which they would be truly husband and wife, anyway. And though panic grabbed at her stomach when she thought of what must happen when the holiday was over and Mama and Papa began to talk about returning home, she would not think of that. She wanted a Christmas to remember.

The Earl of Lisle was no better pleased with his ring.

He knew as soon as he saw it that the original must have had nine sapphires. The arrangement of eight just did not look right. They did not look like a night sky with a single star shining from it.

But it did not matter. Nothing could look quite like the Star of Bethlehem, and this ring was lovely. Perhaps she would know that it was not meant to be a substitute, but something wholly new. Perhaps. He wrapped the little velvet box and carried it about with him wherever he went.

Nicky, in the meanwhile, was feeling somewhat uncomfortable, for several reasons. There was the whole question, for example, of what Mags would do with him if he could get his hands about his throat. And what his new master would do with him if he caught him thieving again. Nicky had the uncomfortable feeling that it would not be a whipping, which would be easy to bear. The governor would force him to look into his eyes for a start, and that would be worse than a beating. He was proving to be not such a soft touch after all.

Then, of course, there was his mother. And Elsie. Were they starving? Was Mags bothering them? He knew what Mags did to help girls to a living. But Elsie was not old enough yet. Nicky did not know what he would do, short of abandoning his family to their fate. Nothing had been said about any money in this new position of his. Plenty of clothes and food, yes, and very light work. But no money.

There was, of course, the shiny shilling the lady had given him the first night she came to him with a cup of chocolate. Nicky had never seen so much money all at once. But he couldn't give that to his mother. He needed it for something else.

And that brought him to the nastiest problem of all. That ring and that diamond almost burned a hole in his stomach every day, pressed between the band of his

breeches and his skin as they always were. He couldn't
sell them to Mags now. It would seem like breaking his
promise, though the things were already stolen when he
had been forced to look into his master's eyes and make
the promise, and though he had never thought of keeping a promise before.

And he couldn't put them back in the lady's room,
though he had thought of doing so. Because she would
tell the governor and he would know the truth. He was
a real sharper, he was. And he would not whip or even
scold. He would look with those eyes. He might even
put a hand on his head again and make him squirm with
guilt.

There was only one thing he could think of doing.
And that would mean leaving his room again during the
night, and the house, after the lady had brought him his
chocolate and kissed him and allowed him to breathe in
the scent of her. And the governor might catch him and
look at him. And the stupid clothes he would be forced
to wear would draw ruffians like bees to a honey pot.
And Ned Chandler might refuse to help him at the end
of it all and might not believe where he had got the
things and what he meant to do with them.

Nicky sighed. Sometimes life was very hard. Sometimes he wished he were all grown up already so that he
would know without any difficulty at all what was what.
And he was getting used to a warm and comfortable
bed and to a full night's sleep. He did not particularly
want to be prancing about the meaner streets of London at an hour when no one would ever hear of him
again if he were nabbed.

Ned Chandler had been a jeweler of sorts at one time.
He still had the tools of his trade and still mended trin-
kets for anyone who came to ask and dropped a few
coins his way. Nicky, as a very small child, had often
crept into the man's hovel and sat cross-legged and

openmouthed on the floor watching him when he was busy.

It was doubtful that Chandler had ever held in his hands a gold ring of such quality set with nine sapphires of such dark luster, and a diamond that must be worth a fortune in itself.

"Where did you get these 'ere, lad?" he asked in the middle of one particular night, not at all pleased at having been dragged from his slumbers and his two serviceable blankets. He held the ring in one hand, the diamond in the other.

"It belongs to my guv'nor's missus," the child said. "I'm 'avin' it mended for 'er. She sent me. She sent me a shillin'."

"A shillin'?" The former jeweler frowned. "And sent yer in the middle of the night, did she?"

Nicky nodded.

"Did you steal these 'ere?" Chandler asked grimly. "I'll whip the skin off yer backside if you did."

Nicky began to cry. His tears were perhaps somewhat more genuine than was usual with him. "She's pretty," he said, "an' she smells like a garden, an' she brings me choc'lut when I'm in bed. An' I'm 'avin' it mended for 'er."

"But she didn't send yer, lad." It was a statement, not a question.

Nicky shook his head. "It's to be a surprise," he said. "Honest, Mr. Chandler. She lost the di'mond, an' she cried, an' I found it. I'm 'avin' it mended for 'er. I'll give you a shillin'."

"I'll do it," Ned Chandler said with a sudden decision, looking ferociously down at the tiny child from beneath bushy eyebrows with a gaze that reminded Nicky uncomfortably of the earl. "But if I 'ear tell of a lady wot 'ad a ring stole, Nick, lad, I'll find yer and whip yer backside. Understood?"

"Yes." Nicky watched in silent concentration as the jeweler's tools were unwrapped from an old rag and the diamond replaced in the ring.

"You can keep yer shillin'," the man said, tousling the boy's hair when the mended ring had been carefully restored to its hiding place. "And you make sure to give that ring back, lad. Don't you be tempted to keep it, or I'll be after yer, mind."

"Take the money," the boy said, holding out his treasure, "or it won't be my present. Please?"

The man chuckled suddenly. "Well," he said. "I'll take it, 'cos it shows me yer must be honest. Off with yer then, lad. Be careful on your way back."

Nicky grinned cheekily at him and was gone.

Christmas Eve. It had always been Estelle's favorite day of the season. It was on Christmas Day, of course, that the gifts were opened and that one feasted and sat around all day enjoying the company of one's family. But there had always been something magical about Christmas Eve.

On Christmas Eve there was all the anticipation of Christmas.

And this year was to be no exception. There was all the hustle and bustle of the servants and all the tantalizing smells coming from the kitchen, that of the mince pies being the most predominant. And there was Alma pretending to forget a dozen times during the day that the mistletoe was hanging in that particular spot, and standing beneath it. Especially when Estelle's unmarried brother, Rodney, happened to be in the room.

And there was Papa working everyone's excitement to fever pitch, as he did every year, with hints dropped about the presents, hints that stopped just short of telling one exactly what the gift was. And Mama sitting with her needlepoint having a comfortable coze with

Allan's mother. And the children rushing about getting under everyone's feet, and their parents threatening halfheartedly to banish them to the nursery even if it was Christmas.

And the men playing billiards. And the girls whispering and giggling. And Papa tickling any child who was unwise enough to come within arm's length of him. And Allan relaxed and smiling, playing the genial host. And Nicky following the tea tray into the drawing room with a plate of cakes and pastries, looking fit enough to eat himself, and the pleased way he puffed out his chest when Estelle caught his eye and smiled and winked at him.

And the group of carolers who came to the door before the family went to church and were invited inside the hall and stood there and sang, their cheeks rosy from the cold outside, their lanterns still lit and in their hands. And the noisy and cheerful exchange of season's greetings before they left again.

And the quiet splendor of the church service after the hectic day. And the Christmas music. And the Bible readings. And Bethlehem. And the star. And the birth of the baby, the birth of Christ.

And suddenly the meaning of it all, the quiet and breathless moment in the middle of all the noisy festivities surrounding it.

The birth of Christ.

Estelle was seated beside her husband, their arms almost touching. She looked at him, and he looked back. And they smiled at each other.

The drawing room was noisy again when they went back home, even though the children had been put to bed before they went to church. But finally the adults too began to yawn and make their way upstairs. After all, someone said, it would be a terrible tragedy if they were too tired to enjoy the goose the next day.

Estelle smiled rather regretfully at her husband when they were alone together. "It's going so quickly," she said. "One more day and it will all be over."

"But there are always more Christmases," he said.

"Yes." Her smile did not brighten.

"Are you tired, Estelle?" he asked.

She shrugged. "Mm," she said. "But I don't want the day to end. It has been lovely, Allan, hasn't it?"

"Come and sit down," he said, seating himself on a love seat. "I want to tell you about Nicky."

"About Nicky?" She frowned. And Allan wanted to talk to her?

One of his arms was draped along the back of the love seat, though he did not touch her when she sat down beside her. "I have been making some plans for him," he said. "I spoke with him in my study this morning. He seemed quite agreeable."

"Plans?" Estelle looked wary. "You are not going to send him away, Allan? Not another apprenticeship? Oh, please, no. He is too young."

"He is going to live with his mother and his sister," he said.

She looked her incomprehension.

"I am glad to say the orphanage was a fabrication," he said. "To win your sympathy, I do believe."

"He lied to me?" she said. "He has a family?"

"I am afraid he became the victim of a villainous character," he told her gently. "Someone who was willing to set him up in life, buy his apprenticeship to a chimney sweep in exchange for stolen items from the houses that a climbing boy would have access to."

Estelle's eyes were wide with horror. She did not even notice her husband take one of her hands in his.

"I told him I would not tell you," he said. "But I have decided to do so, knowing that you will not blame Nicky or think the worst of him. I caught him at it a week ago, Estelle, though I already had my suspicions."

She bit her upper lip. There were tears in her eyes.

"The money from his stolen goods—or some fraction of it—was going to the upkeep of his mother and sister," he said. "It seems the father took himself off sometime ago."

"Oh, the poor baby," she whispered.

"I have spoken with the mother." He was massaging her hand, which had turned cold, in both of his. "I had her brought here yesterday. I had from her the name of the villain who has been exploiting the child in this way and have passed it on with some pertinent information to the appropriate authorities. Enough of that. To cut a long story short, the mother has agreed that she would consider life in a country cottage as washerwoman to our house as little short of heaven. Nicky confessed this morning to a lifelong ambition to own a horse. I have suggested that he may enjoy working in our stables— when he is not at school, of course. Somehow he was not nearly so enthusiastic about the idea of school."

"So he is to live on your estate with his mother?" she asked.

"Yes." He raised her hand to his lips, and this time she did notice as she saw it there and felt his lips warm against her fingers. "Do you think it a good solution, Estelle? Are you pleased?" He looked almost anxious.

"And you did all this without a word to me?" she asked in some wonder. "You did it to save me some pain, Allan? Did you do it for me?"

His smile was a little twisted. "I must confess to a certain fondness for the little imp," he said. "But yes, Estelle. I thought it might make you happy. Does it?"

"Yes." She leaped to her feet in some agitation and stood quite unwittingly beneath the mistletoe.

He said nothing for a few moments, but he got to his feet eventually and came to stand behind her. He set his hands on her shoulders. "Now this is an invitation impossible to resist," he said, lowering his head and kissing the back of her neck.

She turned quickly and stared at him in some amazement. He had never—ever—held her or kissed her outside her bed. She had not even quite realized that he was so tall and that he would feel thus against her— strong and warm and very safe.

He lowered his head, and his mouth came down open on hers.

And how could a kiss when one was standing and fully clothed and in a public room that might possibly be entered by someone else at any moment seem every bit as erotic as any of the kisses they had shared in bed, when his hands were beneath her nightgown against her naked flesh and when his body was in intimate embrace with hers?

But it was so. She felt an aching weakness spiral downward from her throat to her knees.

When he removed his mouth from hers, it was only to set his forehead against her own and gaze downward at her lips.

"I want to give you your gift tonight," he said. "Now. I want to do it privately. No one else would understand. May I?"

Her senses were swimming, but she smiled at him. "I feel the same way about mine to you," she said. "Yes, now, tonight, Allan. Just the two of us." She ran across the room to where they had all piled their gifts and came back to him with a small parcel in her hands. He had removed his from a pocket.

"Open mine first," he said, and he watched her face as she did so. They were both still standing very close together, underneath the mistletoe. "It is not the original," he said quickly as she opened the velvet box. "It is not nearly as lovely. There were nine sapphires, were there not? I could not remember, but these do not look right. But I want you to have it anyway. Will you, Estelle? Will you wear it?" He took it from the box and slid it onto her nerveless finger.

"Allan!" she whispered. "But why?"

He was not sure he could explain. He had never been good with words. Especially with her. "You called it the Star of Bethlehem," he said. "I always loved that name, because it suggested Christmas and love and peace and hope. All the things I have ever wanted for you. And with you. I felt I could only tell you with the ring. Never in words. Until now."

He laughed softly. "It must be the mistletoe. I am not the man for you, Estelle. You are so beautiful, so full of life. So . . . glittering! I have always envied those other men and wanted to be like them. And I have been horribly jealous and tried to make your life a misery. But I have not meant to. And after Christmas you can go away with your parents, and no one will know that we are separated. There will be no stigma on your name. But you will be free of my taciturn and morose presence." He smiled fleetingly. "My marble-statue self. But perhaps the ring will help you to remember me a little more kindly. Will it?"

"Allan!" She whispered his name. And looked down at the ring on her finger, the ring that was not the Star of Bethlehem, but that she knew would be just as precious to her. And she noticed the parcel lying forgotten in her hands. She held it out to him. "Open yours."

He was disappointed that she said no more. He tried to keep his hands from trembling as he opened her gift.

He stood smiling down at the silver snuffbox with its turquoise-studded lid a moment later. "It is the very one I could not persuade Humber to sell me," he said. "You succeeded, Estelle? You remembered that I wanted it for my collection? Thank you, my dear. I will always treasure it."

But she was looking anxiously into his eyes. "Open it," she said. "There is something else inside. It is not really a present. I mean, it is not for you. It fits me. But I lost the other—yes, I did, Allan. I lost it all, though I have been afraid to tell you. But I wanted you to have this so that you would know that I did not do so carelessly."

He lifted the lid of the snuffbox and stood staring down at a diamond ring set with nine sapphires. He looked up at her, his eyes wide and questioning.

"I didn't mean to lose it," she said. "I have broken my heart over it, Allan. It was my most treasured possession. Because it was your first gift to me, and because at the time I thought it was a symbol of what our marriage would be. And because I spoiled that hope by going about a great deal with my friends when I might have stayed with you, and by flirting quite deliberately with other men when you were so quiet and never told me that I meant anything to you. Because I wanted you to know that my behavior has never shown my true sentiments. Those other men have meant nothing whatsoever to me. I have never allowed any of them to touch more than my fingers. You are the only person—the only one, Allan—who occupies the center of my world. The only one I can't bear to think of spending my life without.

"Because I wanted you to keep the ring when you send me away after Christmas, so that perhaps you will come to know that I love you and only you. And so that perhaps you will want to bring me home again someday and put it on my finger again." She flashed him a nervous smile. "I have given it to you, you see, in the hope that you will give it back to me one day. Now, is that not the perfect gift?"

He lifted the ring from the snuffbox, slipped the box into a pocket, and took her right hand in his. He slid the ring onto her third finger and looked up into her face. "Perfect," he said. "Now you have two gifts and I have one. I do not need to keep the ring for even one minute, you see, Estelle."

The look in his eyes paralyzed her and held her speechless.

"It is the most wonderful gift I have ever had," he said. "It is yourself you are giving me, is it not, Estelle?"

She nodded mutely.

"Come, then," he said. "Give me your second and most precious gift."

She moved into his arms and laid one cheek against his broad shoulder. She closed her eyes and relaxed all her weight against him.

"Do you understand that my gift is identical to yours in all ways?" he murmured against her ear.

"Yes." She did not open her eyes or raise her head. She lifted her hand to touch his cheek with the backs of her fingers. "Except that your ring has only eight sapphires."

He laughed softly.

"You love me, Allan?" She closed her eyes even more tightly.

"I always have," he said. "I knew it the moment I put the Star of Bethlehem on your finger two years ago. I am not good at showing it, am I?"

She raised her head suddenly and gazed into his eyes. "How is it possible," she said, "for two people to be married for almost two years and live close to each other all that time and really not know each other at all?"

He smiled ruefully. "It is rather frightening, is it not?"

he said. "But think of what a wonderful time we have ahead of us, Estelle. I have so much to tell you, if I can find the words. And there is so much I want to know about you."

"I may find too many words," she said. "You know that I can't be stopped once I start, Allan."

"But always to other people before," he said. "Very rarely to me, because you must have thought that I did not want to hear. Oh, Estelle." He hugged her to him and rocked her.

Her arms were wrapped about his chest. She held up her two hands behind his back and giggled suddenly. "I love my two presents," she said. "One on each hand. But I love the third present even more, Allan. The one I hold in my arms."

"This was an inspired choice of location for mistletoe," he said, kissing her again. "Perhaps we should take it upstairs with us, Estelle, and hang it over the bed."

She flushed as she smiled back at him. "We have never needed any there," she said.

He took her right hand in his, smiled down in some amusement at his Christmas present, which he had placed there, and drew her in the direction of the door and the stairs and—for the first time in their married life—his own bedchamber.

The servants had been called into the drawing room to receive their Christmas gifts, the cook first, as she flatly refused to abandon her kitchen for longer than five minutes at the very most.

The Earl of Lisle allowed his wife to distribute the presents, contenting himself with shaking each servant's hand warmly and conversing briefly with each. He wondered if he was looking quite as glowingly happy as Estelle was looking this morning. But he doubted it. No one was capable of glowing quite like her.

Anyway, it was against his nature to show his feelings on the outside. He doubtless looked as humorless and taciturn as ever, he reflected somewhat ruefully, making a special effort to smile at one of the scullery maids, who clearly did not quite know where to put herself when it became clear that she was expected to place her hand into that of her employer, whom she rarely saw.

But, the earl thought, startling the girl by asking if she had quite recovered from the chill that had kept her in bed for two days the week before and so showing her that he knew very well who she was, it was impossible—quite impossible—for Estelle to be feeling any happier than he was feeling. He hoped that she was *as* happy as he, but she could not be more so.

For he knew that the glow and the sparkle in her that had caused all attention to be focused on her since she had appeared in the breakfast room before they all adjourned to the drawing room to open their gifts—he knew that he had been the cause of it all. She glowed because he loved her and had told her so and shown her so all through what had remained of the night when they had gone to bed.

Indeed, it was amazing that she was not yawning and that she did not have dark rings beneath her eyes to tell the world that she had scarce had one wink of sleep all night. When they had not been making love, they had been talking. They had both tried to cram a lifetime of thoughts and feelings and experiences into one short night of shared confidences. And when they had paused for breath, then they had used even more breath in making love to each other and continuing their conversation in the form of love murmurings and unremembered nonsense.

It seemed that the only time they had nodded off to sleep had been just before his valet had come into his room from the dressing room, as he always did, to pull

back the curtains from the windows. It was fortunate that
the time of year was such that the earl had covered Estelle up to the neck with blankets, because she did not
have a stitch on beneath the covers any more than he did.

Poor Higgins had frozen to the spot when he had
glanced to the bed and seen his master only barely conscious, his cheek resting on a riot of tumbled dark curls.
The poor man had literally backed out of the room. Estelle, fortunately, had slept through the encounter until
he woke her with his kisses a few minutes later. And he
had gazed in amusement and wonder at the blush that
had colored her face and neck—after two years of marriage.

Estelle had just given Nicky his present and, child
that he was, he had to open it right there. She sat down
close to where he stood, one arm about his thin waist,
heedless of the presence of all her guests and many of
the other servants. She looked into his face with a smile
and watched his look of wide-eyed wonder and his
dropped jaw as he saw his watch for the first time.

She laughed with delight. "It is a watch for you,
Nicky," she said, "so that you will always know what
time of day it is. Do you know how to tell time?"

"No, missus," he said in his treble voice, his eyes on
his new treasure.

"Then I shall teach you," she said, hugging him and
kissing his cheek. "And when you move to the country
with your mama and your sister, you will know when it
is time to come to the stables to groom the horses, and
when it is time to go home from school. Happy Christmas, sweetheart."

He traced the silver frame of the watch with one finger, as if he were not quite sure that it was real.

"His lordship and I will be going into the country
after Christmas too," she said. "We will meet your
mama and your sister. What is her name?"

"Elsie," he said, and then added hastily, "missus."

"You will want to run along," she said, kissing his cheek again. "I hear that one of the footmen is to accompany you and carry a basket of food to your mama and then go back for you tonight. Do have a lovely day."

"But he don't need to come for me," the child said with some spirit, "I know the way."

Estelle smiled, and the earl held out his hand gravely. "Happy Christmas, Nicky," he said. "Her ladyship and I are very happy that you have come to us."

The child forced his eyes up to the dreaded ones of his master, but he saw nothing but a twinkling kindness there. He turned to leave, but at the last moment whisked a crumpled rag out from the band of his breeches and almost shoved it into Estelle's hands.

"For you," he said, and was gone from the room before she could react at all.

"Oh, Allan, he has given me his seashell," she said to her husband in some distress before being caught up again in the noise and bustle of the morning.

An hour passed before there was a lull enough that the Earl of Lisle could take his wife by the hand and suggest into her ear that they disappear for half an hour. She picked up the half-forgotten rag as they were leaving the room.

"I wished you a happy Christmas very early this morning under the mistletoe," he said with a smile when the study door was safely closed behind them, "and early this morning after I had quite finished waking you. But I feel the need to say it again. Happy Christmas, Estelle." He lifted her hands one at a time to his lips, kissing first the ring he had given her, and then the one she had given him. "We have established an undying reputation for eccentricity, I believe, with two almost identical rings, one on each of your hands."

"They are identical in meaning too," she said, grip-

ping his hands and stretching up to kiss him on the lips.
"Allan, what am I to do with this seashell? He has treasured it so much."

"He really wanted to give it to you," he said. "Let's
have a look at it, shall we?"

They both stood speechless a few moments later,
their foreheads almost touching as they gazed down at
the Star of Bethlehem nestled on her palm inside the
rag. And then their foreheads did touch and Estelle
closed her eyes.

"Oh," she said, after a lengthy silence during which
neither of them seemed able to find quite the right
words to say, "was there ever such a Christmas, Allan?"

"What I am wondering," he said in a voice that
sounded surprisingly normal considering the emotion
that had held them speechless, "is where we are to find
another finger to put it on."

"I see how it is," she said, clasping ring and rag in one
hand and lifting both arms up about his neck. She made
no attempt to suggest a solution to the problem he had
posed. "The Wise Men lost the star too for a while, but
when they found it again, it was over Bethlehem, and
they found also everything they had ever been looking
for. Oh, Allan, that has happened to us too. It has, hasn't
it? What would we have ever done if Nicky had not
come into our lives?"

He did not answer her. He kissed her instead.

She giggled suddenly after he had lifted his head. "I
have just had a thought," she said. "A thoroughly silly
thought. Nicky came down a chimney and brought us a
Christmas happier than any our dreams could have devised."

He laughed with her. "But I don't think even our
wildest dreams could convey sainthood on Nicky," he
said. "I don't think he can possibly be the real Saint
Nicholas, Estelle. Would a real saint steal both a dia-

mond and a ring, as Nicky of the sharp eyes obviously did, be smitten by a pretty lady who smells pretty, and have the ring mended by some devious means? I think it will be entirely better for my digestion if I don't investigate that last point too closely, though doubtless I will feel obliged to do just that tomorrow. The little imp. Perhaps he is Saint Nicholas after all. Now, do you suppose we should go back upstairs to our guests?"

She hesitated and brushed at an imaginary speck of lint on his shoulder and passed a nervous tongue over her lips.

"What is it?" he asked.

She flushed and kept her eyes on his shoulder. "I have another gift for you," she said. "At least, I am not sure about it, though I am almost sure. And I suppose I should not offer it as a gift until I am certain. But by that time Christmas will be over. And it is such a very special Christmas that I have become greedy and want to make it even more so."

He laughed softly. "Suppose you give it to me," he said, "and let me decide if it a worthy offering or not."

She raised her eyes to his and flushed a deeper shade. "I can't actually give it to you for a little more than seven months," she said. "That is, if I am right about it, anyway. But I think I must be, Allan, because it has been almost a whole month now."

"Estelle?" He was whispering.

"I think it must be right," she said, wrapping her arms about his neck again, "because I am never late except perhaps by a day or two. And I think I have felt a little dizzy and nauseated some mornings when getting out of bed, though that could, of course, be wishful thinking. I think I am with child, Allan. I think so. After almost two years. Can it be true, do you think?"

He did not even attempt to answer her question. He caught her up in a hug that seemed designed to crush every bone in her body, and in the body of their child too. He pressed his face to her neck. Hers was hidden against his shoulder.

For the next several minutes it was doubtful that Estelle was the only one without dry eyes. It seemed that men did sometimes cry—in very exceptional circumstances.

The Best Gift

"*C*hristmas is an unutterable bore," Lady Enid Penn said with an affected sigh. "There is positively no one with whom to amuse oneself except parents and aunts and uncles and cousins by the score and nothing to do except feast and make merry—with one's own family!"

There was a murmur of sympathetic agreement from several other young ladies.

"I shall simply die," the Honorable Miss Elspeth Lynch informed her listeners, "if the Worsleys remain in town for the holiday, as they did last year, instead of returning home. Patricia Worsley is my dearest bosom friend, and Howard Worsley is . . . well, he is interesting." She looked around archly at her companions, who tittered on cue.

"If one were only sixteen instead of fifteen," the Honorable Miss Deborah Latimer said, adding her sigh to everyone else's. "One's parents and aunts and uncles and all their friends have a wonderful time dancing and partaking of the wassail bowl and staying up almost until dawn while one is banished to the nursery and to bed with the children."

"And what about you, Craggs?" Lady Enid turned her head to look at the lady who had sat silently writing at her desk while they talked. "Do you find Christmas a bore, too? Or do you have wonderfully exciting plans? You are older than sixteen, after all."

The other young ladies tittered again, though there was an edge of cruelty to their laughter this time.

"Do you have dozens of beaux, Craggs? *Do* tell," Miss Lynch said, widening her eyes.

Miss Jane Craggs looked up from the journal in which she was writing. Although it was homework hour and school rules stated quite categorically that it was to be a silent hour, she was not enforcing the rule this evening. It was the last day of school before Christmas. Tomorrow all the girls would be going home, most of them with their parents or with liveried servants in sumptuous carriages.

"I believe it would be something of an exaggeration, Elspeth, to count my beaux in the dozens," she said. "Besides, a lady never does tell, you know."

"But you are not a lady, Craggs," one of the younger girls said.

But she won only frowns for her witticism. Everyone knew that Jane Craggs was not a lady, that she had spent most of her life at Miss Phillpotts's school for young ladies, her board and education paid for by an unknown benefactor—undoubtedly her father—until she was seventeen, that she had stayed on afterward as a teacher, though Miss Phillpotts treated her more as a servant than as an instructor. All the girls took their cue from the headmistress. The names of all their teachers were preceded by "Miss" except for Craggs. They treated her with a condescension bordering sometimes on insolence. But there was an undefined borderline beyond which they would not go. It was unladylike to remind Craggs in words that she was no lady.

"I believe," Jane Craggs said, closing her journal and getting to her feet, "we will make a concession to the approaching holiday and end homework hour five minutes early. Would anyone care to argue the point?"

There was relieved laughter and some enthusiastic cheering from the young ladies, who jumped to their feet and made for the door.

"Happy Christmas, Craggs," Deborah Latimer said as she was leaving the room.

Jane Craggs smiled at her and returned the greeting.

She sat down again when she was alone and began deliberately to clean and mend the pen she had been using. And she tried to ignore the knowledge that Christmas was approaching—an impossibility, of course.

No one with whom to amuse oneself except aunts and uncles and cousins and parents. Nothing to do but feast and make merry with one's family members. Such a Christmas was unutterably boring? Jane felt rather like crying, and ruthlessly suppressed the feeling. If only she could once—just once in her life—experience such a Christmas.

She had always hated Christmas. As a child and as a young girl she had also dreaded it. Dreaded the aloneness, with which she had always lived every day of the year but that always assaulted her most cruelly at Christmas. Dreaded the emptiness. Dreaded the excitement of the other girls as they prepared to go home and waited for family members or servants to come and fetch them. Dreaded the departure of Miss Phillpotts and the teachers until she was quite alone in the school with the few servants who were kept on for the holidays—always, it seemed, the most humorless of the servants.

Now she was three-and-twenty years old. The dread had gone. But the aloneness, the loneliness, the emptiness had not. She had heard and read so much about

Christmas. For her there had never been family—she understood that she had spent her early years in an orphanage, a rather expensive one. She believed, though she did not know for sure, that her mother had been a nobody, perhaps a whore, while her father had been a wealthy man who had agreed to support her until she was old enough to support herself. And so there had never been family for her and never Christmas gifts or Christmas parties.

Sometimes she had to remind herself that her name was Jane. A rather plain name, it was true, but her own. She heard it so rarely on anyone's lips that she could not remember the last time. It seemed singularly unfortunate to her that someone—her mother, she supposed— had blessed her with the surname of Craggs.

As a child she had dreamed of Christmas, and the dream had lingered even though she had passed the age of dreams. But did one ever pass the age of dreams? Would life be supportable if one could not dream?

She had dreamed of a large house with three stories in which every window blazed with light. It was always twilight and there was snow outside blanketing the ground and making of the trees and their branches magical creations. Inside there was a large hall, three stories high, with two large fireplaces crackling with log fires, the hall decked out in greenery and bows for the season. It was a house filled with people. Happy, beautiful people. All of whom loved her. All of whom she loved.

As a child she had even given names and faces and personalities to all those people. And in her imagination she had bought or made special gifts for each of them and had received gifts in return.

In her dream there was always a carved Nativity scene in the window of the drawing room, and it was always the focal point of family celebrations. The family always went to church on Christmas Eve, trudging through the snow to get there, filling a number of the pews. They always ran and laughed and ambushed one another with snowballs and rolled one another in the snow on the way home.

The contrast between dream and reality had been almost unbearable when she was a child. Now it was bearable. Jane tidied the already tidy teacher's desk, picked up her journal, her best friend, and clasped it with both hands against her bosom as she left the study room to climb the stairs to her small attic room. Now she was old enough to know that Christmas Day was just a day on the calendar like all others, that it would pass, that before she knew it the teachers and girls would be returning for the spring term. She had learned to be sensible.

She lit a candle in her room, shivered, and began to undress. Oh, no, she had not—she had not learned to be sensible. And it had not become bearable. It had not, it had not.

But she had learned to pretend to be sensible. And she had learned to pretend that it was bearable. She had learned to hold on to her childish dreams.

To say that he was feeling annoyed was to understate the case. He disliked Christmas. He had disliked it for most of his adult years. It was all just a parcel of nonsense as far as he was concerned. He liked to remove himself from town and all other centers of merriment well before the collective madness set in and take himself off to Cosway, his country seat, where he could wait out the season in quietness and sanity.

The trouble was that his family knew it and saw him as being available to care for unwanted relatives. Not that it had ever happened before, it was true, but it was happening this year, and he knew that it would happen again, that he was setting a trend this year that he would regret forever after. His sister and brother-in-law had decided entirely on the spur of the moment to spend Christmas with friends in Italy and had disposed of the minor inconvenience of a fifteen-year-old daughter by informing him—yes, Susannah had told him, not asked him—that she would spend Christmas with him at Cosway.

What, in the name of all that was wonderful, was he going to do with a fifteen-year-old niece for a few weeks? And at Christmas, of all times?

What he would do, he had decided at once, having neglected the obvious solution of telling his elder sister that she must change her plans, that he just would not do it—what he would do was enlist the help of someone else. Some female who had no other plans for Christmas. Someone who would be pleased enough to spend it at Cosway, keeping Deborah out of mischief. And out of his way.

Agatha, in fact. But Agatha, his maiden aunt, had been invited to spend the week of Christmas with her dear friends, the Skinners, in Bath, and while she hated to inconvenience her dear nephew and great-niece, she really could not disappoint the Skinners this close to Christmas.

When Viscount Buckley descended from his carriage outside Miss Phillpotts's school and had himself announced to speak with the headmistress herself, he was scowling. And his mood matched his expression exactly.

"Deborah will be very delighted to learn that her uncle, the viscount, has come in person to convey her home for the holidays, my lord," Miss Phillpotts said to him, smiling graciously.

His lordship sincerely doubted it. Especially when the child discovered that her parents had taken themselves off to Italy without a word to her. He felt sorry for the girl, if the truth were known. But he felt sorrier for himself.

"I suppose, ma'am," he said, without allowing himself to feel even the faintest glimmering of hope, "that there is not another young lady at the school who has nowhere to go for the holiday? Someone who could come with my niece and be company for her over Christmas?"

"I am afraid not, my lord," the headmistress said. "All our girls will be leaving today."

The viscount sighed. "It was a faint hope," he said. "I am not much in practice as far as entertaining very young ladies is concerned, ma'am." Or as far as celebrating Christmas was concerned. And Deborah would doubtless want to celebrate it. *Damn!*

"It is indeed kind of you to be willing to extend your hospitality to another young lady," Miss Phillpotts said. "But the only person who will be remaining at the school apart from three servants is Miss Craggs."

Miss Craggs sounded like an elderly tyrant. But Viscount Buckley was somewhat desperate. "Miss Craggs?" he said.

"One of my teachers," Miss Phillpotts explained.

Undoubtedly a tyrant. Poor Deborah. She would probably hate him forever for asking the question he was about to ask.

"Is there any possibility," he asked, "that she would be willing to accompany us to Cosway?"

"I believe she would be delighted, my lord," the headmistress told him. "Shall I send her down to you? I see that Sir Humphrey Byrde's carriage has arrived." She glanced toward the window, which looked down onto a cobbled courtyard. "I should go to greet him."

The viscount bowed his acquiescence and wandered to the window while Miss Phillpotts left the room to see another of her pupils on her way. *Damn Susannah and Miles!* How could they think of going off to Italy for Christmas when they had a young daughter to care for?

And how could they think of leaving her with him when they knew he did not celebrate Christmas? But then Susannah had always been the flighty, selfish one, quite different from their other two sisters. She was the youngest of the three and by far the most beautiful.

He had a suspicion that Susannah had never wanted children.

He thought briefly of his own child. Had he reminded his secretary to send her a gift? But then Aubrey would remember without a reminder. Part of his job was to remember what his employer was likely to forget.

He turned when the door opened behind him. She was not elderly, and despite her name, she did not look like a tyrant.

"Miss Craggs?" he said.

She inclined her head.

She was not elderly at all. She was probably five or six years younger than he, in fact. She was rather tall, and slender almost to the point of thinness. She had a rather thin, pale face, with fair hair smoothed back into a bun at her neck. Her gray dress was of cheap fabric and was high-waisted but made no other concession to fashion. Only her eyes saved her from being so nondescript that she might have faded entirely into her surroundings. Her eyes were dark gray and long-lashed. And they appeared to have such depth that he had the strange feeling that most of her living must be done very far within herself.

"Miss Craggs." He took a few steps toward her. "I understand that you will be staying here for Christmas?"

"Yes, my lord." Her voice was unexpectedly low and soft.

"You are expecting company?" he asked. "There would be someone to miss you if you were not here?"

Her face did not change expression. And yet he was given the impression that far within herself, where her living was done, she grimaced. "No, my lord," she said.

"I am Deborah Latimer's uncle," he said. "Warren Nash, Viscount Buckley, at your service, ma'am. Would it be possible to persuade you to come with us to my country seat in Hampshire? My sister and her husband, Deborah's parents, have gone to Italy and left her in my care. Frankly, I do not know what I am to do with a fifteen-year-old over Christmas. I need a female companion or chaperon for her. Will you come?"

There was the merest flicker in her eyes. Nothing more. He had never known a woman who was so impassive. He had always thought of women as open books, their emotions as clear to view as the words on a page. He had never had any problem knowing what his various mistresses felt or thought.

"Yes, my lord," she said.

He waited for more, for some questions or conditions. But she said nothing else. Her eyes, he noticed, were focused, not on his, but on his chin or thereabouts.

"I would guess that Deborah is eager to leave," he said. "How soon can you be ready, Miss Craggs?"

"Half an hour?" she said.

Half an hour! Good Lord, most women of his acquaintance would have asked for two or three days. He inclined his head to her. "Would you have Deborah sent to me?" he asked as she turned to leave the room.

Damn Susannah, he thought, too irritated to think of an original way mentally to censure his sister. How was he supposed to break the news to his niece?

Miss Craggs looked as if she had about as much joy in her as would half fill a thimble. A thimble for a small finger.

Damn!

She could not remember going farther from the school than could be accomplished on foot. She could not remember riding in a carriage. She could not re-

member being in company with a gentleman for
longer than a minute or two at a time, except the
dancing master who came in to teach the girls. She
was usually chosen to partner him when he taught
them the steps because he was not allowed to touch
any of the girls, and none of the other teachers was
willing to tolerate his lavishly insincere compliments
and his moist hands.

She was not sure if she was glad or sorry to be where
she was. At first she had been numbed with the strange-
ness and wonder of it. She was going on a holiday. She
was going to spend Christmas at a private home in
Hampshire. The home of Viscount Buckley. She was not
going to be alone at the school, as she always had been
for as far back as she could remember. And then she
had been excited. Her teeth had chattered and her
hands had shaken and her mind had whirled at dizzying
speed as she had packed her few belongings into a
valise she had had to borrow from Miss Phillpotts.

Now, after hours of travel, the luxury of a well-sprung,
lavishly upholstered carriage was no longer able to
mask the discomfort of the near silence that existed
among its three occupants. An unnatural, uncomfortable silence. Deborah was sullen and unhappy. Jane did
not blame her when she had discovered only this morning that her parents had gone away for Christmas and
left her behind. But she feared that part of the sullenness was caused by the fact that she had been appointed
the girl's companion. Craggs, the teacher who was not
really a lady.

The viscount was merely silent. Jane doubted that he
felt uncomfortable. But she did. Dreadfully so. She had
had no experience with maleness. Viscount Buckley
seemed suffocatingly male to her. He was dark, not
much taller than she, elegant. She imagined he was
handsome by any standards. She really had not seen

many men. He seemed to her more handsome than any man she could possibly imagine. And very male.

She was uncomfortable and terrified.

"We are almost there," he said, turning his head and looking at Deborah. "You will feel better after a cup of tea."

"I will *not* feel better," his niece said sullenly. "I hate Christmas. And I hate Mama and Papa."

Jane looked at the girl. She wanted to take her hand and tell her that at least she had an uncle willing to take her in. At least she had someone to whom she belonged and somewhere to go. But such an assurance would not console, she supposed.

"If it is any consolation," the girl's uncle said, "they are not exactly my favorite people at this moment either, Deborah."

"Meaning that you do not want to be burdened with me, I suppose," the girl said, misery overlaying the sullenness. "Everyone knows you do not believe in Christmas, Uncle Warren."

"Well," he said with a sigh, "I shall have to see what I can do to exert myself on your behalf this year, Deborah. Ah, the house. It is always a relief to see it at the end of a long journey."

Jane did not hear the rest of the conversation if, indeed, there was more. She had seen the house. Built within the last century, it had a classical symmetry of line combined with a deceptive simplicity of design. Built of light gray stone, it was rectangular in shape, three stories high, with a domed central portion and a pillared portico with wide marble steps leading up to double doors. It was larger and more magnificent than the house of her dream. And there was no snow, only bare trees and flower beds and grass of faded green. But it was all like enough to the dream house to catch at her breathing.

This was Cosway? This was where she was to spend the holiday?

She was aware suddenly that she had leaned forward and was gazing rather intently through the window. She was aware of the silence of her two companions. She turned her head and met the viscount's dark eyes. She sat back in her seat again and retreated within herself, into that secret place far inside where it never mattered that no one noticed her or respected her or loved her. A secret place she had discovered as a very young child.

"You admire my home, Miss Craggs?" the viscount asked her.

"Yes, my lord," she said. She felt the uncharacteristic urge to babble, to enthuse. She curbed it. "It is very beautiful."

"I think so too," he said.

She felt his eyes on her for a few moments longer. She kept her own eyes firmly on the hands she had clasped in her lap. And then the carriage lurched slightly as it stopped, and the door was being opened and the steps set down. She felt excitement ball in her stomach again.

Was this really happening? To her?

Always as he drove up to the house, and more especially when he stepped inside the great domed hall, he wondered why he did not spend more of his time here. There was always a special feeling of homecoming when returning to Cosway. He loved the hall, especially in the winter, when the log fires in the great twin fireplaces at opposite sides gave welcome and the illusion of warmth. The hall was too large and too high, of course, ever to be really warm in reality.

"Ah, Kemp," he said to his butler, rubbing his hands together as a footman took his hat and his gloves and waited for him to remove his greatcoat. "It is good to be home. I have brought my niece with me, as you see, and her companion, Miss Craggs. You will see that Mrs. Dexter assigns rooms to them? And that their bags are taken up? We will have tea served in the drawing room immediately."

Kemp cleared his throat. "There was a, ah, delivery for you earlier this afternoon, m'lord," he said, nodding his head significantly to one side. "I did not know quite what to do with it but knew you would be arriving yourself before the afternoon was out."

The viscount turned his head toward one of the fireplaces. Beside it, seated on a wooden settle, quite upright and quite still, sat a small child so bundled up inside a large coat and woolen scarf and mittens and so hidden beneath an absurdly large hat that she looked more like a bundle of abandoned laundry than a living child. To the left side of her chest was pinned a square sheet of paper.

"She would not, ah, remove her gloves or her hat, m'lord, or allow either Mrs. Dexter or myself to remove the label," the butler said. "The name on the label is Miss Veronica Weston, m'lord, care of yourself and this house."

Veronica Weston. Oh, good Lord. Viscount Buckley crossed the hall, his booted feet echoing on the marble tiles, and stopped a few feet in front of the child, who looked up at him with eyes that he supposed were very like his own.

He had never seen her before. He had known of her existence since before her birth and had never tried to deny paternity or to shirk the responsibility of providing for her financially. But he and Nancy had parted company before she discovered the pregnancy, and she had moved on to another protector soon after the birth. He himself had never felt any particular human interest in his daughter.

"Veronica?" he asked.

"Yes." She was looking very directly into his eyes. "Are you my papa? I am not to speak to anyone except my papa."

Papa! He had never thought of himself by any such name. He was a father. He had a daughter. He had never been a papa.

"This name is mine." He touched one finger lightly to the label she wore on her chest. "You may speak to me. Your mama sent you here?"

"Mama went away," the child said. "Mrs. Armstrong said I was to come to my papa."

"Mrs. Armstrong?" He raised his eyebrows.

"She looks after me," the child said. "But Mama went away and Mrs. Armstrong said there was no money. I was to come to my papa."

The label was thick. He guessed that there was a letter sealed up within it. Nancy had never neglected the child despite the demands of an acting career. Aubrey had assured him of that. But she had gone away? She had tired of the child?

"Do you have a letter for me, Veronica?" he asked, holding out one hand. He was only just beginning to realize what a coil he was in now. As if things were not bad enough as they were.

The child looked down and laboriously unpinned the label from her coat. She handed it to him. Sure enough, there was a letter. Nancy had been out of town for a weekend party, leaving her daughter with Mrs. Armstrong, a neighbor who frequently cared for the child. Nancy had fallen from an upper gallery in the house she was visiting to the hall below and had died instantly. Mrs. Armstrong, with six children of her own, could not afford to keep the child when there was no chance of payment. She respectfully sent her to her father. She had been to the expense of hiring someone to write the letter for her and of sending the child on the stagecoach. She hoped she would be reimbursed for her pains.

Poor Nancy, he thought. She had been beautiful and a talented actress. And a skilled lover. She had borne his child. And now she was dead. He folded the letter again and looked down at his daughter. She was gazing up at him, quiet and self-contained. And all of four years old.

Lord. Oh, dear Lord. What was he to do?

He turned his head to the two young ladies, who were still standing there, watching him. His eyes instinctively came to rest on Miss Craggs.

"She is my daughter," he said. "Her mother has d— Her mother has gone away and she has been sent here." He looked at her in mute appeal, like a child himself who did not know how to proceed.

"*Uncle Warren!*" Deborah said, shock in her voice.

Miss Craggs came closer, her eyes on the child. "She will want something to eat and a glass of milk," she said. "She will need to remove her hat and her coat and have them and her bag taken to a room that will be hers."

Of course! How practical and how simple. "Are you hungry, Veronica?" he asked.

"Yes, Papa," the child said.

"Come along, then," he said, clasping his hands awkwardly behind him. Good Lord, his illegitimate child, his by-blow, was in his own home with his niece. His servants would be scandalized. His neighbors would be shocked. "Will you give your hat and your coat to Kemp?"

"Will you let me help you, Veronica?" He watched as Miss Craggs went down on her knees before the child, who stood up and allowed her outer garments to be removed. "What a pretty color your scarf is. There—now you will be more comfortable. But we will need to comb those curls of yours before you sit down for your milk and your food." She touched the backs of two fingers to a tangled curl at the child's cheek and smiled at her.

The viscount felt jolted, first by the sight of his daughter without the heavy outer garments—she was little more than a baby—and then by the smile on the face of his niece's teacher. Good God, he thought, he had not noticed that the woman was beautiful. Though he knew even as he thought it that she was not beautiful, that it was merely something from deep within her that for the moment she had allowed to the surface of her face.

"Would you like to hold my hand?" she asked his daughter.

"Yes, please," the child said, looking up at her and suiting action to words.

"Uncle Warren?" Deborah asked faintly.

"She is my child," he told her. He felt almost as if he were realizing it for the first time. It was one thing to know one had fathered a child and to have accepted financial responsibility for her. It was another thing entirely to see the child, tiny and dainty and quiet, her eyes and her hair the color of his own.

"But—" Deborah said.

"She is my daughter," he said firmly. "Shall we go up for tea and get warm again?" He offered her his arm.

"Is this Papa's very own house?" Veronica was asking Miss Craggs.

Her own awkwardness and awe and even her excitement had been forgotten. Although the great hall was the hall of her dream with the addition of a painted and gilded dome, and although the staircase was wide and magnificent and the drawing room large and splendid, Jane noticed them only with her eyes and not with her heart. And her own bedchamber with a separate dressing room was large and richly furnished and far surpassed anything she might have dreamed for herself.

But she merely glanced at it when she hurried in to change her dress for dinner—to change from one drab gray dress to another.

Her time and her attention and her heart were otherwise engaged than in the perusal of a mere house and in the recognition of a dream come true.

She had never had anything to do with very young children. The girls who came to Miss Phillpotts's school were older and more independent and did not really need her for anything outside her capacity as a teacher.

No one had ever needed her. The thought came without any self-pity. It was simply the truth.

Until today. But today she had seen a small child bewildered and frightened by the loss of her mother and by her arrival at the home of the father she had never seen before. And her heart had lurched with all the love she had never been called upon to give.

She had taken a comb from her own reticule in the drawing room and drawn it gently through the soft baby curls. And she had sat by the child and helped her to food and milk. And then she had taken her to the nursery, where a bed had been made up, and had helped her unpack her little bag, which had been full of surprisingly pretty dresses. She had taken the child down to dinner, although she would probably eat in the nursery on future days, and had helped her wash and change into her nightgown afterward. She had tucked her into bed.

A maid was to stay in the nursery next to the bedchamber and sleep on a truckle bed there.

"Good night, Veronica," Jane said as she was leaving. Her heart ached with unfamiliar love and happiness. Someone had needed her for almost half a day and would need her again tomorrow.

"Good night, Miss Craggs," the child said, peering at her with wide eyes over the blanket that had been tucked beneath her chin. "When will Mama be coming back?"

Ah, poor child. Poor child. "Mama had to go away for a long time," she said, walking back to the bed and smoothing her hand over the child's head. "She did not want to leave you, Veronica, but she had to go. She sent you here, where you will be safe."

"Miss Craggs," the child said, "don't leave."

"I'll stay for a while," Jane said, seating herself on the side of the bed. "You are quite safe, dear. My name is Jane. It sounds a little nicer than 'Miss Craggs,' does it not?"

"Miss Jane," the child said, and closed her eyes.

There was a rather painful aching around the heart to hear her name spoken aloud by another person. Jane sat quietly on the side of the bed, waiting for the little girl to fall asleep. But after a few moments the child's eyes opened and she lay staring quietly upward.

And the door opened softly, and when Jane turned her head it was to find Viscount Buckley standing there, his hand on the doorknob.

"She is still awake?" he asked after a few moments.

"Yes," Jane said.

He came to stand beside her and gazed down at his daughter. A daughter he had had with a mistress. A child he had never seen until today. And a child he seemed not to know what to do with. What *would* he do with her? Jane felt fear for the defenseless baby who was still staring quietly upward.

"Veronica?" he said. "Is there anything you need?"

"No, thank you," the child said, not moving the direction of her gaze.

"You are tired?" he asked.

"Yes."

"Go to sleep, then." He leaned forward rather jerkily to lay the backs of his fingers against her cheek for a moment. "You are quite safe now. I will arrange something for you."

The child looked at him finally. "Good night, Papa," she said.

"Are you coming, Miss Craggs?" he asked, looking at Jane.

"I will stay until she falls asleep," Jane said.

He inclined his head to her. "Deborah is having an early night," he said. "Will you join me in the library as soon as you may? I need to talk with you."

Veronica was asleep no more than ten minutes later, not having spoken or moved since her father left the room. Jane got carefully to her feet, bent down after a moment's hesitation to kiss the child's forehead, and tiptoed from the room.

How wonderful it must be, she thought, how wonderful beyond imagining, to be a mother.

He sat in the library resisting the urge to refill his brandy glass for the second time. If he drank any more he would be foxed. The thought had its definite appeal, but getting drunk would solve nothing. He had learned that much in his almost thirty years of living.

Deborah was sullen and unhappy—and angry.

"How could you, Uncle Warren?" she had said just before going to bed. "How could you let her stay here and announce for all the world to hear that she is your daughter? Mama will be furious with you. Papa will kill you."

Yes, they would be a trifle annoyed, he conceded. But it served them right for foisting their daughter on him without so much as a by-your-leave.

What was he to do? How did one go about finding a good home for a young child? Aubrey would doubtless know, but Aubrey was in London, about to take a holiday with his family. Perhaps Miss Craggs would have some idea. He hoped so.

He was relieved when she was admitted to the library less than half an hour after he had left her in the nursery. He rose to his feet and motioned her to a chair. She sat straight-backed on the edge of it, he noticed, and clasped her hands in her lap. Her face had the impassive, empty look again now that Veronica was no longer present.

"These things happen, Miss Craggs," he said. He wondered how shocked this prim schoolteacher was beneath the calm exterior.

"Yes, my lord," she said. "I know."

"Can you blame me for taking her into my own home?" he asked. "What was I to do?"

She looked fully into his eyes but did not reply. He shifted uncomfortably. He had never encountered eyes quite like hers.

"Send her back where she came from?" he asked. "I could not do it, ma'am. She is my own flesh and blood."

"Yes, my lord," she said.

"What am I to do, then?" he asked. "How does one find a home for a child? A home in which one can be quite sure she will be well cared for. It is an infernally awkward time of year. Everything will be complicated by the fact that it is Christmas. What am I to do?"

"Perhaps, my lord," she said, "you should celebrate Christmas."

He frowned at her.

"You have a young niece," she said, "who is unhappy at being abandoned by her parents at this of all times. And you have a small child who is bewildered at the disappearance of her mother. Perhaps it is the very best time of year. Let Christmas bring some healing to them both."

He might have known it. For all her drab appearance and seemingly sensible manner and bearing, she was a sentimentalist. Christmas bringing healing, indeed! As if there was something inherently different in that day from all others. Besides, how could Christmas bring any sort of happiness to four such very different people— Deborah, Veronica, Miss Craggs, and himself?

"You believe in miracles, Miss Craggs?" he asked. "Do you have any suggestions as to how this healing can be effected?"

She leaned slightly forward in her chair, and there was a suggestion of eagerness in her face. "We could decorate the house," she said. "I have always dreamed of . . . There must be greenery outside that we can gather."

"Holly and such?" he asked, still frowning.

"And mistletoe," she said, and interestingly enough she blushed.

"And that will do it?" he asked, a note of sarcasm in his voice. "An instant miracle, Miss Craggs?"

"Deborah needs company," she said. "She is of an age at which it seems that life is passing her by unless she has company of her own age and activities to keep them busy and happy."

He grimaced. "Company of her own age?" he said. "From memory and experience I would say that young people of Deborah's age are usually ignored at Christmastime—and all other times of the year, for that matter. Adults want nothing to do with them, yet they are too old to enjoy being with the children. It is an unfortunate time of life that has to be endured until it passes."

"Perhaps," she said, "there are other young people in the neighborhood who would be only too happy to get together independently of either the adults or the children."

"Are you seriously suggesting that I visit all my neighbors within the next few days, seeking out the young and organizing a party here?" he asked, aghast.

"I think that a wonderful suggestion, my lord," she said.

He should have left the woman where she was, he thought. She was definitely dangerous.

"You would doubtless be left to organize and chaperon such an affair," he warned her. "I will be invited to join a sane adult party." And he would accept too, though he usually sent his excuses.

"I am accustomed to supervising young people, my lord," she reminded him.

"Very well, then," he said. "On your own head be it." He was feeling decidedly annoyed. Except that her suggestion made sense. And it would definitely solve the problem of Deborah. "I will have to postpone making a decision about Veronica until after Christmas. I suppose it will not matter greatly. She is a quiet and well-behaved child."

"She is hiding," Miss Craggs said quietly.

"Hiding?" he frowned.

"She suspects that something dreadful has happened to her mother," she said. "And she knows that you are a stranger, although you are her father. She is not at all sure that she is safe, despite your assurances to her and my own. She does not know what is going to happen to her. And so she has found a hiding place. The only one available. She is hiding inside herself."

The notion was thoroughly preposterous. Except that he recalled his impression that morning that Miss Craggs herself did most of her living far inside herself. What was her own story? he wondered briefly. But there was a topic of more pressing importance on which to focus his mind.

"But she must know," he said, "that I will care for her, that I will find her a good home. I always have cared for her."

"Why must she know any such thing?" Miss Craggs asked. "She is four years old, my lord. A baby. Financial care and the assurances of a good home mean nothing to her. Her world has rested firmly on one person, and that person is now gone."

"Miss Craggs," he asked quietly, though he already knew what her answer was going to be, "you are not suggesting that I keep the child here, are you?"

She looked down at the hands in her lap. "I am suggesting nothing, my lord," she said.

But she was. She obviously knew nothing about life. She knew nothing about the types of relationships that might exist, between a man and his illegitimate offspring.

And yet, even as he thought it, he recalled the totally unfamiliar experience of standing in the nursery looking down at his own small child in the bed there, lying still and staring quietly upward, in a most unchildlike way. And he felt now, as he had felt then, an unidentifiable ache about his heart.

She was his child, the product of his own seed. She was his baby.

"Miss Craggs." He heard the irritability in his voice as he got to his feet. "I see clearly that nothing can be done and no decisions can be made until Christmas is over. It is looming ahead of us, a dark and gloomy obstacle, but one that must be lived through. Make of it what you will, then. Load the house with greenery if you must. Do whatever you will. And in the meantime I shall call upon my neighbors and try to organize that unheard-of phenomenon, a preadult party." He felt thoroughly out of sorts.

"Very well, my lord," she said, and looked up at him.

He felt almost as if he might fall into her eyes.

"Come," he said, extending an arm to her even though he had brought her here as more of a servant than a guest, "I will escort you to your room, Miss Craggs."

She got to her feet and looked at his arm with some

misgiving before linking her own through it. Her arm
was trembling quite noticeably though she did not feel
cold, and she stood as far from him as their linked arms
would allow.

Good Lord, he thought, had she been shut up inside
that school for so long?

He stopped outside her dressing room and opened
the door for her. "Thank you," he said, "for agreeing to
accompany Deborah here. And thank you for showing
kindness and gentleness to Veronica. Good night."

"Good night, my lord," she said, her eyes on a level
with his neckcloth. And she moved hastily into the
dressing room and closed the door behind her even as
he prepared to take her hand to raise to his lips.

He was glad then that she had not given him a chance
to do it. She was, after all, merely a servant. What was
her first name? he wondered. He hoped it was something more fortunate than her surname. Though it was
of no concern to him. He would never have reason either to know it or to use it.

Jane helped Veronica get dressed the following morning and brushed her curls into a pretty style while the
child sat very still on a stool, her legs dangling over its
edge. They were breakfasting together in the nursery
when Mrs. Dexter, the viscount's housekeeper, arrived
there to ask Miss Craggs what her orders were regarding the Christmas baking and cooking.

"What my orders are?" Jane asked, bewildered.
"Should you not be consulting his lordship, Mrs. Dexter?"

"He said I should come to you, miss," the housekeeper said, looking somewhat dubious. "He said that
whatever you wanted was to be supplied."

Oh, dear. He really meant what he had said last night,
then. She was to do whatever she wanted to celebrate

Christmas. The thought was dizzying when at the age of three-and-twenty she never had celebrated the season. She was to have a free hand?

"Where is his lordship?" she asked.

"He has gone visiting with Miss Deborah, miss," the housekeeper said. "He said you were to wait until this afternoon to gather greenery so that he can help you carry it."

"Oh, dear," Jane said. "What is usually cooked for Christmas, Mrs. Dexter?"

The housekeeper raised her eyebrows. "Anything that will not remind his lordship that it is Christmas," she said. "The cook threatens every year to resign, miss, but she stays on. It is unnatural not to have a goose and mince pies, at the very least."

Goose and mince pies. The very thought of them was enough to set Jane's mouth to watering. "Perhaps," she said, "I should go down to the kitchen and consult the cook."

"Yes, miss," Mrs. Dexter said. But she paused as she was about to leave the room. "It is time Christmas came back to this house. It has been too long gone. And it needs to be celebrated when there is a child in the house, poor little mite." She nodded in Veronica's direction.

Jane wondered what had happened to banish Christmas from Cosway. She could not imagine anyone deliberately deciding not to celebrate it. She looked at Veronica and smiled.

"Shall we go down to the kitchen and talk to Cook?" she asked.

The child nodded and got down from her stool to hold out her hand for Jane's. Jane, taking it in hers and feeling its soft smallness, wondered if there could be a greater happiness in life.

The cook was so overjoyed at the prospect of Christmas baking that Jane found she did not need to make any suggestions at all. She merely sat at the kitchen table with a cup of tea and approved every suggestion made. The cook lifted Veronica to the table, placed a large, shiny apple in her hand, and clucked over her and talked about the delight of having a child in the house again.

"I do not care what side of the blanket she was born on, if you take my meaning, miss," she said to Jane. "She is a child, and children have a right to a home and a right to be loved. Chew carefully, ducky. You do not want to choke on a piece."

Veronica obediently chewed carefully.

"It will do his heart good to have her here," the cook said, jerking her head toward the ceiling. "He does not love easy, miss, and when he do, his heart is easy to break."

Jane could not resist. "Was his heart broken once?" she asked.

The cook clucked her tongue. "By his childhood sweetheart," she said. "You never saw a man so besotted, miss, though she were a flighty piece, if you was to ask me. Their betrothal was to be announced on Christmas Day here at a big party. A big secret it was supposed to be, but we all knew it, miss. And then halfway through the evening, just when his lordship were excited enough to burst, a stranger who had come home with her brother a month before stood up and announced *his* betrothal to her. And she smiled at him as sweet as you please without so much as a guilty glance at our boy— or at her papa, who was as weak as water, as far as she was concerned. Six years ago it was, miss. His heart don't heal easy. But this is one to mend any heart."

She nodded at Veronica, who had spotted a cat curled beside the fire and had wriggled off the table to go and kneel beside it and reach out gingerly to pat its fur. The cut purred with contentment.

"A blessed Christmas gift she is for any man," the cook said.

Yes. Jane remembered sitting alone with him in the library last evening. She alone with a man! And talking with him. Being consulted on what he should do with his daughter. And having the temerity to give her opinion and her suggestions. She would have expected to have been quite tongue-tied in a man's presence. But she had made a discovery about this particular man. He was not the infallible figure of authority she had thought all men were. He was an ordinary human being who did not have all of life's answers or even the most obvious of them.

He did not know that all his child needed—all!—was love. The love of her father. And he did not know that good, docile behavior in a child did not necessarily denote a happy child. He had turned to her, Jane, for help. Even a man could need her in some small way for one small moment of time.

It was the thought she had hugged to herself in bed. And also the memory of how it had felt to touch him. To feel his strongly muscled, unmistakably male arm with her own. To smell the unfamiliar odor of male cologne. To feel the body heat of a man only inches away from her own body. And to know that the yearning she had suffered and suppressed in herself for years had a definite cause. It was the yearning for a man, for his approval and his support and companionship. And for something else, too. She did not know quite what that something else was except that outside her dressing room, when he had stopped and thanked her for coming and for giving her attention to Veronica, she had felt suffocated. She had felt that there was no air in the corridor.

She had felt the yearning for . . . for *him.* She still could not express the need less vaguely than that.

And so she had fled into her room like a frightened rabbit.

"And there." The cook's hand patting her shoulder felt strangely comforting. There had been so few physical touches in her life. "He would be a blessed Christmas gift for some lady too, missy."

But you are not a lady, Craggs. She heard again the words that had been spoken in the homework room just two days before. No, she was no lady. She smiled and got to her feet.

"You are going to be busy if you are to make everything you have suggested," she said. "Oh, I can hardly wait for all the smells and all the tastes. I can hardly wait for Christmas."

The cook chuckled. "It will come, miss, as it always does," she said.

But it had never come before. This would be her first-ever Christmas. She could scarcely wait. At the same time, she wanted to savor every moment as it came. They were to gather greenery during the afternoon, she and Veronica and perhaps Deborah. And Lord Buckley was to come to help carry the loads.

Veronica was sitting cross-legged on the stone floor, smoothing the cat's fur.

He could not quite believe that this was himself. Himself up a tree, balanced precariously on a branch, feeling hot and disheveled and dusty. His boots, he was sure, though he did not look down at them, must be in a condition to give his valet heart palpitations. Below him Miss Craggs stood with arms partly spread as if to catch him if he fell, Deborah had her hands to her mouth and was alternately squealing and giggling, and Veronica was gazing gravely upward.

"Miss Craggs believes that in addition to all the holly we have gathered and all the pine boughs we have cut down we need some mistletoe," he had said to his daughter a short while before. "What do you think, Veronica? Do we need mistletoe?"

"Yes, please, Papa," she had said.

And Deborah had giggled—she had started giggling during their morning visits and had scarcely stopped since—and had added her voice to everyone else's. It just would not be Christmas, it seemed, unless there was some mistletoe hanging in strategic places so that one might be caught beneath it accidentally on purpose.

So here he was up a tree.

And then down with a sizable armful of mistletoe and a tear on the back of one kid glove and a scrape so deep on the inside of his left boot that it would never be the same again.

And all in the name of Christmas.

"Do you know why I have risked life and limb just to gather this?" he asked Veronica, frowning.

"Because Miss Jane wanted it?" she asked.

Jane. He might have guessed that she would have such a name. And yet it suited her. It was quietly, discreetly pretty.

"Not at all," he said. "This is what it is used for." He held one sprig above the absurd hat, which Nancy had doubtless thought suitably flamboyant for the daughter of an actress, stooped down, and kissed her soft, cold little cheek. And took himself quite by surprise. Now why had he done that?

"Any gentleman has the right to kiss any lady he catches beneath the mistletoe," he said, "without fear of having his face slapped. It is a Christmas custom. You see?" And he straightened up and repeated the action with Deborah, who giggled. "Now we have to carry all this greenery back to the house."

"What about Miss Jane?" a grave little voice asked him.

And he knew he was caught. Caught in the act of maneuvering. For when he had demonstrated the use of mistletoe on his daughter and his niece, he had really wanted to use Miss Craggs as his model. Even though she was prim and gray and every inch the schoolteacher. Though that was not the whole truth this afternoon. Since they had left the house there had been a light in her eyes that had touched him. She was enjoying all this just like a child.

"Oh, it works with Miss Craggs too," he said, turning to her and raising his sprig of mistletoe again. And he felt suddenly and stupidly breathless. She was standing very still and wide-eyed.

He kissed her lightly and briefly, as he had kissed the other two. Except that foolishly he kissed her on the lips. And ended up feeling even hotter than his excursion up the tree had made him.

She turned hurriedly away before their eyes could meet and began energetically arranging the heap of holly they had gathered into three bundles.

"Here, Veronica," he said, "you may carry the mistletoe, since it will not prick you all to pieces. Deborah, take that bundle of holly. I'll take this one."

His hand brushed Miss Craggs's as he gathered up the largest bundle and belatedly their eyes met. Her own were still large and bright. Brighter. Was it the cold that had brought the tears there? Or was it the kiss? Surely she had been kissed before. Surely that had not been her first kiss.

Had it? Once again he wondered about her past, about her life. Impoverished parents and the need to go out and make her own living? But she had not been planning to go home for Christmas.

"I will send someone back with a wagon for the pine boughs," he said.

"'Deck the halls with boughs of holly,'" Deborah

sang suddenly with loud enthusiasm and no musical talent whatsoever.

"'Fa la la la la la la la la,'" Miss Craggs sang with her in a rather lovely contralto voice.

"'Tis the season to be jolly.'" He joined his tenor voice to their singing and looked down at Veronica.

"'Fa la la la la la la la la.'" She piped up with them, off-key.

"'Don we now our gay apparel.'" Three of them sang out lustily while the fourth continued with the fa-la-las.

And the damned thing was, Viscount Buckley thought, that it could grab at one quite unawares. Christmas, that was.

Jane had never been very assertive, even as a teacher. She had never been the type who liked to boss and organize people. And yet over the next couple of days she seemed to be transformed into a wholly different person.

It was she who directed the decorating of the house—of drawing room, staircase, and hall. The viscount had suggested that the servants could do it, but she had exclaimed in horror and disappointment before she could stop herself, and he had meekly agreed that perhaps they could do it themselves, the four of them.

"But I have no eye for design, Miss Craggs," he had told her. "You will have to tell us what you want."

And she had told them. She stood in the middle of the drawing room giving orders like a sergeant with a company of soldiers. Boughs and sprigs and wreaths were hung exactly where and exactly how she directed, and if she did not like the look of them when the deed was done, then she directed their replacement. And everyone obeyed, even the viscount, who was given all the climbing to do. He balanced on chairs and tables and ladders in his shirtsleeves, decking out pictures and

mirrors and door frames while she stood critically
below him, head to one side, examining the effects of his
handiwork and criticizing any slight error on his part.

She felt so happy by the time they were finished that
she thought she might well burst with it. She was surrounded by Christmas—by the sights and smells of it.
She could smell the pine boughs, and there were interesting smells wafting up from the kitchens. Particularly
the smell of Christmas puddings.

"Oh, it is so very beautiful," she said, her hands
clasped to her bosom when they were all finished and
were all standing admiring their efforts. "If only we had
some ribbons for bows."

"Oh, yes," Deborah said. "Red ones and green ones."

Viscount Buckley sighed. "Ribbons and bows," he
said. "And bells, too, I suppose? Doubtless you will find
what you need in the village, Miss Craggs. Go there if
you must and purchase whatever you need and have the
bill sent to me."

"Oh." She turned to him with glowing eyes. "May I?
Oh, thank you, my lord."

He looked at her and made her a little mocking bow.
And she remembered the earth-shattering feeling of his
lips touching hers and wondered if he realized what an
enormous treasure this Christmas was going to be to her
in memory. The most precious treasure of her life.

Veronica was tugging at her skirt. "May I come too,
Miss Jane?" she asked.

"Of course, sweetheart," she said, hearing in some
surprise the unexpected endearment she had used. "I
will need you to help me choose."

"And I will come too, Craggs," Deborah said. But she
flushed suddenly and added, "*Miss* Craggs." And then
she extended both arms and twirled into the steps of a
waltz. "Uncle Warren," she said, "do you think we may
dance on Christmas Day?"

Deborah had completely changed since the visits she had paid with her uncle during the morning. She had come rushing into the house on their return home to announce to Jane that she was to have a party of her very own on Christmas Day. Fifteen young people were to come during the afternoon for walks and games and were to stay for the evening while their parents—and her uncle—engaged in an adult party at the home of the Oxendens. Even the seventeen-year-old and very dashing George Oxenden had decided to come to Cosway, though his parents had agreed to allow him to attend the adult party if he wished.

Jane saw the viscount grimace. "A dance?" he said. "And who is to provide the music, pray?"

But Deborah made it instantly clear that the idea had not come to her on the spur of the moment. "Mr. George Oxenden told me that his aunt plays the pianoforte rather well," she said, "and that she would be only too pleased to be with the young people rather than with the adults on Christmas Day."

Her uncle looked skeptical. "I will have to see what can be arranged," he said.

"Oh, thank you, Uncle Warren," she said, darting back across the room to hug him. "This is going to be the best Christmas ever, after all, I just know it."

The viscount raised his eyebrows and looked at Jane. Jane could only agree with his niece.

But there was work to be done. The village shop had to be visited and yards of the widest, brightest ribbon to be chosen and measured. Jane felt guilty when she was told the total cost, but she did not change her purchases. Viscount Buckley was a wealthy man, was he not? When Veronica gazed admiringly and rather longingly at some porcelain bells, she even added three to her purchases, a dreadful extravagance. But they would look lovely hanging from the holly on the mantel in the drawing room.

And then she discovered during a visit to the kitchens that the servants were murmuring over the fact that there was to be no Yule log. The head gardener was only too delighted to go in search of the largest one he could find when Jane insisted that they must have one. A Yule log! She had not even thought of it. She knew so little about Christmas.

During the same visit she learned that one of the grooms was skilled with his hands and loved to whittle on wood whenever he had a few spare moments. When Jane admired a spoon he was carving for his girl in the village, he offered to carve a small crib for the drawing room. And that other detail of her dream returned to Jane. Time was short, but the groom agreed to try to carve a baby Jesus to go inside the crib, and a Mary and Joseph to kneel beside it, and perhaps even a shepherd or two and an animal or two to worship and adore.

The decorations would be complete, Jane decided, standing alone in the drawing room after the ribbons and bells had been added to all the greenery, if only there could be a Nativity scene in the window.

Oh, Christmas would be complete. She twirled around and around rather as Deborah had done and thought of the little bonnet and muff for Veronica and the small bottle of perfume for Deborah she had had set aside in the village shop as Christmas gifts. They would take all the meager hoard of money in her purse, but she could not resist. She had never bought Christmas presents before. She had nothing for Viscount Buckley, but it would be inappropriate anyway to give a gentleman a gift.

For Deborah's sake she was going to make this a wonderful Christmas. And for Veronica's sake. Veronica was quietly obedient, but Jane knew that the child was still hiding inside herself. And she knew from long experience how that felt. She was going to do her very best to see that Christmas brought the child out of herself again, even if it was only to a realization of her grief and her insecurity. At least then she could be properly comforted.

If there could be any meaningful comfort. Jane stopped twirling. Her heart chilled to the memory of the viscount's asking how he was to find his daughter a good home. He intended to send the child away again to be cared for by strangers. They would be strangers, no matter how kindly they might be.

Oh, for the viscount's sake too, this must be a wonderful Christmas. He must be made to see that love was everything, that family was everything. Why could people who had always had family not see that? Why could he not see that his daughter was his most priceless possession?

And for her own sake she was going to see that this Christmas was celebrated to the limit. It was her first and might well be her last. It was going to be a Christmas to remember for a lifetime.

Yes, it was. Oh, yes, indeed it was.

She twirled again.

Christmas Eve dawned gray and gloomy, and Viscount Buckley, surrounded by all the foolish sights of Christmas, his nostrils assailed by all the smells of it, felt his irritation return. Because she—Miss Jane Craggs, the tyrant—had persuaded him into the madness of allowing a party for young people to take place in his home tomorrow, he had been faced with the necessity of absenting himself from that home. And so he was facing the unspeakable monotony of a Christmas gathering at the Oxendens'. He was being forced to enjoy himself.

Well, it could not be done. Just look at the weather. He did just that, standing at the window of his bedchamber, gazing out at raw, cheerless December.

But one hour later he felt foolish. How was it he had recognized none of the signs when they had been as plain as the nose on his face? For of course the grayness and the gloom were harbingers of snow, and before the morning was even half over, it was falling so thickly that he could scarcely see six feet beyond the window. And it was settling too, just like a white blanket being spread.

Good Lord, snow! He could not remember when it had last fallen at Christmastime. Certainly not the year Elise had humiliated him and broken his foolish young heart. It had been raining that year and blowing a gale. Typical British winter weather. This was not typical at all. He wondered if Veronica had seen the snow, and was halfway up the stairs to the nursery before he realized how strange it was that he had thought of sharing the sight of snow with a child. But he continued on his way.

They were all in there, Veronica and Deborah kneeling on the window seat, their noses pressed against the glass, Miss Craggs standing behind them.

"Look, my lord." She was the only one who had glanced back to see who was coming through the door. "Snow. We are going to have a white Christmas. Can you conceive of anything more wonderful?"

Sometime before she returned to Miss Phillpotts's school he was going to have to sit down and have a good talk with Miss Jane Craggs. There was something deep inside the woman that could occasionally break through to her face and make her almost incredibly beautiful. She was beautiful now, flushed and wide-eyed and animated. And all over the fact that it was snowing for Christmas.

He found himself wondering quite inappropriately what her face would look like as he was making love to her. Totally inappropriately! He had a mistress waiting for him in London with whose services he was more than satisfied. He had had her for only two months. He had not even begun to tire of her yet.

"I am trying," he said in belated answer to her question. "And at the moment I can think of nothing."

She smiled at him and his heart and his stomach danced a pas de deux.

Good Lord, he wanted her, the gray and prim Miss Craggs.

"Look, Papa," his daughter was saying. "Look at the trees. They are magic."

He strolled over to the window and stood almost shoulder-to-shoulder with Jane Craggs, looking out on a Christmas wonderland.

"And so they are," he said, setting his hand on the child's soft curls. "I have just had a thought. There used to be sleds when I was a boy. I wonder what happened to them."

"Sleds?" Deborah turned her attention to him, "Oh, Uncle Warren, could we go sledding tomorrow. A sledding party. Do you think so? How many are there?"

"Wait a minute," he said, holding up one hand. "I am not even sure they still exist. I suppose you are going to insist that I get on my greatcoat and my topboots and wade out to the stables without further delay."

Yes. Three pairs of eyes confirmed him in his suspicions. And then three voices informed him that they were coming with him, and Jane Craggs was bundling Veronica inside her coat and winding her inside her scarf and burying her beneath her hat while Deborah darted out to don her own outdoor clothes.

"I knew," Miss Craggs said, looking up at him with a face that was still beautiful, "that this was going to be a perfect Christmas. I just knew it."

How could it be perfect for her, he wondered, when she had been brought here merely as a glorified servant to chaperon a sullen girl and then had been saddled with the responsibility of caring for an illegitimate child, whose presence in the house might well have offended her sensibilities? How could it be perfect when she was away from her own family?

But there was that light in her eyes and that beauty in her face, and he knew that she was not lying.

And he knew suddenly that for the first time in many years there was hope in him. The hope that somehow she might be right, that somehow this might be the perfect Christmas.

That somehow the magic might come back.

There were four sleds, three of them somewhat dilapidated. But he was assured that by the morrow they would be in perfect condition.

"Well, Veronica," he said as they were wading back to the house with the snow falling thickly about them and onto them, "are you going to ride on a sled tomorrow too? Faster than lightning down a hill?"

"No, Papa," she said.

"With me?" he asked her. "If I ride with you and hold you tight?"

"Yes, Papa," she said gravely.

He could not ask for a more docile and obedient child. Nancy had brought her up well. And yet he could not help remembering what Jane Craggs had said about her—that she was hiding inside herself. And wondering how she could know such a thing, if it were so. But he was beginning to believe that perhaps it was true. Over the past few days the child had joined in all the activities, and she had made a great friend of the kitchen cat, whom he had found curled impertinently in his favorite chair in the drawing room, of all places, just the day before. But there had been no exuberance in her as there had been in Deborah and even in Miss Craggs.

He was beginning to worry about Veronica. The sooner he found her a good home to go to, the better it would be for her. She needed a mother and father to care for her. As soon as Christmas was over he must set Aubrey to work on it. It must take priority over all else.

"Look at me," Deborah shrieked suddenly, and she hurled herself backward into a smooth drift of snow, swished her arms and legs to the sides, and got up carefully. "Look. A perfect angel."

"Which you assuredly are not," he said, looking at the snow caked all over her back.

She giggled at him. "I dare you to try it, Uncle Warren," she said.

"It certainly does not behoove my dignity to be making snow angels," he said.

But he did it anyway because it had never been his way to resist a dare. And then they were all doing it until they had a whole army of angels fast disappearing beneath the still-falling snow. Like a parcel of children, he thought in some disgust, instead of two adults, one young person, and one child.

"This must be the multitude of the heavenly host that sang with the angel Gabriel to Mary," he said. "I do not know about the rest of you, but I have snow trickling down my neck and turning to water. It does not feel comfortable at all. I think hot drinks at the house are called for."

"Veronica has made the best angels," Deborah said generously. "Look how dainty they are."

It was the first time she had mentioned his daughter by name, the viscount thought.

"That is because she is a real little angel," he said, stooping down impulsively and sweeping the child up into his arms. "Are you cold, Veronica?"

"A little, Papa," she admitted.

She weighed almost nothing at all. He tightened his hold on her and realized something suddenly. He was going to miss her when she went away. He was always going to be wondering if she were happy, if she were being loved properly, if she were hiding inside herself.

"Snuggle close," he said. "I shall have you inside where it is warm before you know it."

Miss Craggs, he noticed, was watching him with shining eyes—and shining red nose. She looked more beautiful than ever. Which was a strange thought to have when, really, she was not beautiful at all.

At first she was going to go to church alone. It was something she had always done on Christmas Eve and something she wanted to do more than ever here. She had seen the picturesque stone church on her journeys to the village. And the thought of trudging through snow in order to reach it was somehow appealing. It would bring another part of her dream to life.

She asked Veronica at dinner—the child still ate in the dining room with the adults—if she would mind not being sat with tonight until she slept. Jane explained her reason.

"I promise to look in on you as soon as I return," she said.

But Veronica looked at her rather wistfully. "May I come too, Miss Jane?" she asked.

It would be very late for a child to be up, but Viscount Buckley immediately gave his permission and announced his intention of attending church, too. And then Deborah wondered aloud if Mr. George Oxenden would be at church, blushed, and declared that anyway she always enjoyed a Christmas service.

And so they walked together the mile to the church, the snow being rather too deep for the carriage wheels, Veronica between Jane and the viscount, holding to a hand of each, while Deborah half tripped along beside them. And they sat together in church, Veronica once again between the two adults until, after a series of yawns, she climbed onto Jane's lap and snuggled close. Jane was unable to stand for the final hymn, but she sat holding the child, thinking about the birth of the Christ child and understanding for the first time the ecstasy Mary must have felt to have her baby even though she had had to give birth far from home and inside a stable.

Christmas, Jane thought, was the most wonderful, wonderful time of the year.

They walked home after the viscount had greeted his neighbors and Deborah had chatted with her new friends, the Oxenden sisters, and had been rewarded with a nod and a smile and a Christmas greeting from their elder brother. Jane sat holding the sleeping child on her lap while she waited for them.

And then Viscount Buckley was bending over her in the pew and opening his greatcoat and lifting his daughter into his own arms and wrapping the coat about her. Jane smiled at him. Oh, he felt it too. What a tender paternal gesture! He loved the child and would keep her with him. Of course he would. It was something she, Jane, would be able to console herself with when she was back at Miss Phillpotts's. Though she would not think of that. Not yet. She was going to have her one wonderful Christmas first.

And wonderful it was too, she thought as they approached the house in a night that was curiously bright despite the fact that there were clouds overhead—more snow clouds. It was her dream come true, even though not every window in the house blazed with light. But close enough to her dream to make her believe for once in her life in miracles.

Deborah was yawning and ready for bed by the time they reached the house. She went straight to her room. Veronica stirred and grumbled in her father's arms as he carried her upstairs. Jane followed him and undressed the child in her bedchamber while he waited in the nursery. He came to stand in the doorway as he always did after Jane had tucked her up in bed. She was only half-awake.

"Good night, Mama," she said.

Jane could hardly speak past the ache in her throat. "Good night, sweetheart," she said softly.

"Good night, Papa."

"Good night, Veronica," he said.

Jane sat for a few minutes on the side of the bed, though it was obvious that the child had slipped back into sleep. She was too embarrassed to face the viscount. But when she rose and turned to leave the room, she found that he was still standing in the doorway.

"I ordered hot cider sent to the library," he said. "Come with me there?"

She longed to be able to escape to her room. Or a part of her did, anyway—that part that was flustered and even frightened at the thought of being alone with him. But the other part of herself, the part that was living and enjoying this Christmas to the full, leaped with gladness. She was going to sit and talk with him again? She only hoped that she would be able to think of something to say, that her mind would not turn blank.

When they reached the library, he motioned her to the chair she had occupied once before. He ladled hot cider into two glasses and handed her one before seating himself at the other side of the fire.

She had never drunk cider before. It was hot and tasted of cinnamon and other, unidentified spices. It was delicious. She looked into the glass and concentrated her attention on it. She could not think of anything to say. She wished she had made some excuse after all and gone to bed.

"You were going to spend Christmas alone at the school?" he asked her.

"Yes." She looked up at him unwillingly.

"Where does your family live?" he asked. "Was it too far for you to travel?"

She had never talked about herself. There was nothing to talk about. She could be of no possible interest to anyone except herself.

"I have no family," she said. She was not particularly given to self-pity, either. But the words sounded horribly forlorn. She looked down into her drink again.

"Ah," he said, "I am sorry. Have they been long deceased?"

"I believe," she said after rejecting her first impulse, which was to invent a mythical warm and loving family, "I was the product of a union much like yours and Veronica's mother's. I do not know who my mother was. I believe she must have died when I was very young. Or perhaps she merely did not want to be burdened with me. I do not know my father, either. He put me into an orphanage until I was old enough to go to Miss Phillpotts's school. He supported me there until I was seventeen. I have earned my way there since."

He said nothing for a long time. She kept her eyes on her drink, but she did not lift it to her mouth. She knew her hand would shake if she tried it.

"You have never known a family," he said very quietly at last.

"No." But she did not want him to think that she was trying to enlist his pity. "The orphanage was a good one. The school is an expensive one. He cared enough to make sure that my material needs were catered to and that I had a good enough education to make my way in the world."

"But you stayed at the school," he said. "Why?"

How could she explain that, cold and cheerless as it was, the school was the only home she had known, that it was the only anchor in her existence? How could she explain how the thought of being cast adrift in unfamiliar surroundings, without even the illusion of home and family, terrified her?

"I suppose," she said, "I drifted into staying there."

"In an environment that is wholly female," he said. "Have you never wanted to find yourself a husband and have a family of your own, Miss Craggs?"

Oh, it was a cruel question. How could she find a husband for herself? Even if she left Miss Phillpotts's, what could she hope to do except teach somewhere else or perhaps be someone's governess? There was no hope of matrimony for someone like her. And a family of her own? How could she even dream of a family when there was no possibility of a husband?

To her annoyance, she could think of no answer to make. And in her attempt to cover up her confusion, she lifted her glass to her lips, forgetting that her hand would shake. It did so and she had to lower the glass, the cider untasted. She wondered if he had noticed.

"How did you know," he asked, seeming to change the subject, "that Veronica hides inside herself? I begin to think you must be right, but how did you realize it?"

"She is too quiet, too docile, too obedient for a child," she said.

"Did you know it from experience?" he asked.

"I . . ." She swallowed. "Is this an interrogation, my lord? I am not accustomed to talking about myself."

"Why not?" he asked. "Does no one ever ask you about yourself? Does Miss Phillpotts believe she does you a favor by keeping you on at the school? And do the teachers and pupils take their cue from her? Do they all call you Craggs, as Deborah did until recently? Does no one call you Jane?"

For some reason she felt as if she had been stabbed to the heart. There was intense pain.

"Teachers are not usually called by their first names," she said.

"But teachers should have identities apart from their career," he said. "Should they not, Jane? For how long have you been in hiding?"

"Please." She set her hardly tasted cider on the small table beside her and got to her feet. "It is late, my lord. It is time for me to say good night."

"Have I been very impertinent, Jane?" He too stood, and somehow he possessed himself of both her hands. "No, you do not need to answer. I have been impertinent and it has been unpardonable of me when you are a guest in my home and when you have been very kind to both Deborah and my daughter and when you have brought Christmas to this house for the first time in years. Forgive me?"

"Of course," she said, trying to draw her hands free of his without jerking on them. She felt again as if she were suffocating. His closeness and his maleness were overpowering her. "It is nothing, my lord."

"It is something," he said. "It is just that you have intrigued me during the past few days, Jane. You are like two people. Much of the time you are a disciplined, prim and—forgive me—plain teacher. But sometimes you are eager and warm and quite incredibly beautiful. I have been given the impression that the latter person has come bubbling up from very deep within. Is she the real person, the one you hide from the world, the one you have never had a chance to share with anyone else?"

"Please." She dragged at her hands but was unable to free them. Her voice, she noticed in some dismay, sounded thin and distressed. She sounded on the verge of tears.

"He was a fool, your father," he said. "He had you to love and let opportunity pass him by."

She forgot herself instantly. She looked up into his face, her eyes wide. "And are you going to make the same mistake?" she asked. "You too have a daughter to love."

"But the situation is different," he said. "I am not going to abandon her to an orphanage or a school. I am going to find her the very best parents I can."

"But she is four years old," Jane said. "Do you not think she will remember, however hazily? She will remember that her mother disappeared mysteriously and she will try to persuade herself that she died and did not merely abandon her. You need to tell her the truth. However cruel it seems now, she needs to know. And she will remember that her father was titled and wealthy and that he cared enough to provide for her physical needs but did not care enough to provide for the only need that mattered."

"And that is?" He was frowning and she thought that perhaps he was angry. But so was she. She would answer his question.

"The need for love," she said. "The need to know that to someone she means more than anything else in the world."

"But she is illegitimate." He was almost whispering. "She is the daughter I fathered on a mistress. Do you understand, Jane? Do you know anything about what is acceptable and what is not in polite society?"

"Yes," she said. "Oh, yes, I know, my lord. I am such a daughter too, remember. No one in my memory has ever wanted to know me as a person. No one has ever hugged me. Or kissed me. No one has ever loved me. I am three-and-twenty now, old enough to bear the burdens of life alone, but I would not want another child to have to live the life I have lived. Not Veronica. I hope she will remember that you have kissed her cheek and rubbed your hand in her hair and carried her home from church inside your greatcoat. I am not sure it will help a great deal, but I hope she remembers even so. I wish I had such memories."

"Jane," he said, his voice shaken. "Oh, my poor Jane."

And before she knew what was to happen or could do anything to prevent it, his hands had released hers and grasped her by the shoulders instead, and he had pulled her against him. And before her mind could cope with the shock of feeling a man's warm and firmly muscled body against her own, his mouth was on hers, warm and firm, his lips slightly parted.

For a moment—for a fleeting moment after her mind had recovered from its first shock—she surrendered to the heady physical sensation of being embraced by a man and to the realization that she was experiencing her first real kiss. And then she got her palms against his chest and pushed firmly away from him.

"No," she said. "No, my lord, it is not poor Jane. It is poor Veronica. She has a father who could love her, I believe, but who feels that the conventions of society are of greater importance than love."

She did not give him a chance to reply though he reached for her again. She whisked herself about and out of the room and fled upstairs to her bedchamber as if being pursued by a thousand devils.

It had snowed a little more during the night. The viscount stood at his window, eager to go downstairs to begin the day, yet wanting at the same time to stay where he was until he could safely escape to the Oxendens' house. He wanted to go downstairs because he had told her the truth last night. She had brought Christmas to his home for the first time in many years, and he found himself hungry for it. And yet he dreaded seeing her this morning after his unpardonable indiscretion of the night before. And he dreaded seeing

Veronica. He dreaded being confronted with love. He had decided six years ago to the day that he must be incapable of loving enough to satisfy another person. He had confined his feelings since then to friendships and to lust.

She was wrong. It was not that he put the conventions of society before love as much as that he did not believe he could love his daughter as well as a carefully chosen couple would. He wanted Veronica to have a happy childhood. Because he loved her. He tested the thought in his mind, but he could not find fault with it. He did love her. The thought of giving her up to another couple was not a pleasant one. And that was an understatement.

He was the first one downstairs. Before going to the breakfast room he went into the drawing room to take the parcels he had bought in a visit to a nearby town two days before and a few he had brought home with him and to set them down beside the rudely carved but curiously lovely Nativity scene with its Mary and Joseph and babe in a manger and a single shepherd and lamb. They had been set up last night. He was seeing them for the first time.

He looked about the room. And he thought of his irritation at finding himself saddled with his niece for Christmas and of her sullenness at being abandoned by her parents and left to his care. And of the terrible aloneness of Veronica as she had sat in his hall, like a labeled parcel abandoned until someone could find time to open it.

Yes, Jane had transformed his home and the three of them who lived in it with her. Under the most unpromising of circumstances she had brought the warmth and joy of Christmas. He wondered if it was something she was accustomed to doing. But he knew even as he thought it that that was not it at all. If she had been about to spend Christmas alone at the school this year, then surely she must have spent it alone there last year and the year before. His heart chilled. Had she ever spent Christmas in company with others? Had she always been alone?

Was all the love of her heart, all the love of her life being poured out on this one Christmas she was spending with strangers? With three other waifs like herself? But she was so much stronger than they. Without her, he felt, the rest of them would have wallowed in gloom.

But his thoughts were interrupted. Deborah burst into the room, parcels in her hands. She set them beside his and turned to smile at him.

"Happy Christmas, Uncle Warren," she said. "Veronica is up. Craggs—*Miss* Craggs—is dressing her and brushing her hair. They will be down soon. I wish they would hurry. I have presents for everyone. I bought them in the village shop. And you have presents too. Is there one for me?"

"Yes." He grinned at her. "Happy Christmas, Deborah."

And then they came into the room, hand in hand, Jane and Veronica, and his heart constricted at sight of them. His two ladies. Jane was carrying two parcels. Veronica was saucer-eyed.

And finally it was there again, full-grown—the glorious wonder of Christmas in a young child's eyes, which were fixed on the Nativity scene and on the parcels beside it. He hurried across the room to her and stooped down without thought to lift her into his arms.

"Happy Christmas, Veronica," he said, and kissed her on her soft little lips. "Someone brought the baby Jesus with his mama and papa during the night. And someone brought gifts, too. I will wager some of them are yours."

Jane, he saw, had hurried across the room to set down her parcels with the rest.

"For me?" Veronica asked, her eyes growing wider still.

He sat her on his knee close to the gifts, feeling absurdly excited himself, almost as if he were a boy again. And he watched her as she unwrapped the dainty lace-edged handkerchief Deborah had bought for her and held it against her cheek, and the pretty red bonnet and muff Jane had bought her, both of which she had to try on. And then he watched her, his heart beating almost with nervousness, as she unwrapped his exquisitely dressed porcelain doll.

"Oh!" she said after staring at it in silence for a few moments. "Look what I have, Papa. Look what I have, Miss Jane. Look, Deborah."

Viscount Buckley blinked several times, aware of the acute embarrassment of the fact that he had tears in his eyes. And yet when he sneaked a look at Jane, it was to find that her own eyes were brimming with tears.

"She is beautiful, Veronica," she said.

"Lovely," Deborah agreed with enthusiasm.

"Almost as beautiful as you," her father assured her. "What are you going to call her?"

"Jane," his daughter said without hesitation.

And then Deborah opened her gifts and exclaimed with delight over the perfume Jane had given her and with awe over the diamond-studded watch her parents had left for her and with warm appreciation over the evening gloves and fan her uncle had bought for her—because she was as close to being adult as made no difference, he explained. She declared that she would wear them to the dance that evening.

Viscount Buckley unwrapped a linen handkerchief from Deborah and a silver-backed brush and comb from his sister and brother-in-law.

And he watched as Jane unwrapped her own lace-edged handkerchief from Deborah and smiled rather teary-eyed at the girl. And then he watched more keenly as she took out his cashmere shawl from its wrapping and held it up in front of her, its folds falling free. She bit her lip and shut her eyes very tightly for a few moments.

"It is the most beautiful thing I have ever seen," she said before turning to him, her face looking almost agonized. "Thank you. But I have nothing for you. I did not think it would be seemly."

Veronica had wriggled off his lap and was gazing down with Deborah into the manger at the baby Jesus, her doll clutched in both arms. Deborah was explaining to her what swaddling clothes were.

"You have given me a gift beyond price, Jane," he said quietly, for her ears only. "You have opened my eyes to Christmas again and all its meanings. I thank you."

She gazed back at him, the shawl suspended in front of her from her raised arms.

But Deborah had decided it was time for breakfast and was assuring Veronica that she could bring her doll along and they would find it a chair to sit on and a bowl to eat from. His niece seemed to have quite got over her shock at being exposed to the company of his illegitimate daughter.

"Come," he said to Jane, getting to his feet and extending a hand to her, "let us eat and then we must have the servants up here for their gifts. They will doubtless be happy to see that I can do it without a frown this year."

He smiled at her and she smiled rather tremulously back.

Once, when she was seventeen, Miss Phillpotts had given her a porcelain thimble in recognition of her new status as a teacher. It was the only gift she had ever received—until today. Jane set down her handkerchief and her shawl carefully on her bed, as if they too were of porcelain and might break, smoothed a hand over each, and swallowed back her tears so that she would not have to display reddened eyes when she left her room.

But the best gift of all was what he had said to her. *You have given me a gift beyond price, Jane.* And he had smiled at her. And he had held Veronica on his knee and had looked at her with what was surely tenderness.

Going back to Miss Phillpotts's, being alone again, was going to be more painful than ever, she knew, now that she had had a taste of family life, now that she had fallen in— No, that was a silly idea. That she would have fallen in love with him was thoroughly predictable under the circumstances. It was not real love, of course. But however it was, she would put up with all the pain and all the dreariness, she felt, if only she could know that he would keep Veronica with him. She would give up all claim to future Christmases without a murmur if only she could be sure of that.

It was a busy day, a wonderfully busy day. There were the servants to greet in the drawing room while Viscount Buckley gave each of them a gift, and toasts to be drunk with them and rich dainties to eat. And there were gifts from almost all of them for Veronica to open. It was certainly clear that his staff had taken the viscount's young daughter to their hearts. And there were carols to sing.

After the Christmas dinner, taken *en famille* in the dining room very early in the afternoon, there were the young guests to prepare for. There was no containing Deborah's excitement. As soon as they had arrived, all of them bright and merry at the novel prospect of a party all to themselves without adults to spoil it and tell them to quieten down or to stay out of the way, they were whisked out-of-doors.

They engaged in an unruly snowball fight even before they reached the hill where the sledding was to take place. Deborah, Jane noticed with indulgent interest, was almost elbow-to-elbow with Mr. George Oxenden, the two of them fighting the common enemy, almost everyone else. But before she knew it, Jane was fighting for her own life, or at least for her own comfort. A soft snowball splattered against her shoulder, and she found that Viscount Buckley was grinning smugly at her from a few yards away. She shattered the grin when by some miracle her own snowball collided with the center of his face.

Jane found herself giggling quite as helplessly as Deborah was doing.

The sleds were much in demand when they reached the hill as the young people raced up the slope with reckless energy and then zoomed down two by two. Nobody complained about the cold even though there was a great deal of foot stamping and hand slapping against sides. And even though everyone sported fiery red cheeks and noses.

Veronica stood quietly watching, holding Jane's hand.

"Well, Veronica," her father said, coming to stand beside them, "what do you think? Shall we try it?"

"We will fall," she said, looking gravely up at him.

"What?" he said. "You do not trust my steering skills? If we fall, we will be covered with snow. Is that so bad?"

"No, Papa," she said, looking dubious.

"Well." He held out a hand for hers. "Shall we try?"

"Can Miss Jane come too?" Veronica asked.

Jane grimaced and found the viscount's eyes directed at her. They were twinkling. "It might be something of a squash," he said. "But I am willing if you two ladies are."

"I . . . I . . ." Jane said.

"What?" His eyebrows shot up. "Do we have a coward here? Shall we dare Miss Jane to ride on a sled with us, Veronica?"

"Yes, Papa," his daughter said.

And so less than five minutes later Jane found herself at the top of the hill, seating herself gingerly on one of the sleds, which suddenly looked alarmingly narrow and frail, and having to move back to make room for Veronica until her back was snug against the viscount's front. His arms came about her at either side to arrange the steering rope. And suddenly, too, it no longer seemed like a cold winter day. She was only half aware of the giggles of the young ladies and the whistles and jeers and cheers of the young gentlemen. She set her arms tightly about Veronica.

And then they were off, hurtling down a slope that seemed ten times steeper than it had looked from the bottom, at a speed that seemed more than ten times faster than that of the other sledders when she had watched them. Two people were shrieking, Veronica and herself. And then they were at the bottom and the sled performed a complete turn, flirted with the idea of tipping over and dumping its load into the snow, and slid safely to a halt.

Veronica's shrieks had turned to laughter—helpless, joyful, childish laughter. The viscount, the first to rise to his feet, scooped her up and held her close and met Jane's eyes over her shoulder. Perhaps it was the wind and the cold that had made his eyes so bright, but Jane did not think so.

Oh, how good it was—it was the best moment so far of a wonderful Christmas—how very good it was to hear the child laugh. And beg to be taken up again. And wriggle to get down and grab at her father's hand and tug him impatiently in the direction of the slope. And to watch her ride down again with him, shrieking and laughing once more.

And how good it was—how achingly good—to see him laughing and happy with the little child he had fathered almost five years before but had not even seen until a few days ago.

Chilly as she was—her hands and her feet were aching with the cold—Jane willed the afternoon to last forever. He was to go to the Oxendens' for dinner and he was to spend the evening there and perhaps half the night too. Once he had gone she would be the lone chaperon of the group, apart from the lady who was coming to play the pianoforte. She was going to feel lonely.

But she quelled the thought. She had had so much, more than she had ever dreamed. She must not be greedy. This evening was for the young people.

And then, just before it was mutually agreed that it was time to return to the house to thaw out and partake of some of Cook's hot Christmas drinks and mince pies, Veronica was borne off by Deborah to ride a sled with her and Mr. Oxenden, and Viscount Buckley took Jane firmly by one hand and led her toward the slope.

"If you stand there any longer," he said, "you may well become frozen to the spot. Come and sled with me now that I have relearned the knack of doing it safely."

She savored the moment, this final moment of her very own Christmas. But alas, this time they were not so fortunate. Perhaps the constant passing of the sleds had made the surface over which they sped just too slippery for successful navigation. Or perhaps there was some other cause. However it was, something went very wrong when they were halfway down the slope. The sled went quite out of control, and its two riders were unceremoniously dumped into a bank of soft, cold snow. They rolled into it, arms and legs all tangled together.

They finally came to rest with Jane on the bottom, flat on her back, and Viscount Buckley on top of her. They were both laughing and then both self-conscious. His eyes slid to her mouth at the same moment as hers slid to his. But for a moment only. The delighted laughter of the young people brought them to their senses and their feet, and they both brushed vigorously at themselves and joined in the laughter.

Jane was tingling with warmth again. If only, she thought shamelessly. If only there had been no one else in sight. If only he had kissed her again. Just once more. One more kiss to hug to herself for the rest of her life.

Oh, she really had become greedy, she told herself severely. Would she never be satisfied?

An unwanted inner voice answered her. No, not any longer. She never would.

But it was time to take Veronica by the hand again. It was time to go back to the house.

Viscount Buckley went upstairs to change into his evening clothes while the young people played charades in the drawing room and Jane played unobtrusively in one corner with Veronica and her new doll, the kitchen cat curled beside them, apparently oblivious to the loud mirth proceeding all about it. He had lingered in the room himself, reluctant to leave despite the squeals from the girls and loud laughter from the boys that just a few days before he had welcomed the thought of escaping. But he could delay no longer if he were to arrive at the Oxendens' in good time for dinner.

Yet despite the fact that he was pressed for time, he wandered to the window of his bedchamber after his valet had exercised all his artistic skills on the tying of his neckcloth and had helped him into his blue evening coat, as tight as a second skin, according to fashion. He stood gazing out at twilight and snow, not really seeing either.

He was seeing Veronica in her red Christmas bonnet, her muff on a ribbon about her neck. He was seeing her rosy-cheeked with the cold, bright-eyed and laughing, and tugging impatiently at his hand. Looking and sounding like a four-year-old. And he was thinking of her next week or the week after or the week after that, going away to settle with her new family.

He was going to be lonely. He was going to grieve for her for the rest of his life. And if Jane was correct, he was not even doing what was best for Veronica.

Jane! He could see her too, animated and giggling—yes, giggling!—and beautiful. Ah, so beautiful, his prim, plain Jane. And he thought of her the week after next, returning to Miss Phillpotts's school with Deborah, returning to her life of drudgery and utter aloneness. She had never been hugged or kissed or loved, she had said—not out of self-pity but in an attempt to save Veronica from such a fate.

He was going to be lonely without Jane. He thought of his mistress, waiting for him in London with her luscious, perfumed body, and of the skills she used to match his own in bed. But he could feel no desire, no longing for her. He wanted Jane with her inevitable gray dress and her nondescript figure and her face that was plain except when she stopped hiding inside herself. Jane, who did not even know how to kiss—she pursed her lips and kept them rigidly closed. She probably did not know what happened between a man and a woman in bed.

He wanted her.

And he wanted to keep Veronica.

His valet cleared his throat from the doorway into his dressing room and informed him that the carriage was waiting. The viscount knew it was waiting. He had been aware of it below him on the terrace for at least the past ten minutes. The horses, he saw now when he looked down, were stamping and snorting, impatient to be in motion.

"Have it returned to the carriage house," he heard

himself say, "and brought up again after dinner. I had better stay here and help Miss Craggs with the young people at dinner. They are rather exuberant and unruly."

That last word was unfair. And what the devil was he doing explaining himself to his valet?

"Yes, m'lord," the man said, and withdrew.

Well, that was the excuse he would give the Oxendens later, he thought, as he hurried from the room and downstairs to the drawing room, lightness in his step. It would seem an eminently believable excuse.

And so he sat at the head of the table during dinner, the second of the day, while Jane sat at the foot, Veronica beside her, and the young people were ranged along the two long sides. And he listened indulgently to all their silly chatter and laughter without once wincing with distaste. And he feasted his stomach on rich foods, which it just did not need, and feasted his eyes on his two ladies, who were both making sure that the doll Jane was having her fair share of each course.

And then it was time for the young people and their chaperon to adjourn to the drawing room. The servants had rolled back the carpet during dinner, and Mrs. Carpenter had arrived to provide music for the dancing. Vernoica was to be allowed to stay up and watch until she was sleepy. And he was to go to the Oxendens'. The carriage was waiting for him again.

But what if any of the silly children decided to imitate their elders and disappear in couples to more remote locations? What if young George Oxenden, in particular, decided to become amorous with Deborah? They had been flirting quite outrageously with each other all afternoon. He had even spotted the young man kissing her beneath the mistletoe she had deliberately stood under. How could Jane handle all that alone when she had Veronica to look after too?

No, he could not leave her alone. It would be grossly unfair when he was the master of the house—and when Susannah and Miles had entrusted Deborah to his care.

"Have the carriage sent away," he told his butler. "I will not be needing it this evening after all." He smiled fleetingly in self-mockery. This was the most blatant example of rationalization he had ever been involved in. And he must have windmills in the brain. He was choosing to party with young people rather than with sane adults?

No, actually he was choosing to party with his lady and his daughter.

They had danced a quadrille and numerous country dances. All the young people danced every set. They were clearly enjoying the novelty of being able to use the skills they had learned from dancing masters in the setting of a real ball—or what was almost a real ball.

Jane was feeling wonderfully happy as she watched and as she played with an increasingly tired Veronica. The child did not want to give in to suggestions that she be taken up to bed. At the moment she was seated cross-legged on the floor beside the Nativity scene, rocking her doll to sleep in her arms and looking as if she was not far from sleep herself.

But what completed Jane's happiness was the fact that for some reason Viscount Buckley had not gone to the Oxendens' after all but had stayed at the house. He had mingled with the company and chatted with Mrs. Carpenter between dances and had not been near Jane and Veronica. But it did not matter. Just having him in the room, just being able to feast her eyes on him, was enough. He looked even more splendidly handsome than usual in a pale blue evening coat with gray knee breeches and white linen and lace.

She thought with secret, guilty wonder of the fact that

she had been kissed by this man. And that she had his gift, the lovely shawl, to hug about her—literally—for the rest of her life.

He was bending over Mrs. Carpenter, speaking to her, and she was nodding and smiling. He turned to his young guests and clapped his hands to gain their attention.

"This is to be a waltz, ladies and gentlemen," he said. "Do you all know the steps?"

They all did. But the young ladies in particular had not expected to be able to dance them in public for many years, until they had made their come-outs and had been approved by the patronesses of Almack's in London. There was a buzz of excitement.

Jane knew the steps of the waltz too. She remembered with an inward shudder demonstrating it for the girls at school with the dancing master, whose hands had always seemed too hot and too moist, and who had always tried to cause her to stumble against him. But it was a wonderful dance. Wonderfully romantic—a couple dancing face-to-face, their hands touching each other.

"Jane?" Suddenly he was there before her, bowing elegantly as if she were the Duchess of Somewhere, and extending a hand toward her. "Will you do me the honor?"

"Me?" she said foolishly, spreading a hand over her chest.

He smiled at her and something strange happened to her knees and someone had sucked half the air out of the room.

"Thank you." She set her hand in his and he looked down at Veronica.

"Do you mind if I steal Miss Jane for a few minutes?" he asked. "Will you watch us dance?"

Veronica yawned.

Jane had dreamed of happiness and romance and pleasure. But never until this ten-minute period had she had even the glimmering of a notion of what any of the three might really feel like. They were almost an agony. She danced—he was an exquisite dancer—and felt that her feet scarcely touched the floor. She danced and did not even have to think about the steps. She danced and was unaware that the room held anyone else but the two of them and the music. She was too happy even to wish that time would stop so that forever she would be caught up in the waltz with the man she had so foolishly fallen in love with.

To say it was the happiest ten minutes of her life was so grossly to understate the case that the words would be meaningless.

"Thank you," she said when it was over, coolly, as if it really had not meant a great deal to her at all. "I think I should take Veronica up to bed, my lord. She is very tired."

"Yes," he said, glancing down at his child. "Take her up, then. I will come in ten minutes or so to say good night to her."

And so the magic was gone and the day was almost over. She took the sleepy child by the hand and led her up to the nursery, undressed her and washed her quickly, helped her into her nightgown, and tucked her into bed beside her doll.

"Good night, sweetheart," she said, smoothing back the child's curls with one gentle hand. "Has it been a happy Christmas?"

Veronica nodded, though she did not open her eyes and she did not speak. And then Jane's heart lurched with alarm. Two tears had squeezed themselves from between the child's eyelids and were rolling diagonally across her cheeks.

Jane turned instinctively toward the door. He was

standing there, as he did each night. When he saw her face, he looked more closely at his daughter. Jane could tell that he could see the tears. His face paled and he came walking across the room toward the bed.

He did not know what to do for a moment. She had seemed so happy for most of the day. She had been laughing and excited during the afternoon. What had happened to upset her? And how could he cope with whatever it was?

"Veronica?" He touched his fingers to her cheek. "What is it?"

She kept her eyes closed and did not answer him for a while. But more tears followed the first. There was something horrifying about a child crying silently. Jane had got up from the bed to stand behind him.

"Why did Mama not come?" his daughter asked finally. "Why was there no present from Mama?"

Oh, God. Oh, dear Lord God, he could not handle this. He sat down on the bed in the spot just vacated by Jane. "Mama had to go far away," he said, cupping the little face with his hands and wiping the tears away with his thumbs. "She would be here if she could, dear. She loves you dearly." He rejected the idea of telling her that the doll was from her mother. Children were usually more intelligent than adults gave them credit for.

His daughter was looking at him suddenly. "Is she dead?" she asked.

A denial was on his lips. And then Jane's words came back to him. She needed to know. Ultimately it would be worse for her not to know, for her to grow up believing that her mother had just tired of her and abandoned her. He stood up for a moment, drew back the bedclothes, scooped up his daughter in his arms, and sat down again, cradling her against him.

"Yes," he said. "She died, Veronica. But she sent you

to Papa. And Papa loves you more than anyone or anything else in this world."

She was sobbing then with all of a child's abandoned woe. And he, rocking her in his arms, was crying too. Crying over his daughter's loss and grief. Crying over the truth of the words he had just spoken, and over the treasure he had so very nearly given carelessly away.

She stopped crying eventually and lay quietly in his arms. "You are not going to send me away, Papa?" she whispered.

"Send you away?" he said. "How could I do that? What would I do without my little girl? Who would there be to make me happy?"

She looked up at him with a wet and swollen face so that he was reaching into his pocket for a handkerchief even as she spoke. "Do you really love me, Papa?"

"You are my little Christmas treasure," he said, drying her eyes and her cheeks. "The best gift I ever had. I love you, dear."

She reached up to set one soft little hand against his lips. He held it there and kissed it and smiled at her. She yawned hugely and noisily. "Is Miss Jane going to stay too?" she asked.

He felt Jane shift position behind him.

"Yes," he said, "if I can persuade her to. Would you like that?"

"Yes, Papa," she said.

And in the way of children she was asleep. Asleep and safe and loved in her father's arms. He held her there for a few minutes until he was quite sure she would not wake and then stood to set her down carefully in her bed. Jane held the bedclothes back for him and then stepped aside again.

By the time he had tucked the blankets snugly about his daughter and bent to kiss her little mouth, Jane had disappeared.

*   *   *

It had been agreed that the young people could stay at Cosway until midnight. It was no surprise to anyone, then, when they did not actually leave until thirty minutes after the hour. After all, there had to be just one more dance to follow the last and then one more to follow that.

It was the best, the very best Christmas she had ever known, Deborah declared, dancing before her uncle and Jane in the hall after everyone had finally gone.

"But do not tell Mama and Papa," she said to the viscount, giggling, "or they will be hurt."

"It will be our secret," he said dryly. "Upstairs with you, now. It is long past your bedtime."

She pulled a face at him before kissing his cheek and dancing in the direction of the stairs. But she came back again and kissed Jane's cheek too, a little self-consciously. "I am glad you came here with me, Miss Craggs," she said. "Thank you."

"Good night." Jane smiled at her. And then, when the girl was only halfway up the stairs, Jane turned, fixed her eyes on the diamond pin Viscount Buckley wore in his neckcloth, and wished him a hasty good night too.

She was already on her way to the stairs when she felt her hand caught in his.

"Coward!" he said. "You really are a coward, Jane."

"I am tired," she said.

"And a liar," he said.

She looked at him indignantly. He was smiling.

"Into the library," he said, giving her no chance to protest. He was leading her there by the hand. "I have a job to offer you."

As Veronica's nurse? She was too afraid to hope for it, though he had assured his daughter that he would try to persuade her to stay. Oh, would he offer her the job? Could life have such wonder in store for her? After the child no longer needed a nurse, perhaps he would keep her on as a governess. But it was too soon to dream of the future when she was not even sure of the present.

"Jane." He closed the library door behind him and leaned against it. He was still holding her hand. Someone had lit the branch of candles in there.

"You really do not have to persuade me to stay," she said breathlessly. "Veronica will not even remember in the morning that you promised to do so. If you think me unsuitable for the job of nurse, I will understand. I have had no experience with young children. But I do love her, and I would do my very best if you would consider hiring me. But you must not feel obliged to do so." She stopped talking abruptly and looked down in some confusion.

"A nurse," he said. "I do indeed consider you unsuitable for the job, Jane. It was not what I had in mind at all."

She bit her upper lip, chagrined and shamed. Why, oh, why had she not kept her mouth shut?

"I was hoping you would take on the job of mother," he said. "Mother of Veronica and mother of my other children. My future children, that is."

She looked up at him sharply.

"And wife," he added. "My wife, Jane."

Oh. She gaped at him. "Me?" she said foolishly. "You want *me* to be your wife? But you cannot marry me. You know who and what I am."

"You and my daughter both," he said, smiling. "Two treasures. I love you, Jane. I have Veronica, thanks to your words of admonition and advice, and she is a priceless possession. But you can make my happiness complete by marrying me. Will you? I cannot blame you if you do not trust me. I am new to love. I have not trusted it for a long time. But I—"

"Oh," she said, her eyes wide, her heart beating wildly. "You *love* me? You love *me*? How can that be?"

"Because," he said, still smiling, "I have been playing hide-and-seek, Jane. I have not yet discovered all of you there is to discover. You have done an admirable job over the years of hiding yourself. But what I have seen dazzles me. You are beautiful, inside and out, and I want you for myself. Yes, I love you. Could you ever feel anything for me?"

"Yes," she said without hesitation. "Oh, yes. Oh, yes, my lord. I love you with all my heart."

Somehow his arms were clasped behind her waist and hers behind his neck. Only a part of her mind had grasped what he was saying to her and what he was asking of her. She knew that it would take a long time before the rest of her brain caught up to the knowledge.

"It is going to have to be Warren," he said. "Say it before I kiss you."

"Warren," she said.

It was a kiss that lasted a scandalous length of time. Before it was over she had allowed him to bend the whole of her body against his and she had responded to the coaxing of his lips and softened her own and even parted them. Before it was over she had allowed his tongue into her mouth and his hands on parts of her body she would have thought horrifyingly embarrassing to have touched. Before it was over she was weak with unfamiliar aches of desire.

"My love," he was saying against her mouth, "forgive me. I would not have you for the first time on the library floor. It will be on my bed upstairs on our wedding night. If . . ." He drew his head back and gazed at her with eyes that were heavy with passion and love—for her. "If there is to be a wedding night. Is there? Will you marry me?"

"Yes," she said, stunned. Had she not already said it? "Warren—"

But whatever she was about to say was soon forgotten as his mouth covered hers again and they moved perilously close after all to anticipating their wedding night.

After all, it was Christmas and they had both just discovered love and joy and romance. And the treasure of a child to love and nurture together.

It was Christmas. Christmas after a long, long time for him. The first Christmas ever for her.

It was Christmas.

Playing House

*T*he logs in the fireplace were crackling and shooting sparks up into the chimney. The fire's warmth felt good to the young lady who had just come in from the cold and the wind and rain. She held her hands out to the blaze.

But she could not draw a great deal of comfort from the fire. She caught sight of the hem of her wool dress. It was heavy with wetness and streaked with mud. Her half-boots looked no better. And she wished she had not removed her bonnet and handed it to the footman with her cloak. Her hair was hopelessly damp and flattened to her head. And she knew that her nose as well as her cheeks must be glowing red.

It was cold outside, and the mile-and-a-half walk across the park to Bedford Hall had been taken into the teeth of the wind and into the driving force of the rain and had seemed more like five miles.

Lilias lowered her hands from the blaze and brushed nervously at her dress. The darned patch near the hem was more noticeable now that the fabric was wet. She looked down at her right wrist and twisted her sleeve so that the darn there would be out of sight.

She should not have come. She had known that as soon as the footman had opened the front doors and asked her, after she stepped inside, if he could take her to Mrs. Morgan. But no, she had replied with a firmness that had been fast deserting her, she was not calling on the housekeeper today. She wished to speak with his lordship, if it was convenient.

She should not have come, a single lady, alone, to speak with a single gentleman. She knew she would never have dared to do so if she were in London or some other fashionable center. Even here in the country it was not at all the thing. She should have brought someone with her, though there was no one to bring except the children. And she did not want them to know she was paying this call.

And who was she, even if she had had a respectable companion, to be paying a call on the Marquess of Bedford? She was wearing her best day dress, yet it was patched in three places. She had had to walk from the village because she owned no conveyance or even a horse or pony. In two weeks' time she was to be a servant.

She should have come to the kitchen entrance, not to the main doors.

Lilias took one step back from the fireplace, suddenly feeling uncomfortably warm. If she hurried, she could grab her cloak and bonnet from the hallway and be outside and on her way home before any more harm was done. The rain and wind would be at her back on the return journey.

But she was too late. The door to the salon in which she had been asked to wait opened even before she could take one more step toward it, and he stepped inside. Someone closed the door quietly behind him.

The Marquess of Bedford.

Lilias swallowed and unconsciously raised her chin. She clasped her hands before her and dropped into a curtsy. She would scarcely have known him. He looked taller, and he was certainly broader. He bore himself very straight, like a soldier, though he had never been one. He was immaculately and fashionably dressed. His hair was as thick as it had ever been, but its darkness was highlighted now by the suggestion of silver at the temples. But he was not thirty yet.

His face was what had changed most. It looked as if carved out of marble, his jaw firm and hard, his lips thin and straight, his blue eyes above the aquiline nose heavy-lidded and cold. One eyebrow was arched somewhat higher than the other.

He made her a stiff half-bow. "Well, Miss Angove," he said in a voice that was softer, colder than the voice she remembered, "what an unexpected pleasure. You are the first of my neighbors to call upon me. All alone?"

"Yes, my lord," she said, clasping her hands more firmly before her and consciously resisting the impulse to allow them to fidget. "This is not a social call. I have a favor to ask."

His one eyebrow rose even higher and his lips curved into the suggestion of a sneer. "Indeed?" he said, advancing farther into the room. "Well, at least you are honest about it. Have a seat, ma'am, and tell me how I may be of service to you."

She sat on the very edge of the chair closest to her and clasped her hands in her lap. Someone had tamed his hair, she thought irrelevantly. It had always waved in a quite unruly manner and had forever fallen across his forehead. It had been a habit of his to toss it back with a jerk of the head.

"It is not precisely a favor," she said, "but more in the way of the calling in of a debt."

He seated himself opposite her and looked at her inquiringly. His eyes had never used to be like this. They had been wide and sparkling eyes, mesmerizing even. But then, they were compelling now too. They regarded her with cynical contempt. Lilias glanced down nervously at her sleeve to find that the darned patch was staring accusingly up at her. But she did not twist the sleeve again. Perhaps he would not notice if she kept her hands still. Except that she felt that those eyes saw everything, even the larger darned patch beneath her left arm.

"When you were at school," she said, "and found your Latin lessons difficult, Papa helped you during your holidays. You used to come to the rectory every morning for two successive summers. Do you remember?" She did not wait for a reply. "You would not tell your own papa for fear that he would be disappointed in you. And Papa would accept no payment for your tuition. You told him—I was there when you said it—that you would always consider yourself in his debt, that you would repay him one day."

"And so I did say," he said in that quiet, cold voice. His expression did not change at all. "Your father has been dead for well over a year, has he not, Miss Angove? But I take it that the day of reckoning has come. What may I do for you?"

"I think less than the tuition for two summers would have cost you," she said hastily, wishing that she could keep her voice as cool as his. "I would not put myself in your debt."

His eyelids appeared to droop even lower over his eyes. "What may I do for you, ma'am?" he asked again.

"I want a Christmas for my brother and sister," she said raising her chin and looking very directly into his face. She could feel herself flushing.

Both his eyebrows rose. "An admirable wish," he said. "But it would seem that if you wait patiently for one more week, Christmas will come without my having to do anything about the matter."

"They are still children," she said. "My parents' sec-

ond family, people have always called them. Philip and
I were two years apart, and then there were eleven
years before Andrew was born. And Megan came two
years after that. They are only eleven and nine years old
now. Just children. This is our last Christmas together. In
two weeks' time we will all be separated. Perhaps we
will never be together again. I want it to be a memorable Christmas." She was leaning forward in her chair.
Her fingers were twining about one another.

"And how am I to help create this memorable Christmas?" he asked. His mouth was definitely formed into a
sneer now. "Host a grand party? Grand parties are not
in my style."

"No," she said, speaking quickly and distinctly. "I
want a goose for Christmas dinner."

There was a short silence.

"Papa was not a careful manager," she continued.
"There was very little money left when he died and now
there is none left, or at least only enough to pay for our
journeys in two weeks' time. The people of the village
would help, of course, but they were so used to finding
that Papa would not accept charity in any form that
they now do not even offer. And perhaps they are
right." Her chin rose again. "I have some of his pride."

"So," he said, "instead of asking charity, you have
found someone who is in your debt."

"Yes," she said, and swallowed awkwardly again.

"And you want a goose for Christmas," he said. "Your
needs are modest, ma'am. That is all?"

"And a doll for Megan," she said recklessly. "There is
the most glorious one in Miss Pierce's window—all
porcelain and satin and lace. I want that for Megan. She
has never had a doll, except the rag one Mama made for
her when she was a baby. I want her to have something
really lovely and valuable to take with her."

"And for your brother?" he asked softly.

"Oh." She gazed at him wistfully. "A watch. A silver watch. But there are none in the village, and I would not know how to go about purchasing one for him. But it does not matter. Andrew is eleven and almost not a child any longer. He will understand, and he will be happy with the scarf and gloves I am knitting for him. The cost of a goose and the doll will not exceed the cost of tuition for two summers, I don't believe. Will it?"

"And for yourself?" he asked even more softly.

Lilias gazed down at her hands and reached out to twist the offending sleeve. "I don't want anything that will cost money," she said. "I want only the memory of one Christmas to take with me."

"Where are you going?" he asked.

She looked up at him. "Into Yorkshire," she said. "I have a post as a governess with a family there."

"Ah," he said. "And your brother and sister?"

"I have persuaded my grandfather to take Andrew," she said. "It took several letters, but finally he agreed to take him and send him to school. Sir Percy Angove, that is, Papa's father. The two of them never communicated after Papa's marriage."

The marquess nodded curtly.

"And Megan is going to Great-aunt Hetty in Bath," Lilias said. "I am afraid I pestered her with letters too. But it will be only until I can earn enough money to bring us all together again."

Bedford got to his feet and looked down at her from cold and cynical eyes. "Ah, yes," he said. "A suitably affecting story, Miss Angove. I must congratulate you on the manner in which you have presented it."

Lilias looked up at him in some bewilderment.

His bearing was military again, his manner curt, his eyes like chips of ice. "You will have your goose, ma'am," he said, "and your sister her doll. Your brother will have his watch too—I shall see to it. You will have your Christmas and the memory of it to take into York-shire with you. I shall wish you good day now."

Victory? Was it to be so easy? Was she to have more than a Christmas dinner to give the children? Was Megan to have her doll? And Andrew his watch? Andrew was going to have a watch! All without any struggle, any persuasion, any groveling?

Was this victory?

Lilias scrambled to her feet and looked up at the tall, austere figure of the Marquess of Bedford. She curtsied. "What can I say?" she said breathlessly. "Thank you sounds so tame."

"You need not say even that," he said. "I am merely repaying a debt, after all. You will wait here, ma'am, if you please. I shall have tea sent to you while you await the arrival of my carriage to take you home. I take it you walked here?"

He would not take no for an answer, although there was no apparent kindness at all in his manner. Lilias found herself gazing once more into the fire a few minutes later, having been left to take her refreshments alone. And after drinking her tea, she was to have a warm and comfortable—and dry—ride home.

She should be feeling elated. She *was* feeling elated. But uncomfortable and humiliated too. As if, after all, she were taking charity. She blinked back tears and stared defiantly into the flames. She was not taking charity. She was merely accepting what was hers by right.

He seemed to be made of stone to the very heart. Not once had he smiled. Not once had he given any indication that theirs was no new acquaintance. And he had called her explanation an affecting story. He had said so with a sneer, as if he thought it contrived and untrue.

It did not matter. She had got what she had set out to get. More. She had not even been sure she was going to ask for the doll. But as well as that, Andrew was to have a watch. It did not matter that he had not smiled at her or wished her a happy Christmas.

It was at Christmastime he had first kissed her. It had been one of those magical and rare Christmases when it had snowed and there was ice on the lake. They had been sledding down a hill, he and she the last of a long line of young people, all of whom had been trekking back up again by the time they had had their turn. And she had overturned into the snow, shrieking and laughing, and giggling even harder when he had come over to help her up and brush the snow from her face and hair.

He had kissed her swiftly and warmly and open-mouthed, stilling both her laughter and his own until he had made some light remark and broken the tension of the moment. It had been Christmastime. Christmas Eve, to be exact. She had been fifteen, he one-and-twenty.

It did not matter. That had been a long time ago, almost exactly seven years, in fact. He was not the same man, not by any means. But then, she was not the same, either. She had been a girl then, a foolish girl who had believed that Christmas and life were synonymous.

She turned and smiled at Mrs. Morgan, who was carrying a tray into the salon.

He had a daughter somewhere in the house, Lilias thought for the first time since her arrival.

The child tugged at her father's hand, trying to free her own.

"The water is running down my arm, Papa," she complained. A few minutes before she had told him that the rain was running down the back of her neck. "I want to go home now. Pick me up."

The Marquess of Bedford stooped down and took his daughter up in his arms. She circled his neck with her own arms and burrowed her head against the heavy capes of his coat.

"We'll be home in a twinkling, poppet," he said, admitting to himself finally that he was not enjoying tramping around his own grounds any more than she, being buffeted by winds and a heavy drizzle that seemed to drip into one's very bones. "The snow will come before Christmas, and we will build snowmen and skate on the lake and sled on the hill."

"Your coat is wet, Papa," she said petulantly, moving her head about as if in the hope of finding a spot that the rain had not attacked. "I'm cold."

He was clearly fooling only himself, Bedford thought, unbuttoning the top two buttons of his coat so that his daughter might burrow her damp head inside. Christmas would not come. Not this year or ever again. December the twenty-fifth would come and go, of course, this year and every year, but it would not be Christmas for all that.

Christmas had come for the last time six years before, when his father had still been alive, and Claude too. When he had been a younger son. When Philip Angove had still been alive. Before Spain had taken Claude and Waterloo, Philip. When life had been full of hope and promise.

Christmas in that year and in all the years preceding it had invariably been white. Always snow and skating and sledding and snowball fights. And Yule logs and holly and mistletoe. And family and laughter and the security of love. And food and company and song.

Christmas had always been white and innocent. How could there ever be Christmas again?

His brother—his great hero—had died at Badajoz. And his father less than a year later. And soon after that he had discovered that the world was not an innocent or a pleasant place in which to do one's living. Suddenly he had had friends by the score. And suddenly women found him irresistibly attractive and enormously witty.

And suddenly relatives he had hardly known he had developed a deep fondness for him.

In his innocence he had been flattered by it all. In his innocence he had fallen for the most beautiful and most sought-after beauty of the London Season. He had married her before the Season was out.

Lorraine. Beautiful, charming, and witty. The only thing she had lacked—and she had lacked it utterly— was a heart. She had made no secret of her affairs right from the beginning of their marriage and had merely laughed at him and called him rustic when he had raged at her.

"Papa, open another button so that I can get my arms in," his child said, her voice muffled by the folds of his cravat.

He kissed one wet curl as he complied with her demand. He was not even sure that she was his, though Lorraine had always insisted that she was.

"Darling," she had said to him once, when she was very pregnant and fretful at being confined to home, "do you think I would go through all this boredom and discomfort for any other reason than to give you your precious heir?"

She had been very angry when Dora was born.

Lorraine had drowned two years later in Italy, where she had been traveling with a group of friends, among whom was her latest lover.

And the lures had been out for him again for almost all of the two years since. Women gazed at him with adoration in their eyes. Women cooed over a frequently petulant and rather plain-faced Dora.

The Marquess of Bedford ran thankfully up the marble steps in front of his house and through the double doors, which a footman had opened for him.

"Let's see if there is a fire in the nursery, poppet, shall we?" he asked, setting his daughter's feet on the tiled floor and removing her bonnet and cloak. "And buttered muffins and scones?"

"Yes, if you please, Papa," she said, raising a hand for his. But her tone was petulant again as they climbed the stairs side by side. "When will Christmas come? You said there would be lots of people here and lots to do. You said it would be fun."

"And so I did," he said, his heart aching for her as he looked down at her wet and untidy head. "But Christmas is still five days away. It will be wonderful when it comes. It always is here. You will see."

But he was lying to her. The dolls and the frilled dresses and the bows would not make a happy Christmas for her. The only real gift he would be able to give her was his company. The choice had been between any of a number of house parties to which he had been invited alone, and Christmas spent, for the first time ever, with his child. He had chosen the latter. But he was not at all sure that that was not more a gift to himself than to her.

Where was the snow? And the young people? And the laughter and song?

"When will the rain end, Papa?" the child asked, echoing his own thoughts.

"Soon," he said. "Tomorrow, probably."

"But it has rained forever," she said.

Yes it had. For all of a week, at least.

He should not have come. He had not been home for almost six years. Not since leaving in a hurry with his father when the news about Claude had come. He should have kept that memory of home intact, at least. That memory of something perfect. Something pure and innocent. Something beyond the dreariness and the corruption of real life.

But he had been fool enough to come back, only to discover that there was no such place. And perhaps there never had been. Only a young and innocent fool who had not yet had his eyes opened.

The rain was bad enough when he had been expecting the magic of his childhood Christmases. Worse by far had been that visit two days before.

Even Lilias.

She had been his first real love. Oh, he had lost his virginity at university and had competed quite lustily with his fellow students for the favors of all the prettiest barmaids of Oxford. But Lilias had been his first love.

A sweet and innocent love. Begun that Christmas when he had first become aware of her as a woman and not just as the fun-loving and rather pretty sister of his friend, Philip Angove. And continued through the following summer and the Christmas after that.

It had been an innocent love. They had never shared more than kisses. Sweet and brief and chaste kisses. He had been very aware of her youth—only sixteen even during that second Christmas. But they had talked and shared confidences and dreamed together.

A sweet and uncomplicated love.

He wished he had kept that memory untainted. But the world had come to her too. He had wondered about her when he had decided to come home, wondered if he would see her, wondered what it would be like to see her again. He had been amazed to be told on his second day home that she was waiting downstairs in the salon for him. And he had hoped with every stair he took that it would not be as he suspected it would.

It had been worse.

The wet and muddy hem of her gown; the darned patches on the hem and sleeve—the second brought to his attention by the artful design to conceal it; the damp and untidy hair; the thin, pale face; the sad, brave story; the modest appeal for assistance; the ridiculous mention of a debt unpaid. He had seen worse actresses at Drury Lane.

He had been furious enough to do her physical harm. She had come to his home to arouse his pity and his chivalry, and in the process she had destroyed one of his few remaining dreams.

Could she find no more honest way of finding herself a husband? Did she really imagine he was so naive? She had not even had the decency to wait awhile. She had been the first to come.

"Papa," Dora was saying. She had climbed unnoticed onto his lap beside the fire in the nursery and was playing with the chain of his watch, "it is so dull here. I want to go somewhere."

"Tomorrow, poppet," he said. "Mr. Crawford has two little boys, who will surely be pleased to see you. And the rector has a family of five. Maybe there are some little ones among them. We will call on them tomorrow, shall we?"

"Yes, please, Papa," she said.

"And I have another errand to run in the village," he said, staring down at his watch, which she had pulled from his pocket. "To see a little boy and girl, though they are not quite as little as you, Dora."

"Tomorrow?" she said. "Promise, Papa?"

"I promise," he said, kissing her cheek. "Now, Nurse wants to dry and comb your hair again. And I need to change my clothes and dry my own hair."

Lilias set three pairs of mud-caked boots down outside the door of her cottage and looked down at them ruefully. Would it be better to tackle the job of cleaning them now, when the mud was still fresh and wet, or later, when it had dried? She glanced up at the sky. The clouds hung heavy and promised that the rain was not yet at an end, but for the moment it had stopped. The boots would not get wet inside just yet.

She was closing the door when her eye was caught by

the approach of a carriage along the village street. The very one she had ridden in just three days before. She closed the door hastily. She did not want to be caught peeping out at him as he rode past. But she could not prevent herself from crossing to the window and standing back from it so that she could see without being seen.

"Ugh," Megan said from the small kitchen beyond the parlor. "It is all soaking wet, Lilias."

"Ouch," Andrew said. "Is there any way to pick up holly, Lilias, without pricking oneself to death?"

"Oh, mercy on us," Lilias said, one hand straying to her throat, "he is stopping here. And descending too. One of the postilions is putting down the steps."

The dripping bundles of holly, which they had all just been gathering at great cost to fingers and boots, were abandoned. Megan and Andrew flew across the room to watch the splendid drama unfolding outside their window.

"The marquess?" Megan asked, big-eyed. "And is that his daughter, Lilias? What a very splendid velvet bonnet and cloak she is wearing."

Andrew whistled, an accomplishment he had perfected in the past few months. "Look at those horses," he said. "What prime goers!"

Lilias licked her lips and passed her hands over hair that was hopelessly flattened and untidy from her recent excursion outdoors. The watch? Had he come to bring the watch in person? The doll had been delivered by a footman the day before, fortunately at a time when the children had gone over to the rectory to play with the children there. It had been carefully hidden away after she had smoothed wondering fingers over the lace and the soft golden hair. And the butcher had informed her that she might pick up a goose on Christmas Eve.

She wished she were wearing her best day dress again. She crossed to the door and opened it before anyone had time to knock. And she saw with some dismay the row of muddy boots standing to one side of the doorstep. She curtsied.

"How do you do, ma'am?" the Marquess of Bedford said. He looked even larger and more formidable than he had looked three mornings before, clad as he was in a many-caped greatcoat. He held a beaver hat in one hand. "I have been taking my daughter about to meet some of the children of the neighborhood."

"Oh," Lilias said, and looked down at the small girl standing beside him, one hand clutched in his. She was handsomely dressed in dark red velvet, though she was not a pretty child. "I am pleased to make your acquaintance, my lady."

"This is Miss Angove, Dora," the marquess said.

The child was looking candidly up at Lilias. "We have brought you a basket of food from the house," she said, tossing her head back in the direction of the postilion, who was holding a large basket covered with a white cloth.

"Won't you come inside, my lord?" Lilias asked, standing hastily to one side when she realized that she had been keeping them standing on the doorstep. "And there really was no need." She glanced at the basket and took it reluctantly from the servant's hand.

"We have taken one to each of the houses we have called at," he said. "A Christmas offering, ma'am." He looked at her with the hooded blue eyes and the marble expression that she had found so disconcerting a few days before. "Not charity," he added softly for her ears only.

His daughter was eyeing Megan and Andrew with cautious curiosity.

"Do you think girls are silly?" she asked Andrew after the introductions had been made and Lilias was ushering the marquess to a seat close to the fire.

Andrew looked taken aback. "Not all of them," he said. "Only some. But then, there are some silly boys too."

"Mrs. Crawford's sons think girls are silly," Dora said.

"They would," Andrew said with undisguised contempt.

"And do you squeal and quarrel all the time and run to your mama with tales?" Dora asked Megan.

Megan giggled.

"Dora," her father said sharply, "watch your manners."

"Because the children at the rectory do," Dora added.

"We have no mama to run to," Megan said. "And when Drew and I quarrel, we go outside and fight it out where Lilias cannot hear us and interfere." She giggled again. "We have been gathering holly. It is all wet and prickly. But there are so many berries! Do you want to see it? You may take your coat off and put on one of my pinafores if you wish."

"Megan," Lilias said, her voice agonized. One of Megan's faded pinafores on Lady Dora West?

"What is the holly for?" Dora asked. "And, yes, please." She looked at her father on an afterthought. "May I, Papa? Where did you find it? I wish I could have come with you."

"No, you don't," Andrew said. "My fingers look like one of Miss Pierce's pincushions. We found some mistletoe too. It is in the kitchen. Come and look."

Lilias found herself suddenly seated opposite the marquess in the small and empty parlor, the object of his silent scrutiny. She jumped to her feet again.

"May I offer you tea?" she asked.

"No," he said. "That is not necessary. We had tea at the rectory not half an hour since."

She flushed. "I am afraid I have nothing else to offer," she said.

"Sit down," he said. He looked over his shoulder into the kitchen, where the voices of the children mingled. "One of my men has been sent into town for your brother's watch, among other things. I shall have it delivered tomorrow."

Lilias felt herself flush even more deeply. "You are kind," she said. "And thank you for the other things."

More than ever she felt that she had begged from him and had been given charity. There was no unbending in his manner, not the merest hint of a smile on his lips or in his eyes. He was regarding her with what looked uncomfortably like scorn.

"Dora is lonely," he said. "She has never had children to play with. Until less than a year ago she lived with her grandparents."

Lilias did not reply. She could think of nothing to say.

"Unfortunately," he said, "when she does find playmates, she demands perfection. She wants them to be the sort of friends she would like to have. I am afraid our visits this afternoon have not been a great success."

Lilias smiled fleetingly.

"Look, Papa." Dora was back in the room, holding up one small index finger for her father's inspection. A tiny globe of blood formed on its tip. "I pricked myself." She put the finger in her mouth even as the marquess reached into a pocket for a handkerchief. "Megan and Andrew are going to put the holly all about the house for Christmas. May I stay and watch?"

"It is time to go home," he said.

"But I don't want to go home," she said, her lower lip protruding beyond the upper one. "I want to stay and watch."

"We shall gather holly too, shall we?" he asked. "And decorate our house with it?"

"But it will be no fun," she said mulishly, "just you and me. I want to watch Megan and Andrew. And I want to watch Andrew carve the Bativity scene he is making. We don't have a Bativity scene, do we?"

"No," he said, getting to his feet, impatience showing itself in every line of his body, Lilias thought as she too rose from her chair, "we don't have a Nativity scene, Dora. Take off the pinafore now. I shall help you on with your cloak and bonnet."

"They have mistletoe, Papa," Dora said, making no attempt to undo the strings of her pinafore. "They hang it up and kiss under it. Is that not silly?"

"Yes," he said, undoing the strings for her, "very silly."

"Can we have some, Papa?" she asked.

"Yes," he said. "We will find some tomorrow."

"But it will be no fun," she said again.

"We will come with you," Megan offered, glancing at her brother. "Won't we, Drew? We know all the best places to look. Or rather, Lilias does, and she showed us today. Shall we come with you?"

The child looked almost pretty for a moment, Lilias thought, as her face lit up with eagerness. "Yes, you come too," she said. "We will need ever so much holly because our house is much bigger than yours. Isn't it, Papa? And mistletoe for every room. And Andrew can carve a Bativity scene just for me."

"No," Andrew said, "there will not be time. But I will bring the shepherd with me to show you. It will be finished by tomorrow."

Lilias found herself suddenly gazing into the marquess's eyes across the heads of the children and feeling decidedly uncomfortable. His eyes were cold and penetrating. And for the first time there was a half-smile on his lips. But she wanted to shiver. The smile had nothing to do with either amusement or friendship.

"Well, Miss Angrove," he said, "it would be quite too bad if you were the only one to miss this merry outing. I shall send my carriage for the three of you after luncheon tomorrow and we will all go holly gathering together. You will do us the honor of taking tea with us afterward."

He did not ask questions, Lilias noticed. He did not even make statements. He gave commands. Commands that she would dearly have liked to refuse to comply with, for if one thing was becoming clear to her mind, it was that he disliked her. Quite intensely. Perhaps it was her temerity in reminding him of a long-forgotten debt that had done it. She could think of no other reason for his hostility. But it was there nonetheless.

And she was glad suddenly that he had come home, glad that she had seen what he had become, glad that she could put to rest finally a dream and an attachment that had clung stubbornly long after he had left in such a hurry the very day after they had spent two hours together strolling the grounds of his home, hand in hand, looking at the flowers of spring and planning what they would do during the summer.

She was glad he had come back, for he no longer lived, that gentle and sunny-natured young man whom she had loved. He was dead as surely as his older brother was dead. As surely as Philip was dead. He had died six years before. She had just not known it.

He was holding her eyes with his own. He was obviously waiting for an answer, though he had asked no question. And how could she answer as she wished to do when there were three children standing between them, all eagerly anticipating the treat that the morrow would bring?

"Thank you, my lord," she said. "That would be very pleasant."

Very pleasant indeed, the Marquess of Bedford was thinking the following afternoon as the five of them descended the steps of his house and set off past the formal gardens and the lawns and orchards to the trees and the lake and the hill and eventually the holly bushes.

She was wearing a cloak that looked altogether too thin for the weather. And beneath it he could see the same wool dress she had worn for her first interview with him. Except that he had realized the day before that it could not, after all, be her oldest gown. The cotton dress she had worn when he and Dora had called upon her was so faded that it was difficult to tell exactly what its original color had been.

The children were striding along ahead, one Angove on each side of Dora, Megan holding her hand. Dora had had a hard time getting to sleep the night before. He had sat with her, as he had each night since their coming into the country, until she fell asleep. He had sat there for almost an hour.

"We won't forget the mistletoe, Papa?" she had asked after he had tucked her comfortably into her bed.

"No," he had assured her, "we won't forget the mistletoe."

"Will you kiss me, Papa?" she had asked.

He had leaned over her again and kissed her.

"Under the mistletoe, silly," she had said, chuckling uncontrollably for all of two minutes.

"Yes, I will kiss you, poppet," he had said. "Go to sleep now."

But she had opened her eyes several minutes later. "Do you think Andrew will remember the shepherd, Papa?" she had asked.

"I expect so," he had said.

He had thought her asleep ten minutes after that. He had been considering getting up from his chair, tiptoeing out of the room, and leaving her to the care of her nurse.

"Papa," she had said suddenly, frowning up at him, "what is a Bativity scene?"

"A Nativity scene," he had said. "I'll tell you some other time. It is time to sleep now."

"It won't rain tomorrow, Papa, will it?" she had asked plaintively.

She had been excited about the promised outing with the Angoves. More excited than he had seen her since taking her from Lorraine's parents early the previous spring, a thin and listless and bad-tempered child.

Damnation! he thought now, and offered his arm to Lilias. Events could not have turned more to her advantage if she really had planned them. The afternoon before he had thought she had, but he had been forced to admit to himself later that she could not have done so. Too much had depended upon chance. She had not even known that he and Dora were going to call on her.

But she would take full advantage of the cozy family outing. He supposed he would be forced to listen to patient cheerfulness about the prospective post as governess and tender lamentations on the fact that the family was about to be broken up. Doubtless she would confide again her intention of reuniting them when she had made her fortune as a governess.

Lilias. He had not expected her to come to this. He looked down at her as she walked silently at his side. She had not grown since the age of sixteen. Her head still barely passed his shoulder. Her hair was still smooth and fair beneath her bonnet. But she was thinner. Her hand, even inside its glove, was too slender on his arm. Her face was thin and pale. Her dark-lashed gray eyes seemed larger in contrast. She really did look as if she were half-starved.

Damnation!

"I wanted Christmas for my daughter," he told her, realizing with a jolt as he heard his own words that that was exactly what she had said to him four days before about her brother and sister. "Christmas as I remembered it. I thought I would find it here. But I chose just the year when there is no snow. Only this infernal cold and damp."

"But it did not always snow," she said, looking up at him. "Just very rarely, I think. It was especially lovely when it did. But Christmas was always wonderful anyway."

"Was it?" He frowned.

She drew breath as if to speak, but she seemed to change her mind. "Yes," she said.

"I have your watch," he said. "It is at the house. I shall see that you have it before you leave after tea."

She looked up at him again, bright-eyed. "Thank you," she said.

Here we go, he thought. He had supplied her with the perfect opportunity to heap upon his head reflections on how happy the boy would be during the coming years and how he would be able to remember his sisters and their life together every time he pulled the watch from his pocket. He clamped his teeth together and felt his jaw tighten.

He felt guilty suddenly. She so obviously *was* very poor, and it was so obviously true that the three of them were to be separated after Christmas. He just wished she had not decided to use the pathos of her situation to win herself a rich and gullible husband.

Except that he was not gullible. Not any longer.

She half-smiled at him and shifted her gaze to the three children, who were now quite a distance ahead of them. She said nothing.

Dora was skipping along, he was surprised to notice when he followed the direction of Lilias's eyes.

"This is where we got the holly yesterday," Megan announced a while later when they came up to the thicket. And then she looked at Lilias, a hand over her mouth, and giggled.

Andrew was laughing too. "We were not supposed to say," he said, darting a mischievous look at the marquess. "We were trespassing."

Lilias was blushing very rosily, Bedford saw when he glanced at her. She looked far more as she had looked as a girl.

"But these ones don't have as many berries as yours," Dora complained.

"All the good branches are high up," Andrew said. "We could not reach them yesterday. Even Lilias."

"It seems that I am elected," the marquess said. "Thank goodness for leather gloves. This looks like certain self-destruction."

Megan giggled as he stepped forward and his coat caught on the lower branches of holly. He had to disengage himself several times before he could reach up to cut the branches that were loaded with berries. His upturned face was showered with water. Dora was giggling too.

Lilias had stepped in behind him to take the holly as he handed it down. Her gloves and cloak were not heavy enough to protect her from hurt, he thought, and clamped his lips together as he was about to voice the thought.

"Ouch," Dora cried excitedly, and giggled even more loudly. "I have almost as big an armful as you, Andrew. I have more than Megan. Oh, ouch!"

"You must not clutch them," Andrew said. "Just hold them enough that they do not drop."

"Well," the Marquess of Bedford said when he paused and looked behind him. "You look like four walking holly bushes. Do you think you can stagger back to the house with that load? Only now does it strike me that we should have had a wagon sent after us."

"Oh, no," Andrew said. "That would spoil the fun."

"This is such fun, Papa," Dora said.

"Let me take some of this load," Bedford said, reaching out to take some from Lilias's arms, "before you disappear entirely behind it."

Her eyes were sparkling up at him.

"But, Papa," Dora wailed. "The mistletoe."

"Oh, Lord," he said, "the mistletoe. I shall go and get some. You all start back to the house." But she was loaded down. She would never get back without being scratched to death. "Better still, drop your load, Lilias, and show me where this mistletoe is. You children, on your way. We will catch up to you."

God, he thought, turning cold as she did what she had been told—considering her load, she had had little choice—he had called her Lilias. *The witch!* Her wiles were working themselves beneath his guard despite himself. His jaw hardened again.

She led him around past the thicket of holly bushes, past the old oaks, to the mistletoe, which he had forgotten about. The old oaks! He had climbed them with her, to sit in the lower branches, staring at the sky and dreaming aloud with her. He could remember lifting her down from the lowest branch of one—he could not remember which—and kissing her, her body pressed against the great old trunk, her hands spread on either side of her head, palm to palm against his. He could remember laughing at her confusion because he had traced the line of her lips with his tongue.

"It was all a long time ago," he said abruptly, and felt remarkably foolish as soon as the words were spoken. As if he had expected her to follow his train of thought.

"Yes," she said quietly.

He gave her the mistletoe to carry, being very careful not to lift it above the level of her head as he handed it to her. And on the way back he took the large bundle of holly into his own arms, against her protests, to carry to the house.

"My coat and my gloves are heavier than yours," he said.

She brushed her face against the mistletoe as they walked.

"I suppose," he said harshly after a few silent minutes, "you do not get enough to eat."

She looked up at him, startled. "My lord?" she said.

"Your brother and sister do not look undernourished," he said. "I suppose you give all your food to them."

Her flush was noticeable even beneath the rosiness that the wind and cold had whipped into her cheeks.

"What a ridiculous notion," she said. "I would have starved to death."

"And have been doing almost that, by the look of you," he said, appalled at his own lack of breeding and good manners.

"What I do is my own business, I thank you, my lord," she said. Her voice was as chill as his own, he realized. "I do not choose to discuss either my appetite or my means with you."

"You were quite willing to do so a few days ago," he said.

"Only enough to explain why I had to bring up the matter of that old debt," she said. "And I take it unkindly in you to refer again to a topic I confided only with embarrassment and reluctance."

He strode on, knowing that he was walking too fast for her, but doing nothing to slacken his pace.

"Stephen," she said. She sounded close to tears. "Why do you hate me?"

Stephen. No one had called him by his given name for years, it seemed. Lorraine had never called him anything but Bedford. He slackened his pace so that she was no longer forced almost to run at his side.

It was clever. Very clever. It almost unnerved him. It was too clever. She had overplayed her hand.

"I do not hate you, ma'am," he said, thankful to see the house close by. The children must be inside already. "What possible reason would I have to hate you?"

"I don't know," she said.

He gritted his teeth against the trembling of her voice. It was too overdone. Too contrived.

Lilias, he thought, and remembered the oak trees. And remembered Lorraine and dozens of admiring female eyes and more dozens of obsequious hangers-on. All with their various wiles and arts, and not a few of them with their sad stories and their outstretched hands.

Life might have been so different if only Claude had not died, he thought bitterly, standing aside so that Lilias might precede him up the steps and through the doors into the hallway of his home.

Lilias was putting the final stitches in a strip of faded blue cloth for Mary's robe while Megan was painstakingly lining the manger with straw. Andrew was whittling away at a sheep that insisted on looking more like a fox, he complained, a deep frown between his eyes.

"But Joseph is quite splendid, Drew," Megan said loyally. "He looks quite like a real man."

"And how lovely it will be," Lilias said, "to have our own Nativity scene when everyone else has to go to church to see one. What shall we sing?"

"'Lully, lulla, thou little tiny child,'" Megan began to sing, and Lilias joined her, while Andrew held his sheep at arm's length and regarded it with half-closed eyes.

They all stopped what they were doing when there was a knock at the door. Lilias rose to answer it.

Lady Dora West was dressed in dark blue velvet this time, in a small but dashing riding outfit. Her eyes shone and her cheeks were flushed with color. She was clutching her father's hand as she had two days before.

"We rode here on Pegasus," she announced as soon as

the door was opened, and Lilias could see beyond her a magnificent black stallion tethered to the fence. "Papa said we might call and see your decorations and see Joseph if he is finished."

"I do beg your pardon if you are busy." The Marquess of Bedford was looking at her with hooded and wary eyes, Lilias saw when she lifted her own reluctantly to his face.

Why had he come? The afternoon before had been unspeakably embarrassing, especially after her outburst, when she had called him by his given name and asked him such a foolish question. Instead of sitting in the drawing room after tea while the children ran excitedly about first that room and then the nursery, placing the holly, and giggling over where to hang the mistletoe, they had trailed almost silently after. Afraid to be alone together.

She had not expected to see him again.

"Dora has quite taken to your brother and sister," he said. "She can derive no excitement from her nurse's company or from mine. She will be satisfied with ten minutes, I believe."

But by the time he entered the cottage, Dora had already thrown aside her hat and riding jacket and had run into the kitchen to lift from a hook behind the door the pinafore she had worn the last time.

"Oh, the holly," she cried. "It looks so lovely in here because the room is small. And the mistletoe is right in the center." She stood beneath it and chuckled. "Kiss me, Papa."

He did so, bending from his great height to take the upturned face between his hands and kiss the puckered mouth. Lilias turned away, a curious churning in her stomach.

"But that is supposed to be just for Christmas," he said. "Not for another two days, poppet."

Listening to his voice as he spoke to the child, not seeing him, she thought he sounded like Stephen. But no, she would not think that. It was not true.

Dora was soon exclaiming over Joseph and laughing delightedly over the sheep when Andrew told her that it looked like a fox. She noticed Mary, who was already dressed in her blue robe.

"Oh, pretty," she said, fingering it.

Bedford seated himself, uninvited, his eyes on his daughter.

"We were singing when you came," Megan said, and began singing the same carol that had been interrupted by the arrival of their guests. Dora smiled and stroked Mary's robe. "You sing too, Lilias."

Lilias flushed. "Later, Megan," she said, and glanced in some embarrassment at the marquess, whose eyes had shifted to her. His expression was unfathomable.

"You used to sing," he said. "All the time."

She smiled fleetingly and wished she still had Mary's robe to stitch at. She had not yet started Joseph's.

"You used to go caroling," he said, frowning as if the memory had only just come back to him. "On Christmas Eve. We all used to go—Claude, Philip, Susan and Henrietta Price, the Hendays. But you used to lead the singing."

Lilias bit her lip. "We still go," she said. "Some of the villagers and I. The children too. We go around the village before church at eleven, and out to some of the cottages too if we know that someone is too unwell to come to church."

"Tomorrow night," Andrew said, looking up briefly from his work. "We had great fun last year. Mr. Campbell gave us all hot cider before he realized that some of us were children and ought not to be drinking it."

Megan giggled. Then she looked up, arrested by some bright thought. "You ought to come too this year," she said. "Dora can come. I will hold her hand. And you too, sir," she added magnanimously.

"May I, Papa?" Dora had leaped to her feet. She looked definitely pretty, Lilias thought, untidy hair and faded pinafore notwithstanding. "May we?" She danced up and down on the spot in an agony when he did not answer immediately. "Oh, please, please, Papa, may we?"

"You do not know any of the carols, poppet," he said. "And it will be too late for you. It will be past your bed-time."

"But Megan will teach me," she said. "Won't you, Megan? And Miss Angove. Won't you, Miss Angove? And I will go to sleep tomorrow afternoon, Papa, and sleep all afternoon and be very good. Oh, may we go too? Please."

"We will have to talk about it further," he said stiffly. He looked almost angry, Lilias saw at a glance. "Right now we are interrupting work, Dora. And I have some errands to run in the village."

"But I don't want to go," she said. "You will stop to talk to people, Papa, and I will be dull. You go and do your errands and I will stay here. Miss Angove will teach me the carols."

The marquess stood up resolutely. "Put your pinafore away where you found it, now," he said, "and I shall help you on with your coat."

She stared at him, her lower lip protruding beyond the upper.

"We will be very happy to have her stay, if you will agree," Lilias said softly. "It is good to have children here at Christmastime."

His eyes turned on her, hooded, inscrutable. He inclined his head. "Very well, then, ma'am," he said. He turned back to his daughter. "You may stay for an hour, Dora," he said. "But you must come without protest when I return."

Megan and Dora clapped their hands. Even Andrew looked pleased.

Lilias, standing at the door a minute later, watching the marquess swing himself into the saddle of his horse and proceed along the village street, was not sure if she had done the right thing or not, interfering between a father and his daughter. He had paused in the doorway and looked down at her.

"Another debt to call in?" he had said softly and icily.

She had not comprehended his meaning until he was riding down the pathway to the gate, and even then she was not sure he had meant what she thought he had meant. She hoped he had not. And she wondered again, though she wished with all her heart that she had not asked it, why he hated her.

They sang for almost the whole hour, sometimes the same carol over and over, while Andrew tackled the final feature of the Nativity scene, the baby Jesus, and Megan arranged and rearranged the items already completed. Dora first helped and then stood at Lilias's elbow, staring fascinated at the tiny robe for Joseph that she was making.

Lilias smiled at her after a few minutes, when they were between carols. "Why don't you pull up that stool?" she said.

"Papa told me the story," Dora said when she was seated. "About the baby and the stable and the manger and the smothering clothes."

"The swaddling clothes," Lilias said with a smile. "That is what I will be making next."

"He is going to tell me again tonight," Dora said. "I like that story. I am going to learn to sew next year when I am five."

"Are you?" Lilias smiled again. "Will you like that?"

"Nurse is to teach me," Dora said. "But I am going to

ask Papa if you can teach me instead. It would be fun with you."

Megan began singing another carol.

The caroling was not the only part of Christmas he had forgotten, Bedford discovered the following morning. And he really had forgotten that. He had always remembered Christmas as a white and outdoor affair. Everything else had become hazy in memory.

But there had always been the caroling and the lanterns and the rosy cheeks and laughter, and the glasses of cider and wassail until not one of them had been quite sober by the time they got to church. None of them had ever been precisely drunk—just smiling and warm and happy. How could he have forgotten? And how everyone had wanted to stand next to Lilias because she had such a sweet voice and such perfect pitch. He had won almost all of those battles.

Dora, restless in the morning because it seemed such a long wait until the evening—he had promised her the night before, much against his better judgment, that they would join the carolers—wandered down to the kitchen to watch the cook roll the pastry for the mince pies. And she fell into conversation with Mrs. Morgan, who was delighted to have a child in the house again.

And that encounter led, unknown to Bedford until later, to a visit to the attic to find the relics of Christmases past.

"Papa!" Dora burst into the library, where Bedford was trying to read, though it was hard to bring his thoughts to bear on the book opened before her. She was moving at a run past the footman who held the door open for her, and her face was flushed and pretty with an excitement that she could barely contain. "Papa, come to the attic with me. We have been looking at

Christmas. The dearest bells. And the star! May we have an evergreen bough, Papa? Mrs. Morgan says there were always evergreens. May we? Do put down the silly book and come."

He put down the silly book and came. Or rather was dragged by an insistent little hand and a voice brimming with an excitement he had thought her incapable of.

And of course, he thought as soon as he looked into the opened boxes in the attic and dismissed a rather uncomfortable and apologetic Mrs. Morgan . . . Of course. How could he have forgotten? The evergreen boughs, decorated with crystal balls and bells that tinkled and twinkled every time a door was opened or a draft blew down a chimney. The evergreen boughs that had brought the smell of Christmas right inside the house.

And one year the candles on the boughs, until they had been forbidden forever after . . . after the great fire, when the branch had been singed black and a whole circle of carpet ruined, for he had collided with the bough during blindman's buff and tipped it over . . . They must be only thankful that he had not burned too, his mother had said, hugging him while his father had scolded. And someone had been smothering hysterical giggles through it all. Lilias.

"May we have an evergreen bough, Papa? May we?" Dora's voice was almost a wail, there was so much anxiety in her tone.

"There are enough decorations here for a whole forest of boughs," he said with a laugh. "There used to be some in the nursery and dining room as well as a whole great tree in the drawing room."

"A tree, Papa. Just one whole tree in the nursery," she said, and reached up her arms to be picked up when he smiled down at her.

"Just one, then," he said. "We will go out and find one

ourselves and cut it down, shall we? I think the rain stopped about an hour ago."

"Yes," she said, hugging his neck and kissing his cheek.

It was only when they were outside and she was tripping along at his side, her gloved hand firmly clasped in his, that she had her great idea. Though to her it seemed quite natural.

"We will take one for Megan and Andrew and Miss Angove as well," she announced. "Just a little one because they have such a small room. But there are so many bells and balls. We will take them before luncheon, Papa, so that I may still have my sleep ready for tonight. They will be happy, won't they?"

"I think they have enough, poppet," he said. "They are making their own Christmas. They will not want our offerings."

"Oh, yes, they will," she said happily. "You said Christmas is for giving, Papa. They will be happy if we give them a whole evergreen tree. Besides, I want to see the baby Jesus. He was not finished yesterday. Such a dear little manger, Papa. Miss Angove was going to make the smoth—the swathering clothes."

"Was she?" he said, his heart sinking. Christmas was for giving, he had told her, and she had just thrown it back in his teeth. How could he refuse to give his daughter happiness?

"Just a little tree, then," he said. "Papa has only two hands, you know."

She chuckled. "But they are big hands, Papa," she said. "Miss Angove is going to teach me to sew when I am five."

"Is she?" he said, his lips tightening.

"Yes," she said. "It will be more fun with her than with Nurse."

And so they found themselves little more than an

hour later yet again knocking on the door of the cottage, Bedford found, Dora at his side, jumping up and down.

"I want to tell, Papa," she told him. The evergreen and the box of decorations, including the great star, were still inside the carriage.

And she did tell, rushing through the door, tearing at her cloak, and whisking herself behind the kitchen door for the pinafore just as if she had lived there all her life. And soon Megan was squealing and giggling and Andrew was exclaiming in delight and offering to accompany the marquess into the garden to fetch a pail of earth to set the tree in—a whole tree, and not just a bough!—and Lilias was clearing a small table and covering it with a worn lace cloth close to the window.

And there he was, Bedford discovered half an hour later, his coat discarded, his shirtsleeves rolled up, his neckcloth askew, balanced on a kitchen chair and pounding a nail into the ceiling. For the great star, it seemed, had not been brought for the Christmas tree at all—"How silly, Papa," Dora had said with a giggle. "It would be too big"—but to hang over the Nativity scene.

"Just look at the darling baby Jesus," Dora was saying in a voice of wonder while everyone else was gazing upward at the star Bedford was suspending from the nail.

And then they were all standing in the room, gazing about them at all the splendor and wonder of Christmas, just as if it had come already: the holly boughs and the tree hung with bells and crystal balls, all catching the light from the outdoors and from the fire and the rudely carved Nativity scene with its bright and outsize star and its minute baby wrapped in swaddling clothes.

"Lilias is standing beneath the mistletoe," Megan said suddenly and in great delight.

Dora clapped her hands and laughed.

And he met her eyes from three feet away and saw

the dismay in them and the flush of color that rose to her cheeks, and he was no longer sure that it was all artifice. It was a thin and large-eyed face. It was beautiful.

"Then I had better kiss her," Andrew said in a tone of some resignation. "Again." He pecked her noisily on the cheek and she moved swiftly to the window to still a bell that was swaying and tinkling.

"Time to go, poppet," the Marquess of Bedford said.

There was a chorus of protests.

"All right, then," he said. "Dora may stay for another half hour. But no caroling and no church tonight."

Five minutes later he sank thankfully back against the velvet upholstery of his carriage. He had thought himself hardened to all feeling. He had thought that he could never be deceived again, never caught out in trusting where he should not trust. He would never be caught because he would never trust anyone ever again. It was safer that way.

His saner, more rational, more cautious, more hardened self told him that it was all a ruse, that she was an opportunist who was using all her feminine wiles to trap him and save herself and her brother and sister from a dreary and impoverished future.

His madder, more irrational, more incautious, more gullible self saw a mental image of her eyes lighting up when she saw the tree and the ornaments and their effect on the two children in her charge. And saw her below him as he stood on the chair, her arms half raised as if she expected to be able to catch him if he fell. And saw the look of Christmas in her eyes as she stood in the middle of her living room looking about her. And the flustered look of pure beauty when she realized that she was standing beneath the mistletoe.

Had she known that she stood there? It was impossible to tell. And it made all the difference in the world. Had she known or had she not?

Even more important, did he care either way? Did he still regret that it had been her brother who had stepped forward to kiss her?

No, he must not, he thought, closing his eyes. He must not. He must not.

"Must I sleep all afternoon?" Dora asked him. "May we decorate our evergreen first, Papa?"

"We will do it immediately after luncheon," he said, opening his eyes and looking at her sternly. "And then you are going to sleep all afternoon."

"Yes, Papa," she said.

For the past few years Lilias had been the oldest of the carol singers. But none of the others had been willing for her to retire.

"But, Miss Angove," Christina Simmonds had protested when she had suggested it two years before, "what would we do without you? You are the only one who can really sing."

"Besides," Henry Hammett had added, with a wink for his friend, Leonard Small, "if one of the other girls were to start the carols, Miss Angove, the rest of us would have to either dig a trench to reach the low notes or carry a ladder around with us to hit the high ones."

A deal of giggling from the girls and rib-digging from the young men had followed his words, and Lilias had agreed to stay.

She was not to be the oldest this year, though. Most of the young people were inclined to be intimidated when they first saw the Marquess of Bedford as one of their number. Most of them had only glimpsed him from a distance since his return home, and most of them were too young to remember that during his youth he had joined in all the village activities.

However, after singing at a few houses and consuming a few mince pies and a couple of mugs of wassail, they no longer found him such a forbidding and remote figure. And the usual jokes and laughter accompanied them around the village.

The younger children formed their own group, Dora firmly in the middle of them, clinging to Megan's hand. The marquess carried one of the lanterns and held it each time they sang, as he had always used to do, above Lilias's shoulder so that she could see her music.

She was very aware of him and wished she were not. Apart from the fact that the other faces around them had changed, there was a strange, disturbing feeling of having gone back in time. There was Stephen's gloved hand holding the lantern above her, and Stephen's voice singing the carols at her right ear, and Stephen's hand at the small of her back once as they crossed the threshold into one home.

She had to make a conscious effort to remember that he was not Stephen, that he was the Marquess of Bedford. She had to look at him deliberately to note the broadness of his shoulders and chest beneath the capes of his coat, showing her that he was no longer the slender young man of her memories. And she had to look into his face to see the harsh lines and the cynical eyes—though not as cynical as they had been a week before, surely.

She brought her reactions under control and bent over a very elderly gentleman in a parlor they had been invited into who had grasped her wrist with one gnarled hand.

"Miss Lilias," he said, beaming up at her with toothless gums, "and Lord Stephen." He shook her arm up and down and was obviously so pleased with what he had said that he said it again. "Miss Lilias and Lord Stephen."

Lilias smiled and kissed his cheek and wished him a happy Christmas. And the marquess, whom she had not realized was quite so close, took the old man's free hand between both of his and spoke to him by name.

In the voice of Stephen, Lilias thought, straightening up.

The children were all very tired by the time they had finished their calls and the church bells had begun to ring. But not a single one of them was prepared to admit the fact and be taken home to the comfort of a bed.

Dora was yawning loudly and clutching Lilias's cloak.

"I'll take you home, poppet," Bedford said, leaning down to pick her up. "Enough for one day."

But she whisked herself behind a fold of Lilias's cloak and evaded her father's arms. "But you promised, Papa," she said. "And I slept all afternoon. I was good."

"Yes, you were good," he said, reaching out a hand to take one of hers. "You may see the day out to its very end, then."

And somehow, Lilias found, the child's other hand made its way into hers and they climbed the steps to the church together, the three of them, just as if they were a family. People turned from their pews to look at the marquess, and nodded and smiled at them. Megan and Andrew were already sitting in their usual pew, two seats from the front.

Lilias smiled down at Dora when they reached the padded pew that had always belonged to the marquess's family, and released her hand. She proceeded on her way to join her brother and sister.

"But, Papa," she heard the child say aloud behind her, "I want to sit by Megan."

A few moments after Lilias had knelt down on her kneeler, she felt a small figure push past her from behind and heard the sounds of shuffling as Megan and Andrew moved farther along the pew. And when she rose to sit on the pew herself, it was to find Dora sitting between her and Megan, and the Marquess of Bedford on her other side. She picked up her Psalter and thumbed through its pages.

There were candles and evergreen branches and the Nativity scene before the altar. And the church bells before the service, and the organ and the singing during it, and the Christmas readings. And the sermon. And the church packed with neighbors and friends and family. There were love and joy and peace.

It was Christmas.

Christmas as it had always been—and as it would never be again. She had to concentrate all her attention on her Psalter and swallow several times. And a hand moved toward her so that she almost lifted her own to meet it halfway. But it came to rest on his leg and the fingers drummed a few times before falling still.

She was saved by a loud and lengthy yawn and a small head burrowing itself between her arm and the back of the pew. She turned and smiled down at Dora and slipped one arm behind her and the other under her knees so that she could lift her onto her lap and pillow the tired head against her breast. The child was asleep almost instantly.

The marquess's eyes, when Lilias turned her head to look into them, were very blue and wide open. And quite, quite inscrutable. When the organ began to play the closing hymn, and before the bells began to peal out again the good news of a child's birth, he stood and took his child into his own arms so that Lilias could stand and sing.

His carriage was waiting outside the church, but Lilias refused a ride for herself and her brother and sister.

"It is such a short distance to walk," she said.

He set the still-sleeping Dora down on the carriage seat and turned back to them. "I shall say good night, then," he said. He held out a hand for Megan's. "Thank you for inviting Dora. I don't think you know how happy you have made a small child." He took Andrew's hand. "You may come to the house the day after to-morrow, if your sister approves, and we will take that ride I have promised you."

"Oh, ripping," Andrew said excitedly.

Bedford turned to Lilias and took her hand in his. He searched her face with his eyes and seemed about to say something. But he merely clasped her hand more tightly.

"Happy Christmas, Lilias," he said.

"Happy Christmas, Stephen."

She had said the words and heard them a hundred times that evening, Lilias thought as she turned away and made her way along the street with the two tired children. But the last two times burned themselves on her mind, and she felt herself smiling and happy . . . and swallowing back tears.

Christmas Day. Chill and dry but heavy with gray clouds out-of-doors. Warm with the glow and the smells and the goodwill of the season indoors. It did not matter that there was no soft white snow to trudge through, no snow to form into snowballs to hurl at shrieking relatives, no hills of snow to slide down and fall into, no ice to skate on. It did not matter. Christmas was indoors.

The goose was cooking, and the vegetables, saved from the summer's garden, were simmering. The plum pudding, part of the contents of the basket that had come from the hall, was warming. The light from the fire and the window was glinting off the crystal balls on the tree and off the star suspended from the ceiling. The bells occasionally tinkled when someone walked by and created a draft. And the baby Jesus, wrapped warmly in swaddling clothes in his manger, was being adored by Mary and Joseph, the Three Kings, an angel with one wing larger than the other, one shepherd, and one sheep, which might as easily have passed for a fox.

Megan was seated cross-legged on the floor close to the fire, rocking her new doll to sleep and gazing in wonder at the porcelain perfection of its face. Andrew was jerking his new watch from a pocket every five minutes to make sure that the goose was not being overcooked. And Lilias sat watching them, a smile on her face.

It was their last Christmas together, at least for a very long time. And their best for several years. She did not regret for a moment the humiliation she had had to suffer in going to the hall to beg for what she had needed to make it a memorable Christmas. And she did not regret that he had come to despise her and even hate her for that begging.

It did not matter. For now it was Christmas, and she had one week left in this cottage and with these children. And she had seen the wonder in their eyes when they had seen their presents that morning. They would have a day together that she would hug to herself in memory for many long months to come.

If there was a restlessness, an emptiness, a strange sense of something missing, then she would not think of it. For she could not bring back Papa or Philip, or Mama from even longer ago. She could not bring back the Christmases at the hall with their charades and blindman's buff and forfeits and sometimes their dancing. She could not bring back those rare and magical white Christmases when they had all spilled outdoors and been reluctant to go back inside even for the foods of Christmas.

And she could not bring Stephen back. For though he had stood beside her last evening when they had gone caroling and sat beside her at church, and though he had taken her hand in his at the end of the evening and wished her a happy Christmas and called her by her

name, he was not Stephen. He was the Marquess of
Bedford, serious and aloof. And he disliked her, even
hated her, perhaps.

She must count her blessings—so many of them—and
keep all her attention and all her love and hope within
these four walls for today. She would not think of either
the past or the future today.

She glanced across the room to the small table where
the evergreen stood, and beneath it the box with the ill-
fitting lid that Andrew had carved for her, and the carefully hemmed cotton handkerchief with the
embroidered forget-me-not that Megan had made for
her during stolen private moments over the past few
weeks. She smiled again.

"I wish Dora could see my doll," Megan said. "Do
you think she has had anything as grand, Lilias?"

"I can hardly wait for tomorrow," Andrew said, consulting his watch once more. "Do you think his lordship
will let me ride one of his prime goers, Lilias?"

Dora was playing quietly with her own new doll. Indeed, she looked almost like a doll herself, her father
thought, glancing across the nursery at her. She was dressed
all in her Christmas finery with quantities of satin and lace,
and large pink satin bows in her hair, which her nurse had
dressed painstakingly in masses of shining dark ringlets.

The child was singing one of her newly learned carols
to the doll.

They had opened their own gifts and distributed gifts
to the servants, but it was still barely midmorning. Bedford turned to stare out the window. A gray world met
his eyes. Those were surely snow clouds overhead, but
they were stubbornly retaining their load. If only it had
snowed, he thought. He could have taken Dora outside.
He could have played in the snow with her all day long
and seen that flush of color in her cheeks and that light

of pleasure in her eyes that he had not seen a great deal during her short life.

Perhaps he should, after all, have organized some sort of party at the house. There had always used to be a large gathering there for Christmas. But he had come late and without a great deal of warning. Most of the neighbors had made their plans for the day already.

Perhaps he should have accepted one of the numerous invitations he had received since his arrival. But none of them had seemed to be for family gatherings. It would have meant packing Dora off upstairs to someone's nursery with other children while he was entertained by the other adults. With cards, doubtless, or dancing. He had been greedy for a Christmas spent with his daughter. He loved her with an almost fierce ache, he had discovered when he had finally taken her from her grandparents' home the previous spring.

But perhaps he should have accepted one of those invitations. Perhaps Dora would have enjoyed being with other children instead of with him or her nurse all day long. Perhaps he had been selfish.

Christmas Day suddenly seemed to stretch for many long hours ahead of him. What were they to do for the rest of the day? Their Christmas dinner was not to be served until the evening.

"Papa," Dora said from beside him. She was still cradling her doll in her arms. "Will you tell me a story?"

"Yes, I will," he said. "What will it be?" He leaned down and swung both child and doll up into his arms. "Shall we go for a walk or a drive afterward? Perhaps take your doll for some fresh air?"

"To Megan's?" she asked eagerly.

"It is Christmas Day," he said. "We must not disturb them today, poppet. Tomorrow Andrew is coming to ride with me. We shall have Megan come over to play with you, shall we?"

"But I want to see her today," she said. "I want to go now. I want to show Miss Angove my doll."

"Tomorrow," he said, hugging her. "You still have not told me which story you want."

"I want to go now," she said petulantly. "I want to see the holly and the tree and the baby Jesus and the star."

"But we have our own decorations and our own evergreen," he said, sitting down with her and settling her on his lap.

"But it's not the same," she said. "They are so much more cozy, Papa. Please may we go. Please!"

One thing he had discovered about himself in the past year, Bedford thought ruefully: He was incapable of exercising the proper control over his child. He knew that it was not good always to give in to her whims; he knew that he must stand up against her, for her own good as much as for his. But he could not bear to see pleading in her eyes and dash it to pieces.

He had so much to atone for: almost four years when he had scarcely seen her but had left her to the not-so-tender care of her grandparents. Lorraine had not wanted her; she had had no use for a daughter. Now he had to be both mother and father to her. There was no soft, motherly presence to bring her the love and security so necessary to a small child. He had to provide that care himself. But he knew that he was allowing her to rule him, that eventually she would suffer from having no one to take a firm stand with her.

He sighed as he looked down into the pleading eyes of his child. Perhaps it would be easier to say no if he did not wish so desperately to go himself. This house was altogether too large and cheerless for two people, especially at Christmas. The cottage in the village was like a magnet to him.

Lilias was like a magnet. But he put the thought ruthlessly from his mind.

"We will take the carriage, then," he said, "and go immediately. Just for half an hour, to wish them a happy Christmas. No longer, poppet, because they will be busy preparing their dinner, and they will want to enjoy one another's company."

Dora's face lit up and she slid from his knee. "May I take my new muff?" she said. "May I, Papa? And may we take them gifts? I am going to give Megan my little pearls and Miss Angove my diamond brooch. What shall we take for Andrew?"

The marquess laughed. "Slow down," he said. "Gifts are a good idea, Dora, but nothing too valuable, or we will embarrass them."

She looked crestfallen, but her brow puckered in thought. "May I give Megan the new blue ribbon you bought for my bonnet?" she asked.

"I think that is a splendid idea," he said.

"And I could give Miss Angove the painting I did of you on your horse," she said. "Is it good enough, Papa?"

"I am sure she will be pleased," he said, hoping that his daughter would forget to identify the horseman when she presented the gift.

"But what can we give Andrew?" She was frowning.

"I'll wager he would like that seashell we found at Brighton," he said. "The one you can hold to your ear to hear the tide. Can you bear to part with it?"

Dora's face lit up again, and she darted off to find the three treasures. Bedford watched her go.

He really should not have given in on this occasion, should he? He must be the last person Lilias would want to see on this of all days. But just for half an hour. It would not quite ruin her day, surely. And it would make Dora's day.

It was Christmas morning, too early for the carriages of those going visiting for the afternoon. The street had been silent all morning. But it was no longer silent. It was Andrew who first remarked on the sound of horses and who crossed to the window to look out. Megan joined him there when it became clear that there was also a carriage approaching.

"It is Lord Bedford's carriage," Andrew cried. "And it is stopping here, Lilias. Oh, ripping! He will see that I have a watch, just like a man."

"Dora is with him," Megan cried. "How pretty she looks. And she has a doll with her. Do come and look, Lilias."

"I think one of us should think of opening the door," Lilias said, getting to her feet with a smile. And she passed nervous hands over her apron, realized she was wearing it, and removed it hastily. She was pleased that she was wearing her blue silk. It was true that it was no longer fashionable, but it had been worn so sparingly in the last few years that it was barely faded and not patched at all. She was wearing the lace collar that had been Mama's. And she had taken special care with her hair that morning because it was Christmas.

He was holding himself very straight. His expression was wooden. She would have said he was embarrassed if she had thought him capable of such feelings. But she had little time in which to stare.

"We have called for half an hour to wish you all a merry Christmas," he said stiffly.

But Dora was jumping up and down at his side and then pushing her way through the door. "We have brought you presents," she said in a voice that seemed designed to be heard by someone at the other end of the street. "And I have a new doll, Megan. Oh, and you do too. Ooh, she is pretty. What is her name? And see my new muff, Miss Angove? Papa bought it in London for me, though I did not know until this morning. I wanted to see the star again. Oh, it does look lovely.

What smells so good? Does it not smell delicious, Papa? And here are your gifts. Open them. Oh, open them."

"Quieten down, poppet," the marquess said, bending down to remove her muff and undo her coat. He kissed her on the cheek, and Lilias felt that churning in her stomach she had felt before.

Megan and Andrew were soon exclaiming over their gifts while Dora shouted them both down, explaining that the ribbon had been meant for her but she had wanted to give it to Megan. And the shell she and Papa had found their very own selves on the beach at Brighton. And couldn't Andrew just hear the tide at Brighton when he held it to his ear?

Lilias sat down before removing the ribbon from the paper and unrolling her painting.

"Ah," she said. "How lovely. And you painted it yourself."

"Yes, I did," Dora said, climbing up onto Lilias's lap so that she could see the picture too. "That is Papa, but he does not look very much like him, does he? Papa is more handsome, isn't he? That is Papa's horse. His one leg is white, you see? Really he is not quite black, but I had to paint him black because my brown paint was not dark enough. I painted a sun, see?"

"It is beautiful," Lilias said, burying her face in the child's ringlets for a moment. "Quite the loveliest painting I have ever owned. I shall treasure it."

"Will you?" Dora looked up at her. "This is pretty." She laid one small forefinger against the lace collar. "Do you like my muff?"

But she did not wait for an answer. She wriggled down to the floor again in order to exchange exclamations of delight with Megan over their dolls.

The marquess was bent over Andrew, meticulously examining his watch, for all the world as if he had never seen it before, Lilias thought.

Dora accepted a mince pie, another of the offerings from the hall; the marquess did not. Dora sat very straight on a chair close to the Nativity scene, her usual pinafore protecting her dress from crumbs, her feet dangling above the floor.

"I like Christmas in your house," she told Lilias and Megan after telling them all about the distributing of gifts to the servants that morning. "I wish we could stay here all day."

The marquess, Lilias could hear with some delight, was telling Andrew about Tattersall's. He would make a friend for life. Andrew had a passion for horses.

"You *can* stay all day," Megan said. "Can't they, Lilias? Our goose is ever so big and there are enough vegetables to feed the five thousand. Lilias said so just a short while ago. We could play house all day. I could be mother and you could be elder sister. And the two dolls can be the babies. Andrew could be the father, but I don't suppose he will want to be. But that does not matter, does it?"

"I am sure his lordship must have other plans for the day," Lilias said quietly to Megan, but Dora had already slipped from her chair and crossed the room to stand beside her father's. She stood there, pulling at his sleeve.

"Papa," she said, "Miss Angove and Megan want us to stay for the rest of the day. There is lots of food, Miss Angove says, and Megan and I are going to play house all day. May we, Papa? Please, may we?"

"Yes," Andrew said with some enthusiasm.

Wide-open blue eyes were turned on her, Lilias saw. Accusing? Assessing? Hostile? Incredulous? It was impossible to tell. She felt herself flushing.

"Impossible, Dora," the marquess said, getting to his feet. "We could not so impose. You agreed to half an hour, and that must be just about up."

There was a chorus of disappointed protests from the three children.

"You would be very welcome," Lilias found herself saying. "There really is plenty of food, and it would be such a treat for the children to have company."

His eyes burned into hers from across the room. *And for me too,* she told him silently. For suddenly there was no longer that elusive sense of something missing. There was excitement in the house and happiness. And Christmas was somehow complete.

And *he* was there. And there was a chance—she clasped her hands in front of her very tightly—that he would be there for the whole day. Her memorable Christmas would be memorable indeed, for she would remember him as Stephen. No matter how much he was this withdrawn and austere and even hostile marquess, in memory she knew she would erase all facts except the essential one: He was Stephen. And she had never stopped loving him. Maybe she never would.

If he stayed, she would be able to carry him with her in memory with all the other memories of this last Christmas with her family. It would all be complete.

"This is preposterous," he said, sitting back down again and looking distinctly uncomfortable. "Whatever will Miss Angove think of us, Dora?"

"Hurrah," Andrew shouted out. "He is going to say yes."

The girls squealed and jumped up and down on the spot. And when Dora climbed onto her father's lap to hug him and kiss him, Megan climbed onto his other knee and smiled adoringly into his face.

"Thank you," she said. "Oh, thank you, sir."

"Your sister is going to throttle me, little imp," he said, and to Lilias's amazement, he hugged the child close with one arm and kissed her cheek. "I had better go outside and dismiss my coachman. He might die of boredom and cold if we leave him out there for the rest of the day."

The children were enjoying themselves quite noisily. Even Andrew had been prevailed upon to join in the game of house and was currently sitting on a stool having his hair combed and parted down the wrong side by Dora.

They were having a good time, and that was what really mattered, Bedford thought. But what on earth must Lilias think of him for agreeing so weakly to stay for dinner and even for the rest of the day? He had instructed his coachman to return for him and Dora at eight o'clock.

Or perhaps he should not be feeling guilty, but angry. A few days before he would have been angry and suspicious. It would have been very easy for her to set the children to trapping him into this domestic situation and leading him on to making her an offer.

But he found it hard to believe still that her every action since his homecoming had been conniving. And if it were, was it so despicable? She and the children really were in a desperate situation, and they really were facing a bleak future. Would it be so wrong of her to scheme to win for herself a husband who could lift the burden from her shoulders?

"I have never done this before, you know," he said now, looking rather dubiously at the goose she had asked him to carve. "The meat seems to want to come away in clumps rather than in neat slices."

Lilias laughed. "I have never done it either," she said. "That is why I asked you." She was stirring the gravy. But she paused and looked at him in some concern. "If any of that grease gets on your shirt, it will be ruined."

He looked down at his white shirt. He had already removed his coat and waistcoat and rolled up his sleeves to the elbow.

"What you need is an apron," she said, and crossed to the hook on the kitchen door to fetch one.

"But my hands are greasy," he protested when she held it out to him.

"Lower your head, then," she said with a giggle he had not heard for years, and she slipped the neck strap over his head. She moved behind him, and there was a moment when her arms came around his waist to grasp the ties of the apron so that she could secure it behind him.

"There," she said, coming around to the front of him again to survey her handiwork. His hands were greasy, and he held them suspended in the air. "The Marquess of Bedford in heavy disguise." She laughed. "Oh, you do look funny, Stephen."

But the smile froze on her face and faded, and color rose up her neck and into her cheeks, and he watched her swallow. The children's voices seemed very distant, even though they were just beyond the open door between the kitchen and the parlor. His eyes strayed to her lips.

"The goose awaits," he said lightly.

"The gravy will be lumpy," she said simultaneously.

They worked together in the small kitchen in an awkward silence.

The tension eased when they all sat down to dinner. But there was a heightened awareness that Bedford did not find altogether unpleasant. They sat at either end of the table, Andrew on one side of them and Megan and Dora on the other. Just like a family, all of them playing house in the warm and cozy little cottage. He met Lilias's eyes across the table and smiled. She looked down hastily and then back at him.

"Will you say grace, my lord?" she asked.

He had never in his life washed dishes. But when the plum pudding was finally eaten and they were all groaning with the good foods they had stuffed into themselves, he rolled up his sleeves and put on the apron again. The children giggled.

"Oh, you must not," Lilias said, flustered. "Please sit

down in the parlor, my lord. The children and I will see to the dishes."

"No, this is famous," Andrew exclaimed. "You wash, sir, and Megan and I will dry."

"My thoughts entirely," the marquess said. "Your sister thinks I am incapable, you see, Andrew. We will show her, won't we? You may clear away the food, ma'am, and then we will all have something to do."

"I want to dry too." Dora had climbed onto a chair to make herself noticed.

"Oh, sweetheart," Lilias said, "you may help me put away. I really need assistance with that. Will you?"

Doing dishes had never been so much fun, Andrew declared half an hour later when the wet towels were being hung up to dry. Megan and Dora were still giggling over the cup that had slipped from the marquess's wet hand and smashed on the floor.

"Let's play house again," Megan said.

"Let's go for a walk," Andrew said.

"Yes." Dora jumped up and down on the spot. "Go for a walk."

"I am sure we all need a brisk walk of at least five miles," the marquess said, patting his stomach. He turned to Lilias. "You have been busy all morning, ma'am. Would you care to have a rest while I take the children walking?" He looked down at her hopefully. "Or would you care to join us?"

"I shall join you," she said. "Fresh air sounds wonderful."

Steady, Bedford told himself as he buttoned Dora's coat a few minutes later and pulled on his own greatcoat. He must not become too mesmerized by the feeling of family he had had for the past few hours. Only Dora was his family. The other children belonged to Lilias, and she was not his family at all.

*   *   *

Perhaps she should have refused, Lilias thought as she drew her cloak about her and tied the strings of her bonnet. Perhaps she needed an hour alone in which to clear her head of this seductive feeling of warmth and belonging she had had in the past few hours. Perhaps she should not go walking with him, just as if they were one close and happy family.

But there was so little time left. Less than a week, and then a long and lonely life as someone's governess. And the long illusion that one day she would earn enough money to gather her family back around her again. Less than a week left with Megan and Andrew. Less than a week with Stephen and Dora.

No, she thought, pulling her gloves on resolutely, she was not doing the wrong thing. He had ordered the carriage for eight. That left them with six hours. Six hours. It was not long. She was going to enjoy every minute of it, even if to do so was only to invite future pain. She did not care about the future. Only the present mattered.

Dora attached herself to one of her hands, Megan to the other. Dora skipped rather than walked, and entertained her companions with stories of all that her papa had shown her in London and Brighton. Andrew and the marquess were striding along ahead, deep in conversation—doubtless about horses, Lilias thought with a smile. She was glad for Andrew. He needed more male company than he had had in the past two years. But then, of course, soon he would have nothing but male company, their grandfather during holidays, other boys of his own age during term time. She shut the thought from her mind.

They walked to the lake on the grounds of Bedford Hall. It was looking very bleak and even had a thin layer of ice covering it.

"Yes," Andrew was saying excitedly as Lilias and the girls came up to him and the marquess. "If it stays cold like this, we will be able to slide on the ice in a few days' time."

The children were soon running around the bank, gazing eagerly at the film of ice.

Lilias had not realized how cold it was until she stopped walking. The wind cut at her like a knife. She glanced up at the heavy clouds.

"Snow clouds," the marquess said. "Are they just teasing, do you suppose? But I think not. I believe we are going to have our snow yet."

"Yes," Lilias said, "I think you are right." Her teeth were chattering. She shivered. She could feel him looking at her. She sought in her mind for something to say. There was an awkwardness when they were alone. They needed the presence of the children to create an atmosphere of ease between them.

"Lilias," he said. His voice was tight and withdrawn, the voice of the Marquess of Bedford again, despite his use of her given name, "your cloak is too thin. It must be quite threadbare. When did you last have a new one?"

She looked jerkily up at him. "It is quite adequate, I thank you," she said. "It is just this standing still that is making me cold."

"When did you last buy yourself anything?" he asked. His voice sounded angry. "Has everything been for the children in the last few years? Your lips are quite blue."

"Don't," she said. His face had that shuttered look it had had the first few times she had seen him. "It is none of your concern."

"Your dress," he said. "It was quite fashionable six years ago when it was new. You wore it for Christmas then. Had you forgotten?"

She stared at him, though she did not see him at all. She was blinded by hurt and humiliation. She *had* forgotten. She had felt pretty that morning. Pretty for him. She turned quickly away.

"It is none of your business," she said. "What I wear and what I spend on myself and the children is none of your concern at all. I am not answerable to you."

"No, you are not," he said, moving closer to her so that he stood between her and the wind. He lifted his head and his voice suddenly. "Andrew," he called, "your sister and I are going to begin the walk home. You may bring the girls along behind us. Don't let anyone set even a single toe on that ice."

"No, I won't, sir," Andrew called back.

He took her arm through his and hugged it close to his side. He walked at a brisk pace. And he plied her the whole way home with questions about her governess post: where it was and who the family were and how many charges she would have and how arduous the duties were likely to be. And he asked about Andrew, about what school he was to attend, how well he was likely to be treated by his grandfather, how much he looked forward to being away from home. He wanted to know about Great-aunt Hetty in Bath and how suitable a home she would be able to offer a nine-year-old child.

Lilias answered as briefly as she could.

"Why would your grandfather not take all of you?" he asked as they entered the village again.

"Papa defied him when he married Mama," she said. "He has never recognized us. I was fortunate to be able to persuade him to take Andrew."

"You are his grandchildren," he said. "He ought to have taken you. Did you ask him to?"

She shook her head. "I will not answer any more questions," she said. "I have arranged everything to my own satisfaction, my lord."

"In other words, it is none of my business, again," he said, his voice still angry. "You are right. But those children need you, Lilias. They are still very much children."

She stared stonily ahead to the cottage. The temptation to tip her head sideways to rest against his shoulder, to sag against the strength of his arm, to close her eyes and pour out all her pain to him was almost overwhelming. She was only thankful that for the return walk he had chosen to be the Marquess of Bedford rather than Stephen. She might not have been able to resist letting down her guard with Stephen.

He put fresh logs on the fire when they went indoors while she filled the kettle. By the time they were ready to settle into an uncomfortable silence, the children were home, and they brought with them again all the joy and laughter of Christmas—and, yes, the warmth too, despite rosy cheeks and reddened fingers and noses.

"Tell the Nativity story again, Papa," Dora begged when all outdoor garments had been removed and put away, climbing onto his knee.

"Again?" he said. "You have heard it three times already, poppet."

"Tell it again," she said, fingering the diamond pin in his neckcloth.

Megan was standing beside them. The marquess smiled at her—Lilias's heart did a complete somersault—and reached out his free arm to draw her onto his other knee. He told both girls the story, and Andrew too, who was sitting at his feet whittling away at the sheep again, trying to improve its appearance. Lilias busied herself getting tea.

The time went too fast. He willed it to hold still; he willed eight o'clock never to come. But of course it did come. Stories and singing and charades and forfeits had passed the time merrily. Megan and Dora were bright-cheeked and bright-eyed and very giggly long before eight o'clock came, a sure sign that they were very tired.

"But I don't want to go, Papa," Dora said, yawning very loudly. "One more hour?"

"One more?" Megan pleaded.

Lilias was sitting in a chair opposite his own, her feet resting on the hearth. She was smiling. She looked very beautiful. Why had he not told her that out at the lake? Why had he not told her that she looked even lovelier this year in the unfashionable blue gown than she had looked six years before? Why had he allowed himself to get angry instead? Angry at a fate that could treat her so? He wanted her to have everything in the world, and instead, she had almost nothing. Why had he not told her she looked beautiful?

"Not even one more minute," he told the girls. "And, as it is, that coach of ours is late. Wherever can it be?"

He got up from his chair and crossed the room to the window. He pulled back the curtains, which they had closed as soon as they had returned from their walk, and leaned past the evergreen in order to peer out into the darkness. Not that he had really needed to lean forward, he realized immediately. It was not completely dark outside.

"Good Lord," he said. "Snow."

It must have started in great earnest the moment they had pulled the curtains. And it must have been snowing ever since. There were several inches of it out there.

"Snow!" There were three identical shrieks, and three human missiles hurled themselves against him and past him in order to see the spectacle. "Snow!" There was a loud babble of excitement.

"Well," he said, "at least we know what has delayed the coach. It is still in the coach house and the horses in the stable, if Giles has any sense whatsoever."

Dora shrieked and bounced at his side. "We can stay, then, Papa?" she asked. "We can stay all night?"

He turned to see Lilias standing before the fireplace.

"She can share Megan's bed," she said hastily. "There will be room for the two of them. You must not think of taking her out if the snow really is too deep for your carriage."

"And you can share mine," Andrew said brightly.

The marquess laughed. "Thank you, Andrew," he said, "but I shall walk home. For days I have been longing to set my feet in snow. But I will be grateful to leave Dora here until morning. Thank you, ma'am." He looked at Lilias.

She went upstairs almost immediately with Megan to get all ready. He took Dora onto his lap to explain to her that he would go home alone and return for her in the morning. But he need not have worried. She was so tired and so excited at the prospect of spending the night with Megan that she seemed not at all upset at being separated from him. He took her upstairs.

The door to one small bedroom was open. Megan was crying. The marquess stood still on the stairs and held his daughter's hand more tightly.

"Hush," Lilias was saying. "Oh, hush, sweetheart. You know we had a pact not to talk of it or even think of it until Christmas was well and truly over. Hush now. It has been a lovely Christmas, has it not?"

"Ye-e-es," Megan wailed, her voice muffled. "But I don't want to go, Lilias."

"Sh," Lilias said. "Dora will be here in a minute. You don't want her to see you cry, do you?"

"No-o-o."

The marquess looked down into the large eyes of his daughter and held a finger to his lips. He frowned. Then he stepped firmly on the next stair. "Here we are," he said cheerfully. "Two little girls to squash into one little bed."

Megan giggled.

"Four little girls," Dora corrected him, indicating the doll clutched in her own arms and pointing to Megan's, which was lying at the foot of the bed.

Both girls giggled.

"Four, then," he said. "In you get."

Andrew was no less tired than the girls. He went to bed only ten minutes later. Ten minutes after that the giggling and whisperings stopped. It seemed that all were asleep.

The marquess was standing at the window, looking out into the curiously lightened world of freshly falling snow. Lilias was seated silently at the fire.

"Lilias," he said. He could no more think of the right words to say than he had been able to twenty minutes before. He continued to look out the window. "You must marry me. It is the only way. I cannot let you take on the life of a governess. And Andrew and Megan must not be separated from each other, or from you. You must marry me. Will you?" He turned finally to look across the room at her. And knew immediately that he had done it all wrong, after all.

She was quite pale. She stared up at him, all large eyes in her thin face. "No," she said, and her voice was trembling. "No, I will not accept charity. No."

But she must be made to accept. Did she not realize that? He felt his jaw harden. He retreated behind the mask that had become almost habitual with him in the past few years.

"I don't think you have any choice," he said. "Do you seriously think that, as a governess, you will ever again have a chance to see your brother and sister? Do you imagine that you will be able to save even enough money to travel to where they are to visit? It will not happen. When you leave here, you will see them for perhaps the last time."

She was sitting on the very edge of her chair, her back straight, her hands clasped tightly in her lap.

"Do you think I do not know that?" she said.

"Andrew will not even be allowed to see you again,"

he said. "He will be taken back into the fold, and he will be taught to despise you. Do you realize that?"

"Yes."

He saw the word forming itself on her lips. He did not hear it. "Megan will be an old woman's slave," he said. "She will have a dreary girlhood. She will probably end up like you, a governess or a paid companion. Have you thought of that?"

"Yes," she said.

"Then you must marry me," he said. "For their sakes, if not for your own. You will be able to stay together." His eyes strayed down her body. "And you will be able to have some new clothes at last."

He ached to buy her those new garments, to see the pleasure in her eyes as he clothed her in silks and lace and warm wool. He wanted to hang jewels about her neck and at her ears. He wanted to put rings on her fingers.

"You *must* marry me," he said.

She rose to her feet. He knew as soon as she did so that she was very angry. "Must I?" she said softly. "Must I, my lord? Is this what your title and wealth have done for you? Do you talk to your servants so? Do you talk to everyone so? And does everyone kiss the ground at your feet and do what they must do? Is this how you persuaded your first wife to marry you? And did she instantly obey? Well, not me, my lord. I do not have to marry you, or anyone else. And if it is true that my brother and sister will live less than perfect lives according to the arrangements I have made for them, then at least we will all be able to retain our pride and hold our heads high. I will not sell myself even for their sakes."

The Marquess of Bedford had trained himself not to flinch outwardly under such scathing attacks. He merely stared at her from half-closed eyelids, his teeth and lips firmly pressed together.

"Pride can be a lonely companion," he said.

"Perhaps so," she said. "But charity would be an unbearable companion, my lord."

He nodded. "I will wish you good night, then," he said. "Thank you for giving Dora a bed. And thank you for giving her the loveliest day of her life. I know I do not exaggerate. I hope we have not spoiled your day."

"No," she said. The fire of battle had died in her eyes. She looked smaller and thinner even than usual. "You have not spoiled our day. The children have been very happy."

The children. Not she. The marquess half-smiled, though he feared that his expression must look more like a sneer. He picked up his greatcoat and pulled it on.

"Good night," he said again, pulling his collar up about his ears. "Don't stand at the door. You will get cold."

He did not look at her again. He concentrated his mind on wading through the soft snow without either falling or losing his way.

She sat back down on the edge of her chair and stared into the fire. She would not think. She would not remember . . . or look ahead. She would not think. She would not. She would sit until some warmth seeped into her bones, and then she would go to bed and sleep. She felt bone-weary. But she would not think at all. Tomorrow she would work things out.

She would sit there until she was warm and until she could be sure that her legs would support her when she stood up. And until she could see to climb the stairs. She blinked her eyes determinedly and swallowed several times.

But she would not think.

She sat there for perhaps fifteen minutes before leaping to her feet suddenly and flying to the door to answer a loud hammering there. She pulled it open, letting in cold and snow. And she closed it again, setting her back to it, and watching in a kind of stupor as Bedford stamped the snow from his boots and tore off his coat and hat and threw them carelessly aside.

"Listen to me, Lilias," the marquess said fiercely, turning to her. But he stopped talking and looked at her in exasperation. He reached out and took one of her hands in a firm clasp. "No, don't listen to me. Come with me."

He did not take her far, only to the middle of the parlor. She looked up at him in mute inquiry.

"You will not even be able to slap my face," he said, drawing her against him with his free arm. He glanced upward at the mistletoe. "It is a Christmas tradition, you see." He bent his head and kissed her.

She stood still, rigid with shock. It was a hard and fierce kiss.

"Don't," he said against her lips. His very blue eyes were gazing into hers. "Don't, Lilias. Don't shut me out."

And then she could only cling to him and sag against him and eventually reach up to hold him more firmly by the shoulders and about the neck. He was no longer a slender boy, kissing her with the eager kisses of a very young man. He had a man's body, hard and firmly muscled. And his kisses were a man's kisses, deep and experienced and full of a knee-weakening promise.

But he was the same, nonetheless. He was Stephen as she remembered him, as she had dreamed of him and cried for him, and as she had consigned to the most treasured memories of her young life. He was Stephen as she had longed for him and yearned for him through six years when she might have married any of several other worthy men. Stephen, whom she had loved at the age of fifteen, and whom she would love at the age of ninety, if she lived that long.

She did as he asked. She did not shut him out. At long last, she lowered her guard and did not shut him out.

"Lilias." He held her head against his shoulder and looked down into her face. "I said it all wrong. I did it all wrong. Right from the start. Six years ago. How could I ever have left you? After Claude died, my father impressed upon me that I was now his heir, that I must put behind me all that was humble and beneath the dignity of a future marquess. And when he died soon after, I was dazzled by my own importance and popularity. I forgot you. I married Lorraine."

"I understood," she said, reaching up a hand and touching his cheek with her fingertips. "I did not expect any different. Even before you left, I never expected more from you. Only friendship and an innocent romance. I was very young. Too young to have any expectations of anything beyond the moment."

"I never allowed myself to think of you," he said. "You just became part of the dream of a perfect childhood and boyhood."

"I know," she said. "You became my dream, too."

"I did only one good and worthy thing in all those years," he said, "and had only one claim to happiness: I begot Dora."

"Yes," she said. "I know."

"I have had her only since last spring," he said. "And as Christmas approached, I knew I had to bring her here. I remembered that Christmases here were always perfect. I thought it was the snow and the sledding and skating. Memory can sometimes be so defective. I was wrong about that. But not wrong in the main. Christmas *was* always perfect here, and it has been perfect this year, even though the snow has only just come. It was because of you, Lilias. Because you were always there. And because you were here this year."

She turned her face to his shoulder. "I wanted Christ-

mas for the children," she said. "I did not know how I
was to do it. But when I heard that you had come, I
knew that you would be able to provide it. Not just with
money, though that is what I ended up asking for and remembering that ridiculous incident of the Latin lessons.
I just felt that I had to go to you and that you would
make everything all right. But you had changed. I was
frightened when I saw you."

"Lilias," he said, and held her head more firmly
against his shoulder. "How can I say it this time without
saying quite the wrong words again? If not for your own
sake and your brother's and sister's, will you do it for
mine? Marry me, I mean. Though I don't deserve it. I
left you without a word. For Dora's, then? She needs a
mother. You would not believe what a sullen and bad-
tempered child she was when I first took her, and how
petulant she can still be when she does not have her
way. And I cannot say no to her, though I know I must
learn how. She needs you, Lilias. And she loves you already. Have you seen that? I want you to be her mother.
Will you? Will you marry me?"

She pulled her head free of his hand and looked up
into a face that was anxious and vulnerable.

"No," she said, shaking her head. "Not for Dora's
sake, Stephen. It would not be enough. And not for Andrew's and Megan's. That would not be enough either.
And not for my need. Somehow I will survive as a governess."

He opened his mouth to protest. She set one finger
lightly over his lips.

"For one reason only," she said. "For the only reason
that would make it work. Only if we love each other.
Both of us."

Wide blue eyes looked down into hers. "You have
been there for six long and unhappy years," he said.
"The dream of you. I brought my child to you this

Christmas, though I did not realize when we left London quite why I was bringing her here. The dream has come alive again. Like a greedy child, I have Christmas and want to keep it forever here in my arms. I don't want it to disappear tomorrow or the next day. I don't want that dreary world back, Lilias. I don't want to live without you. Yes, I love you. I always have, but like a fool, I have repressed the knowledge for six years. Will you have me?"

"So many times," she said, "I have told myself how foolish I was not to let go the memory of you. I had the well-being of two children to see to, and my own, and I have had two offers since Papa died. We could have been comfortable, the three of us. But I could not let you go, even though I was so very young when you left. Now I know I was not foolish, after all. For whether you marry me or leave me forever tomorrow, Stephen, you will always be a part of me. I will never love any other man. There is only you."

He was quite the old Stephen suddenly, his eyes dancing, his mouth curved into a grin. "Now, let me get this straight," he said. "Was that yes or no?"

She laughed back into his eyes. "It was yes," she said.

"Was it?" He stooped down suddenly and she found herself swung up into his arms. He carried her over to the fire and sat down on a chair with her. "God, Lilias, you weigh no more than a feather. The first thing I am going to do with you, my girl, is fatten you up."

She clung to his neck and laughed.

"And the next thing I am going to do," he said, "is take you to London and buy you so many clothes it will take you a year to wear them all. And so many jewels that it will take two footmen to lift you from the ground."

Her laughter turned to giggles.

"But there," he said, shrugging his shoulder so that

her face was turned to his again, "I was always a fool, wasn't I, love? The costliest gown in London could not look lovelier on you than this blue silk. And anyway, those things are going to have to come second and third. A very distant second and third. There is something else I must do first."

"What?" she asked, reaching up to touch the silver hairs at his temples.

"I'll show you in just a moment," he said. "But first you had better tell me what time you are planning to kick me out of here."

"Mm," she said. "Give me time to think about it. What were you going to show me, Stephen?"

He rubbed his nose against hers. "How to play house properly," he said, grinning at her once more before seeking her mouth with his own again.

No Room
at the Inn

*T*he White Hart Inn, somewhere in Wiltshire—it had never been important enough for anyone to map its exact location on any fashionable map or in any guidebook, fashionable or otherwise—was neither large nor picturesque nor thriving. It was not a posting inn and had no compensating claim to fame—not its location, nor the quality of its ale or cuisine, nor the geniality of its host, nor anything, in short. It was certainly not the type of place in which one would wish to be stranded unexpectedly for any length of time.

Especially at Christmastime.

And more especially when the cause was not a heavy snowfall, which might have added beauty to the surroundings and romance to the adventure, but rain. Torrential, incessant rain, which poured down from a leaden sky and made a quagmire of even the best-kept roads. The road past the White Hart was not one of the best-kept.

The inn presented a picture of squatness and ugliness and gloom to those who were forced to put up there rather than slither on along the road and risk bogging down completely and having to spend Christmas inside a damp and chill carriage—or risk overturning and celebrating the festive season amidst mud and injuries and even possibly death.

None of the travelers who arrived at the inn during the course of the late afternoon of the day preceding Christmas Eve did so by design. None of them did so with any pleasure. Most of them were in low spirits, and that was an optimistic description of the mood of a few of them. Even the landlord and his good lady were not as ecstatic as one might have expected them to be under the circumstances that they had rarely had more than one of their rooms filled during any one night for the past two years and more. Before nightfall all six of their rooms were occupied, and it was altogether possible that someone else might arrive after dark.

"What are we going to give 'em to eat?" Letty Palmer asked her husband, frowning at the thought of the modest-size goose and the even more modest ham on which the two of them had planned to feast on Christmas Day. "And what are we going to give 'em to drink, Joe? There is only ale, and all of 'em are quality. Not to mention the coachmen what brought 'em 'ere."

"It'll 'ave to be ale or the rainwater outside," Joseph Palmer said, a note of belligerence in his voice, as if his guests had already begun to complain about the plain fare at the White Hart. "And as far as vittles is concerned, they'll 'ave to eat what we 'as and be thankful for it too."

But the guests had not yet begun to complain about the food and drink, perhaps because they had not yet had an opportunity to sample the fare on which it seemed likely they would have to celebrate Christmas.

Edward Riddings, Marquess of Lytton, cursed his luck. He had been fully intending to spend the holiday season in London as he usually did, entertaining himself by moving from party to party. The ladies were always at their most amorous at Christmastime, he had found from experience. Yes, even the ladies. There was always pleasure to be derived from a sampling of their charms.

But this year he had been persuaded to accept one of the invitations that he always received in abundance to a private party in the country. Lady Frazer, the delectable widow, was to be at the Whittakers' and had given him an unmistakable signal that at last she would be his there. He had been laying determined siege to her heart, or rather to her body, since she had emerged from her year of mourning during the previous spring. She had the sort of body for which a man would be willing to traverse England.

Yet now it was evident that he was neither to reach that body in time for Christmas nor to return to London in time to console himself with the more numerous but perhaps less enticing pleasures of town. Even if the rain were to stop at this very instant, he thought, looking out of the low window of the small and shabby room to which he had been assigned at the White Hart, it was doubtful that the road would be passable before Christmas Day at the earliest. And there were still twenty miles to go.

The rain showed no sign of abating. If anything it was pounding down with greater enthusiasm than ever.

If he were fortunate—but events were not shaping up to bring any good fortune with them—there would be a beautiful and unattached lady of not quite impeccable virtue also stranded at this infernal inn. But he would not allow himself to hope. There could not be more than five or six guest rooms, and he had already seen five or six of his fellow strandees, none of whom appeared even remotely bedworthy.

It was going to be some Christmas, he thought, gritting his teeth and pounding one fist against the windowsill.

Miss Pamela Wilder gazed from the window of her room and felt all the misery of utter despair. She could not even cry. She could not even feel all the awkwardness of her situation, stranded as she was at a public inn without either maid or chaperon. It did not matter. Nothing mattered except that her first holiday in more than a year was to be spent here at this inn, alone. She thought of her parents and of her brothers and sisters, and she thought of Christmas as she had always known it—except last year—at the rectory and in the small church next to it. There was warmth and light and wonder in the thought, until nostalgia stabbed at her so painfully that the memories could no longer bring any comfort.

They did not know she was coming. It was to be a surprise. Lawrence, one of Sir Howard Raven's coachmen, had been given a few days off for Christmas and had even been granted permission to take the old and shabby carriage that was scheduled for destruction as soon as the new one was delivered. And his home was not ten miles from the rectory where Mama and Papa lived. Pamela had broached the subject very tentatively and quite without hope, first with Lawrence and then with Lady Raven, and wonder of wonders, no one had raised any objection. It seemed that a governess was not particularly needed at Christmastime, when young Hortense would have cousins with whom to play and greater freedom to mingle with the adults.

Pamela was free until two days after Christmas. Free to go home. Free to be with her family and spend that most wonderful time of the year with them. Free to see Wesley and hope that finally he felt himself well enough established on his farm to offer for her. Free to hope that perhaps he would at least ask her to betroth herself to him even if the wedding must be postponed for a long time. Having an unspoken understanding with him had not soothed her loneliness since she had been forced to take her present post more than a year before. She craved some more definite hope for the future.

Yet now she was to spend Christmas at the White Hart, eight miles—eight impossible miles—from home. Even if the rain were to stop now, there seemed little chance that she would make it home for Christmas Day. But the rain was not going to stop now or before the night was over at the very earliest. There was no point in even hoping otherwise.

She was hungry, Pamela realized suddenly, even though she was not at all sure she would be able to eat. How could she do so, anyway? How could she go downstairs alone to the dining room? And yet she must. She was not of any importance at all. There seemed little hope of persuading anyone to bring up her dinner on a tray.

What a Christmas it was going to be, she thought. Even last year had been better—that dreadful Christmas, her first away from home, her first in the status of a servant and yet not quite a servant. She had been able to celebrate the coming of Christ with neither the family nor the servants. Perhaps after all she would be no more alone this year than last, she thought in a final effort to console herself.

Lord Birkin stood at the window of his room, his lips compressed, his hands clasped behind him and beating a rhythmic tattoo against his back. What a confounded turn of events.

"We should have come a week ago, like everyone else," Lady Birkin said, "instead of staying in London until the last possible minute."

She was seated on the edge of the bed behind him. He knew that if he turned and looked at her, he would see her the picture of dejection, all her beauty and animation marred by the rain and the poverty of her surroundings. She would hate having to spend Christmas here when they had been on their way to spend it with the Middletons and more than twenty of their relatives and friends.

"You would have missed the opera and the Stebbins' ball," he said without turning.

"And you would have missed a few days at your club," she said, a note of bitterness in her voice.

"We could not have predicted the rain," he said. "Not in this quantity anyway. I am sorry that you will miss all the Christmas entertainments, Sally."

"And you will miss the shooting," she said, that edge still in her voice. "And the billiards."

He turned to look at her at last, broodingly. Marriage had turned out to be nothing like what he had expected. They were two people living their separate lives, he and Sally, with the encumbrance of the fact that they were legally bound together for life.

Were things quite as bad as that? They had been fond of each other when they had married, even though their parents on both sides had urged the match on them. He still was fond of her, wasn't he? Yes, he was still fond of her. But somehow marriage had not drawn them closer together. The occasional couplings, now no more frequent than once or twice a month, though they had not been married much longer than three years, brought with them no emotional bond. They both behaved on the mornings after the couplings as if they had never happened.

"I am sorry about the sparsity of rooms," he said. "I am sorry we must share."

His wife flushed and looked about the room rather than at him. It was going to be dreadful, she thought. Dreadful to be alone with him for what would probably be several days. Dreadful to have to share a room with him and a bed for that time. They had never shared a bed for longer than ten minutes at a time, and even those occasions had become rarer during the past year.

She had married him because she loved him and because she had thought he loved her, though he had never said so. *Foolish girl.* She must have appeared quite mousy to such a blond and beautiful man. He had married her because it was expected of him, because the connection was an eligible one. She knew now that she had never attracted him and never could. He rarely spent time with her. Their marital encounters were a bitter disappointment, and so rare that she did not even have the consolation of having conceived his child.

She knew about his mistresses, though he did not know that she knew. She had even seen his latest one, a creature of exquisite beauty and voluptuous charms. She herself had come to feel quite without beauty or charm or allure.

Except that she had not allowed herself to give in to self-pity. She had had a choice early in her marriage. Either she could retreat into herself and become the mousy, uninteresting thing he saw her as, or she could put her unhappiness and disappointment behind her and live a life of busy gaiety, as so many married ladies of her acquaintance did. She had chosen the latter course. He would never know for what foolish reason she had married him or what foolish hopes had been dashed early in their marriage.

"There is no point in apologizing for what cannot be helped, Henry," she said. "Under the circumstances I suppose we are fortunate to have a roof over our heads. Though I could wish that it had happened at some other time of the year. It is going to be an unimaginably dull Christmas."

She wondered what it would be like to lie all night in the large and rather lumpy bed with him beside her. Her breathing quickened at the thought, and she looked up at him with an unreasonable resentment.

"Yes," he said. "Whoever heard of Christmas spent at an inn?"

"It would not have happened," she said, hearing the irritability in her voice and knowing that she was being unfair, "if we had come a week ago, like everyone else."

"As you keep reminding me," he said. "Next year we will do things differently, Sally. Next year we will see to it that you are surrounded by friends and admirers well before Christmas itself comes along."

"And that you have plenty of other gentlemen and gentlemen's sports with which to amuse yourself," she said. "Perhaps there will be some gentlemen here, Henry. Perhaps you will find some congenial companions with whom to talk the night away and forget the inconvenience of such congested quarters."

"I can sleep in the taproom if you so wish," he said, his voice cold.

They did not often quarrel. One or the other of them usually left the room when a disagreement was imminent, as it was now.

"That would be foolish," she said.

He was leaving the room now. He paused, with his hand on the doorknob. "I doubt there is such a luxury as a private parlor in this apology for an inn," he said. "We will have to eat in the public dining room, Sally. I shall go and see when dinner will be ready."

An excuse to get away from her, Lady Birkin thought as the door closed behind him. She concentrated on not crying and succeeded. She had perfected the skill over the years.

It was an excuse to get away from her, Lord Birkin thought as he descended the stairs. Away from her accusing voice and the knowledge that the worst aspect of the situation for her was being forced to spend a few days in his dull company. She did not sleep with any of her numerous admirers. He did not know quite how he could be sure of that, since he had never spied on her, but he did know it. She was faithful to him, or to their marriage, at least, as he was not. But he knew equally that she would prefer the company of any one of her admirers to his.

But she was stuck with it for several days. And at Christmas, of all times.

The Misses Amelia and Eugenia Horn, unmarried ladies of indeterminate years, had left their room in order to seek out the innkeeper. The sheets on their beds were damp, Miss Amelia Horn declared in a strident voice.

"Perhaps they are only cold, dear," Miss Eugenia Horn suggested in a near whisper, embarrassed by the indelicate mention of bedsheets in the hearing of two gentlemen, not counting the innkeeper himself.

But her elder sister was made of sterner stuff and argued on. They were bitterly disappointed, Miss Eugenia Horn reflected, leaving the argument to her sister. They would not make it to dear Dickie's house fifteen miles away and would not have the pleasure of their annual visit with their brother and sister-in-law and the dear children, though the youngest of Dickie's offspring was now seventeen years old. How time did fly. They would all be made quite despondent by her absence and dear Amelia's. Dickie was always too busy, the poor dear, to have them visit at any other time of the year.

Miss Eugenia Horn sighed.

Colonel Forbes, a large, florid-faced, white-haired gentleman of advanced years, was complaining to Lord Birkin, the innkeeper's attention being otherwise occupied at the time. He deplored the absence of a private parlor for the convenience of his wife and himself.

"General Hardinge himself has invited us for Christmas," the colonel explained. "A singular honor and a distinguished company. And now this blasted rain. A fine Christmas this is going to be."

"We all seem to be agreed on that point, at least," Lord Birkin said politely, and waited his turn to ask about dinner.

Sometimes the most dreaded moments turned out not to be so dreadful after all, Pamela realized when the emptiness of her stomach drove her downstairs in search of dinner. Although the dining room appeared alarmingly full with fellow guests and she felt doubly alone, she did not long remain so. Two middle-aged ladies looked up at her from their table, as did all the other occupants of the room, saw her lone state, and took her beneath their wing. Soon she was tucked safely into a chair at their table.

"Doubtless you expected to be at your destination all within one day, my dear," Miss Eugenia Horn said in explanation of Pamela's lack of a companion.

"Yes, ma'am," she said. "I did not expect the rain."

"But it is always wiser to expect the unexpected and go nowhere without a chaperon," Miss Amelia Horn added. "You would not wish to give anyone the impression that you were fast."

"No, ma'am." Pamela was too grateful for their company to feel offended.

The Misses Horn proceeded to complain about the dampness of their bedsheets and their threadbare state.

"I suppose," Miss Amelia Horn said, "that we should have expected the unexpected, Eugenia, and brought our own. It is never wise to travel without."

The rain and all being stranded at the very worst time of the year had appeared to draw the other occupants of the room together, Pamela noticed. Conversation was becoming general. She looked about her with some curiosity, careful not to stare at anyone. A quiet gentleman of somewhat less than middle years sat at the table next to hers. He said very little, but listened to everyone, a smile in his eyes and lurking about his mouth. He was perhaps the only member of the party to look as if he did not particularly resent being where he was.

An elderly couple sat at another table, the man loudly and firmly condemning England as a place to live and declaring darkly that if the government did not do something about it soon, all sensible Englishmen would take themselves off to live on the Continent or in America. He did not make it clear whether he expected the government to do something about the excessive amount of rainfall to which England was susceptible or whether he was referring to something else. Whatever the cause, he was very flushed and very angry. His wife sat across the table from him, quietly nodding. Pamela realized after a while that the nodding was involuntary. They were Colonel and Mrs. Forbes, she learned in the course of dinner.

A young and handsome couple sat at another table, perhaps the most handsome pair Pamela had ever seen. The lady was brown-haired and brown-eyed and had a proud and beautiful face and the sort of shapely figure that always made Pamela sigh with envy. Her husband, Lord Birkin, was like a blond Greek god, the kind of man she had always found rather intimidating. They were clearly unhappy both with each other and with a ruined Christmas. Apparently they were on their way to a large country party. They were the sort of people who had everything and nothing, though that was a flash judgment, Pamela admitted to herself, and perhaps unfair.

There was another gentleman in the room. Pamela's eyes skirted about him whenever she looked up. On the

few occasions when she looked directly at him, her uncomfortable impression that he was staring at her
was confirmed. He was not handsome. Oh, yes, he was,
of course, but not in the way of the blond god. He was
more attractive than handsome, with his dark hair and
hooded eyes—they might be blue, she thought—and a
cynical curl to his lip. She had met his like a few times
since becoming a governess. He was undressing her with
his eyes and probably doing other things to her with his
mind. She had to concentrate on keeping her hands
steady on her knife and fork.

"Oh. On my way home, ma'am," she said in answer to
a question Mrs. Forbes had asked her. "To my parents'
home for Christmas. Eight miles from here."

Everyone was listening to her. They were sharing stories, commiserating with one another for the unhappy
turn of events that had brought them all to the White
Hart. Only the quiet gentleman seemed to have had no
Christmas destination to lament.

"I am a governess, ma'am," she said when Miss Eugenia Horn asked her the question. "My father is a clergyman." The gentleman of the lazy eyelids—the innkeeper
had addressed him as "my lord"—was still staring at
her, one hand turning his glass of ale.

The conversation turned to the food and a spirited
discussion of whether it was beef or veal or pork they
were eating. There was no unanimous agreement.

A governess, the Marquess of Lytton was thinking,
daughter of a clergyman. A shame. A decided shame.
Governesses were of two kinds, of course. There were
the virtuous governesses, the unassailable ones, and
there were the governesses starved for pleasures of the
sexual variety and quite delightfully voracious in their
appetites when one had finally maneuvered them between bedsheets or into some other satisfactory location. He judged that Miss Pamela Wilder was of the

former variety, though one never knew for sure until one had made careful overtures. Perhaps she would live up to her name.

She was certainly the only possibility at the inn. There had not appeared to be even any chambermaids or barmaids with whom to warm his bed. He had the uncomfortable feeling that he might be facing an alarmingly celibate Christmas if Miss Wilder were saving herself for a future and probably illusory husband. There was the delectable Lady Birkin, of course, but then he had never made a practice of bedding other men's wives or even flirting with them, whether the husband was in tow or not.

Miss Pamela Wilder was the only possibility then. And a distinct possibility she was, provided she was assailable. She was slim, perhaps a little slimmer than he liked his women when there was a choice, but there was a grace about her figure and movements that he found intriguingly feminine and that stirred his loins, though he had drunk only two tankards of the landlord's indescribably bad ale. Her face was lovely—wide-eyed, long-lashed, with a straight nose and a soft, thoroughly kissable mouth. Her hair was smooth and tied in a simple knot at her neck, as one would expect of a governess, but no simplicity of style could dim its blond sheen.

Two nights, probably three, at this inn, he thought, if they were fortunate. She could help Christmas pass with relative comfort, perhaps with enormous comfort. She might console him for the fact that the consummation of his lust with Lady Frazer must be postponed beyond the festive season.

The innkeeper and his wife did not seem to feel it would be diplomatic to discuss private business in private. Mr. Joe Palmer was refilling the gentlemen's glasses with ale when the inevitable new arrivals came

to the inn, looking for a room. Mrs. Letty Palmer came
and stood in the doorway to discuss the matter with him
just as if the room were not full of guests who had their
own conversations to conduct.

"We don't 'ave no room for 'em," Mr. Palmer said
with firm decision. "They'll 'ave to go somewhere else,
Letty."

"There's nowhere else for 'em to go," Mrs. Palmer
said. "We're full with quality and their servants. They
aren't quality, Joe. I thought p'raps the taproom?"

"And 'ave 'em rob us blind as soon as we goes to
bed?" Mr. Palmer said contemptuously, earning a roar
of fury from Mr. Forbes when he slopped ale onto the
cloth beside that gentleman's glass. "We don't 'ave no
room, Letty."

"The woman's in the fambly way," Mrs. Palmer said.
"Looks as if she's about to drop 'er load any day, Joe."

"Oh, dear," Miss Eugenia Horn said, a hand to her
mouth. Such matters were not to be spoken aloud in
genteel and mixed company.

Mr. Palmer put his jug of ale down on the cloth and
set his hands on his hips. "I didn't arsk 'er to get in the
fambly way, now, did I, Letty?" he said. "Am I 'er
keeper? What are they doin' out in this weather anyway
if she's close to 'er time?"

"'Er man's in search of work," Mrs. Palmer said.
"What shall we do with 'em, Joe? We can't turn 'em
away. They'll drowned."

Joe puffed out his cheeks, practicality warring with
compassion.

"I won't 'ave 'em in 'ere, Letty," he said. "There's no
room for 'em and I won't risk 'aving 'em steal all our
valuables. And all these qualities' valuables. They'll 'ave
to move on or stay in the stable. There's an empty stall."

"It's cold in the stable," she said.

"Not with all 'em extra 'orses," the innkeeper said.

"It's there or nowhere, Letty." He picked up his jug and turned determinedly to the quiet gentleman. "They comes 'ere expectin' a body to snap 'is fingers and make new rooms appear." His voice was aggrieved. "And they probly don't 'ave two 'a'pennies to rub together."

The quiet gentleman merely smiled at him. Poor *devils,* the marquess thought, *having to sleep in the stable.* But it was probably preferable to the muddy road. He would not think of it. It was not as if the inn itself offered luxury or even basic comfort. The dinner they had just eaten was disgusting, to put the matter into plain English.

"Poor people," Lady Birkin said quietly to her husband. "Imagine having to sleep in a stable, Henry. And she is with child."

"They will probably be thankful even for that," he said. "They will be out of the rain, at least, and the animals will keep them warm."

She stared at him from her dark eyes with an expression that never failed to turn his insides over. She had a tender heart and carried out numerous works of charity, though she always fretted that she could do so little. She was going to worry now about the two poor travelers who had arrived at safety only to find that there was no room at the inn. He wanted to reach across the table to take her hand. He did not do so, only partly because they were in a public place.

"Will they?" she said. "Be warm, I mean? The landlord was not just saying that? But it will smell in there, Henry, and be dirty."

"There is no alternative," he said, "except for them to move on. They will be all right, Sally. They will be safe and dry, at least. They will be able to keep each other warm."

Her cheeks flushed slightly, and he felt a stabbing of desire for her—the sort of feeling that usually sent him off in search of his mistress and an acceptable outlet for his lust.

"I am going back upstairs," she said, getting to her feet. He walked around the table to pull back her chair. "Are you coming?"

And impose his company on her for the rest of the evening? "I'll escort you up," he said, "and return to the taproom for a while."

She nodded coolly, indifferently.

Her movement was the signal for everyone to get up except the quiet gentleman, who continued to sit and sip on the bad ale. But Lord Birkin did not wait for everyone else. He escorted his wife to their room and looked about it with a frown.

"You will be all right here, Sally?" he asked. "There is not much to do except lie down and sleep, is there?"

"I am tired after the journey," she said.

He looked at the bed. It did not look as if it were going to be comfortable. He was to share it with her that night. For the first time in over three years they were to sleep together, literally sleep together. The thought brought another tightening to his groin. He should have slept with her from the start, he thought. He should have made it the pattern of their marriage. Perhaps the physical side of their marriage and every other aspect of it would have developed more satisfactorily if he had. Perhaps they would not have drifted apart.

He did not know quite why they had done so, or even if *drifted* were the right word. Somehow their marriage had never got properly started. He did not know whose fault it was. Perhaps neither of them was to blame. Perhaps both of them were. Perhaps she had really been as fond of him as he was of her at the beginning. Perhaps they should have put their feelings into words. Perhaps he should not have given in to the fear that she found him dull and his touch distasteful. Perhaps he should not have treated her with sexual restraint, as his father and other men had advised, because she was a lady and ladies were supposed to find sex distasteful. Perhaps he should have taken her with the desire he felt—surely it was not disrespectful to show pleasure in one's wife's body.

Perhaps. Perhaps and perhaps.

"I'll be up later," he told her. "Don't wait up for me." *You may sleep. I'll not be demanding my conjugal rights.* He might as well have said those words too.

She nodded and turned away to the window, waiting for the sound of the door closing behind her and the feeling of emptiness it would bring. And the familiar urge to cry. It was Christmas, and he preferred being downstairs drinking with strangers to being alone with her.

She looked down into wet darkness and shivered. Those poor people—trying to get warm and comfortable in a dirty and drafty stable, trying to sleep there. She wondered if the man loved his wife, if she loved him. If he would hold her close to keep her warm. If he would offer his arm as her pillow. If he would kiss her before she slept so that she would feel warm and loved even in such appalling surroundings.

She wiped impatiently at a tear. She did not normally give in to the urge to weep. She did not usually give in to self-pity.

The Misses Horn were busy agreeing with Mrs. Forbes that indeed it was dreadful that those poor people had to find shelter in a stable on such a wet and chilly night. But what could the husband be thinking of, dragging his poor wife off in search of work when she was in a, ah, delicate situation? There was a deal of embarrassed coughing over the expression of this idea and furtive glances at the gentlemen to make sure that none of them was listening. She would give the man a

piece of her mind if she had a chance, Miss Amelia
Horn declared.

The Marquess of Lytton got to his feet.

"Allow me to escort you to your room, Miss Wilder,"
he said, offering her his arm and noting with approval
that the top of her head reached his chin. She was taller
than she had appeared when she entered the dining
room.

She looked calmly and steadily at him. At least she
was not going to throw a fit of the vapors at the very
idea of being conducted to her bedchamber by a rake.
He wondered if she knew enough about the world to
recognize him as a rake, and if she realized that all
through dinner he had been compensating for the ap-
pallingly unappetizing meal by mentally unclothing her
and putting her to bed—with himself.

"Thank you," she said, and rested her hand on his
arm, a narrow, long-fingered hand. An artist's hand. Either she was a total innocent or she had accepted the
first step of seduction. He hoped for the latter. He
hoped she was not an innocent. It was Christmas, for
God's sake. A man was entitled to his pleasures at that
season of the year above all others.

"This is an annoyance and a discomfort that none of
us could have forseen this morning," he said.

"Yes." Her voice was low and sweet. Seductive,
though whether intentionally so or not he had not yet
decided. "Do you suppose they are dreadfully cold out
there? Was there anything we could have done?"

"The couple in the stable?" he said. "Very little, I suppose, unless one of us were willing to give up his room
and share with someone else."

She looked up into his eyes. Hers had a greenish hue,
though they had looked entirely gray from a farther distance. "I suppose that was a possibility," she said. "Alas,
none of us thought of it."

He had, though he did not say so. Of course, if they did share a room that night, they could hardly go and advertise the fact to the Palmers. The poor devils were doomed to their night in the stables regardless. A governess. A quiet, grave girl instead of Lady Frazer. A poor exchange, perhaps, though not necessarily so. The quiet ones were often the hottest in bed. And this one was definitely stirring his blood.

She knew that he had offered his escort not out of motives of chivalry, but for other reasons. Her employers entertained a great deal. She had learned something about men during the year of her service. She might have had half a dozen lovers during that time. She had never been tempted.

She was tempted now. She was twenty-three years old, eldest daughter of an impoverished clergyman, a governess. In all probability she was headed for a life of drudgery and humiliation and spinsterhood. She did not believe in her heart that Wesley would ever feel himself in a secure enough position to take her as a wife. Or perhaps he used insecurity as an excuse to avoid a final commitment. The hope of marriage with him was just the frail dream with which she sustained her spirits. It was in truth a dreary life to which she looked forward.

And now even the promised brief joy of this Christmas was to be taken away from her. Except that she could spend it with this incredibly attractive man. She did not doubt that he wanted her and that he would waste no time in sounding out her availability. She had even less doubt that he knew well how to give pleasure to a woman. She could have a Christmas of unimagined pleasure, a Christmas to look back upon with nostalgia for the rest of her life. Now, within the next few minutes, without any chance for her mind and her conscience to brood upon the decision, she could discover what it was like to be with a man, what it was like to be desired and pleasured.

She was tempted. The realization amazed her—she did not even know him. She did not know his name. But she was tempted.

She stopped outside her door and looked up at him. "Thank you, sir," she said. "The innkeeper called you 'my lord'?"

"Lytton," he said. "The marquess of. Green eyes, gray—which are they?"

"A little of both, my lord," she said. *A marquess. Oh, goodness.* He was tall, broad-shouldered. "Thank you," she said again.

He opened the door for her, but when she stepped inside he followed her in and closed the door behind his back. She had been expecting it, she realized. And she realized at the same instant that this was the moment of decision. She did not have any time in which to think, not even a minute.

"It is likely to be a lonely Christmas," he said. "You away from your family, me from my friends."

"Yes." One of his hands had come up so that he could touch her cheek with light fingertips. She felt his touch all the way to her toes. His eyes—yes, they were blue— were keen beneath the lazy lids. She looked into them.

"Perhaps," he said, "we can make it less lonely together."

"Yes." But no sound came out with the word.

She had been kissed before—twice, both times by Wesley. But the experience had not prepared her at all for the Marquess of Lytton's kiss. It was not that it was hard or demanding. Quite the opposite, in fact. His lips rested as lightly against hers as his fingertips had against her cheek a few moments before. But they were parted, warm and moist, and they moved over hers, feeling them, caressing them, softening them, even licking at them. When his hands came to her waist to bring her against him, she allowed herself to be embraced and rested her body against his—against this hard, muscled, warm male.

He felt wonderful. He smelled wonderful. And he was doing wonderful things to her body, though his hands were still at her waist and his lips still light on hers. Then his hands moved up to her breasts and she knew that now—now, not one moment later—was the point of no return. Now she must stop it or move on to new experiences, to a new state of being.

She would be a fallen woman.

She was incredibly sweet. He had never known innocence, had never imagined how arousing it could be. She was yielding without being in any way aggressive. She held still to his touch without being in any way cringing. She was his, he knew, with a little skill and a little care. And yet he knew equally that she was an innocent despite having allowed him inside her room and having allowed his kiss without any hesitation or coyness.

Her waist was soft, warm, small, with the promise of feminine hips below. He slid his hands up to her breasts. They were not large, but they were firm and soft all at the same time. Her nipples, he found when he tested them with his thumbs, were already peaked. She was his, he knew, despite the almost imperceptible stiffening he felt when his hands moved. He felt her indecision, but knew what that decision would be. He raised his head and looked down at her. She gazed back, wide-eyed.

"I had better say good night," he said, "before I go too far and get my face slapped. Yes, perhaps we can make each other less lonely for Christmas, Miss Wilder. I look forward to conversing with you tomorrow."

"Yes," she said, but he could not tell from her expression if she had been fooled. Did she really believe that he had meant nothing more than pleasant conversation and almost chaste good-night kisses as the means of soothing their loneliness at Christmas? Did she believe that he had not entered this room to bed her?

"Good night," he said, inclining his head to her and letting himself out of her room. Fortunately there was no one to witness his leaving it.

Fool! he thought, his lip curling into a cynical half smile. He had been issued the sort of invitation he had never before in his life refused, and yet he had done just that. He had wanted her. He still did. And yet he had put her from him and pretended that he had meant nothing more than a good-night kiss. He did not believe he had ever kissed a woman good night and not expected more.

She would have had him, too. And she would have been sweet despite her innocence and inexperience. Of course, there would have been her virginity to take—he would wager his fortune that she was a virgin. Perhaps that had been the problem, he thought, shrugging and turning in the direction of the staircase and the taproom. The thought of taking someone's virginity frankly terrified him. He might be a rake, but he was not a corrupter of innocence. Especially when the girl was lonely and unhappy and incapable of making a rational decision.

All the men were in the taproom, though it seemed likely that they were seeking out one another's company rather than their landlord's ale, the marquess thought, grimacing as he tasted it again. Christmas would be beginning now at the Whittakers', with all its rich and tasty foods and drinks and with all its congenial company. He pictured Lady Frazer and put the image from his mind with a mental sigh.

Lord Birkin did not stay long. He could not concentrate on the conversation. It was true that she did not seem to find his company of any interest, and equally true that she must be horrified at the thought of sharing a bed with him all night. But even so it seemed somehow wrong to sit belowstairs, making conversation with the other gentlemen guests while she was forced to be alone in their small and shabby bedchamber.

A candle still burned in their room, though she was lying far to one side of the bed with her eyes closed. He could not tell if she slept or not. He undressed, wondering if she would open her eyes, finding it strange to think that they had never allowed themselves to become familiar with each other physically. They had never seen each other unclothed. He wished again that it were possible to go back to the beginning of their marriage. He would do so many things differently. Now it seemed too late. How did one change things when patterns had been set and habits had become ingrained?

He blew out the candle and climbed into bed, keeping close to the edge. But it was impossible to sleep and impossible to believe that she slept. She was too still, too quiet. He almost laughed out loud. They had been married for longer than three years and yet were behaving like a couple of strangers thrown together in embarrassing proximity. But he did not laugh; he was not really amused.

"Sally?" He spoke softly and reached out a hand to touch her arm.

"Yes?"

But what was there to say when one had been married to a woman for so long and had never spoken from the heart? Patterns could not so easily be broken. Instead of speaking he moved closer and began the familiar and dispassionate ritual of raising her nightgown and positioning himself on top of her.

All their actions, hers and his, were as they always were. There were never variations. She allowed him to spread her legs, though she did not do it for him, and she lifted herself slightly for his hands to slide beneath. He put himself firmly inside her, settled his face in her hair, felt her hands come to his shoulders, and worked in her with firm, rhythmic strokes until his seed sprang. He was always careful not to indulge himself by prolonging the intercourse. She never gave the slightest sign of either pleasure or distaste. She was a dutiful wife.

And yet he wondered, after he had disengaged himself from her and settled at her side, why he carried out the ritual at all, since it brought neither of them any great pleasure and was not performed frequently enough for there to be any realistic expectation that she would conceive. Why did he do it at all when his desires and energies could be worked out on women who were well paid to suffer the indignity?

Perhaps because he needed her? Because he loved her? But of what use was his love when he had never been able to tell her and when he had never taken the opportunity to cultivate her love at the beginning, when she had perhaps been fond of him?

Lady Birkin lay still, willing sleep to come. Were they reasonably warm and comfortable in the stable? she wondered. Did the man care for his wife? Was she lying in his arms? Was he murmuring words of love to her to put her to sleep? Did her pregnancy bring her discomfort? What did it feel like to be heavy with child—with one's husband's child? She burrowed her head into the hard pillow, imagining as she often did at night to put herself to sleep that it was an arm, that there was a warm chest against her forehead and the steady beat of a heart against her ear. Her hand, moving up to pull the pillow against her face, brushed a real arm and moved hastily away from it.

Breakfast was late. It was not that the night before had been busy and exciting enough to necessitate their sleeping on in the morning. And it was certainly not that the beds were comfortable enough or the rooms warm and cozy enough to invite late sleeping. It was more, perhaps, lethargy, and the knowledge that there was not a great deal to get up for. Even if the rain had stopped, travel would have been impossible. But the rain had not stopped. Each guest awoke to the sound of it beating against the windows, only marginally lighter than it had been the day before.

And so breakfast was late. When the guests emerged from their rooms and gathered in the dining room, it seemed that only the quiet gentleman had been sitting there for some time, patiently awaiting the arrival of his meal.

Greasy eggs and burned toast accompanied complaints about other matters. Eugenia was sure to have taken a chill, Miss Amelia Horn declared, having been forced to sleep between damp sheets. Miss Eugenia Horn flushed at the indecorous mention of sleep and sheets in the hearing of gentlemen. Colonel Forbes complained about the lumps in his bed and swore there were coals in the mattress. Mrs. Forbes nodded her agreement. The Marquess of Lytton lamented the fact that the coal fire in his room had been allowed to die a natural death the night before and had not been resuscitated in the morning. Lord Birkin wondered if they would be expected to make up their own beds. Lady Birkin declared that the ladies could not possibly be expected to sit in their rooms all day long. In the absence of any private parlors, the gentlemen must expect their company in the taproom and the dining room. The other ladies agreed. Even Pamela Wilder nodded her head.

"That is the most sensible suggestion anyone has made yet this morning," the Marquess of Lytton said, nodding his approval to Lady Birkin and fixing his eyes on Pamela.

The innkeeper's wife was pouring muddy coffee for those foolish enough or bored enough to require a second cup. The innkeeper appeared in the doorway.

"You'd best come, Letty," he said. "I told yer we should 'ave nothing to do with 'em. Now look at what's gone and 'appened."

"What 'as 'appened?" The coffee urn paused over the quiet gentleman's cup as Mrs. Palmer looked up at her husband. "'Ave they gone and stole an 'orse, Joe?"

"I wish they 'ad," Mr. Palmer said fervently. "I wish they 'ad, Letty. But no such luck. 'E's in the taproom." He jerked a thumb over his shoulder. "She's 'aving 'er pains. In our stable, mind."

"Oh, Lord love us," Mrs. Palmer said. The quiet gentleman was still waiting for his coffee. "She can't 'ave it there, Joe. Who ever 'eard of anyone 'aving a baby in a stable?"

The quiet gentleman smiled and appeared to resign himself to going without his coffee.

"Oh." Lady Birkin was on her feet. "The poor woman. How dreadful." She looked at her husband in some distress. "She must be taken extra blankets."

"There ain't no extra blankets," Mrs. Palmer said tartly. "We 'ave a full 'ouse, my lady."

Lady Birkin looked appealingly at her husband. "Then she must have the blankets from our bed," she said. "We will manage without, won't we, Henry?" She reached out a hand to him and he took it.

"Perhaps one from your bed and one from ours, Lady Birkin," Mrs. Forbes said. "Then we will both have something left."

"I have a shawl," Miss Eugenia Horn said. "A warm woolen one that I knitted myself. I shall send it out. Perhaps it will do for wrapping the baby when it is, ah, born." She flushed.

"And I will send out my smelling salts," Miss Amelia Horn said. "The poor woman will probably need them."

"I have a room," Pamela said quietly. "She must be carried up there."

"We don't 'ave no other room to put you in, miss," Mrs. Palmer said.

"And I won't 'ave no one in the taproom," Mr. Palmer added firmly.

"Then I shall sleep in the stable tonight," Pamela said.

The Marquess of Lytton got to his feet. "Is the husband large and strong?" he asked the innkeeper. "If not, I shall carry the woman in from the stable myself. To *my* room. Miss Wilder may keep hers. And you will, my good man, have someone in the taproom. Tonight. Me."

Mr. Palmer did not argue.

"I'll lend a hand," Lord Birkin said, and the two gentlemen left the room together, followed by Mr. Palmer.

"Perhaps," Lady Birkin said, looking at the innkeeper's wife, who appeared to have been struck with paralysis, "you should have coals sent up to Lord Lytton's room to warm it."

"Lord love us," Mrs. Palmer said, "I 'ave breakfast to clear away, my lady, and dishes to wash before I gets to the rooms."

Colonel Forbes puffed to his feet. "I have never heard the like," he said. "I never have. An inn with no help. Where are the coals, ma'am? I shall carry some up myself."

Mrs. Forbes nodded her approval as her husband strode from the room.

"I shall go up and get the bed ready," Pamela said, "if you will tell me which room is Lord Lytton's, ma'am." She flushed rosily.

"That would be improper, dear," Miss Eugenia Horn said. "Though, of course, it is not his lordship's room any longer, is it? I shall come with you nevertheless."

"Thank you," Pamela said.

"And I shall go and fetch your shawl, Eugenia, and my smelling salts," Miss Amelia Horn said.

"You will send for a midwife?" Lady Birkin said to Mrs. Palmer.

"Oh, Lord, my lady," Mrs. Palmer said. "There is no midwife for five miles, and she wouldn't come 'ere anyhow for no woman what can't pay as like as not."

"I see," Lady Birkin said. "So we are on our own. Have you ever assisted at a birth, Mrs. Palmer?"

The woman's eyes widened. "Not me, my lady," she said. "Nor never 'ad none of my own neither."

Lady Birkin's eyes moved past the Misses Horn and Pamela to Mrs. Forbes. "Ma'am?" she said hopefully.

Mrs. Forbes ceased her nodding in order to shake her head. "I was forty when I married Colonel Forbes," she said. "There was no issue of our marriage."

"Oh," Lady Birkin said. She looked around at the other ladies rather helplessly. "Then I suppose we will have to proceed according to common sense. Will it be enough, I wonder?"

Pamela smiled at her ruefully and left the dining room so that Lord Lytton's former room would be ready by the time he carried up the woman from the stable. Pamela had been surprised by his offer both to give up his room and to carry the woman up to it. She would not have expected compassion of him.

The quiet gentleman picked up the urn, which Mrs. Palmer had abandoned on his table, and poured himself a second cup of coffee.

Lisa Curtis's baby did not come quickly. It was her first and it was large and it appeared determined both to take its time in coming into the world and to give its mother as much grief as possible while doing so. Tom Suffield, the father, was beside himself with anxiety and was no help to anyone. Big, strapping young man as he was, he made no objection to the marquess's carrying his woman into the inn and up the stairs, Lord Birkin hovering close to share the load if necessary. Tom was rather incoherent, accounting perhaps for his lack of wisdom in admitting to his unwed state.

"We was going to get married," he said, hurrying along behind the two gentlemen while Lisa moaned, having had the misfortune to suffer a contraction after the marquess had picked her up. "But we couldn't afford to."

And yet, Lord Lytton thought, wincing at the girl's obvious agony, they could afford a child. An unfair judgment, perhaps. Even the poor were entitled to their pleasures, and children had a habit of not waiting for a convenient moment to get themselves conceived.

A strange scene greeted them at the entrance to his former inn room—had he really given it up in a chivalrous gesture to counter Miss Wilder's brave offer to sleep in the stable? Miss Amelia Horn was hovering at one side of the doorway, a woolen shawl of hideous and multicolored stripes clutched in one hand and a vinaigrette in the other. Mrs. Forbes was hovering and nodding at the other side. The room itself was crowded. He had not realized that it was large enough to accommodate so many persons.

Colonel Forbes was kneeling before the grate, blowing on some freshly laid coals and coaxing a fire into life. Both his hands and his face were liberally daubed with coal dust. He was looking as angry and out of sorts as he always did. Miss Eugenia Horn was at the window, closing the curtains to keep out some draft and a great deal of gloom. Lady Birkin was in the act of setting down a large bowl of steaming water on the washstand. Pamela Wilder was bent over the tidied bed, plumping up lumpy pillows and turning back the sheets to receive its new occupant. Lord Lytton, despite the weight of his burden, which he had just carried from the stable into the inn and up the stairs, pursed his lips at the sight of a slim but well-rounded derriere nicely outlined against the wool of her dress.

What a fool and an idiot he had been the night before! He might by now be well familiar with the feel of that derriere. She turned and smiled warmly at the woman in his arms. He found himself wishing that her eyes were focused a little higher.

"The bed is ready for you," she said. "In a moment we will have you comfortable and warm. The fire will be giving off some heat soon. How are you feeling?"

"Oh, thank you," Lisa said, her voice weak and weary as the marquess set her gently down. "Where's Tom?"

"Here I am, Leez," the young man said from the doorway. His face was chalky white. "How are you?"

"It's so wonderfully warm in here," the girl said plaintively, but then she gasped and clasped a hand over her swollen abdomen. She opened her mouth and panted loudly, moaning with each outward breath so that all the occupants of the room froze.

"Who is in charge?" the marquess asked when it appeared that the pain was subsiding again. He had felt his own color draining away. "Who is going to deliver the child?"

The one Miss Horn, he noticed, had disappeared from the doorway, while the other had turned firmly to face the curtained window. Obviously not them, and obviously not Miss Wilder. He must take her downstairs, away from there. But it was she who answered him.

"There is no one with any experience," she said. She flushed. "And no one who has given birth. We will have to do the best we can."

Hell, he thought. *Hell and damnation! No one with any experience. A thousand devils!*

"Sally," Lord Birkin said, "let me take you back to our room. Mrs. Palmer is doubtless the best qualified to cope."

"Mrs. Palmer," she said, her eyes flashing briefly at him, "has the breakfast to clear away and the dishes to wash and the rooms to see to. I'll stay here, Henry." She turned to the girl, who was sitting awkwardly on the side of the bed, and her expression softened. "The stable must have been dreadfully dirty," she said. "I have brought up some warm water. I will help you wash yourself and change into something clean. I have a loose-fitting nightgown that I believe will fit you." She looked up. "Will you fetch it, Henry? It is the one with the lace at the throat and cuffs."

He looked at her, speechless. She, the Baroness Birkin, was going to wash a young girl of low birth who at present smelled of rankly uncleaned stable? She was going to give the girl one of her costly nightgowns? But yes, of course she was going to. It was just like Sally to do such things, and with such kindness in her face. He turned to leave the room.

"I'll help you, my lady," Pamela said. She stooped over the girl on the bed. "Here, I'll help you off with your dress once the gentlemen have withdrawn. What is your name?"

"Lisa," the girl said. "Lisa Curtis, miss."

"We will make you comfortable as soon as we possibly can, Lisa," Pamela said.

Miss Eugenia Horn coughed. "You must come with me away from this room, my dear Miss Wilder," she said. "It is not fitting that we be here. We will leave Lisa to the care of Lady Birkin and Mrs. Forbes, who are married ladies."

The Marquess of Lytton watched Pamela's face with keen interest from beneath drooped eyelids. She smiled. "I grew up at a rectory, ma'am," she said. "I learned at an early age to help my fellow human beings under even the most difficult of circumstances if my assistance could be of some value."

It was a do-gooder sentiment that might have made him want to vomit, the marquess thought, if it had not been uttered so matter-of-factly and if her tone had not been so totally devoid of piety and sentiment.

"I think it will survive without your further help, Forbes," the marquess said, looking critically at the crackling fire. "Let us see if our landlord can supply us with some of that superior ale we had last night, shall we? Join us, Suffield."

He was rewarded with a grateful smile from Pamela Wilder. Lady Birkin was squeezing out a cloth over the bowl of water and rubbing soap on it. Miss Eugenia Horn was preparing to leave the room and sights so unbecoming to maiden eyes.

It was strange, perhaps, that for the rest of the day all the guests at the White Hart Inn could not keep their minds away from the room upstairs in which a girl of a social class far beneath their own, and a girl moreover who was about to bear a bastard child, labored painfully though relatively quietly. Her moans could be heard only when one of them went upstairs to his own room.

"They should have stayed at home," Colonel Forbes said gruffly. "Damn fool thing to be wandering about the countryside at this time of year and with the girl in this condition."

"Perhaps they could not afford to stay at home," Lord Birkin said.

Tom could not answer for himself. He had returned to the stable despite the offer of ale and a share of the fire in the taproom. He was pacing.

"The poor child," Miss Eugenia Horn said, having decided that it was unexceptionable to talk about the child, provided she ignored all reference to its birth. She was sitting in the taproom, knitting a pair of baby boots. "One cannot help but wonder what will become of it."

"Tom will doubtless find employment and make an honest woman of Lisa, and they and the child will live happily ever after," the marquess said.

Mrs. Forbes nodded her agreement.

"It would be comforting to think so," Lord Birkin said.

Mrs. Palmer, looking harried, was emerging from the kitchen, where she had given the guests' servants their breakfast and washed the dishes, and was making her way upstairs to tidy rooms.

They were all increasingly aware as the day dragged on that it was Christmas Eve and that they were beginning to live through the strangest Christmas they had ever experienced.

"We might decorate the inn with some greenery," Miss Amelia Horn said at one point, "but who would be foolhardy enough to go outside to gather any? Besides, even if some were brought inside, it would be dripping wet."

"As far as I am concerned," Colonel Forbes said, "there is enough rain outside. We do not need to admit any to the indoors." No one argued with him.

They all began to think of what they would have been doing on that day if only they had had the fortune or wisdom to travel earlier and had reached their destinations. But the images of elegant and comfortable homes and of relatives and friends and all the sights and sounds and smells of Christmas did not bear dwelling upon.

Lord Birkin went back upstairs with his wife when she appeared briefly early in the afternoon to fetch more water from the kitchen. She had reported to all the gathered guests that there was no further progress upstairs. Poor Lisa was suffering cruelly, but appeared no nearer to being delivered than she had done that morning.

Lord Birkin took his wife by the arm when they reached the top of the stairs and steered her past Lisa's room and into their own.

"Sally," he said, "you are going to tire yourself out. Do you not think you have done enough? Should it not be Mrs. Palmer's turn? Or Mrs. Forbes's?"

She sat down on the edge of the bed and he seated himself beside her.

"Mrs. Palmer is frightened by the very thought of becoming involved," she said. "I can tell. That is why she is keeping so busy with other things. And Mrs. Forbes is quite inept. Well-meaning but inept. The few times she has come inside the room she has stood close to the door and nodded sweetly and clearly not known what she should do."

"And you *do* know?" he said.

She smiled. "Some things come by instinct," she said. "Don't worry about me, Henry."

"But I do worry," he said, taking her hand and holding it in both of his. "And I blame myself for not bringing you from London sooner than I did. This is Christmas Eve, Sally. Have you realized that? You should be with Lady Middleton and all your friends and acquaintances now. You should be in comfort. The partying should have begun—the feasting and caroling and dancing. Instead we are stuck here. Not only stuck, but somehow involved with a girl who is giving birth. This is no Christmas for you."

"Or for you," she said. "It really does not seem like Christmas at all, does it? But we cannot do anything about it. Here we are and here Lisa is. I must return to her."

"What is going to happen when it comes time for her to deliver?" he asked.

He had struck a nerve. There was fear in her eyes for a brief unguarded moment. "We will jump that hurdle when we come to it," she said.

"You are afraid, Sally?" he asked.

"No, of course not," she said briskly. But then she looked down at their clasped hands and nodded quickly. Her voice was breathless when she spoke again. "I am afraid that in my ignorance I will cause her death or the baby's."

He released her hand, set an arm about her shoulders, and drew her toward him. She sagged against him in grateful surprise and set her head on his shoulder.

"Without you and Miss Wilder," he said, "she would be alone in the stable with the hysterical Tom. You are being very good to her, Sally. You must remember that, whatever happens. I wish I could take you away from here. I wish I had not got you into this predicament."

She nestled her head on his shoulder and felt wonderfully comforted. If this had not happened, they would be caught up in the gaiety of Christmas at this very moment, surrounded by friends. Except that they would not be together. As like as not, he would be off somewhere with some of the other gentlemen, playing billiards, probably, since the weather would not permit shooting.

"Don't blame yourself," she said. "Besides, it is not so very bad, is it? If we were not here, I fear that Pamela would have to cope alone. That would be too heavy a burden on her shoulders. She is wonderful, Henry. So calm and brave, so kind to Lisa. Just as if she knew exactly what she was doing."

"You sound like two of a kind, then," he said.

She looked up at him in further surprise. His face was very close. "Do you think so?" she said. "What a lovely thing to say—and very reassuring. I feel quite inadequate, you see."

He dipped his head and kissed her—swiftly and firmly and almost fiercely. And then raised his head and looked into her eyes as she nestled her head against his shoulder again. He very rarely kissed her. She ached with a sudden longing and put it from her.

"I must go back," she said. "Pamela will be alone with Lisa."

"If there is anything I can do," he said, "call me. Will you?"

Her eyes sparkled with amusement suddenly. "You will spend the rest of the day in fear and trembling that perhaps I will take you at your word," she said.

He chuckled, and she realized how rarely he did so these days. She had almost forgotten that it was his smile and the way his eyes crinkled at the corners when he laughed that had first attracted her to him. "You are probably right," he said.

He escorted her back to Lisa's room, though he did not go inside with her. She felt refreshed, almost as if she had lain down and slept for a few hours. Pamela was leaning over a moaning Lisa, dabbing at her brow with a cool, damp cloth. She looked around at Lady Birkin.

"Two minutes," she said. "The pains have been two minutes apart for more than an hour now. It must be close, don't you think, Sally?"

But it was not really close at all. There were several more hours of closely paced contractions and pain to live through.

Everyone moved from the taproom into the dining room for afternoon tea, just so that they might have a welcome change of scenery, Colonel Forbes said with a short bark of laughter. Lord Birkin, strolling to the window, announced that the rain appeared to be easing and that he hesitated to say it aloud but the western horizon looked almost bright.

"But it is happening too late, my lord," Miss Amelia Horn said. "Christmas has been ruined already."

Mrs. Forbes sighed and nodded her agreement.

And yet they were all making an effort to put aside their own personal disappointments over a lost Christmas. They were all thinking of the baby who was about to be born and of the child's destitute parents. Miss Eugenia Horn was still busy knitting baby boots. Mrs. Forbes, having recalled that she had no fewer than eight flannel nightgowns in her trunk, flannel being the only sensible fabric to be worn during winter nights, declared that she did not need nearly as many. She was cutting up four of them into squares and hemming them so that the baby would have warm and comfortable nappies to wear. Miss Amelia Horn was cutting up a fifth to make into small nightshirts. She had already painstakingly unpicked the lace from one of her favorite caps to trim the tiny garments.

Even the gentlemen were not unaffected by the impending event. Colonel Forbes was thinking of a certain shirt of which he had never been overly fond. It would surely fit Tom and keep him warm too. By good fortune the garment was in the trunk upstairs—for the simple reason that it was one of his wife's favorites. Lord Birkin thought of the staff at his London house and on his country estate. There really was no room for an extra worker. His wife had already foisted some strays upon him. He was definitely overstaffed. Perhaps some banknotes would help, though giving money in charity always seemed rather too easy. The Marquess of Lytton turned a gold signet ring on his little finger. It was no heirloom. He had bought it himself in Madrid. But it had some sentimental value. Not that he was a sentimentalist, of course. He drew it slowly from his finger and dropped it into a pocket. Sold or pawned, it would provide a family of three with a goodly number of meals. The quiet gentleman withdrew to the stable after tea to stretch his legs and breathe some fresh air into his lungs.

Pamela Wilder appeared in the dining room doorway

when tea was over and immediately became the focus of attention. But she could give no news other than that Lisa was very tired and finding it harder to bear the pains. Miss Wilder looked tired too, the Marquess of Lytton thought, gazing at her pale and lovely face and her rather untidy hair. Lady Birkin had sent her downstairs for a half-hour break, having had one herself earlier.

"The tea is cold, dear," Miss Eugenia Horn said. "Let me get you a fresh pot. There is no point in ringing for service. One might wait all day and all night too if one did that."

But Pamela would not hear of anyone else's waiting on her. She went to the kitchen herself. The marquess was sitting in the taproom when she came out again, carrying a tray.

"Come and sit down," he said, indicating the chair next to his own, between him and the fire, which he had just built up himself. "It is quieter in here."

She hesitated, but he got to his feet and took the tray from her hands. She sighed as she sat down and then looked at him in some surprise as he picked up the teapot and poured her cup of tea.

"Is she going to deliver?" he asked. "Or is there some complication?"

He liked watching her blush. Color added vibrancy to her face. "I hope not," she said. "Oh, I do hope not."

"Do you have any idea what to do?" he asked. "Or does Lady Birkin?"

"No," she said, and she closed her eyes briefly. "None at all. We can only hope that nature will take care of itself."

Oh, Lord. There was a faint buzzing in his head.

"You are a clergyman's daughter," he said. "You were never involved with such, er, acts of nature?"

"No," she said. "My mother made sure that I had a very proper upbringing. I wish I knew more." She looked down at her hands. "I hope she does not die. Or the baby. I will always blame myself if they die."

A thousand hells and a million damnations! He reached out and took one of her hands in his. "If they die—and probably they will not," he said, "they will die in a warm and reasonably comfortable inn room instead of in a stable, and tended by two ladies who have given them unfailingly diligent and gentle care instead of by a hysterical boy."

She smiled at him rather wanly. "You are kind," she said.

He looked down at her hand and spread her fingers along his. "You have artists' hands," he said. "You must play the pianoforte. Do you?"

"Whenever I can." She looked wistful. "We always had a pianoforte at the rectory. I played it constantly, even when I should have been doing other things. I was often scolded."

"But there is no instrument at your place of employment?" he asked.

"Oh, yes," she said. "A beautiful one with the loveliest tone I have ever heard. I give my pupil lessons and try to steal a few minutes for myself whenever I can."

He felt angry suddenly. "They have to be stolen?" he asked. "They are not granted?"

She smiled. "Mrs. Raven, my employer, suffers from migraine headaches," she said. "She cannot stand the sound of the pianoforte."

His jaw tightened. "It is not a good life, is it," he said, "being a governess?"

She stiffened and withdrew her hand from his. She reached out to pick up her cup and raised it to her lips. "It is a living, my lord," she said, "and a reasonably comfortable one. There are many women, and men too, far worse off than I. We cannot all choose the life we would live. You do not need to pity me."

He looked at her broodingly. Her hand was shaking slightly, though she drank determinedly on. Did he pity her? He was not in the habit of pitying other mortals. No, he did not think it was pity. It was more admiration for her and anger against employers who evidently did not appreciate her. It was more the desire to protect her and see happiness replace the quiet discipline in her face—the desire to give her a pianoforte for Christmas, all wrapped about with red ribbons. His lip curled in self-derision. Was this unspeakably dull Christmas making him sentimental over a governess?

"What would you be doing now," he asked her, "if it had not rained?"

She set her cup down in its saucer and smiled down into it, her eyes dreamy. "Decorating the house with the children," she said. "Helping my mother and our cook with the baking. Finishing making gifts. Delivering baskets to the poor. Helping my father arrange the Nativity scene in the church. Getting ready to go caroling. Looking forward to the church service. Running around in circles wishing I could divide myself into about twelve pieces. Christmas is always very busy and very special at home. The coming of Christ—it is a wonderful festival."

He took her hand again, almost absently, and smoothed his fingers over hers. He was the Marquess of Lytton, she reminded herself, and she a mere clergyman's daughter and a governess. Last night he had held her and kissed her, and she had almost gone to bed with him. She was still not sure if she would have allowed the ultimate intimacy or if she would have drawn back at the last moment. But he had drawn back, and now they were sitting together in the taproom, talking, her hand in his. This was a strange, unreal Christmas.

"What would *you* be doing?" she asked. "If it had not rained, I mean."

He raised his gaze from their hands, and she was struck again by the keenness of his blue eyes beneath the lazy lids. They caused a strange somersaulting feeling in her stomach. "Stuffing myself with rich foods," he said. "Getting myself inebriated. Preparing to make merry and to drink even more. Flirting with a lady I have had my eye on for some time past and wondering if I would be spending tonight with her or if she would keep me waiting until tomorrow night." One corner of his mouth lifted in an expression that was not quite a smile. "A wonderful way to celebrate the coming of Christ, would you not agree?"

Pamela found herself wondering irrelevantly what the lady looked like. "I cannot judge," she said. "We all have our own way of enjoying ourselves."

"Yours is a large family?" he asked.

"I have three brothers and four sisters," she said, "all younger than myself. It is a very noisy household and frequently an untidy one, I'm afraid."

"I envy you," he said. "I have no one except a few aunts and uncles and cousins with whom I have never been close." He raised one hand and touched the back of a finger to her cheek. "I am sorry you have not been able to get home for Christmas."

"I believe that everything that happens does so for a purpose," she said. "Perhaps I was meant to be trapped here for Lisa's sake."

"And perhaps I was meant to be trapped here with you for . . . for what purpose?" he asked.

His eyes were looking very intently into hers. She could not withdraw her own. "I don't know," she said.

"Perhaps," he said, and his voice was very soft, "to discover that innocence can be more enticing than experience. And far more warming to the heart."

He raised her hand while she watched him with widening eyes and warming cheeks, and set his lips to it.

"I must be going back upstairs," she said.

"Yes." He lowered her hand. "You must."

But the next moment they were both on their feet. Lady Birkin had appeared at the top of the stairs. She was looking distraught and was beckoning urgently.

"Pamela," she called. "Oh, thank heaven you are there. Something is happening. Oh, please come." And she turned and hurried out of sight again.

Pamela could feel the color draining from her face as she rushed across the room toward the staircase. She scarcely heard the quite improper expletive that was the marquess's sole comment.

"Bloody hell!" he said.

The bed was soaked. Fortunately Mrs. Palmer had given them a pile of old rags and told them to spread some over the sheets. There was something about waters breaking, she had mumbled before scurrying away about some real or imagined chore. Pamela and Lady Birkin stripped away the wet rags and replaced them with dry ones. But Lisa was in severe distress. She was panting loudly and thrashing about on the bed. Her moans were threatening to turn into screams.

"Hot water," Lady Birkin said, trying to keep her voice calm. "I have heard that hot water is needed."

"Lisa," Pamela had a cool cloth to the girl's brow. "What may we do for you? How may we help?"

But there was a feeling of dreadful helplessness, an almost overpowering urge to become hysterical or simply to rush from the room.

And then the door opened. Both Lady Birkin and Pamela looked in some surprise at the Marquess of Lytton, who stood in the doorway, his face pale. Perhaps they would have felt consternation too, if they had not been feeling so frightened and helpless.

"I think I can help," he surprised them both by saying.

And he grimaced and turned even paler as Lisa began to moan and thrash again. He strode over to the bed. "I think she should be pushing," he said. "The pain will subside soon, will it not? Next time we must have her in position and she must push down. Perhaps the two of you can help her by lifting her shoulders as she pushes."

The two ladies merely stared at him. Lisa screamed.

"The Peninsula," he said. "I was a cavalry officer. There was a peasant woman. There was a surgeon too, but he had just been shot through the right hand. He instructed a private soldier and me. The private held her and I delivered."

Lisa was quiet again, and the marquess turned grimly back to the bed. "Raise your knees," he told her, "and brace your feet wide apart on the bed. The next time the pain comes, I want you to bear down against it with all your strength. This little fellow wants to come out. Do you understand me?"

Through the fog of weakness and pain, the girl seemed to turn instinctively to the note of authority and assurance in his voice. She looked up at him and nodded, positioning herself according to his instructions. And then the fright came back into her eyes and she began to pant again.

"Now!" he commanded, and he pushed his hands forward against her knees through the sheet that still covered her to the waist while Lady Birkin and Pamela, one on each side of her, lifted her shoulders from the bed and pushed forward. Lisa drew a giant breath and bore down with all her might, pausing only to gasp in more air before the pain subsided again.

"Send down for hot water," Lord Lytton said while Lisa relaxed for a few moments. "Go and give the instruction yourself, Pamela, but come right back. Someone else can bring it. But wait a moment. She needs us again."

He was going to forget something, he thought as he pushed upward on the girl's knees. He would forget something and either she or the child was going to bleed to death. Or there was going to be a complication, as there had not been with the Spanish peasant girl. This girl was already weak from a long and hard labor. Soon—perhaps after the next contraction—he was going to have to take a look and pray fervently that it was the child's head he would see. He could recall the surgeon's talking about breech births, though he had given no details.

And then between contractions, as he was about to draw the sheet back, there was a quiet voice from the doorway. It almost did not register on his mind, but he looked over his shoulder. He had not been mistaken. The quiet gentleman was standing there.

"I am a physician," he repeated. "I will be happy to deliver the child and tend the mother."

Anger was the Marquess of Lytton's first reaction. "You are a physician," he said. "Why the hell have you waited this long to admit the fact? Do you realize what terrors your silence has caused Lady Birkin and Miss Wilder in the course of the day?"

"And you too, my lord?" The quiet gentleman was smiling. He had strolled into the room and taken one of Lisa's limp hands in his. He spoke very gently. "It will soon be over, my dear, I promise. Then the joy you will have in your child will make you forget all this."

She looked calmly back at him. There was even a suggestion of a smile in her eyes.

But the marquess was not mollified. Relief—overwhelming, knee-weakening relief—was whipping his anger into fury. "What the hell do you mean," he said, "putting us through all this?" He remembered too late the presence in the room of three women, two of them gently born.

The quiet gentleman smiled and touched a cool hand to Lisa's brow as she began to gasp again. "How could I spoil a Christmas that had promised to be so dismal for everyone?" he asked, and he moved to draw the sheet down over the girl's knees. "The blood will probably return to your head faster, my lord, if you remove yourself. The ladies will assist me. Have some hot water brought up to us, if you will be so good."

Lord Lytton removed himself, frowning over the physician's strange answer to his question. Lady Birkin and Pamela, moving back to their posts, puzzled over it too. What had he meant? Christmas might have been dismal but was not? Because of what was happening?

"Set an arm each about her back to support her as you lift her," the quiet gentleman said. "Your labors too, will soon be at an end, ladies, and you will experience all the wonder of being present at a birth. Ah. I can see the head, my dear. With plenty of dark hair."

"Ohhh!" Lisa was almost crying with excitement and exhaustion and pain.

But all sense of panic had gone from the room. Both Lady Birkin and Pamela were aware of that as the physician went quietly and efficiently about his work and Lisa responded to his gentleness. Her son was born, large and healthy and perfect—and crying lustily—early in the evening. They were all crying, in fact. All except the doctor, who smiled sweetly at each of them in turn and made them feel as if it were not at all the most foolish thing in the world to cry just because one more mouth to be fed had been born into it.

Lisa was exhausted and could scarcely raise her arms to Tom when he came into the room several minutes later, wide-eyed and awed, while Lady Birkin was washing the baby and Pamela was disposing of bloodstained rags. Lisa accepted the baby from Lady Birkin and looked up with shining eyes into Tom's face while he reached out one trembling finger to touch his son. But she had no energy left.

"I'll take him," Lady Birkin said, "while you get some sleep, Lisa. You have earned it."

"Thank you, mum." Lisa looked up at her wearily. "I'll always remember you, mum, and the other lady." Her eyes found Pamela and smiled. "Thank you, miss."

And so Lady Birkin found herself holding the child and feeling a welling of happiness and tenderness and . . . and longing. *Ah, how wonderful,* she thought. How very wonderful. She acted from instinct. She must find Henry. She must show him. Oh, if only the child were hers. Theirs.

Word had spread. Everyone was hovering in the hallway outside Lisa's room. The birth of a little bastard baby was the focus of attention on this Christmas Eve. The ladies oohed and aahed at the mere sight of the bright stripes of the shawl in which it was wrapped. But Lady Birkin had eyes for no one except her husband, standing at the top of the stairs close to the Marquess of Lytton and gazing anxiously at her.

"Henry," she said. "Oh, look at him. Have you ever seen anything so perfect?" She could hear herself laughing and yet his face had blurred before her vision. "Look at him, Henry."

He looked and smiled back up at her. "Sally," he whispered.

"He weighs nothing at all," she said. "How could any human being be so small and so light and so perfect and still live and breathe? What a miracle life is. Hold him, Henry."

She gave him no choice. She laid the bundle in his arms and watched the fear in his eyes soften to wonder as he smiled down at the baby. The child was not quite sleeping. He was looking quietly about him with unfocused eyes.

Lord Birkin smiled. What would it be like, he wondered, to look down like this at his own child? To have the baby placed in his arms by its mother? By his wife?

"Sally," he said, "you must be so tired." She was pale and disheveled. He had a sudden image of how she should be looking now, early in the evening of Christmas Eve, immaculate and fashionable and sparkling with jewels and excitement and ready to mingle with their friends far into the night. And yet he saw happiness now in her tired eyes—and breathtaking beauty.

The ladies wanted to hold the baby. And so he was passed from one to another, quiet and unprotesting. He was cooed over and clucked over and even sung to, by Miss Amelia Horn. The occasion had made even the Palmers magnanimous.

"Well," Mr. Palmer said, rubbing his hands together and looking not unpleased. "I never did in all my born days."

"I mean to tell Mr. Suffield," Mrs. Palmer said in a voice loud enough for all to hear, "that we are not even going to charge 'im for the room."

No one saw fit to comment on this outpouring of incredible generosity.

The Marquess of Lytton reached out both hands to Pamela when she came from the room. She set her own in them without thought and smiled at him. "Have you seen him?" she asked. "Is he not the most beautiful child you have ever set eyes on?"

"I'm sorry," he said to her, squeezing her hands until they hurt. "I ripped up at the physician for keeping quiet so long, and yet that is exactly what I had been doing all day. You and Lady Birkin were wonderfully brave. I am sorry my own cowardice made me hide a fact that might have made your day less anxious."

"I don't think," she said, gazing up into his eyes, her own filling with sudden tears, "that I would change one detail of this day even if I could. How glad I am that it rained!"

His eyes searched hers. "And so am I," he said, raising both hands to his lips and continuing to regard her over them. "More glad than I have been of anything else in my life."

"Anyway," Colonel Forbes's voice was declaring gruffly over the babble of voices in the hallway; it seemed that Mrs. Forbes had been trying to force him to hold the baby. "Anyway, this was a damned inconvenient thing to happen. What would have been the outcome if one of our number had not turned out to be a doctor, eh? Whoever heard of any woman having a baby at Christmas?"

The babble of voices stopped entirely.

The Marquess of Lytton's eyes smiled slowly into Pamela's. "Good Lord," he said, and everyone kept quiet to listen to his words, "a crowd of marvelous Christians we all are. Did any of us realize before this moment, I wonder? We have, in fact, been presented with the perfect Christmas, have we not? Almost a reenactment of the original."

"'How could I spoil a Christmas that had promised to be so dismal for everyone?'" Pamela said quietly. "I think someone realized, my lord."

"The child was very nearly born in a stable," Lady Birkin said.

"It is uncanny enough to send shivers up one's spine," Miss Eugenia Horn said.

"I hope you have not caught a chill from the damp sheets, Eugenia," Miss Amelia Horn said.

"I wonder," Lord Birkin said, "if above the heavy rain clouds a star is shining brightly."

"Fanciful nonsense," Colonel Forbes said. "I am ready for my dinner. When will it be ready, landlord, eh?

Don't just stand there, man. I would like to eat before midnight—if it is all the same to you, of course."

Lady Birkin took the baby from Mrs. Forbes's arms. "I'll take him back to his mother," she said, tenderness and wistfulness mingled in her voice.

"Back to his manger," Lord Birkin said, laughing softly.

"Well, anyway," Mrs. Palmer said to the gathered company as she cleared away the plates after dinner, "we didn't keep 'em in the stable like them innkeepers did in the Bible. We gave 'em one of our best rooms and aren't charging 'em for it neither."

"For which deeds you will surely find a place awaiting you in heaven," the Marquess of Lytton said.

"And yet it give me quite a turn, it did, when the colonel said what 'e did and we all thought of that other babe what was born at Christmas," Mr. Palmer said. He was standing in the doorway of the dining room, busy about nothing in particular. "I was all over shivers for a minute."

"I am sure in Bethlehem there was not all this infernal rain," Colonel Forbes commented.

"The kings would have arrived in horribly soggy robes and dripping crowns," the marquess said. "And the heavenly host would have had drooping wings."

"I am quite sure their wings were more sturdy than to be weakened by rain, my lord," Miss Amelia Horn said. "They were angels, after all."

Mrs. Forbes nodded her agreement.

"I think it would be altogether fitting to the occasion," Miss Eugenia Horn said, "if we read the Bible story together this evening."

"And perhaps sang some carols afterward," Lady Birkin said. "Does everyone feel Christmas as strongly as I do tonight despite all the usual trappings being absent?"

There were murmurings of assent. Mrs. Forbes nodded. The quiet gentleman smiled.

"Does anyone have a Bible?" Lord Birkin asked.

There was a lengthy pause. No one, it seemed, was in the habit of traveling about with a Bible in a trunk.

"I do," the quiet gentleman said at last, and he got to his feet to fetch it from his room.

And so they all spent a further hour in the dining room, far away from friends and families and parties, far from any church, far away from Christmas as any of them had ever known it. There were no decorations, no fruit cake or mince pies, no cider or punch or wassail. Nothing except a plain and shabby inn and the company of strangers become acquaintances. Nothing except a newborn baby and his mother asleep upstairs, cozy and warm because they had been taken from the stable and given a room and showered with care and with gifts.

The quiet gentleman himself read the story of the birth of another baby in Bethlehem, and they all listened to words they had heard so many times before that the wonder of it all had ceased to mean a great deal. They listened with a new understanding, with a new recognition of the joy of birth. Even the one man who rarely entered a church, Lord Lytton, was touched by the story and realized that perhaps Christmas had not been meant to be an orgy of personal gratification.

Singing that might have been self-conscious, since there was no instrument to provide accompaniment, was, in fact, not self-conscious at all. Lady Birkin, Pamela Wilder, Colonel Forbes and, surprisingly, Miss Amelia Horn all had good voices and could hold a tune. Everyone else joined in lustily, even the tone-deaf Mrs. Forbes.

Lord Birkin left the room after a while. He found

Tom Suffield in the kitchen, where he had been eating with the guests' coachmen. Lisa and the baby were asleep, Tom explained, scrambling to his feet, and he did not want to disturb them. Lord Birkin took Tom through into the taproom.

"I don't know what you are good at, Tom," he said. "I can't offer much in the way of employment, I'm afraid, but I can send you to my estate in Kent and instruct my housekeeper to find you work in the stables or in the gardens. I doubt there will be an empty cottage, but we will find somewhere where you and Lisa can stay for a while, at least."

Tom shifted his weight awkwardly from one foot to the other. "That be awf'ly good of ye, sir," he said, "but Mr. Cornwallis needs a cook and a handyman and have offered the jobs to me and Lisa."

"Mr. Cornwallis?" Lord Birkin raised his eyebrows.

"The doctor, sir," Tom said.

"Ah." It was strange, Lord Birkin thought, that even though they had all introduced themselves the evening before, he had thought of Mr. Cornwallis ever since only as the quiet gentleman. "I am glad, Tom. I hated to think of your taking Lisa and your baby to one of the industrial towns with no job waiting for you there."

"Aye, sir," Tom said. "Everyone is right kind. Thanks again for the money, sir. We will buy new clothes for the baby with it."

Lord Birkin nodded and returned to the dining room.

The Marquess of Lytton found Tom just ten minutes later. "Having a woman and child and no home or employment is a burdensome situation to find yourself in, Tom," he said.

"Aye, that it is, sir," Tom said. "But I feels like a wealthy man, sir, with all the gifts. And with your gold ring, sir. And a home and a job from Mr. Cornwallis." He told his tale again.

"Ah," the marquess said. "I am glad to hear it, Tom. I was prepared to give you a letter of introduction to a friend of mine, but now I see you will not need it. I would like to give you a small sum of money, though. Call it a Christmas gift to you personally, if you will. It is the price of a license. You must marry her, Tom. Such things are important to women, you know. And you would not wish to hear anyone calling your son a bastard."

"Bless you, sir," Tom said, flushing, "but Mr. Cornwallis is to marry us, sir, as soon as we gets to his home."

"The physician?" the marquess raised his eyebrows.

"He's a clergyman, sir," Tom said.

"Ah." The marquess nodded pleasantly to him and returned to the dining room. The quiet gentleman, he thought, was becoming more intriguing by the moment. Was he a physician or a clergyman? Or both? Or neither?

Lord Lytton seated himself beside the quiet gentleman and spoke to him while everyone else was singing. "You are a clergyman, sir?" he asked.

The quiet gentleman smiled. "I am, my lord," he said.

"And a physician too?" The marquess frowned.

"It is possible to be both," the quiet gentleman said. "I am a clergyman, but not of a large and fashionable parish, you see. My time is not taken up by the sometimes tedious and meaningless duties I would have if I belonged to a large parish, and certainly not by the social commitments I would have if I had a wealthy patron. I am fortunate. My time is free to be devoted to the service of others. I am not distracted by the trappings of the established faith." He chuckled. "I have learned to deliver babies. It is the greatest delight and the greatest privilege a man could experience. You discovered that once upon a time, I believe."

"And the greatest terror," the marquess said fervently. "I dreaded facing it again today. There was the terror of becoming the instrument of death rather than of life."

"Ah," the quiet gentleman said, "but we must learn to accept our limitations as part of the human condition. It is our Lord who controls life and death."

The marquess was quiet for a while. "Yes," he said. "We are all of us too busy, aren't we? Especially at Christmastime. Too busy enjoying ourselves and surrounding ourselves with the perfect atmosphere to remember what it is all about. This unexpected rainstorm has forced us to remember. And you have helped too, sir, by sitting back and allowing us to face all the terror of imminent birth."

"Without suffering there can never be the fullness of joy," the quiet gentleman said.

The Misses Horn were rising to retire for the night, and everyone else followed suit. But they did not part to go to their separate rooms without a great deal of hand-shaking and hugging first.

"Happy Christmas," they each said a dozen times to one another. But the words were not the automatic greeting they had all uttered during all their previous Christmases, but heartfelt wishes for one another's joy. Suddenly this Christmas—this dull, rainy disaster of a Christmas—seemed very happy indeed. Perhaps the happiest any of them had ever known.

And so Christmas Eve drew to an end. A baby had been born.

It was a little different when they were alone together in their room. Some of the magic went from the evening. It was all right for her, Lady Birkin thought. She had been busy all day and directly involved in the wonder of the baby's birth. Men were not so concerned about such matters. It must have been a dreadfully dull day for him.

"Henry," she said, looking at him apologetically, as if everything were her fault, "I am so sorry that this is such a dull Christmas for you."

"Dull?" He looked at her intently and took a step toward her so that he was very close. "I don't think I have ever celebrated Christmas until this year, Sally. I am very proud of you, you know."

Her eyes widened. "You are?" He so rarely paid her compliments.

"You worked tirelessly all day to help that girl," he said. "You and Miss Wilder. I don't know how Lisa would have managed without you."

"But there was a physician in the house, after all," she said. "What we did was nothing."

He framed her face with his hands. "What you did was everything," he said. "The doctor gave his skills. You gave yourself, Sally, despite being frightened and inexperienced."

"Oh," she said. She felt like crying. She had tried so hard to impress him since their marriage, dressing to please him, talking and smiling to please him. And losing him with every day that passed. And yet now he was looking at her with unmistakable admiration and . . . love?

"Henry," she said, and on impulse she put her arms up about his neck. "What is it about this Christmas? It is not just me, is it? Everyone has been feeling it. You too? What is so wonderful about it? This inn is not *the* inn, after all, and the baby is not Jesus, not even born in the stable."

He slipped his hands to her waist. "We have all seen to the core of Christmas this year," he said. "We are very fortunate, Sally. We might so easily have never had the chance. We have no gifts for each other. They are somewhere with our baggage coach. And this inn has provided us with nothing that is usually associated with the season. We had all come to believe that Christmas could not possibly be celebrated without those things. But this year we have been forced to see that Christmas is about birth and life and love and giving of whatever one has to give, even if it is only one's time and compassion."

She should not say it, she thought. She might spoil everything. They never said such things to each other. There seemed to be a great embarrassment between them where personal matters were concerned. But she was going to say it. She was going to take a chance. That was what the whole day seemed to have been about.

"Henry," she said. She was whispering, she found. "I love you so very much."

He gazed into her eyes, a look of hunger in his own. He drew breath but seemed to change his mind. Instead of speaking he lowered his head and kissed her—an openmouthed kiss of raw need that drew an instant response of surprise and desire. She tightened her arms and arched herself to him. There was shock for a moment as she felt his hands working at the buttons down the back of her dress, and then a surge of happiness.

"I always have," she said against his mouth. "Since the first moment I saw you. I have always worshiped you."

She gasped when he lowered her bodice and her chemise to her waist, and her naked breasts came back against his coat. And then his hands were on them, cupping them and stroking them, and his thumbs and forefingers were squeezing her nipples, rolling them lightly until she felt such a sharp stab of desire that she moaned into his mouth.

"Henry," she begged him, her eyes tightly closed, her mouth still against his, "make love to me. I have always wanted you to make love to me. Please, for this special day. Make love to me."

She would die, she thought if he merely coupled with her as he had the night before and all those other nights since their marriage. She should not have said what she just had. She should not have given in to the temptation to hope. She should not have begged for what he had never freely given.

But she was on the bed before she could get her thoughts straight, before she could feel shame for her wanton words. She was flat on her back, and he was stripping away her clothes from the waist down, looking at her from eyes heavy with desire as he straightened up and began to remove his own clothes. She was surprised to find that she felt no embarrassment though the candles burned and those passion-heavy eyes were devouring her nakedness. She lifted her arms to him.

She had asked for it, begged for it, wanted it. He would not feel guilt. This was not the way a gentleman used his wife, but they both wanted it. They both needed it. He resisted the urge to douse the candles so that she would be saved from embarrassment. And as he joined her naked on the bed, he rejected the idea of somehow restraining his passion. She wanted him as much as he wanted her. For this one occasion, she had said. So be it, then.

He worked on her mouth with his lips and his tongue and on her breasts with his hands and his fingers. She fenced his tongue with her own and sucked on it. She pushed her breasts up against his hands and gasped when he pinched her nipples, hardening them before rubbing his palms lightly over them. Her own hands explored his back and his shoulders. She wanted him. He felt a fierce exultation. She wanted him. This was not a mistress. This was his wife. This was Sally. And she wanted him.

He moved one hand down to caress her and ready her for penetration. She was hot and wet to his touch, something she had never been before. His temperature soared and his arousal became almost painful.

"Please," she was moaning into his mouth. "Please. Henry, please."

And so he moved on top of her, felt her legs twine tightly about his, lifted his head to look down into her face—her eyes were wide-open and gazing back—and mounted her, sliding deeply into wet heat. *God. Oh, my God. Sally.*

"Love me," she whispered to him. "Oh, please, Henry. There is such an ache."

She was going to come with him, he thought, the re- alization hammering through his temples with the blood. She was going to climax. He had heard that it was possible with some women.

"Tell me when." He lowered himself on his elbows until his mouth was an inch from hers and he began to move slowly and deeply in her. "I'll wait as long as you need."

But she did not have to tell him. He felt the gradual clenching of her inner muscles, the building tension of her whole body. He heard her deep breaths gradually turn to gasps. And he watched the concentration in her face as her eyes closed and her mouth opened in the agony of the final moments before she looked up at him, stillness and wonder in her eyes, and began to tremble.

He lowered himself onto her, held her tightly, held himself still and deep in her, and let himself experience the marvel of his woman shuddering into release be- neath him and crying out his name. Only when he was sure that she had experienced the full joy of the mo- ment did he move again to his own climax.

It was the most wonderful night of her life. She did not care if it was never repeated. She had this to hug to herself in memory for the rest of her days, the most wonderful Christmas that anyone could hope to have. She was nestled in his arms, watching him sleep. After more than three years of marriage she felt like a new bride. She felt . . . oh, she felt wonderful. And she would be satisfied, she swore to herself. She would not demand the moon and the stars. She had the Christmas star, the brightest and best of them all. She would be satisfied with that. Things could never be quite as bad between them now that they had had this night—or this part of a night.

He had opened his eyes and was looking at her. She smiled. *Don't remove your arm,* she begged him with her eyes. *Let's lie like this, just for tonight.*

"You said it," he said. "It seemed to come so easily, though I know it did not. You have not been able to say it in three years, have you? Why have we found it so hard? Why is it so difficult to talk from the heart with those closest to us?"

"Because with them there is most fear of rejection?" she said. "Because we have to protect our hearts from those who have the power to break them every day for the rest of our lives?"

"I do not have your courage," he said, one hand stroking lightly over her cheek. "I still don't. Sally, my love . . . Ah, just that. My love. Did I hurt you? Did I disgust you?"

"Say it again," she said, smiling at him. "Again and again. And do it again and again. I want to be as close to you as I can be, Henry. Close to your body, close to your heart, close to your mind. Not just for tonight. I am greedy."

"My love." He drew her closer to him, set his lips against hers. "It is what I have always wanted, what I have always yearned for. But I have wanted to treat you with respect. Foolish, wasn't I?"

"To think that being respectful meant holding me at arm's length?" she said. "And giving much of what I have longed for to mistresses? Have I made you flush?

Did you think I did not know? Yes, you have been foolish, Henry. And I have been foolish not to fight for your
love and not to put you straight on this ridiculous notion that gentlemen seem to have about women."

"Would this be happening if we had reached the Middletons' before the rain came?" he asked her.

"No," she said. "No, it would not. Perhaps it never
would have happened. We would have kept drifting
until perhaps we would have lived apart. Henry . . ."
There was pain in her voice.

He rubbed his lips against hers and drew back his
head to smile at her. "But it did happen," he said.
"Christmas happened almost two thousand years ago,
and it has happened this year for us. Love always seems
to blossom at the most unexpected times and in the
most unexpected places. This was meant to happen,
Sally. We must not shudder at the thought of how nearly
it did not happen. It was meant to be."

"Do you think we will ever have a child?" she asked
him wistfully, snuggling closer to the warmth and safety
of him. "I wanted so much today for that baby to be
mine, Henry. Ours. Do you think we ever will?"

"If we don't," he said, and he chuckled as he drew her
closer still, "it won't be for lack of trying."

"Oh," she said.

"Shall we try now?" he said to her. "And perhaps
again later?"

"And again later still?" she asked.

He laughed. "After all," he said, "dawn comes late in
December. And there does not seem to be a great deal
to get up early for at this apology for an inn, does there?
Especially not on Christmas morning."

"Christmas morning is for babies," she said.

"The making of them as well as the birthing of them,"
he said, turning her onto her back and moving over her.

She smiled up at him.

"Sally," he said, serious again as he lowered his mouth and his body to hers, "my most wonderful Christmas gift. I love you."

It did not seem quite the same once everyone had gone to bed and he was left alone in the taproom. Even though he built up the fire and sat on a settle close to the heat, the place felt cheerless again. Christmas had fled again.

He thought of the Whittakers' large and fashionable mansion and of Lady Frazer's enticing beauty. He felt a moment's pang of regret but no more. He did not want to be there, he realized with a wry smile directed at the fire. He wanted to be exactly where he was. Well, not exactly, perhaps. There was a room upstairs and a bed where he would rather be. But perhaps not. He could no longer think of her in terms of simple lust. There was a warmer feeling and a nameless yearning when he thought of her. Also a regret for wasted years, for years of senseless debauchery that had brought no real happiness with them.

They would not be able to travel during the coming day, Christmas Day. Probably they would the day after. The rain had finally stopped, and the sky had cleared before darkness fell. He would have one more day in which to enjoy looking at her and in which to maneuver to engage her in conversation. One day—a Christmas to remember.

And then he looked up from his contemplation of the flames in the hearth to find her standing before him, looking at him gravely. She held a blanket and a pillow in her arms.

"I thought you might be cold and uncomfortable," she said, holding them out to him. "It was very kind of you to give up your room for Lisa. You are a kind man."

"I gave up my room," he said, taking the pillow and blanket from her and setting them down beside him, "because you had tried to give up yours and I wanted to impress you with a show of chivalry. Kindness had nothing to do with it. I am not renowned for my kindness."

"Perhaps because you sometimes try not to show it," she said. "But I have seen it in other ways. You came to help Lisa give birth though it terrified you to do so."

He shrugged. "I came for your sake," he said. "And I did not help all day long, while you were exhausting yourself. In the event I did not help at all."

"But you would have," she said. "The intention was there. Tom showed me the ring you gave as a gift for the baby."

He shrugged again. "I am very wealthy," he said. "It was nothing."

"No," she said, still looking at him with her grave eyes, "it was something."

"Ah," he said, "then I have impressed you. I have achieved my goal."

She stared at him silently. He expected her to turn to leave, but she did not do so.

"Do you know how you have affected me?" he asked. "I do not believe I have ever before refused an invitation to bed. That *was* an invitation you were issuing last night?"

She lowered her eyes for a moment, but she lifted them again and looked at him calmly. "Yes," she said. "I suppose so."

"Why?" he asked. "You are not in the habit of issuing such invitations, are you?"

She shook her head. "Sometimes," she said, "I grow tired of the grayness of life. It was so full of color until a little more than a year ago, but there has been nothing but grayness since and nothing but grayness to look forward to. It is wrong of me to be dissatisfied with my lot, and normally I am not. But I thought this was going to be a disappointing Christmas."

"And it has not been?" he asked.

"No." She smiled slowly. "It has been the most wonderful Christmas of all."

"Because of the baby," he said.

"Yes," she said, "because of him. And for other reasons too."

He reached out a hand. "Come and sit beside me," he said.

She looked at his hand and set her own in it. She sat down beside him and set her head on his shoulder when he put an arm about her.

"I wanted you last night," he said. "You know that, don't you? And why I left you, the deed undone?"

"Because you knew I was inexperienced," she said. "Because you knew me to be incapable of giving you the pleasure you are accustomed to. I understood. It is all right."

"Because I realized the immensity of the gift you were offering," he said. "Because I knew I could not take momentary pleasure from you. Because any greater commitment than that terrified me."

"I expected no more," she said.

"I know," he said. "That was the greatness of your gift."

She sighed and set an arm across his waist. "I am going to remember this Christmas for the rest of my life," she said. "It will seem quite unreal when I get back to my post, but I will remember that it really did happen."

He turned his head, found her lips with his own, and kissed her long and lingeringly. Her lips were soft and warm and willing to part for him. He nibbled at them, licked them, stroked them with his tongue. But he would not allow passion to grow. It was neither the time nor the place for passion.

"I am a dreadful rake, Pamela," he said. "My debauched behavior has been notorious for several years. Decent women give me a wide berth."

She raised one hand and touched her fingertips to his cheek.

"But I have never debauched a married woman," he said. "I have always held marriage sacred. I have always known that if I ever married, it would have to be to a woman I loved more than life itself, for I could never be unfaithful to her."

Her finger touched his lips and he kissed it.

"Would you find such a man trustworthy?" he asked her.

"Such a man?" she said. "I don't know. You? Yes. I have seen today, and last night, too, that you are a man of conscience and compassion."

He took her hand in his and brought her palm against his mouth. "How do you think your father would react," he asked, "to the idea of his daughter marrying a rake? Would my title and fortune dazzle his judgment?"

Her eyes grew luminous. "No," she said. "But he would be swayed by kindness and compassion—and by his daughter's happiness."

"Would you be happy, Pamela?" he asked. "Would you take a chance on me?"

She closed her eyes and turned her face to his shoulder.

"It is absurd, isn't it?" he said. "How long have we known each other? Forever, is it? I have known you forever, Pamela. I have just been waiting for you to appear in my life. I have loved you forever."

Her face appeared again, smiling. "I would be happy," she said. "I would take a chance, my lord."

"Edward," he said.

"Edward."

"Will you marry me, my love?" he asked her.

She laughed softly and buried her face again. She hugged his waist tightly. "Yes," she said.

He held her wordless for a while. Then he slid one hand beneath her knees and lifted her legs across his. He reached beside him, shook out the blanket, and spread it over both of them. He settled the pillow behind his head, against the high wooden backrest of the settle.

"Stay with me tonight?" he murmured into her ear. "Just like this, Pamela? It is not the most comfortable of beds, but I will not suggest taking you to your room. I would want to stay with you, you see, and if we were there, I would want to possess you. I want that to wait until our wedding night. I want our bodies to unite for the first time as a marriage commitment. Are these words coming from my mouth?" He chuckled softly. "Are these the words of a rake?"

"No." She turned her face up to his, her eyes bright with merriment. "They are the words of a former rake, Edward—and never to be again. Does that sound dreadfully dull to you?"

He grinned down at her. "It sounds dazzlingly wonderful actually," he said. "Pamela and only Pamela forever after. Are you comfortable?"

"Mm," she said and snuggled against him. "And you?"

"A feather bed could not compete with this settle for softness and ease," he said. He kissed her again, his lips lingering on hers. "Happy Christmas, my love."

"Happy Christmas, Edward," she said, closing her eyes and sighing with warm contentment.

Upstairs, in the room the Marquess of Lytton had occupied the night before, Tom kept watch over the mother of his child, who slept peacefully, and over his newborn son, who fussed in his sleep but did not wake. Tom stood at the window, gazing upward.

A single star almost directly overhead bathed the inn

with soft light and glistened off acres of mud. It was not a pretty scene. Not a noticeably Christmas-like scene. The inn, somewhere in Wiltshire, was neither large nor picturesque nor thriving. No one has ever mapped its exact location.

Penguin Group (USA) Online

What will you be reading tomorrow?

Tom Clancy, Patricia Cornwell, W.E.B. Griffin,
Nora Roberts, William Gibson, Robin Cook,
Brian Jacques, Catherine Coulter, Stephen King,
Dean Koontz, Ken Follett, Clive Cussler,
Eric Jerome Dickey, John Sandford,
Terry McMillan, Sue Monk Kidd, Amy Tan,
John Berendt...

You'll find them all at
penguin.com

*Read excerpts and newsletters,
find tour schedules and reading group guides,
and enter contests.*

Subscribe to Penguin Group (USA) newsletters
and get an exclusive inside look
at exciting new titles and the authors you love
long before everyone else does.

PENGUIN GROUP (USA)
us.penguingroup.com